Praise for *The Forgotten Queen*

"In *The Forgotten Queen*, D. L. Bogdan has given us a thoroughly entertaining novel that vividly captures the turmoil, tensions, passions and intrigue of this period of Tudor and Stewart history. The narrator is Henry VIII's older sister, Margaret, a feisty, endearing heroine, tested by three tumultuous marriages. Here, in this richly woven tale, Bogdan's formidable queen takes her place in history, and not only as the grandmother of Mary, Queen of Scots."

—Sandra Worth, author of *Pale Rose of England*

D1403664

Books by D. L. Bogdan

SECRETS OF THE TUDOR COURT

RIVALS IN THE TUDOR COURT

THE SUMERTON WOMEN

THE FORGOTTEN QUEEN

Published by Kensington Publishing Corporation

The FORGOTTEN QUEEN

D. L. BOGDAN

KENSINGTON BOOKS
www.kensingtonbooks.com

KENSINGTON BOOKS are published by

Kensington Publishing Corp.
119 West 40th Street
New York, NY 10018

All Kensington titles, imprints, and distributed lines are available at special quantity discounts for bulk purchases for sales promotion, premiums, fund-raising, and educational or institutional use.

Special book excerpts or customized printings can also be created to fit specific needs. For details, write or phone the office of the Kensington Special Sales Manager: Kensington Publishing Corp., 119 West 40th Street, New York, NY 10018. Attn. Special Sales Department. Phone: 1-800-221-2647.

Kensington and the K logo Reg. U.S. Pat. & TM Off.

ISBN-13: 978-0-7582-7138-9
ISBN-10: 0-7582-7138-7

First Kensington Trade Paperback Printing: February 2013
10 9 8 7 6 5 4 3 2 1

Printed in the United States of America

Dedicated in loving memory of another sassy redhead:
my mother-in-law, Karen Ann Barton

Acknowledgments

As always, I must first thank my wonderful agent, Elizabeth Pomada, who has worked so hard to help keep making my dreams of living as a working writer come true. I must also thank my editor, John Scognamiglio, for his patience, encouragement, and his ability to meet challenges with tireless grace, along with Paula Reedy and the rest of the magnificent team at Kensington Publishing. A big thanks to Vida Engstrand, my publicist, who is such a joy to work with. I also want to thank the team at the National Archives of Scotland in Edinburgh for their devoted correspondence as I researched this novel. To the authors who became mentors, the bloggers and reviewers who became huge sources of support (you all know who you are!), and the readers who keep me working, my deepest, most heartfelt thanks. I must thank my favorite beta reader, my mother, Cindy Bogdan, who was always up for a late-night phone call as I read her my latest scenes. Not least of all, I must thank my son Quinn for sharing his life and mother with so many historical figures. He knows far more about the Tudors and Stewarts than any twelve-year-old should! To my stepchildren Kristina, Ashley, and Cody (all lucky enough to have grown up and left home, thus avoiding the day-to-day travails of the latest historical obsession), thank you for supporting, respecting, and understanding my work; it means a great deal. And finally, thank you to the love of my life, my best friend, biggest encourager, and shameless promoter: my husband, Kim. I love you, my forever Chief and anchor.

❧ BOOK 1 ❧

Margaret

PROLOGUE

The Flames of Sheen

It began with smoke. His Grace King Henry VII said everything began with smoke, from the fall of the old kings to the rise of the new, when the smoke curled about the mouths of the great cannon as they spewed forth their vengeance on the battlefield, to the love born of a man and a woman, where the smoke rose from the smallest flame in the bedchamber, quite unable to rival that which burns in the human heart, the flames he coveted for his own wife, my mother, Queen Elizabeth of York.

But the night I lost my Sheen, the flames arose from a cause unknown, an errant taper, likely. Sliding across the floor, deft and sleek as a snake were the flames. They licked up the side of the wall, taking in with great satisfaction the new tapestries Her Grace my mother had taken such care in embroidering to cheer the king's chambers that fateful Christmas.

And so watching in awe, I was held fast with helplessness. A cacophony of voices swirled about me, but I was unable to identify their owners.

"The prince!" someone cried. "Remove His Highness, the Prince of Wales!"

Of course it made sense to rescue the treasured heir first. And no one treasured him more than I, his sister. However, I must say a thorn of jealousy twisted in my breast as I watched the guards usher my brother Arthur forth from the chambers, amidst a clamor of frightened dignitaries and courtiers. My mother gathered the other children around her, impetuous Henry and sweet baby Mary, taking flight.

I stood, captivated by the scene. At once my face began to prickle and tingle with the strange sensation that I was being watched. I turned to see him, the man to be feared above all, the man second only to God above. Henry VII, my father, my king. Flames lost their heat in his cool, calm eyes. A small smile lifted the corner of his mouth as his gaze held mine.

"Margaret," he said, his voice low, knowing he as king had no need to raise it. Even the flames stilled to listen.

Only my tears could answer for me.

"We will build another," he assured me.

And then I was in the arms of a guard. I closed my eyes to the flames now devouring my world, insatiable, and my ears to the crackling, creaking timbers that once made up my Sheen, palace of my childhood.

Things were about to change. Somehow I knew then more than ever that I was not ordinary.

❧ 1 ❧

The Wilted Rose

There was no one high enough to intervene on behalf of my immortal soul, my grandmother had cried. I was a shameful creature, she went on, a wilted petal on the Tudor rose. It was time I was made to examine my wicked ways and repent. Grandmother was through with humble chaplains and confessors. I was a Princess of the Blood; the fate of kingdoms may rest in my finding salvation. Thus I was removed to my godfather, the Archbishop of Canterbury himself, where I must come up with an impressive confession. I was certain it wouldn't take much; I had a wealth of sins to choose from.

Lord Chancellor John Morton sat before me in his grand white robes, drumming his slim fingers on his knee waiting, waiting for the recitation of my various sins.

I wrung my hands. Oh, where to begin?

"I hit my brother Henry on the head with a stick," I told him, swallowing my fear as I approached him to lay a hand on his lap. I refused to sit in the confessional. I did not like walls between me and anyone, see-through or not. The archbishop's robe was very soft under my fingertips and I found myself scrunching the material beneath my nails in nervousness.

He offered a grave nod, urging me to continue. "Why would you do such a thing, Princess Margaret?"

"Because Henry is stupid," I explained with impatience. "If you knew him you would surely hit him as well, my lord."

The archbishop's lips twitched. "Pray continue, Highness."

I twisted the material of his gown in my fist, edging closer to him. My tone was conspiratorial. "And then I stuck my tongue out at my tutor because he called me saucy. I am *not* saucy, Your Grace!"

"Indeed?" The smallest smile curved his lips. "Go on."

I swallowed several times, shifting from foot to foot. "And then . . . then I put a frog in my grandmother's slipper—"

"Gracious, Your Highness, that was creative," he observed. "Why should you grieve your gentle grandmother so?"

"Do you *know* my grandmother, Your Grace?" I asked, incredulous that anyone should describe the severe Margaret Beaufort as gentle.

"She is a great lady," said the archbishop. "It would serve you better to respect her." He paused, arching a brow. "Now. Anything else?"

"Well, I also hid Grandmother's hair shirt," I confessed. "I wasn't trying to be bad that time. Honest. I just thought to give her skin a rest—"

"How old are you, Princess Margaret?"

"I am ten," I told him, offering a bright smile to display the pearly row of grown-up teeth that were my pride.

"Do you think a girl of ten should meddle in the affairs of a woman thrice her age?" he asked me in patient tones. "I should say not. The Lord commands us to honor our mother and father; this applies to all elders. Your grandmother is a very spiritual lady and needs none of your . . . intervention. She is an example of faithfulness. Remember, through her loving discipline you are brought to a better understanding of God."

I bowed my head. I hated talking about the Venerable Margaret Beaufort with anyone. I hated even *thinking* about her. Spiritual! How I had suffered for Margaret Beaufort's "spirituality"! If her cane across my back was made to bring about a better understanding of God I could have been an abbess!

"Anything else?"

Summoned to mind was the most grievous sin of all. I sighed. "I asked the king what a whore is."

The priest's eyes widened as he covered his mouth with one large hand. "Did you find out?"

"No! Grandmother slapped me!" I cried, hoping to solicit his sympathy. "I can't begin to imagine why! I only asked because I heard one of the ladies say there were an awful lot of whores about and I feared it was some kind of insect, so I thought it best to find out! I do not want anything crawling on me, after all!"

Archbishop Morton tilted his head back, closing his eyes a long moment. He drew in a deep breath, expelling it slowly. "Anything else, my lady?"

I bit my lip. "I . . . I'm not sure."

"You're not sure?"

I shook my head. "I'm sorry, Your Grace. It's just that I sin with such terrible frequency—I can't seem to keep track. I suppose I should make a list. . . ."

"Highness, has it ever occurred to you that the best way to—er—'keep track' of your sins is to reduce the list or perhaps, to the best of your ability, cease sinning altogether?" he asked.

"Oh, but that would be impossible!" I cried.

"Indeed, we're all human and it is in our nature to sin, but I do not believe reducing the regularity of the habit to be an impossibility—"

"How on God's earth do you expect me to have any fun *that* way?" I cried.

"Charity shall be your penance," said the archbishop in decisive tones as he rose. "I should like you to accompany your grandmother on her charitable exploits. 'Twill teach you humility as well and do your soul much good."

"Yes, Your Grace." I bowed my head in an attempt at humility, though I was much aggrieved at the thought of accompanying Grandmother anywhere. I raised my head, hoping there was some way to endear myself to him. "Thank you ever so!" I cried then, throwing my arms about his waist and resting my chin against his chest, casting adoring eyes to his stern countenance. How I wished he would scoop me up in his arms and carry me off to Lambeth.

Then I could be his little girl most loved. Of course, archbishops couldn't have little girls, so I supposed it would do to place this fantasy with yet another gentleman. Unfortunately, I seemed to be running out.

"Now, now, Highness, that is quite enough!" cried the archbishop as he disengaged himself from me.

Blinking back a sudden onset of tears, I fell to my knees and, in an unusual display of reverence, kissed his grand ring.

"I will pray fervently for your soul, Your Highness," he told me.

I rose. "Your Grace . . . no one ever did tell me . . . what is a whore?"

"Your Highness . . ." The archbishop removed his cap to run a hand through his thinning white hair. "You'll . . . find out when you're older."

I refrained from stamping my foot.

I'd find out when I was older. Everyone's favorite answer when they couldn't tell me a thing. Likely they didn't even know!

Oh, confession was a bore!

I resolved to think of a hundred other fun sins to indulge in just to spite them all.

If anything, it would make the dread chore more interesting. It was rather fun shocking the Archbishop of Canterbury.

I liked shocking everyone.

Christmastide distracted me from my mischievous missions and was all the initiative I needed to remain good. Grandmother said this in itself is a sin; I should be good because I wanted to be good, not because it involved some kind of reward.

"But aren't you being good just so you can get into Heaven?" I countered, recalling my grandmother's famous displays of piety. "That is a reward."

This rewarded me with a clout on the mouth and no satisfactory answer.

We removed from Greenwich to Westminster, where all the family would be together for the first time in many months. Excitement surged through me as I peeked out the curtains of my litter to wave to the throng gathered at the palace gates, who shouted blessings at me.

"Bless the princess!" they called.

"Throw them some coin; that's what they're waiting for," my grandmother urged in stern tones. "Goodness knows they're not really here to see you."

"They are, too!" I returned. "They adore me!"

Just to ensure this, however, I reached into her purse to fish out a handful of sovereigns, tossing them to the awaiting crowd, who scrambled and scuffled over them in the street. My heart lurched as the truth of my grandmother's words rang in my ears.

When at last I was permitted to quit the litter and my grandmother's deplorable company, I ran through the Long Gallery to search out my family. I offered warm greetings to the courtiers and dignitaries who surrounded Father like butterflies around flowers. All rewarded me with smiles and bows.

The Archbishop of Canterbury was there. His dark eyes sparkled with amusement. "Well, Princess Margaret. You have come to grace us with your presence for the holiday season. Let us pray the palace doesn't take fire this year."

My eyes misted as I recalled my precious Sheen, now being re-built as my father had promised into a grand palace he had decided to call Richmond, for our family's seat.

"Well, *I* didn't do it," I assured him, in case that had been his implication.

The archbishop, in a moment of rare tenderness, ruffled my hair as he chuckled. "Of course not, Your Highness. Now. Come with me. You'll be anxious to see your father, no doubt."

"Oh, yes!" I cried, sliding my hand in his and leaning my head on his arm. He disengaged and my arm fell to my side as we progressed through the gallery toward my father's apartments.

We entered King Henry VII's privy chamber to find him hunched over his writing table, scouring documents. He did not put them aside when my presence was announced and I stood among members of the council, who rolled their eyes at each other as if to say, *Here she is again.*

Yes, here I am again and you'll never forget me! I longed to cry. I was not some common street urchin; I was Princess Margaret Tudor and a finer lass they'd never lay eyes upon!

But I said nothing. I sighed and fiddled with the pearls sewn into the neckline of my blue velvet gown. I plaited and unplaited my coppery tresses over my shoulder to busy my fidgety hands until at last the King of England raised his taciturn face toward me. With one slim hand, he gestured for me to come forth.

I made a face at the councilors present, hoping to convey my dislike for them in one charming grimace, and proceeded toward the grand table. I curtsied low.

"Margaret," he muttered in his gruff voice, looking me up and down. "So this is what we have to work with."

I scowled before I could help myself. "Your Grace?"

"Altogether too thin," he mumbled, looking down at his papers. "You had better be able to bear children else you'll be no use at all."

"Your Grace!" I cried. This was not the happy reunion I had envisaged. But then most of my fantasies fell scathingly short of reality. I heaved a deep sigh. "There is no reason to believe I shouldn't be able to bear a wealth of sons, my lord. I am of good Tudor and Plantagenet stock—I will do you proud."

He raised his head at this, offering a rueful smile. "I think I rather like you," he said, as though he were experiencing an epiphany and the idea of actually liking his children was quite novel indeed.

"You'll not let anyone get the best of you, will you?" he mused, rising and rounding the table to lay a hand on my shoulder. "You are of particular interest to me this year, Daughter," he said, his narrow face creasing into a smile. I must say he looked horrible. His auburn hair grazed his shoulders in a straight and sensible mass that did his long features no good at all. I wished he'd cut it. He looked like an old fox wrapped in his furs, an old fox waiting to leap out and, with the slyness associated with the creature, wreak subtle havoc on those who dared oppose him.

And yet without those foxy and wily ways Henry VII would not be Henry VII at all but the obscure Duke of Richmond nobody cared about. Had my father not conspired against (with the help of another fox, my cunning grandmother Margaret Beaufort) and eventually slain the usurper King Richard III at the Battle of Bosworth, the crown of England would not be in Tudor hands and the Wars of the Roses would still be fought in vain. But my father the king, for all his bad hair and fashion sense, swept in and won the day, not only claiming the crown but also uniting the houses of York and Lancaster at last by marrying my fair mother, Elizabeth, ending the wars for good. My father filled the treasury, modernized the government through the appointments of councilors (also men with bad hair and worse fashion sense), ousting all pretenders to the throne with the mightiness of his hand. He was a formidable man, this Henry Tudor, cold and calculating, miserly and cautious. This man, this king, was my father and never was the thought far from my mind that his were the hands that would shape my destiny.

"Everyone out—We should have audience with Our daughter alone!" Father barked, rousing me from my reverie as I watched a room of scrambling servants and councilors all too eager to do his bidding.

Father rounded the desk once more to look out the window, past the gardens, past the Tower, far past the known horizon. He was squinting. I found myself doing the same, though I had no idea what we were looking for.

"You do realize that as a daughter of this house yours is not an ordinary future We have planned," he said. "Margaret, the peace of kingdoms depends on you."

"Oh, if this is about me sinning again I can tell you I have been good for at least a week!" I cried.

He silenced me with a hand. "Margaret, I've news on your suit."

I began to tremble. My suit. I braced myself. What prince had my father chosen for me? To what distant land would I be sent?

"We need an end to these frays with Scotland and one of the ways of achieving that is by forming an alliance," he explained. "D'you understand?"

I shook my head, though against my will comprehension was settling upon me, clutching my heart in its merciless talons until I became short of breath.

"Don't swoon on me now, child," Father commanded. "You've never been a fainting girl and now is no time to start." He rested his hands on my shoulders. "Margaret. You are going to be what unites our kingdoms. You are going to bring about a better understanding between us. You are meant for greatness, perhaps a greatness that surpasses even your own brother the Crown Prince Arthur, because yours is a task that is far from easy." With this he shook me somewhat, not in cruelty, but to illustrate his passion. Fear coursed through me. "Margaret, my child, this is your purpose: You are to become the Queen of the Scots."

Had I been a fainting girl, that would have been the time.

I did not know how to feel, what to think. Queen . . . But I knew I would be a queen; Princesses of the Blood are primed from birth for this function. From cradle to table I had been told that I would marry a prince, that I must bear him many sons, else be deemed a failure. And so with this in mind I prepared for my role as political breeder.

The night I learned I was to become Queen of Scots—Scots, as if he couldn't find a more glamorous country than where that lot of barbarians reside!—there was none with whom I could find comfort. For a while I climbed into bed with little Princess Mary, my three-year-old sister, cuddling her close. This golden princess would have a charmed life, I was certain. She was so agreeable and adorable; as yet she showed none of my sinful inclinations and everyone fawned over her.

At once I rose from the bed of the favored princess, stirred to anger as I thought of the wonderful marriage Father would arrange for her. No doubt she would live in some glorious court where there would be artists and musicians to entertain her all day long—likely she'd get to live in sunny Spain or romantic France while I wasted away in the North, freezing in some drafty castle surrounded by fur-clad courtiers who spoke as though they had something obstructing their throats . . . ! I dared not think on it anymore. I crossed the rush-strewn floor on bare feet, wringing my hands and blinking back tears. I, Margaret Tudor, was going to be Queen of the Scots . . . those frightening, monstrous Scots. . . .

I retrieved a wrap and sneaked out of the nursery, down the hall. I would see my brother Arthur. Gentle, sweet Arthur, so unlike fiery Henry and docile Mary, would be able to guide me.

The guards stood aside to admit me into the apartments of the Prince of Wales. He was lying across some furs before his fire, thumbing through *The Canterbury Tales*. When he saw me, his handsome, scholarly face lit up with a smile.

"Sister," he said in his handsome voice. "A midnight visit. What an unexpected pleasure. Won't you sit? Take some wine." He held the book up for me to see. "I know, I shouldn't be indulging myself in such fancy, but the naughty parts are too delightful to ignore!"

The tears that had settled in my throat since learning of my impending betrothal were replaced by a smile as I sat beside my brother. There was no one like Arthur the world over, I was convinced. He was the gentlest, sweetest prince in Christendom and would no doubt be a fine king. He was not athletic like Henry, nor did he possess my younger brother's fleet dancing feet. Arthur was an intellectual; content to study, to ponder, to think. His beauty was delicate and whenever I was with him I could not help but feel the need to protect him, nurture him, just as he had always protected and nurtured me.

The smile faded at the thought, replaced by fresh tears. "Oh, Arthur," I began. "I hate that I never get to see you. With you living in Ludlow and me here with nobody but Henry to annoy me and Grandmother to torture me . . . it is a miserable existence!"

"So I suppose it best to dispense with the obligatory 'how are you?' " Arthur teased, his blue eyes sparkling as he reached out to cup my cheek. "Now, now, Sister, is it as bad as all that? Far be it for me to disagree with you about Grandmother, but our Henry means well enough. He may be annoying, but his love and devotion are fierce and you do have sweet little Mary—"

"Henry's love and devotion are fierce only when you're in his favor and we're rarely in each other's favor . . . and Mary is favored by everyone. I pale under the glory of her sun. She is the flawless little Tudor rose and I am the thorn they long to cut out," I pouted.

"So intense!" Arthur cried, sitting up and putting his book aside.

"But since it would be unseemly to cut the thorn they shall send her to the land of the thistles—to Scotland!" I cried, scowling. "Can you believe it, Arthur? *Scotland?* They may as well be sending me to Hell!"

Arthur chuckled, but I took no pleasure in the handsome sound. It mocked my misery and my brow ached from furrowing it at him. "So that is what this display is about," he said. "Come here, darling girl." He held out his arm and I scooted in next to him. He gathered me close, stroking my hair. "We are special people, Margaret," he told me. "Special people with very special responsibilities. You know well; your whole life has been preparing you for this zenith. It seems unfair; princes are allowed to stay in their native countries for the most part while our sacred princesses must scatter to the four winds, their sacrifice in order to secure sound alliances for the countries to which they are bound. We are God's chosen, though, my dearest. Chosen to lead His people, chosen to defend them and honor them. You are going to be a *queen*, Margaret. An anointed queen. No one can ever take that away from you. You have the power to do so much good. I know Scotland is not the land you dreamed of spending your life in. They are very different from us; but Father would not send you if he thought you would come to harm. He longs to bring about a good alliance between our two countries. Think of the role you can play in securing that glorious peace! Think of the legacy you will leave! The mark you will make! Margaret, there has not been peace between our two countries in one hundred and seventy years. You have the opportunity of setting things right."

"I don't want to set anything right! I don't want to go away! I want to stay with you!" I cried, burying my head in his chest.

Arthur chuckled again. "You must be brave, lass, *brave*. Take heart and look sharp! A thistle can outlast a thousand roses. Father sends his little thorn to the wilds of Scotland because he knows she is strong enough to bear it."

I pulled away, looking into his face. "It is just so very far, Arthur. When will I see you and Mother? What if they don't like me there?"

"Not like you?" Arthur cried, as though this was impossible to conceive. "Why, no one can resist you."

I brightened at this.

"The Scots will fall madly in love with you," he went on. "And, think, pretty one, of all the clothes and jewels you will have as queen. There are going to be songs written about you, poems dedicated to you . . . there is so much to look forward to!"

"Oh, I hadn't thought of that!" I cried, envisioning bolts of velvet and silk, kirtles of cloth of gold, and kid gloves. "I suppose I will be able to eat whatever I want all the time, too."

"All the time," he assured me. "Just mind that you don't become fat. Nobody likes fat queens!"

I laughed. "Oh, no, I shall not! I'll be a beautiful queen and will set a new standard of elegance for the Scots. All the ladies will want to dress like me—"

"That's the spirit!" he cried, slapping me on the back as though I were one of the lads.

I seized my brother's slim hands. "And you'll write me all the time?"

"All the time," he said, chucking my chin.

"No one loves me like you do," I said in a small voice as I regarded my one true champion.

He waved a dismissive hand, flushing. "Nonsense. Everyone loves you." He smiled. "Now, enough of this fretting. You act as though you're the only one to have a foreign prince inflicted on you. As yet you've expressed no sympathy regarding my suit."

I cocked my head, puzzled.

"Have you forgotten my marriage to the Infanta, Catalina of Aragon?" he asked.

I shook my head. "Oh, no. But at least she's coming to you. And I hear she's very fine and sweet."

"And I hear the King of Scots is lusty and robust!" he returned. "We'll do fine, Sister, you'll see. We'll usher our European brothers into a New Age!"

"A New Age . . ." I repeated, enchanted by the concept of being a luminary. "Do you think we can?"

"I know we can!" he cried. "Now! Enough. Sit with me and I'll read you a story to divert you. 'The Miller's Tale' . . ."

I laughed at the thought of hearing the scandalous tale that Grandmother said was a sin to even listen to. Knowing this made me want to hear it all the more.

I covered up with one of the furs and warmed myself by the fire, enveloped in the solace and reassurance I had been seeking, knowing there was none luckier than I, to have such a sweet brother as Arthur, Prince of Wales.

❧ 2 ❧

The Song of Loss

Oh, it was going to be a wonderful year! I was twelve then and beautiful—everyone told me so. Though I was tiny and lacked the curves of some of my contemporaries, I was assured that my daintiness evoked just as much admiration. The worst part about entering womanhood, however, was the menses—how I hated it!

"I do not understand its necessity!" I once confessed to the old archbishop. "There is no fairness in it."

"Things would be different had Eve not led Adam into sin," he explained, bowing his head to conceal his flushing face.

"So Adam did not have a mind of his own?" I cried. "If he was witless enough to yield to Eve's temptation then it is *his* stupidity that warrants the curse!"

"Madam, you tread on blasphemy!"

"Oh, you don't want to hear it," I lamented. "You are on his side."

And so there was nothing to do but bear it. Fortunately, there were plenty enough diversions to occupy me. The Princess Catalina had arrived! Oh, but she was lovely, so fair and sweet. How I pitied her when her name had to be Anglicized. Now she would be forever known as Catherine of Aragon. How much a princess gave up when leaving her home—her family, her customs, her way of life, even her very name.

I was at least fortunate to be removing to an English-speaking country, for the most part, and would keep possession of my name.

I tried my best to offer friendship to my future sister-in-law. She was all Spanish; it oozed from her, reflected in her piety, her thick accent, and her manner of dress. Father was disappointed.

"Guide her, Margaret," he told me. "Show her what it is to be an English princess."

I was thrilled at this charge and complied with enthusiasm. Catherine was four years my senior but yielded to my instruction, eager to please her new countrymen. Though she demonstrated a strength of character that suggested she would not be manipulated, she agreed to conform to some of the English customs. I enjoyed acquainting myself with her and took to making plans.

"I shall come visit you in Wales," I assured her. "And when I live in Scotland I will write you all the time. We will organize meetings between the royal houses that will unite our countries in friendship—it will be so grand! There'll be masques and entertainments and jousting. England has the best jousters in the world!"

Catherine offered a kind smile. "It all sounds so lovely. May it come to pass just as you imagine it."

Thrilled with the companionship of the princess, I removed to her betrothed that I might tell him of her.

"She is so lovely, Arthur," I reported the night before their wedding. "I just know you are going to be happy!" I clasped my hands to my heart and scrunched up my shoulders in glee.

Arthur was reading abed in his apartments. He offered a lazy smile, then covered his mouth with his handkerchief as his body was seized by a wracking coughing fit. I took to his side, reaching out to feel his forehead.

"You're burning up!" I cried. "Oh, Arthur, are you well?"

He nodded. "No worries, sweeting. I'm just caught up in all the excitement and am a bit worn out."

"You must recover yourself for the wedding night!" I teased. My brother Henry had just informed me of the goings-on between a man and maid. He had heard it from Charles Brandon, who was told by Neddy Howard. It sounded horrid and naughty and a little delightful.

"Remember yourself, Princess!" Arthur commanded, but his tone was good-natured. "Now, you better hurry off to bed!"

I rose, then paused, curling my hand about the post. "Arthur . . ."

"What is it, lamb?" he asked.

"Will you still love me even when you are married?"

He laughed again. "You are a silly creature; of course I will. My first daughter will be named for you, how is that?"

I clapped my hands. "Oh, but it would be lovely! And may I stand as godmother to your first son?"

"You are a demanding little wench," he said.

"I must be; I am going to be a queen, after all!" I returned.

Arthur nodded. "Well, then. I suppose no one would be a better godmother to my first son than you, my dear."

"Ha! I can't wait to tell Mary!" I said. "She will be so jealous!"

With this I dashed off to the nursery, brimming with excitement as I anticipated the future of the glorious Tudors.

Arthur and Catherine were married on 14 November at St. Paul's Cathedral in London. Oh, what a lovely pair! Broad-shouldered Henry, who could at ten could pass for fourteen, escorted the bride to her groom. He strutted like a peacock, did Henry, and to look at him one would think the day was all about him. Of course if it were up to Henry every day would have been about him. He had thrown a fit over the fact that I should take precedence at public ceremonies since I would soon be Queen of the Scots, stamping his foot, making quite a proper fool of himself.

I supposed I could not blame him—I was guilty of basking in whatever attention given me and as I was the future queen everyone deferred to me before Henry, who was merely the Duke of York and would be nothing more than a glorified landlord and knight. I did not envy him at all.

Rivalries were dismissed at the wedding of Arthur and Catherine, however, and all eyes were upon them. They were a sweet couple and seemed engulfed in happiness. Catherine emanated a sincere desire to be a good English princess, though at her wedding feast she and her Spanish ladies entertained us with the spirited dances of their homeland.

"I must learn those dances!" I told Henry. "See how their feet glide—oh, they're so graceful!"

He laughed, a sound as infused with merriment as any, and reached for my hand. "Come, Margaret—we will show them all how the *English* dance!" he cried, and before I could protest we were skipping and alighting about the floor. The onlookers clapped and exclaimed over our prowess.

"At last Father has deemed fit to throw a real party!" Henry said as we twirled about. "They're so few and far between—he cannot bear to part himself from a few crowns!"

"Oh, Henry, you do talk scandalous!" I teased. "But too true!"

Father was sitting under his canopy of state with his chin in his hand, the fixed smile upon his narrow face forced. He was not a man for frivolities. But he must dazzle the Spanish ambassadors with displays of our wealth and hospitality. It was our obligation to show the world we were a power to be reckoned with, and nothing bespoke power like money and nothing bespoke money like an elaborate entertainment.

At last I found Arthur, who was pleased to watch the dancers rather than participate overmuch.

"Are you happy, Arthur?" I asked him.

He nodded. "I could not have hoped for a more beautiful princess," he told me. "I wish you the same joy upon your marriage."

"I wish you didn't have to go to Ludlow," I pined. "It's so cold and far away."

"Be brave, Margaret," Arthur said, his blue eyes sparkling with unshed tears. "Always remember what I've told you. Remember who you are."

In turn I offered my bravest smile. It was my last private moment with Arthur.

Upon his removal to the border of Wales my Arthur perished four months after his wedding, a victim of the terrible sweat. . . .

Oh, Arthur, you were supposed to be reveling in your princess. You were supposed to be giving me a godson and a namesake to follow. You were going to be happy. . . . We were going to usher in a New Age. . . . Oh, Arthur, who would ever love me like you?

The bells that had exclaimed my brother's joy rang out a song of mourning that resonated deep within me; my heart pounded in time with each heavy toll, its own mourning anthem a constant, aching reminder of hope lost. I kept my own counsel during that time, crying soft tears when afforded the privacy to do so. The kind archbishop tried to coax from me confessions of my anger and hurt over my brother's death, but I could not talk to him. There were no words that would bring my Arthur back.

The Crown Prince was dead, his beautiful bride widowed, and I was not the only one to feel the void of his loss. Mother took to her bed, inconsolable. Henry and little Mary clung to each other, but I noted a grim flicker in Henry's blue eyes. Was it satisfaction? Surely not. And yet I could not doubt he was relishing the fact that he was now the Crown Prince; Arthur's demise afforded him with the once unforeseen destiny of becoming King of England. *Oh, Henry, there is something missing in you,* I wanted to scream, but had no strength. He was but ten and I supposed everything was all a little unreal to a ten-year-old boy, who was so very behind a twelve-year-old girl in everything.

Father was devastated by the loss. Arthur was his pride. He loved him. Now his love was showered upon Henry; he became overprotective and strict, determined to prepare the boy for a life never anticipated for him. I almost pitied Henry as he adopted his new role. There was talk he would become betrothed to Catherine, which would at least enable her to remain my sister-in-law. Though the thought comforted me, I found it strange to think that Henry would have all of Arthur's leavings, right down to his own wife.

Mother's way of combating the grief was by proving her fertility. She was with child. Thus far she had been pregnant seven times, suffering stillbirths and miscarriages in addition to the loss of our beloved Arthur. Perhaps she hoped to ensure the succession by giving England another healthy prince in case Henry should meet with the same fate. . . . Oh, I could not bear to think of that.

Father was delighted, and though he was not a demonstrative man, he showered her with gifts.

"What can bring us more comfort than the hope new life brings?" he asked me, his stern countenance yielding to a rare smile that revealed more wistfulness than cheer.

The baby arrived but was short-lived. Our little Prince Edward was born a month premature and died within his first weeks of life. I did not cry this time. The state of my fear was too great, and as I regarded my gentle, fair-haired mother, her head bent in prayer, I pondered my fate. Was this what it meant to be a queen? To give and give and give of oneself and only lose in return? Your girls were sent abroad, your boys were set apart for their glorious educations, and God claimed the rest. . . . Surging through me was a fear cold as ice. I trembled. I was so gripped by nausea I could not abide the sight of food and became even tinier.

It seemed despite everything, kings enjoyed the glory while queens bore the pain.

It was a heady thing.

Mother wasted no time grieving and in the winter of 1502 her belly swelled yet again. This time I could not contain my anxiety. Nerves caused me to take to my bed with dreadful headaches. The nurse brought this to Mother's attention and she alighted to my side one evening over Christmastide.

"Margaret, darling, what is happening to you?" she asked in her soft voice. Ah, her voice. There was none like it; it was akin to a gentle wind, warm and sweet, never raised. There existed in the world no gentler a mother and tears streamed down my cheeks at the thought of causing her distress of any kind.

I sat up in my bed and wrapped my arms about her neck, burying my head in her shoulder. She began to sway, stroking my hair.

"Margaret," she murmured. "What is it? Tell me."

"Oh, my lady, I am so afraid!" I confided. "What if you lose this baby, too? How will your poor body bear it? You're so delicate and pale." I reached up to stroke a flaxen curl away from her alabaster cheek.

Mother pulled away, cupping my face in her hands. "You mustn't worry about me, darling. This is what I was made for. God's will be done."

"I am afraid of God's will," I confessed.

"You must not be afraid, for He intends only the very best," she told me. "Now enough fretting. You do not want to spoil your beauty for the Scottish Embassy; we can't have them telling King James his bride's face is tearstained, that she is beside herself with nerves. You must be strong. Arthur would want you to be strong," she added, her eyes knowing as she confronted my deepest grief.

"Arthur . . ." I covered my eyes to ward off a vision of my gentle brother, a vision that taunted me by being forever unattainable. "Then the baby. Oh, Mother, I am so sorry about the baby." I drew in a shuddering breath. "I watch you endure and you're so gracious and strong. I want to be like you, but I am so afraid I will never live up to your queenly example. I am afflicted with such fear—all I can think of is childbearing and what it'd be like if I were in your place. How would I bear losing my Crown Prince and all those babies? How would I go on?"

"You go on because it is your duty," she said. "I will not pretend that it doesn't break my heart; sometimes I think I lose a little more of myself with each passing." Her tone became thoughtful. "But we cannot bury ourselves with our loved ones. As queens we have a duty to our countries. We must provide heirs as long as we are able."

"What a business!" I sniffed, anger replacing my tears. "We are good for nothing else!"

"We are good for a great many things," she told me. "A subtle queen can advise her husband and be involved with the politics of the land if she is clever enough to make him think he does not know how much he relies upon her."

I smiled. "Do you think I will be such a queen?"

"I hope so," she said with her gentle smile. "Now you must try and stop grieving, lamb. In a few days the Scots will arrive and you

shall be married by proxy in a grand ceremony. The king is sending you all kinds of marvelous gifts."

"Gifts? Oh, gifts!" I exclaimed. At once my head felt much better. "What do you suppose a Scot gives his bride?"

"With any luck, a Scottish bairn!" cried Mother, taking me in
her arms. We dissolved into laughter as I anticipated my impending nuptials.

The proxy ceremony was held on 15 January in my mother's
presence chamber. My northern groom was most generous, sending me a magnificent trousseau from Paris and a gown worth 160
pounds. I almost swooned with delight—what a splendid prince
he must be!

How grand everyone looked, even Father, so solemn and stern
in his black velvet, and Mother a serene picture of fertility and
grace, her golden hair piled beneath her hood in an array of glossy
curls.

I was bedecked in grand state robes of crimson velvet trimmed
with ermine, my throat encircled in jewels, and almost every slim
finger ornamented with rings. My copper tresses tumbled to my
waist in thick waves and I walked in slow, measured steps, my
back straight, my head erect, proud as a Tudor should be.

The Scots did not look as odd as I imagined. There was something alluring about these men; there was an energy in their presence. They were *alive*. A thrill coursed through me as I pondered
my future husband, wondering if he was as handsome and lusty as
they said.

Patrick Hepburn, Earl of Bothwell, served as proxy, looking
most fierce and proud as he took my trembling hand before the
Archbishop of Glasgow.

The archbishop regarded my parents on the dais and asked
them if they knew of any impediment other than what had been
dispensed. They said they did not. When I was asked I responded
in a clear, strong voice that I, too, knew of nothing to impede my
marriage to King James.

Lord Bothwell's hand was warm in mine and I found myself
squeezing it. He squeezed it in turn, glancing at me sideways and

offering a quick smile as if to reassure me. The archbishop asked if it was in the King of Scots' will and mind that he marry me in his name, to which the earl answered with a confident yes.

The archbishop turned his eyes to me. "And you, Princess. Are you content, without compulsion, and of your own free will?"

No! I wanted to scream. Who in their right mind was content with the idea of being exiled to Scotland of all bloody places? But I remained calm and composed. I was a Princess of the Blood.

"If it pleases my lord and father the king and lady mother the queen," I said, making certain my voice resonated throughout the chambers. I would show these Scots that their queen would be strong and able.

"It is my will and pleasure," my father rumbled, his expression wistful as he beheld me.

Lord Bothwell repeated his vows after the archbishop, and I strained against his thick Scots brogue, trying to understand the words through the rolling *r*'s and guttural, throaty tones of speech. To think a whole country talked like that and I had to head them up!

My back ached from standing so straight, but I drew myself even straighter as I repeated after the archbishop, "I, Margaret, first-begotten daughter of the right excellent, right high and mighty prince and princess, Henry by the Grace of God King of England and Elizabeth queen of the same, wittingly and of deliberate mind, having twelve years complete in age in the month of November last past, contract matrimony with the right excellent, right high and mighty prince, James, King of Scotland and therefore I plight and give to him in your person of whom Patrick, Earl of Bothwell, as procurator aforesaid, my faith and troth."

At once the trumpets sounded and the minstrels burst into song. A bubble of laughter caught in my chest as I turned to the earl.

"Many congratulations, Your Grace," he told me, dipping into a bow.

Your Grace! I was a *Grace!* I shot a smug look at my brother, Henry, who was all too eager to sit on the throne. He scrunched his nose up at me but was smiling. I expected both of us were eager to dazzle our guests with our dancing.

Father led the band of Scots to his apartments while Mother approached me, sliding her hand into mine. "Your Grace," she said, and her tone of reverence humbled me. She curtsied before me. I curtsied in turn.

We were no longer simply mother and daughter but two queens, two great monarchs.

Two Graces!

This was something I could not revel in long, however, for Mother was now leading me to my apartments. I exchanged state robes for a shift and my hair was brushed till it shone. Mother ran her fingers through it and laughed.

"You are all Tudor," she said. "That lustrous red hair is your pride."

I smiled at my reflection in the glass. I may not have been as beautiful as my little sister, but I was comely with my round face, full lips, and wide, lively brown eyes. Mother, accompanied by my gentle aunts and ladies, put me to bed, covering me up to my shoulders, fanning my hair about the pillow in a pleasing array. She uncovered my foot to the ankle, and the crisp air caused me to shiver. I began to bounce my foot in nervousness.

"Be still, love," said Mother. "You must be composed."

With effort I collected myself. It would not do to see the Queen of Scots fidgeting in her bed.

It was not long before male voices were heard approaching, Scots and Englishmen laughing and jesting. None would think from that night that there was a moment's unrest between our two kingdoms.

The men entered my chambers, led in by Father and the Archbishops of Glasgow, York, and Canterbury. I offered a shy smile at the last, feeling peculiar that they should see me in such estate. Patrick Hepburn, my proxy husband, was dressed in naught but his shift and he approached the bed, looking at once imposing and awkward. I resisted the urge to shrink away from him as he exposed his bare leg. I pressed my foot to his thigh, my toes cold against his warm flesh. It was so odd that the act should amount to a legal consummation that I stifled another nervous giggle.

The room erupted into cheers and wine was passed about. The men vacated to take in their share and my aunts surrounded me on the bed laughing and I admitted that I was relieved I was not asked to do anything else but press my foot to Hepburn's hairy leg that night.

The thought of all that a real consummation entailed filled me with as much dread as delight.

All of London was celebrating me! There were masques and jousts and feasting. My hunger was insatiable, rejuvenated after a year of grieving and poor appetite. Henry and I gobbled everything in sight; we could not get enough of the roast boar, the eels, the mutton, the meat pies and puddings, the creamy cheeses, the wine that flowed so readily. We danced, our cheeks glowing and ruddy from spirits and excitement. Only on the floor did my chest clench with a pang of sadness as I recalled Arthur, how we would have celebrated that day, how he would have favored me with words of gentleness and wisdom. Tears filled my eyes, but I blinked them away. I would not have the Scots thinking I was a reluctant queen. I tossed my hair about and commenced to dance with tireless vigor as Henry and I ushered in the dawn.

At the jousts I sat beside Lord Bothwell, waving to the glittering knights, awarding them with tokens and prizes for their command of the lance. Oh, they were so brave and fine, those English knights, and I could not imagine their like existing in Scotland.

The earl asked me to point out the jousters and tell him about them. I did so, waving my hands with enthusiasm as I bragged about their prowess. As I did so I heard a Scots ambassador lean in to his companion and say, "Poor lass, she's just a babe." "Aye," agreed the friend.

My cheeks flushed in anger. I was not a babe! That day, for all intents and purposes, I was a bride and a queen.

I would show them that this babe was no one to trifle with.

My sister Catherine was born dead on 2 February, just a few short weeks after my wedding. A few weeks prior the town was alive with celebration. Now it mourned once more. Mother was weak, lying in the land of dreams. Nothing and no one could rouse her.

I learned of her death at Richmond Palace. Mother passed on her thirty-eighth birthday. Henry wailed for her; he had always been her pet and only my little sister, Mary, could comfort him. My father shut himself away and would see no one.

Mother was dead. In the space of a year I lost my treasured two brothers, a sister, and now my guide, my light, my mother. What would I do without her? No matter how afraid I had been about the prospect of removing to Scotland, I had always derived a sense of security in the knowledge that she would be in England. She would write to me and advise me. She would counsel me when I became with child and from her I would learn the art of being a true queen. Once again I was cheated; once again another family member was called to God while I remained behind scrambling to figure out why.

We took to Westminster to hear her requiem mass. Grandmother wrapped her arms about Henry's and Mary's shoulders, drawing them close to her small, strong frame, her countenance resolute, determined as always. She had seen death before, many times. It had lost its effect.

I sat alone. My beloved Archbishop Morton, one of the few in whom I would have been able to confide my grief, now also waited for Mother in the next world as well. I had not allowed myself to grow fond of the new one, Warham, who locked eyes with me and offered a sad smile I could not return.

Upon the conclusion of the service I proceeded down the Long Gallery of Westminster. At once it was as though I were swallowed up by the vastness of this hall, which in itself was a small place compared to the whole of England and the wilds of Scotland. And yet I was a queen, which wasn't small at all, and that must account for something. Would anyone remember me hundreds of years from then?

Would anyone remember my mother, herself so small and fair?

I removed to my father's apartments. I needed to find some assurance in my remaining parent, the king.

The guards fixed me with stern gazes. "The king will see no one," one told me.

"I am his daughter," I responded. "He will see me."

The guard shook his head, his mouth drawn into a thin, grim line. "His orders are explicit: He will see no one."

"Great God in Heaven, are We not the Queen of Scots! Has not one sovereign the right to see another? You will obey Us," I ordered, squaring my shoulders. "Or face the displeasure of Our country! We doubt you want to be responsible for a national incident!"

Startled, the men exchanged glances, then after a moment's more hesitation stood aside to permit me entrance. The instant I strode into my father's chambers I lost all confidence. My strong, measured steps became tiny and soft. I approached my father, who sat at his writing table, his head buried in his hands. I had never seen him thus; this was a man who never allowed for vulnerability. There was no time for it. He had a throne to secure, a treasury to fill, a country's confidence to win. There was no time to be faint of heart.

Now he sat before me broken, his long face drawn. He had been crying; tears stained his weathered cheeks. At once my breath caught. I had never seen him cry before.

"Your Grace . . ." I said, bowing my head and curtsying. "I am sorry . . . I did not mean to burst in."

"I must say it was well done," he commented, offering a sad half smile.

We gazed at each other a moment, immobilized by sorrow. I could not lament to him as I did to Mother; there was no railing against the fates or questioning God. We faced each other, two monarchs, and would address our grief with dignity, not drama.

"I came to comfort you," I said in soft tones.

"My comfort will be in this alliance," he told me, extending his hand. I took it. It was so large that mine was made invisible when enfolded within it. "Be a good queen, Margaret, as your mother was. Beget many sons. And remember: You are a daughter of England before you are a wife to Scotland. Do whatever it takes to ensure peace between our kingdoms."

"I shall," I promised, forcing strength into my voice as I swallowed my tears. I was determined to face him with stateliness. "I shall honor my mother's memory and do you proud."

Father rose. He rested his hands on my shoulders. "You have." He leaned forward and very gently kissed my forehead. I closed my eyes, reveling in the newfound bond between monarchs, vowing to be every inch the queen my mother was while encompassing the strength of my father, the founder of this Tudor dynasty.

❧ 3 ❧

The Progress

Father whiled away his hours in the White Tower, absorbed in the decorating of the new chapel off Westminster Abbey in which Mother was entombed. It was a magnificent structure, its spires stretching toward Heaven, its elaborate stained-glass windows depicting scenes of Christ's life in vivid detail. Despite its splendor never was the thought far from my mind that it was a tomb. This was where my father planned to lay himself down, and as he worked, so diligent in his attention to every facet of the imposing building, I feared he planned to yield to his eternal rest sooner than later. Mother's death had aged him; every act of state became an effort. It was enough for him to get through the daily task of living.

Henry was given his own household resplendent with every luxury. He had companions by the score, the best tutors and priests. Father would prepare him the way of a king. But Father did not offer his own hand that he might lead him. Henry, who was ever a candle to Arthur's flaming torch, remained as alienated from Father as before. Father could not seem to give of himself anymore. He was not cold; he was not cruel. He was silent, isolated, and immobile, save for what must get done. He would keep England as peaceful and powerful as possible while remaining true to his cautious and frugal nature by filling the treasury in the hopes that his son and his country would never be left wanting.

One way of maintaining peace was through the Anglo-Scots alliance. Father determined it was then prudent for me to be sent to my husband in the north.

I panicked. I was not yet fourteen; the treaty expressly stated that I was not to leave England until I was fourteen! But traveling to Scotland after November was a fool's journey. No one wanted to battle the cold and it was this point that convinced me of the necessity of an earlier arrival. As it was I would reach Edinburgh by August.

Everything was arranged. I would be accompanied by a glittering entourage of liveried guards, attendants, courtiers, and servants. Carts of gowns and plate completed the baggage train and I smiled through my rising sense of despair.

"You leave England a princess to enter Scotland a queen," said my little sister, Mary, squeezing my hands as I bid farewell at Richmond.

I blinked back tears as I took the little girl in my arms, wondering when I would see her again. I drew back, stroking her golden hair from her face. What was her fate, then? What kingdom would she be sent to? Would any of us who shared the nursery together see each other again?

I left her with a kiss, that I might promenade in the gardens alone with Henry arm in arm in an effort to extend my farewell as long as I could.

"Are you afraid, Henry?" I asked him in soft tones.

Henry laughed. "Afraid of what, Sister?"

"Of being king," I finished with a sigh.

He stopped walking. "I suppose I am." "I want people to respect me and fear me," he said, then in softer tones added, "but I want them to like me, too. Are you afraid, Margaret?"

I nodded. "I know it isn't the same as it is for you; I am the consort and not the ruler of the people. But I will be so far away from you and from everyone I love. I will feel so left out. Mayhap I will not get to attend your wedding or Mary's. . . . Sometimes letters do not seem as though they will be enough."

"They will have to be," Henry told me. He turned toward me, taking my hands in his. He was truly a promising lad, I realized then, putting aside previous rivalry and prejudices. Perhaps he hadn't been as cold as I thought. His blue eyes shone with nothing but sincerity now.

"Just remember I am your brother," he told me. "I will always protect you. And when you are afraid, remember this moment. Come to this very spot in your mind and I will be here to hold your hands. Kings never rest, nor do their queens, yet even God had a seventh day." He laughed, squeezing my hands in his. "So let this be our seventh day," he said. "Whenever you are afraid or it is all too much to bear, take your seventh day in your mind, and we will all be together again. It will give you strength."

I reached out, stroking his cheek. It was a lovely thought to hold on to. "I am sorry if I was ever mean to you, Henry," I was compelled to say.

Henry laughed. "I can take it," he said. "What kind of prince would I be were I not able to handle the women in my life!"

I laughed in turn as he took me in his arms before we made our way back to the rest of the party.

"Farewell, Sister," Henry said when we reached the assemblage. "Hold your own against those barbarians!"

Princess Catherine of Aragon laughed at this. "Now, Your Highness, you must not scare her," she admonished in her gentle tone as we embraced. "May God bless and keep Your Grace."

I was still unused to the title almost two years later and it caused me to start. I offered a quick smile, turning quickly so the ensemble did not see my tears as I was assisted into my splendid litter, trying to focus on the pageantry of the affair rather than the poignancy.

Farewell, dear siblings. . . .

My ladies surrounded me once in the litter, a gaggle of laughing, gossiping girls, and I was rejuvenated at the prospect of making such a grand progress throughout the country.

"We are all with you, Your Grace," said my aunty Anne Howard. Her whimsical nature was so reminiscent of her sister—my mother—that my heart surged with tenderness for the soft-spoken gentlewoman. "We will carry you all the way to Scotland; our love will carry you farther still."

I pressed her hand. "Thank you, my lady," I told her. I pursed my lips, swallowing the painful lump in my throat. "Oh, Aunty," I added, breaking protocol. "Do you think that love is as the poets say?"

"In what regard?" asked Aunty Anne.

"In that it can overcome anything, distance, anger . . . death," I added in soft tones.

Aunty Anne wrapped her arm about my shoulders, drawing me near. "I believe it can, Your Grace. All my life I have lost—from my dear little brothers in the Tower to my own child, my baby Henry. . . ." She blinked several times.

"Oh, Aunty, are we all fated to lose?" I asked, desperation seizing me as I gripped my empty womb, terrified that its crop would yield as tragic as that of those around me. "Sometimes I fear we are all stalked by death, as if it were some ravenous hawk, swooping down on us from above, and we never see it coming. . . ." *Like with Arthur,* I thought to myself, sweet, scholarly Arthur who should have been . . . should have been . . . I shook the should-have-beens away, trying to draw myself from what might have been to the present dilemma.

Aunty Anne's nod was grave. "Yes. We are human beings and our lot is to lose. The sooner we accept what cannot be changed or controlled the happier we will be. And as compensation for our losses God gives us in turn the ability to love and be loved. It is that which sustains us. It is that which sustains me." She offered a gentle smile filled with triumph. "And it will sustain you, too."

"You speak as my mother would," I observed in tremulous tones. For her words she was forever endeared to me. I favored her with a bright smile, determined to lighten the mood. I turned to seek out her husband, Lord Thomas Howard, who sat his charger looking altogether dark and terrifying. "Why, he's so fierce!" I cried to my aunt.

She laughed. "My fierce knight," she said. "And yet when we are alone you should see him . . . there is none gentler." She lowered her eyes. "I loved him from the first time I saw him. I was but a girl just your age." She yielded to another of her whimsical smiles. "I pray it is so with you and His Grace, King James."

I lay back among the plush velvet cushions and tried to envision the King of Scots, thirty years old to my thirteen. He was said to be a lover of women . . . oh, I was terrified! What if he thought my form too childish? Surely he had loved many a beautiful, buxom maid . . . but I was no mere maid. I was a queen and his rightful wife. He would love me as he loved no other.

And so with those thoughts to keep my restless mind active, I departed for my new home, filled with eagerness, excitement, and something like hope.

The first four days of the progress were not unlike any other progress we had made in years past. The distinct difference was that this was a constant celebration and all in my honor. The country and its people were vibrant, rosy, and infused with summer as they rushed out of their homes to greet my entourage. Children sang my praises, pageants were performed, and I was showered with gifts of fruit, sweet wine and beer, little cakes, and trinkets from children, which I cherished most of all.

It all changed at my grandmother's home of Collyweston, however. Father's journey would end there; he was as far from his royal residence as he could go and the rest of the progress would be spent in the keeping of Aunty Anne's father-in-law, the Earl of Surrey.

"Can't he go a little farther?" I asked my grandmother as we prayed in her apartments the evening before I was to leave Collyweston.

Grandmother shook her head. "He has his obligations, Your Grace, just as you have yours." Despite the somber words, I found myself reveling in the fact that she must defer to me as "Your Grace" and no longer as "that impetuous girl."

I was certain to make the most of it whenever in her company. But looking at her at that moment I was struck with the same fancy as when beholding my sister and brother at Richmond: When would I see her again? For all her sternness and strict religious observance she was the grandmother who oversaw my upbringing with tireless devotion. I was overcome with a wave of tenderness for her and reached out to take her thin hand in mine.

For the first time in memory, Grandmother softened, stroking my thumb a moment with her cool finger before extracting the hand. "Come now, I shall see Your Grace to bed," she said, her low voice gentle as she brushed through my coppery hair, then helped me dress. I slid into the large canopied bed, drawing the blankets to my neck despite the warm summer breeze that came in through the window.

Grandmother smiled down upon me. "Make us proud, Queen Margaret," she ordered as she leaned in to kiss me on the forehead. "Good night."

When she exited, I fixed my eyes on the window, on the full moon that reigned over its court of glimmering stars. Did King James even then behold the same moon as I? Did he wonder after his bride; did he long for her? Or did his gut lurch with dread at the thought of having to marry me for the sake of the alliance? My own stomach churned. The moon became a blur.

At once I heard the creak of my door and sat bolt upright. "Who dares enter Our chambers unannounced?"

Soft male chuckling. My heart pounded. A taper was lit to reveal my father standing there in all his majesty, his stern face softened with a smile. "Haughty as a Tudor queen, no less," he commented as he approached to sit on my bed.

I hugged my knees to my chest. "Forgive me—"

He waved a hand in dismissal. "Nonsense, it was quite the right response." He set the taper on my bedside table. "Your Grace," he began, then lowered his eyes. "Margot . . ." Tears caught in my throat at the use of the pet name he alone had used. "Tomorrow we must say good-bye in the formal capacity before the court." He reached out, cupping my cheek in his large hand. "And so for this night we shall put aside our scepters and face each other as father and daughter."

My lip quivered. Tears began their course down my cheeks; it was a slow progress. Father stroked them away with his thumb.

"I would like to tell you a story," he told me, gathering me in his arms. I yielded to the rare display of physical contact; indeed I had always been a loving girl and eager for affection to such an extent that Grandmother had to warn me against the impropriety of sitting on priests' laps when confessing as a wee girl. Now I flung myself into my father's arms without restraint, nuzzling my head against his black velvet doublet, taking solace in the embrace for a long moment before he pulled away. He smoothed my hair against my face and offered a sad smile.

"Come now, enough," he cooed in soft tones. "Lie back and let me cover you," he said as I settled back among my pillows. He drew the covers over my shoulders again, then reached out to stroke my hair. "Will you remember everything I your father the king tell you this night?"

I offered a grave nod.

He smiled. "From the very first day you were born I knew you would be Queen of the Scots. You were born on St. Andrew's Eve. Saint Andrew, as well you know, is the patron saint of Scotland," he added for good measure. I closed my eyes, trying to emblazon his low musical tone in my heart as he continued. How I hoped never to forget the timbre of his voice! "I had you christened the very next day at the church honoring Scotland's Saint Margaret. It was fortuitous, I thought even then. Though it was yet to be addressed, I knew someday, somehow there would be a great alliance between the thistle and the rose through you. And thus it has come to be, and not without its critics," he added with a soft chuckle. "When I was making the treaty there were those who feared that should the fates be cruel and my heirs stolen from me, leaving you to succeed to the throne of England, it would leave

Scotland in control. But I was not in the least bit afraid of such a thing. I told them England will never yield to Scotland but Scotland to England and so it shall someday, and through you. Our crowns are destined to become one. I am convinced of it."

"How do you know?" I asked him in a small voice.

His eyes were filled with wonder as he looked beyond me. "I have seen it in a dream. I have seen it and I believe it." He reached down again to stroke my head. "You must be strong, Margot. What we Tudors are given to endure God gives us the strength to endure. Be a queen before you are a woman always. Always remember that you stand alone; monarchs have no true friends and must act with constant caution. No one will ever truly love you, my child, and I say it not to be cruel. It is a lonely business. . . ." He cleared his throat. "Do not be ruled by your passions; let your head govern you in all that you do. I fear for your brother in that regard." His eyes clouded a moment as he sighed. "Oh, but you are so young. . . ." He shook his head, closing his eyes and biting his lip. "You will never know what it costs me to let you go. I can offer you all the jewels and gowns in my realm as parting gifts; I can give you palfreys and coaches and splendid litters, every material thing that could satisfy your desire. But it would not be enough; nothing in this world would ever be enough to show you how much . . ." His voice caught. "How much I love you."

I sat up, flinging my arms about his neck once more, feeling his tears wet my cheek. "Oh, Father!" I cried, and at once terror gripped me, terror of leaving all that was familiar, terror of governing a foreign land without any guidance, terror of being alone and unloved. . . .

Father pulled away, seizing my chin between thumb and forefinger. Tears streamed down his high-boned cheeks unchecked. "I will never see you again, Margot," he whispered, and for a long moment we sat, memorizing each other's features. "Promise me something," he said then.

"Anything," I sobbed.

"Be the queen you were born to be," he told me.

"I shall," I promised as he urged me to lie back among the pillows once more. He leaned in and kissed my forehead and thus he left me as a father would his little girl.

Tomorrow we would part as monarchs.

There were no tears for this formal farewell. The court gathered about us, their expressions tender as he bestowed upon me his blessing along with a Book of Hours. Though I was never one to be considered devout, I would treasure it always. I opened the cover, where was inscribed: "Remember your kind and loving father in your good prayers." On the page opposite the prayers for December he wrote: "Pray for your loving father, that gave you this book, and I give you at all times God's blessing and mine. Henry R."

I offered a deep curtsy of gratitude. My tears were kept to myself. Today I was composed, dignified.

A queen.

I was surrounded by splendor. The trumpets sounded; the minstrels sang; the banners snapped and fluttered in the breeze; my white palfrey was brushed till she shone like a star. I mounted her and Father passed the reins to the Earl of Surrey. With effort I stilled my quivering lip as I waved to the onlookers and well-wishers. My grandmother stood stoic and thin lipped, but I was certain the sun caught tears reflecting in those hard eyes.

We began our progress to York and I refrained from turning about on my horse to look back at my father. I could not bear the thought that this was the last time. . . .

I will never see you again, he had said.

I did not want to believe it.

But with heart-sinking certainty I knew it to be true.

I refused to think of my family as we made our progress north. I decided to think of this as an extended holiday. I would see everyone again in time; this was just a little journey. It was the only way I could bear it. But every night in my bed I thought back to my last night with Father, of his low, rumbling voice as he made his tearful farewell. I thought of my gentle mother resting in her crypt. I thought of Arthur, dear sweet Arthur. I thought of little Mary, such a sweet child with a bright life ahead. I even missed fiery Henry.

But I blinked my tears away and the face I presented to the court was filled with joy, for how could it not? The progress was wonderful and filled with merriment. I was beset with gifts from all those I encountered en route. I was serenaded by my minstrels and by choirs of children who praised my beauty and charm. I was given so many gifts that my chests overflowed. The bells of the towns tolled for me, Queen Margaret Tudor Stewart, and I hummed and resonated with the bell-song.

The only things I hated about entering new towns were the strange relics of saints I was made to kiss as if my kissing them would make some kind of difference. My Scottish emissary and chief escort, the Bishop of Murray, handed them to me with a kind smile and I refrained from grimacing as I kissed some thighbone or finger or vial of blood . . . it was disgusting!

This was something I did not have to indulge in with frequency, thank God, and as soon as I was able to be discreet Aunty Anne brought me some cool water to wash my lips with.

There were now so many people in my train I was overwhelmed. All of the fine ladies and gentlemen of York rode out to meet me along with Lord Northumberland, a stunning man in red, sporting black velvet boots with gilt spurs. He was quite the sight and I found myself sighing more over his finery than his person.

In my litter my ladies helped me dress for my grand entrance into York. It was cramped and we were all near to tripping over one another as I was dressed in my gown of cloth of gold, made even more resplendent with its cloth of gold sash. My throat was encircled with a collar of gems, and rings were slid up almost every slim finger. I held out my hand in admiration.

"They look too big to be real!" I exclaimed over the rubies, sapphires, and emeralds that graced my fingers. "It is almost all too big to be real . . ." I added, my eyes misting.

The tears were swallowed as I was arranged on my plush cushions, all embroidered with my badges of Tudor roses and coats of arms. The pretty white palfrey from Father was dressed in her best and was led behind me as I was shown into York with great fanfare, my ears ringing with the cheers of the masses.

The first horrid thing I had to do was hear a Mass, and I tried to refrain from wiggling about in restlessness as I listened to the bishop ramble on in Latin. I was not the scholar both Henry and Arthur were and had very little patience or affinity for languages, so the Mass to me was just one endless stream of gibberish. But I remained composed and serene as I imagined a queen should look and complimented the bishop after. His cheeks glowed when I stretched out my hand for him to take and he almost toppled over as he bowed. I stifled a giggle, but my merriment shone through as I lifted him up by the elbow.

Lord and Lady Northumberland were generous in their admiration of me, giving me such feasting and entertainments that I was overwhelmed with exhaustion. Always there was dancing and eating and then more dancing! As much as I loved it, I found myself longing for a nice sleep in a peaceful place. I longed, too, for my mother and the Princesses Mary and Catherine of Aragon.

I longed for home.

I did not have much time to think on it, however, for we quit bustling York on 17 July and I rode my palfrey through the rugged hills of the north. Newcastle greeted me with more choirs of children and I clapped my hands in delight as I listened to the pure, clear voices lifting themselves in my honor.

"I shall give them all presents!" I cried, and passed them rings and precious stones that I was certain they would sell for food, but I cared not. I was making them happy; they smiled at me as if I were the prettiest, grandest lady in the world and that was all that mattered.

"You must not give away your plate, Your Grace!" Lady Guildford admonished gently.

"It is mine to give, is it not?" I returned in haughty tones. "Besides, they love me for it."

"You do not have to reduce yourself to such things to make people love you," she said quietly.

I turned toward the brown-haired, plain lady and grimaced in disgust. "I know I do not have to buy anyone's love, if that is what you are so grossly implying. I'll not hear another word about it."

"Yes, Your Grace," she said, but I liked not the concern in her eyes as she regarded me.

At Newcastle our party was met by Lord Thomas Dacre, deputy to the Warden of the Marches. From first sight I discerned that he would be a friend to me. He was a broad-shouldered man with a gentle face, if a little weak in the chin. But I liked his eyes, soft hazel eyes that seemed as though they would never dream of imparting unkindness upon another living being.

"I am to escort you to Berwick Castle, Your Grace," he told me. "And there we will have a hunt if it pleases Your Grace."

"A hunt?" I cried in delight. "Oh, it seems like forever since I have enjoyed a good hunt!"

"We will have a bearbaiting for the pleasure of Your Grace as well," he added, hazel eyes sparkling as though his first and last wish was to delight me.

I clapped my hands. "Are they big bears?"

He chuckled. "The biggest we could find."

My heart skipped at the thought of the beasts wrangling with their canine counterparts. Though I feigned excitement at the prospect, in truth bearbaitings frightened me. There was so much blood and death. I hated death. . . .

But I would not offend Lord Dacre, so I exclaimed and carried on as though it were the most anticipated event of my life.

When it came time to witness the event, however, I could not refrain from gasping and averting my head as the bear struck the dog with one large paw, tearing into its flesh with its sharp claws.

"You are not happy with this display, Your Grace," Lord Dacre observed, and at once I realized it was not a question.

I turned toward him, offering an apologetic smile.

"I do wish you would have told me; I'd have canceled the whole thing," he said.

"But I couldn't have done that after you went to so much trouble for me," I told him.

"Moving a mountain would be no trouble, were it to be done for you," he said, and my heart stirred in delight. How I adored courtiers!

I hoped the Scottish court was as good to me as Thomas Dacre!

❧ BOOK 2 ❧

Jamie

৵ 4 ৵

Scotland!

The progress was getting too long for me and I was anxious to settle at Edinburgh. What was a joyous journey was now a chore. I grew tired and sore from riding. I wanted to soak in a warm bath for hours and know that for one day I would not have to go anywhere and do anything, not even dress up. Certainly that meant I was exhausted, for I cherished my finery and most any opportunity to don it.

Accompanied by eighteen hundred ladies and gentlemen, dressed so fine they looked more like dolls than people, we approached Lamberton Kirk, where we encountered the Scots. They were the most glamorous barbarians I had ever seen! Surely I did not think them capable of dressing so fine, but they wore their damasks and cloth of gold and silver much like we did. It was only that crude accent that separated us.

My hair and gown were threaded with pearls and I was disconcerted by this, for pearls were a symbol of mourning and I had had my fill of that. I banished these dark thoughts from my mind, however, as I lay in my litter gazing at the assemblage of Scots in wonderment. My eyes could not help but be drawn to some of the men's legs, which their kilts showed to great advantage, and I compared many a well-turned calf. As I admired these rogues I wondered what my husband looked like; I had tried not to think upon him too much during the progress. The thought that I would soon meet him filled me with such fear and excitement that I knew not how to manage it.

After feasting and entertainment, a thousand of these beautiful barbarians joined our entourage and we set to riding again. I was in Scotland now. England was behind me and I knew not if I would ever return. More and more I found myself swallowing tears. This was a wild place, a beautiful land with its rolling hills and emerald fields. But it was not my land and I was frightened of it. What would these people make of me after the novelty of my arrival had worn off? We had been enemies for so long and grudges died hard. . . .

On 3 August I was met at Dalkeith and given the keys to the castle by Lord and Lady Morton. This was my last stop before Edinburgh and I was glad of it. Soon I would be at my new home. I could not wait!

Lady Morton showed my ladies and me to our apartments while the rest of the assemblage sought out their lodgings. Many had to sleep in stables and barns, inns when available, and tents. It was good for me indeed to be queen as I thought of crawling into a comfortable bed with covers and herbs to sweeten my chambers.

Alone with my ladies I kicked off my slippers and twirled about. "I cannot wait to sleep and dream of my coronation! I am so very tired!" I sat on my bed while Agnes Howard, Lady Surrey, brushed my hair. "I should like a hot bath before bed," I yawned, imagining being enveloped in steaming scented water. Perhaps they would put lavender in it. Yes, that would be pleasing. . . .

At once the door burst open and Lady Morton entered, curtsying. "Forgive the intrusion, Your Grace, but the king is approaching!"

"The king?" I asked, dazed. I rose. "The king! No! He cannot come now! I look—well, I am not ready. He wasn't supposed to see me till Edinburgh."

"He will see you now," said Lady Morton, not without a slight note of annoyance in her tone.

I scowled. "Help me with my gown, Lady Surrey, and make certain the pearls are still threaded prettily through my hair."

I stared down my reflection in the metal of the mirror, wishing there were some better way of seeing myself. I held the swells of my breasts. "Not much I can do about these, I suppose," I lamented.

"You'll fill out as you grow, Your Grace," Lady Surrey assured me.

"I wish I'd grow in the next ten minutes," I pouted.

"Come now, you're beautiful," said Lady Guildford in her tiny voice. "He will adore you."

I blinked the hot tears from my eyes, hating the quickness with which they appeared. "Do you think?"

She nodded, along with Lady Surrey.

When I was deemed presentable the room began to fill with courtiers both Scottish and English. I stood by the window, shoulders squared, trying to rein in my trembling. The king . . . my husband. He was coming. . . .

When at last he swept in, I took in the sight of him. Tall and well built, with auburn hair grazing his shoulders in layered waves, his lively eyes a vivid green, his nose aquiline, and the beard that hugged his well-defined jawline framing a sensual mouth, he was the quintessence of regal bearing. He sported his hunting habit of crimson velvet and wore his hawking lure over his shoulder. Upon seeing me he removed his cap. His lips were parted; his eyes were gentle.

I dipped into a deep curtsy as he approached. He bowed and once we were both righted he took my hands. His were strong, with long, tapering fingers. A hunter's hands. A king's hands.

"But you're beautiful," he breathed as he gazed upon me.

Strange warmth coursed through my veins. My cheeks tingled as I looked at him through my lashes.

"Expecting something else?" I asked him.

He laughed. "One never knows." His voice was handsome despite the thick Scots brogue. Somehow when he spoke the accent was far more charming than grating. "And so, Margaret, my beautiful little bride, do you resent very much my impatience at wanting to see you?"

"I should," I told him. "How unkind coming upon me this way!" But I was teasing him and he knew it. His green eyes sparkled with merriment. "You could have found me in my shift!"

"All the more delightful!" he cried, but I noted as he assessed me, his face clouded over. His eyes softened, as though in pity. My heart raced.

"Have I displeased you, Your Grace?" I asked in small tones.

He rested his hands on my shoulders. "No, dear heart, no . . . but you are so very young and so far from home. Are you terribly frightened?"

My lip quivered. How I longed to throw myself in his arms and cry, *Yes, yes, I am frightened! Rock me, hold me, do not let me go till the fear dispels!* But I only offered a smile.

"How can I be frightened, my lord?" I asked him. "You say I am far from home, but I could not be closer. I am in Scotland beside my husband the king. What is there to fear in my true home?"

He tipped back his head, offering a deep belly-shaking laugh. "Well said, my lady, well said!" He cupped my face between his strong hands. "Scotland is your true home and I shall always endeavor to make it feel that way to you."

He leaned forward then and bestowed the gentlest of kisses upon my lips. The courtiers who had been pretending to be absorbed in their own nonsensical chatter grew quiet as the king pulled away, breaking into his boisterous laughter once more as he led me to the assembly.

As I stood next to him I could not stop looking at him. This was my husband and the King of Scotland.

Most important, he was the most wonderful man in the world and he was mine!

That night the bells began to toll and I started. "Mother is dead!" I cried, then, shaking myself to my senses, scrambled out of bed to see what the matter was.

" 'Tis the stables, Your Grace," a servant informed me. I looked out the window into the black pitch of night. The sky glowed with an eerie golden hue. "Up in flames."

"What of my palfreys?" I asked, my heart racing in panic. "What of the palfreys from my father?"

"All gone, Your Grace," she said softly. "I am sorry."

"No!" I cried, throwing myself facedown on the bed and burying my head in my folded arms. All the tears I tried so hard to quell throughout the long progress into Scotland freed themselves; the floodgates of my soul were torn asunder and I sobbed great gulping gasping sobs. I counted my losses . . . Arthur, baby Catherine, Mother, home, and all that was familiar. . . . Now my loyal horses, the beautiful dear horses Father gave me, were gone. It was as though I were allowed to keep nothing from England. I would be all Scot. I would have Scottish palfreys, Scottish gowns, Scottish maids. I was not to be reminded of home, not even in the smallest sense.

The servant departed and it was not long before I was surrounded by the Ladies Surrey, Guildford, and Morton, who petted me and cooed to me as though I were a wee babe. All meant well, but it was of no use. I could not be consoled.

"I want my mother," I sobbed as Lady Surrey collected me in her arms, swaying gently from side to side.

"Oh, darling," she murmured. "Oh, Your poor little Grace, how much you have endured!"

My ladies slept beside me all night, comforting me when I awoke crying for Mother and Arthur, my little palfreys, and a childhood long gone.

The king himself arrived at dawn and admitted himself into my chambers after I donned a green velvet dressing gown.

He gathered me in his strong arms and I buried my head against his ribs, for I was so small that I did not even reach his breast. He stroked my hair as my tears mingled with the black velvet of his doublet.

"My precious Maggie," he said, and I warmed to the new pet name. "Dearest little girl, dinna cry. Please dinna cry. Your Jamie's going to move you to Newbottle, how would that suit you? Then you will not have to look upon where such tragedy befell you. And I am going to buy you all new palfreys, how about that? White and shining, just as good as your old ones, and they'll be outfitted in the prettiest you've ever seen."

I nodded, hiccoughing and shuddering with renewed sobs.

"Now, now, dinna cry, love. Think about all the entertainments! I canna wait to see you dance and hear you play the lute—it is rumored you are of great talent." He kissed the top of my head. "We'll sing together, won't we? Hmm? You can sing, can you not? Why, I know you can, your speaking voice is such a delight."

"Oh, Your Grace—"

"Jamie," he corrected me. "Your Jamie."

I tried to smile, but my lips quivered so much it was a feeble attempt. "Jamie, I'm so tired," I murmured. "Everything has been so wonderful, but I long so much to sleep all day long."

At this request, Jamie lifted me in his arms and carried me to the bed. When he settled me on the mattress he pulled off one slipper, then the other, then drew the coverlet over my body. "And so you shall. Sleep till you can sleep no more and when you awaken I shall have you carried to Newbottle, where I will arrange the most magnificent entertainment in your honor. How does that sound?"

"Wonderful." I yawned.

He leaned down and kissed my forehead. "Till then, sweetheart," he said as he bowed.

"Till then, Jamie," I echoed, casting adoring eyes at his beautiful face.

Oh, but he made me feel better! He was so handsome and chivalrous! Truly he was the incarnation of Lancelot himself!

❧ 5 ❧

Mistress Stewart

My honorable knight was as good as his word and made certain my residence was moved to Newbottle, where I danced and feasted and was treated to the finest spectacles he could arrange. He sent me white palfreys almost as fine as those from my father. I cooed in delight at my new pets as I stroked the velvet saddles, fingering the gold harnesses. Oh, the splendor of it all, oh, the sweetness of my king!

The next day I donned a new cloth of gold gown trimmed in ermine. Again my throat was encircled in jeweled collars of gold and my hands were heavy with the weight of rings. I would be removing to Edinburgh, my new home, at last. Composed and serene as a queen should be, I climbed into my litter, and the last leg of the journey began.

English lords and ladies were paired off with Scots and they formed a dazzling train while the thousands of onlookers cheered my procession. I waved and tossed coins, hoping to endear myself to the people who shouted blessings and sang my praises.

We neared the halfway point, where I was invited to have a shot at a doe Jamie sent for my hunting pleasure.

"I will not hunt without my lord!" I cried, delighted he should think of me. How I longed to draw back my bowstring and show him my prowess! He would be so pleased with me!

At once Jamie arrived attired in purple, sitting a horse dressed in gold. My breath caught in my throat as I beheld him. Oh, but he was a true king! He dismounted, approaching my litter, and, without further ado, swept me up in his arms, planting a firm kiss upon my mouth.

My eyes widened in delighted surprise as I wrapped my arms about his neck. "Oh, Your Grace!" I breathed.

His expression was soft, filled with tenderness. No eyes were kinder, I thought to myself as I gazed upon him. I longed to trace his face, to marvel in its every contour and angle. Never had I seen a man in possession of such noble beauty.

For a while he rode beside me, making certain to ask after my comfort every few moments to the point that I began to giggle at his solicitude.

"I should like very much for you to ride with me into the city," he told me.

"I shall ride one of the new palfreys," I said as the procession came to a halt.

"No. You shall ride with me, holding me about the waist," he added with a smile. How I adored the enthusiasm that caused his voice to crescendo with passion. So infectious was it that I giggled as he continued. "When the people see you thus they will know how pleased their king is by his precious little queen."

"Oh, yes, that would be delightful!" I exclaimed as I was helped from my litter. After it was decided that Jamie's horse wasn't gentle enough for the task, one of the new palfreys was brought forward. I mounted behind Jamie, wrapping my arms about his waist just as he said. My hands encountered something strange then, a heavy belt of iron. I stiffened. "What is this, Jamie?"

" 'Tis nothing to worry your pretty head about, little one," he assured, moving my hands up to rest above the belt on his belly. "Come now, let's ride!"

We began to gallop toward the city. The wind rippled through my copper hair and I laughed, reveling in the freedom of it all. As we rode we were met by pageants and playacting. Knights mock jousted each other for love of a maiden and I was thrilled at all the effort put into these displays.

"It is all for you," the king told me. "All for my little Queen Maggie."

I nuzzled up between his shoulder blades and squealed in enchantment. All for me! This was a state of affairs I could well get used to!

When we entered through the gates of Edinburgh at last I was presented with more revolting relics to kiss, including the arm of Saint Giles. Jamie, who seemed most observant and devout, urged me to kiss the disgusting things first, which I did with as much grace as I could summon, and he followed my lead, pressing his lips to the objects with a sincerity I did not feel. To me a bone was a bone.

Next we were greeted with more pageants. I was presented with the keys to the city by an angel with real feathers for wings. Everywhere about me was opulence and excess; the fountains gushed with red wine and my head throbbed and tingled from the ringing of the bells.

Edinburgh was alive with merriment and song.

And all for me!

It was my wedding day. The proxy ceremony, I realized, had nothing on this. Even if it were overcast the city would be lit by the gold in my procession—my eyes were dazzled by the cloth of gold and jewelry worn by people and horses alike.

My gown was black velvet and white damask with red silk sleeves to match Jamie, who met me with his bonnet in hand as he did whenever I was in his presence as a sign of respect. My heart stirred at the sight of him standing before me so noble and proud.

I wore a crown, the crown of a queen. It was heavy on my head and I trembled as I reflected upon its significance. My father told me this was my destiny—my fate since birth. He knew it then and I knew it now. I stood straight under the weight of this crown, vowing even as I exchanged vows with my king that I would endeavor to be the greatest queen Scotland had ever known.

The Archbishops of Glasgow and York officiated and we shared the Host at the Mass. I started at the trumpets that announced our union and blinked back tears when Jamie handed me the scepter.

Holy oil anointed me then and with this ritual I truly became the Queen of Scots.

Jamie wrapped his arm about my waist as we removed to the banquet at Holyrood House. "One of my favorite residences," Jamie explained as I gazed at the castle towering before me. "I pray you will come to love it as I do."

"I love it already," I said because it sounded so charming. And I was dazzled. But as I entered the great hall I grew more aware than ever that this was not my home. *I will never see you again.* My father's words rang in my ears, as resonating as the church bells celebrating my presence.

Jamie drew me from my wistful reflections by insisting that the gifts be given in my name. He poured my wine with his own hand, attending to my every need as a stream of gifts paraded before us. Goblets and bolts of fabric, jewels and caskets, trinkets and treasures the worth of which was beyond my conception.

"Are you happy, little one?" Jamie asked me in his enchanting brogue. He began to fix our plate, making certain I was served first.

"I am so happy, my lord," I breathed. "But I am happiest knowing I have married the handsomest, most wonderful prince in Christendom!"

He laughed, bringing my hand to his lips.

We ate the splendid fare before us, served from fifty different platters. I could not contain my ravenous appetite and Jamie laughed as he watched me sample the different meats and puddings. He was quite restrained and ate sparingly.

"You think me unbecoming eating this way," I commented, flushing.

"I think you are a growing girl," he said in soft tones, fondness lighting his green eyes.

The evening passed in a whirl. The English and Scots minstrels and musicians battled against each other, each in the hopes of outshining the other, and there was an underlying tension behind the seemingly good-natured competition. We danced till the soles of my feet ached and throbbed. My legs tingled and my face flushed from wine.

At last the moment that held the court breathless with anticipation arrived. We were escorted to our wedding chamber. Separately the king and I were dressed in our shifts.

"Your hands are cold, Your Grace," my aunty Anne observed as she squeezed my icy fingers in hers. "You are afraid?"

I had not allowed myself to think of this moment. Now that it had arrived my heart thudded against my ribs in a painful rhythm. I offered a small nod.

"Have you been instructed on how best to please a man?" Lady Surrey asked.

I shook my head. "My grandmother thought it sinful to discuss such things."

"A wonder King Henry was conceived at all," Lady Surrey muttered with a smile. "In any case, it does not take much to please them—I daresay a man will infiltrate any hole available." I flinched as dozens of scenarios presented themselves before my mind's eye. "Just yield to their fancies, be sweet, and ever ready to serve."

"Don't be afraid, Your Grace," Aunty Anne instructed. "The pain does pass."

"There's pain?" I asked, my throat constricting in panic.

Aunty Anne's eyes widened, as though she was fearful at revealing this unpleasant insight. She stroked my hair. "There is," she informed me. "But it is a pain that yields itself to much joy; it is a communion of the souls that cannot be achieved through any other act and becomes a closeness you will never feel with any other being." Her face was radiant with conviction. I marveled that she should feel this way, wondering if I would ever know the like.

"Ah, Lady Anne, you are a romantic," observed Lady Surrey.

"It is a pretty thought, Lady Surrey," I said. "I like it."

"Then take comfort in it, Your Grace, as you do your duty for Scotland," commanded Lady Surrey as she brushed my hair, arranging it over my shoulders.

I drew in a breath. The moment had come.

The king and I were led to the massive bed of state by giggling courtiers and ladies. The Archbishops of Glasgow and York stood at its foot, two old men of stony countenance. I flushed under their gazes, fearful that they would stay to observe the entire act as some had been known to do.

The covers were turned down and Jamie and I were assisted into the bed, where the covers were then drawn over us to the chest. We were blessed by the archbishops. Jamie folded his hands and squeezed his eyes shut, murmuring a prayer to himself. It seemed almost an intrusion that I should bear witness to his private communion with God, a communion I had never experienced during my prayers.

At the blessing's conclusion, the archbishops, ladies, and courtiers filed out of the chambers, leaving us alone. Jamie turned down the covers and rose, making toward the buffet, where he poured himself a goblet of wine.

"Would you like some, little one?" he asked me, his soft tone ever solicitous.

"I fear I shall fall asleep if I have any more," I confessed with a nervous giggle. I looked about our suite, my eyes wide with awe. Tapestries depicted the grandeur of the court of King Solomon and the strength of Hercules, certain to be two of my king's heroes. The glazed windows bore the arms of Scotland and England, and crowns of interweaving thistles and roses adorned the bosses. I drank it all in with delight.

"Thistles and roses," I observed with a slight sigh, recalling that long-ago conversation with my beloved Arthur when I likened myself to a thorn.

"Entwined as one," Jamie said, but his smile was distracted. He brought his goblet to his lips, downing it. He turned, gazing at me a long moment. I was unable to read his expression; it was distant, wrought with an emotion I could not understand. Pity, confusion perhaps? It did not make sense to me.

"Would you . . . like to sleep, sweetheart?" he asked then, looking down into his goblet.

I shook my head. "Of course not, Your Grace!"

He smiled through pursed lips. Sweat gathered at his brow. He set the goblet on the buffet, making for the window seat, but did not sit. He gazed out and I had the distinct feeling he was viewing nothing of the scenery. He rested his forehead in his hand a moment before letting the hand fall to his side as he drew in a deep breath, expelling it in a sudden *whoosh.*

"Your Grace . . ." I leaned up on one elbow. "Jamie . . . have I done something wrong?"

He shook his head. "No, no, of course not." He crossed to the buffet once more, pouring himself another cup of wine, taking a long draught, then sitting beside me on the bed. He sighed. "I fear for you," he confided. "You're so very small and I'm—" He bit his lip, his face flushing.

"Your Grace?" I asked, screwing my face up in confusion.

He bowed his head. "Tomorrow morning they will inspect the sheets," he explained. "And we must give them the blood proof that our union has been consummated."

"B-blood?" I asked, scrambling up toward the pillow. "Blood from whom? Nobody told me there would be any blood!"

Jamie gathered me in his arms. "Oh, little one, little one, dinna fret. . . ." He swayed to and fro and I took comfort in the steady beat of his strong heart. "We do not have to do it just yet." He paused. "Let me tell you of your new home." His voice grew very soft and low as it did whenever addressing me. "Here in Scotland there is a fog that shrouds the land every morning, very romantic. It softens our hard-edged world. I love to walk in it and look about; it is smoky and a little undefined, like a painting." He smiled. "And we have lochs so calm and clear that you can see straight to the bottom. I shall take you swimming—yes, I fancy swimming and you shall learn to as well, no matter how 'unladylike' they say it is. We will float on our barge, listening to the water lap against its sides, and let the sun warm us as we dip our toes into the water. There are fish to catch and stags to hunt. We will hawk and ride in the Highlands, where it is so green and the air is so clean and crisp." He drew in a breath, as if he were there, breathing in the Highland air. I found myself doing the same. "And there are castles, beautiful castles where you will play and sing and make many friends. You can decorate as you please and throw as many entertainments as you like."

I tilted my face toward his, watching his beautiful mouth move as he described his kingdom and its people, who he promised would love me. He told me of all the pets I would keep, the horses and dogs and birds of prey to be used for my pleasure. All the while his voice rose and fell, alternating between passionate enthusiasm and gentle musing. His was an enchanting voice; I grew lost in it. I grew lost in him.

At last he laid me back against the pillows and stroked my cheek. "I shall be quick," he reassured me. "There will be no need to even uncover yourself. We shall keep our shifts on." He rose and blew out the tapers, cloaking us in darkness. My breath caught in my throat. He returned to me, climbing in bed once more. "There. Mayhap it will be easier this way."

Easier for whom? I wanted to ask. Was it that he could not bear to look upon my underdeveloped form, my nonexistent breasts and narrow hips? Was I so repulsive then? I kept those disturbing thoughts to myself as the king covered my face with gentle kisses but avoided my mouth, even as I sought his. At last I ceased doing so and lay back, praying I had the strength to endure this act that would cement the alliance between England and Scotland.

As promised he did not attempt to remove either of our shifts; he was as gentle as possible. He did not caress any part of my body save for my hips, which he cradled in his strong hands as he commenced, entering quickly. Tears heated my eyes and I cried out— I told myself I would not, but it was terrifying. This thing inside of me was agonizing—a sword bent on ripping me in two. If I could not abide its presence how would I bear a child? Oh, what a disappointment! The king withdrew at once. He was trembling.

"I have hurt you," he whispered. "Oh, my lady, my dear little . . . little . . ." He could not say it.

My legs quaked. I drew the covers over myself and averted my head from his moonlit silhouette.

"Will it always be like this?" I asked, my tone tremulous.

"No," he told me. "As you grow . . ." His voice wavered. "As you grow . . ." He rose and commenced to pour two goblets of wine. "I trust you are ready for some wine now."

I sat up, nodding.

He handed me the goblet and I downed it like a sailor. It was soothing, warming my quivering limbs.

"Do you think you got a child on me?" I asked then.

"Oh, little Maggie . . ." There was no mistaking the pity in his tone. It shamed me and I held out my goblet for more wine, hoping to drink my disgrace away. "There are other things that have to happen to get a child."

"Does that hurt, too?" I asked, my gut lurching in terror.

He gazed into his goblet. "No, it is very pleasurable," he said.

"For the man, you mean," I remarked, unable to keep the pout from my tone.

He laughed. "Aye. But there is much pleasure to be had for the woman as well. You will see."

"Have you loved many women?" I asked him.

He hesitated. His face clouded over. Moonlight reflected glistening tears standing bright in his eyes. "Yes, Maggie. I have loved many women."

I scowled, unable to contain my instant jealousy. It surged through me hotter than any wine. "I suppose they were buxom and wildly curvaceous and knew just what to do."

His lips twitched. "Maggie, we must not speak of such things on our wedding night," he told me, setting his goblet down once more and climbing into bed beside me. "Come lay your head on my chest," he invited as he enfolded me against him. He sighed. "I do not come to our marriage bed an innocent. I wish that I had. Can you forgive me?"

I wiped my tears away, frustrated to have betrayed my jealousy. "I can forgive you anything," I assured him. "So long as you remember who is the true Mistress. Stewart."

He laughed. "Mistress. Stewart?"

I nodded. "Mistress. Stewart—it is a title I relish even more than 'Your Grace.' "

"Ah." He kissed my nose. "Then, may I bid my forever Mistress. Stewart good night?"

Forever. It was a word that rolled nicely off the tongue. I giggled. "Indeed. Good night . . . Master Stewart."

But as we lay there lost in our own respective thoughts I wondered what else my husband had experienced while my childhood was spent preparing to be his bride.

I wondered at my capacity for forgiveness.

As the night waxed into dawn I lay awake listening to my king cry and twitch in his sleep.

"Margaret," he moaned. "Oh, sweet Margaret . . ."

I was reassured. He must have been greatly bothered by our conversation to let it haunt his dreams so.

"I'm here, my love," I assured, reaching out to stroke his bearded cheek. "I'll always be here."

And I wrapped my arm about his broad chest, curling up against him, this man who was to be my world.

The king did not try to repeat our wedding night's unpleasantness and I was just as glad. The longer I could put off that invasion the better. Meantime he was ever solicitous and attentive. Every day I was treated to glittering entertainments. Jamie's Fool, English John, had such a raunchy sense of humor that I was sent into fits of delight, but the poor fellow was scolded for his bawdy witticisms. I was disappointed in the stricture placed upon him.

Every day hoped to outdo the one before in gaiety. There was naught to do but play and be merry and I relished every opportunity to sun myself in the gardens with my ladies. We played at cards and bowls or spread our embroidery about the lawn and stitched away the hours against the music of our own gossip.

One afternoon Jamie descended upon the garden with old Lord Surrey and a group of courtiers. Surrey spent a great deal of time with Jamie and the two seemed to have developed a genuine rapport. I smiled in greeting.

Aunty Anne and Lord Thomas Howard pushed me in my favorite swing as my king approached with long, confident strides. Oh, what a handsome spectacle he was! In his arms were cradled two squat black terriers with coarse fur and long squared-off snouts.

"They're called Skye terriers," Jamie informed me, his voice infused with his infectious enthusiasm as he placed the wriggling creatures in my arms. "Do you know what Skye means?"

I nodded, proud of myself for remembering. "It is Scotland's true name," I said.

"Very good. They are a feisty breed but very affectionate and fiercely loyal."

"Ah, then they will suit their mistress well." I laughed, fingering one pup's gem-studded collar.

"What will you call them?" he asked.

"I shall call the girl Skye," I said. "And the boy will be named . . ." I put my finger to my chin in thought. "Bruce! After Robert the Bruce!"

"Ah, my little Scottish bride!" Jamie cried, leaning in to kiss my forehead. "Are you quite comfortable and taken care of then?"

"Aye, my lord," I answered, flushing.

"Then I shall leave you to get acquainted," he said, offering a deep bow and kissing my hand. After a series of bows and curtsies, he departed with some of his courtiers, leaving me to my pups and my play.

"I suppose we should begin overseeing the details for our return," remarked Lord Surrey.

Startled, I raised my eyes to him. Return. Of course my English court must leave. They could not stay forever. I knew that. Why did my heart lurch in surprise? I turned toward Lady Surrey and Aunty Anne. Would I see them again? A lump swelled my throat.

"Would that you could all stay a little longer," I lamented in soft tones.

"There will be visits," Aunty Anne reassured me.

I bowed my head. Though I appreciated her attempt to cheer me, I knew the likelihood of visiting to be very slim. This was a long, arduous journey; few ever took it twice. I would receive English ambassadors, perhaps an occasional border lord. No friends, no family. They were leaving.

"Come, Thomas," Surrey commanded in his gravelly tone. "Let us commence."

Lord Thomas turned to Aunty Anne, offering a gentle smile as he leaned in to press his lips against hers. For a brief moment I was allowed a glimpse into her world; his face emanated love in its form most pure and I was swept up in it. Would Jamie ever look at me that way? He looked upon me with fondness and affection already, but not quite love. Not yet. Soon, I hoped.

Lord Thomas's expression was fleeting, converting to the stony mask that I had come to associate with him. He offered a bow, kissing my hand as was required, then departed with Surrey.

Though they were soon out of sight, their voices carried on the wind and I heard Surrey mutter, "I've sent word to the king about his new son-in-law."

"What did you tell him?" asked Lord Thomas.

"Ah, that he's a little too hungry for a Crusade—thinks he's a regular King Arthur. Doesn't see things as they are—a hopeless romantic. But I think he's trustworthy enough for a Scot." He sighed. "Well, let's hope he gets a babe on her soon, before one of his bastards gets any ideas."

I rose, clutching the pups to my chest, my flat, childish chest. My face was hot, my breathing shallow. Tears burned my eyes.

"Your Grace—" Lady Surrey reached for my shoulder.

"Hush!" I commanded, straining my ears.

"At least someone had the good sense to remove the Drummond girl or Scotland very well could have had another Margaret as queen," Surrey went on. His voice was growing softer as he grew farther out of earshot.

"A pity the sisters went down with her," Lord Thomas said. "Three girls poisoned at breakfast."

"What's three girls?" Lord Surrey retorted with a brief, joyless laugh.

"Ask their father," Lord Thomas returned, his tone bitter.

Surrey's reply could not be heard. I whirled upon his wife. "Make me understand, for love of God!" I breathed, tears filling my eyes.

Lady Surrey's face was wistful. "It was cruel of my husband to speak of such things when he clearly knew you would hear him." She pursed her lips a moment. "I suppose in his own strange way he means well—in true Howard manner he is trying to prepare you for the situation before the court leaves." She drew in a wavering breath, closing her eyes. "Lady Margaret Drummond was King James's mistress for many years. To remove the possible threat of her usurping your rightful place as queen she was poisoned at her breakfast. Unfortunately, two of her sisters ingested the poison as well and—"

Margaret, sweet Margaret. It was not me he cried for in his sleep but her. Was that why he called me Maggie? Because he could not bear to utter the name of his lost love? Oh, God, my handsome prince . . . Was there any hope that he would ever love me?

With effort I stilled my quivering lip. "Wh-who did it?"

Lady Surrey shook her head. "No one knows, Your Grace. Likely, those who had the interests of Scotland at heart. Someone who did not want the Douglases or the Drummonds to rise to power through the girl. Some even suspect—" She lowered her eyes, biting her lip.

"Who, Lady Surrey?" I demanded through gritted teeth.

"No one, Your Grace," she said quickly.

"I command you to tell me!" I ordered, so angry I was unable to derive pleasure in the fact that I was commanding someone about.

She averted her head, her voice a whisper so soft it was barely audible. "Some suspect your father may have arranged it, Your Grace, to clear your path of obstacles."

I shook my head. I refused to believe this; I could not bear to have my vision of my father, my stoic, honorable father, altered in any way. In firm tones I said, "Careful you do not speak treason against your king. He is not capable of ordering such cruelty. It was not he; do not even suggest it."

"I was not going to until you commanded me, Your Grace," she replied.

"You must not think of it, dearest," Aunty Anne urged in her soft voice. "You are the queen, the only queen, and none can take your place."

"What's more important is I am his wife. His *wife.*" My voice was heated with fervency. "His Mistress Stewart. And I will never let him forget it."

But my confidence was forever shaken. Three girls were poisoned, one for daring to love a king and two because they were in the wrong place at the worst of times. If three lives could be extinguished with such ease and lack of conscience then what could become of me should a party among these wild Scots decide I was less than worthy of sitting beside James IV?

I laid a hand upon my flat belly. A baby. I would have a prince and soon. My throne would be secured. Panic gripped me as another thought assaulted me.

Bastards. Plural.

Jamie, my sweet, handsome Jamie, had children.

With supreme effort, I went through the motions for the rest of the day. I played with my new pups, I ate heartily at supper and laughed at the Fools, ever in competition with each other. I played my lute and led the courtiers in song. It would have been a most merry sport were my mind not viciously taunting me with the afternoon's revelation.

When Jamie and I were alone my temper could no longer be controlled. The moment he entered our chambers I burst into tears.

"Maggie, child, what is it?" he cried, approaching me to place his hands on my shoulders. His face was stricken at my distress and I was glad of it, reminding myself that this could prove a useful technique in future encounters.

"How many, Your Grace?" I seethed, unable to discern his features through my tearful haze.

"How many . . . ?" His face was wrought with confusion. "Maggie, please, child, calm yourself. Tell me what has happened."

"How many children have you sired?" I sniffled, wiping my cheeks with my palms.

Jamie dropped his hands from my shoulders and backed away. "Oh, Maggie . . . I had hoped to spare you of this until I deemed you more equipped to manage such news. But the court relishes their gossip. I should have known it would not take too long before rumors reached you."

"Are they rumors or truths?" I demanded, my chest still heaving with sobs.

He cocked his head, pursing his lips, his eyes making an appeal for an understanding I could not give. After a moment's more hesitation he said, "It is true. I have children."

"How many?" I persisted.

"Five."

"Five?" I cried. "*Five?* God's blood, aren't you the profligate!" I balled my hands into fists. "Two or three I could perhaps understand—perhaps—but five! And all by the same mother?"

He shook his head.

With wild abandon, I began removing pins from my hair and throwing them at him. They bounced off of him, useless as my tears.

"Five little threats to your throne!" I went on, my eyes gone painfully dry with rage. "Did you ever think at all before you brought them into this world of the effect they could have on your future? On Scotland's future? And these women . . . these—these—" I searched for a word, a word nasty enough to encompass what these women were to me, a word unfit to spring forth from a queen's lips, a word I had heard long ago. "These *whores* of yours! Surely they were happy to give you children in the hopes of raising themselves high and the children even higher!"

Jamie remained very quiet during my tirade and when at last I could think of no more insults to hurl forth he approached. I could not read his face. Perhaps I had gone too far . . . perhaps in my unbridled anger I had sabotaged any growing affection he may have harbored for me.

To my astonishment he swept me up in his arms and carried me across the floor to the window seat and, holding me across his lap, he sat, cradling me against his chest.

"Maggie," he began, his intoxicating tone low as he stroked my hair. "Try and remember, little one, that for the whole of your life I have been a grown man. And 'tis true there are many times when my excessively amorous nature ruled over sound logic. I canna speak for the ladies' motivations, but I would like to think they were not so sordid as you imply. But then"—he shrugged—"I do not know. I *do* know that my children, despite whatever favor showered upon them, will never usurp the place of the royal children, neither in my heart nor on the throne of Scotland."

"But you do not know what they could do, what they may be capable of when they grow up and begin to lust for a power they may see as their birthright," I told him, my voice small with fear.

"A legitimate concern, and one I have taken into consideration. But the relationship I promote with my children is a loving one and it is my hope they will be too bound to me through their affection to ever conspire against me," he reasoned.

"And their mothers? Or your enemies? Are they so 'bound to you through their affection' that they will not use them against you?"

Jamie flinched. "There is no way of knowing." He bowed his head. "I was used in such a way. . . ." His eyes clouded over as he shook his head, as though ridding himself of dark and terrible thoughts. "I was prevented from knowing my father . . . and his enemies used me against him in the worst way imaginable."

"How?" I asked, my jealousy yielding to concern as I noted the profound sadness etched upon my husband's features.

"We must not discuss such things, dearest. Only know that I am raising my children in the hopes that our closeness will cultivate a loyalty that the cleverest of my enemies canna permeate. I—I love them, Maggie," he told me. "Can you understand?" Tears welled bright in his green eyes. They sparkled like emeralds. "It is my hope that someday you can meet them and perhaps . . . perhaps grow to care for them. I would never expect you to love them as your own but perhaps . . . Do not think on it; it is a lot to ask now, but . . . someday."

Indeed I could not bear to think of it, but to prevent any discord I said nothing, bowing my head and pursing my lips should they decide to betray me by blurting out something even more unbecoming than had already been spoken.

"What are their names?" I asked at last, unsure if I wanted to know but feigning sincerity to remain in his good graces.

"There is James, Alexander and Catherine, Margaret." This he said with a flinch and I assumed she was by that other Margaret. "And Janet."

I was silent a long time. "Quite the family," I remarked before I could help myself. "Well, someday we'll have our own babies and you will have to love them most," I added with a scowl.

Jamie sighed, said nothing, and began to sway.

My mind raced; my heart pounded. *He is* my *husband!* I wanted to shout to his mistresses, present and former. *Mine and not yours!* And someday I would have the only children who could mean anything to Scotland.

❧ 6 ❧

Margaret the Queen

My English court, my English friends and family, left me. I was alone in this country, an English princess made a Scots queen. I watched the procession depart with all their pomp and fanfare, tears grown cold upon my wind-chapped cheeks. Jamie's arm was about my waist; he squeezed me to him, holding me upright. I was glad of it. I was weighed down by the finery.

"You will make new friends," he reassured me.

I was too numb with sorrow to nod. The procession grew smaller and smaller till it became a distant snake, slithering down the Scottish countryside and out of Edinburgh, out of my life. They returned to my home, to my father, to the places and the people I would not see, not ever again.

I had my adopted country to acquaint myself with. I was given Scottish ladies and as time passed I not only found myself understanding their harsh dialect but also heard myself slipping into it.

I was becoming a Scot.

My husband came to me now and again to repeat the obligatory act we were avowed to perform for the good of our country. But as yet there was no pleasure to be found in it. It did not happen often enough and when it did it was always in the dark. We had been married nigh on two years and I had yet to see my husband as God made him and he had yet to see me.

Yet he was as attentive as he could be. Gifts were showered upon me; we hawked and hunted together and he praised my skill with the bow. As promised we frolicked in the loch; Jamie held me and taught me the forbidden art of the swim, but I found the most pleasure hanging on to his neck while he cut through the water like an eel.

Music was another of our favorite pastimes and we played together. I strummed my lute while his slim fingers danced upon his favorite organ. I adored hearing him sing; at times he talked through the songs as much as sang them and bubbles of laughter collected at the base of my throat as I took him in, enchanted. I sang out in a voice strong and clear and Jamie smiled in genuine appreciation. He was nothing if not genuine.

And ever generous, allowing me to have as many new gowns as I desired. I loved to order costumes for masques. Anything I wanted was brought to me; I lacked nothing. I needed nothing. And yet there was this loneliness, profound and persistent even through the lavish entertainments I hosted for my new friends and family. Scotland was littered with Stewarts and I tried to learn every name. They fussed over me, calling me a pretty thing, but no one demonstrated a genuine love of me yet. Jamie said that was nonsense, everyone loved me. It would be impossible not to. Though I believed this should be the way of it, it remained untrue nonetheless. I felt it. I was tolerated because I was securing peace with their longtime enemy.

There were some I had grown fond of, however, though I could not say they were close to me. The poet William Dunbar, who composed many a verse praising my beauty or simply to entertain, served as a worthy companion and courtier and was always quick to bring a smile to my face. Another was the privateer Sir Robert Barton, a straightforward man with a rather captivating gift for storytelling, and I was always thrilled to be regaled with his adventures on the high seas, and, even better, by the many exotic gifts bestowed upon me as tribute.

None of the women impressed me much, however. Though I conversed and danced with my ladies, I could call none of them friend, not really. My dearest friend was my husband and I spent as much time enjoying him as I did being jealous of him, jealous of his experience, of his age, of those who admired him with as much conviction as I.

I had even grown jealous of God, for Jamie spent a great deal of time with Him, going on pilgrimages to the shrines of Saint Niniane and Saint Duthlac. I hated when Jamie left me and was not shy about making him aware of my displeasure.

"Going to have another conversation with God?" I snapped one morning as he readied himself for his departure in our chambers at my least favorite castle of Edinburgh.

Jamie strode toward me to cup my cheek. "I regret you canna understand my . . . need to be near Him at times."

"Oh, I understand," I said. "Tell me—the technicalities confuse me—do your mistresses accompany you to the shrine or do you visit them after? Or do you all sort of worship together at the altar—or on the altar as the case may be?"

"Maggie!"

"Dinna let me keep you! Go off to your Saint Niniane and leave me here, here in this cold, solitary place and me so lonely I could scream! And you dinna even care about me at all!" I cried.

Jamie took me in his arms, holding me fast. "Never say such things, Maggie, you know it is untrue," he urged.

"Not at all—not at all!" I reiterated, enjoying the effect of my words on my husband and pulling away, folding my arms across my blossoming breasts. At least something was happening there. I wished the process could be sped along so I would be too irresistible to abandon for a shrine and whatever else he might be devoting himself to.

"Please do not go," I pleaded in soft tones, my anger fading to misery as my arms dropped to my sides.

"I must, little one, but only for a short time," he told me, taking me in his arms and kissing the top of my head. "When I get back we shall go on progress, how about that? To Falkland Palace, our favorite. Would you like that?"

I nodded at the thought of the vast, sprawling deer park and lush forest.

"And we'll hunt together," he went on. "We shall make quite a merry sport of it, a contest. I trust you will practice your archery while I am gone so that you might hit all your marks. Perhaps you shall kill more stags than I!"

He disarmed me. Already I was thinking of the gowns and jewels I would pack for the journey.

"We shall pass a merry spring there," he said. "You must plan a grand banquet—would you like to attend to all the special details, to make certain you have everything just as you wish it?"

I offered a nod of eagerness. "Oh, yes! English John and Scotch Dog shall help me. And Dunbar shall amuse us with witty verse!" I cried with delight, enthused about my task.

"My sweet little girl," Jamie said, kissing my cheeks and touching the tip of my nose with his forefinger. "Plan a wonderful entertainment then and I will come home to you soon."

"Yes, you always come home to me," I remarked with a confident smile.

"Always." And with this Jamie departed. I sat on my bed, bowing my head.

No doubt he visited his children as well on these trips.

I rose, squaring my shoulders. It was no matter. I remained above bastards and would not reduce myself to thinking of them. When our child was born they would be forgotten.

"Scotch, I want your best dressmakers to fashion me a gown," I informed my wardrobe keeper, James Doig, utilizing his pet name.

He was all smiles at the prospect. "What kind of gown would Your Grace be needing?" he asked in his thick burr.

I clasped my hands together as I stood before the mirror in my privy chamber at Edinburgh. "A riding habit—but not an ordinary riding habit. This particular habit must be as enchanting as a ball gown but as seductive as a shift." To my delight his eyes widened at this shocking revelation.

He stood behind me. In the mirror I noted his eyes slowly traveling from my slippers to my hood. There was no lechery in them. He was assessing his project. "I think I know just the thing," he said in decisive tones. "Might I be permitted to surprise Your Grace?"

I broke into a smile. "Of course," I agreed, turning about to take his hands in mine. "Make it a good one, Scotch—the Stewart line is depending on it!"

Scotch's lips twitched a moment before he yielded to a burst of laughter. It rang in my ears like the tinkling of chimes. His blue eyes sparkled bright with mirth against his rosy complexion as he squeezed my hands. "Be assured, Your Grace, that this will be the finest habit you will ever lay eyes upon!"

He bowed over our joined hands, then made his retreat.

I smiled to myself. My first step in seducing my husband the king had been put into action.

There were to be no entertainments at Falkland Palace. I had not planned one, not a single one, for while we were there I wanted no distractions. Jamie would be shared with no one, not even his own courtiers.

The castle was sweetened and scrubbed. I made certain Jamie's favorite organ was brought so that he might play at his leisure. Twenty-three carts of gowns, jewels, and other supplies necessary for diversion were brought on our progress and when everything was unpacked I waited for Jamie to come to me.

I planned a hunt. Together we would ride through the thick forest that surrounded the palace; the sweet spring air would fill our lungs until we were rendered breathless. The clomping of the horses' hooves would pound against the forest floor, mirroring the blood pounding in our ears. Our bodies would thrill with the stretch of the bowstrings as we drew them back to hit our mark, the regal stag. Oh, the hunt!

Jamie arrived to find me and a handful of courtiers waiting. As usual he removed his cap and played the chivalrous knight, ever solicitous, ever caring. I did not offer any challenges about his previous whereabouts but celebrated his presence, reminding myself that he may love a hundred common women but only one queen.

The morning of the hunt a smiling Scotch Dog visited my apartments. Two servants followed with a chest that was set before me.

"Your habit, Your Grace," he announced with a dramatic hand gesture before stooping down to open the chest. He commenced to reveal the most beautiful riding habit I had ever beheld. The low-cut velvet gown was deep claret, with an orange kirtle the color of autumn leaves and fitted sleeves to match. Resplendent velvet oversleeves were claret to match the gown, and the boyish velvet cap with a claret ribbon sported a black feather that Scotch advised me to wear at a jaunty angle.

"Oh, Scotch!" I breathed, clutching the soft velvet of the oversleeve and rubbing it against my cheek. "It's perfect! Tell me it is easy to remove."

Scotch laughed. "Very," he informed me as he showed me where it laced up.

"Excellent work, Scotch!" I commended.

"Happy hunting, Your Grace," he retorted with a wink of his twinkling blue eye.

I giggled. "This is one prey I'm not letting get away from me!"

Scotch departed with another bow and I was assisted into my gown, shocking my ladies with the knowledge that I wore nothing beneath it.

"Your Grace, it simply isn't done!" they cried.

"Then I am setting a precedent," I replied. "Soon everyone will be doing it and think me quite a visionary."

They clicked their tongues and shook their heads but obeyed and I admitted to a certain freedom as I slipped into the gown without the bother of all those petticoats.

My hair was left flowing over my shoulders, streaming to my waist in a rippling copper mane. The cap was set upon my head at an angle, the claret ribbon tied beneath my chin. I smiled at my reflection, pleased. The gown accentuated my developing curves, and even my ladies gasped in appreciation.

Satisfied with my appearance, I removed to the stables, choosing my favorite palfrey and riding her to where Jamie awaited at the edge of the forest. I rode at a deliberate speed, with purpose.

When Jamie beheld me his eyes widened, his lips parting. "Maggie . . ." he breathed.

"Your Grace," I replied, flashing him a bright smile. "Shall we make for the forest?"

He nodded. To my delight he was unable to remove his eyes from me. I pretended not to notice but thrilled with pleasure.

We commenced into the forest. Anticipation made me alert to every noise. It was not long before we were on the tracks of a stag, discovering him grazing in a clearing. He raised his majestic head, heavy with its crown of antlers. His brown gaze fell upon us, cautious, questioning. He was still, his muscles tense. At last he flicked his tail and leapt into the forest. The chase began in earnest and I readied my bow as I followed him, my husband in tow.

The stag turned once more and I drew back, my shoulder aching with the tension in the string. I let it snap. The arrow swished through the air, piercing through the chest of the animal. Brilliant crimson stained his fur as he dropped. A lump swelled in my throat as it did with every kill—as exhilarating as the hunt was for me, I could not help but be moved by the creature's sacrifice.

"Wonderful, Maggie!" Jamie cried as he dismounted. He instructed his courtiers to remove the stag to the palace for our evening's supper. With this executed we stood alone. Our breathing was heavy, the thrill of the kill still surging through our veins. I quivered, trembling with excitement.

Jamie approached me, taking my hands in his. They were hot, slick with sweat. He shook his head as though in disbelief. "My God, Maggie . . . You're so beautiful."

I smiled, drawing him nearer to me. "Jamie . . ."

He wrapped his arms about me, his lips descending upon mine in our first true kiss. His lips were hungry, inflamed with a passion I did not know he possessed as he devoured mine. I returned the kiss, matching his passion with my own. His hands roamed my body and I found myself boldly unlacing his breeches and removing his doublet. Freed of our bonds, we stood before each other as God made us, shining with sweat, our chests heaving. I took in Jamie's body, drinking in its beauty—all angles, all muscles, taut and fine. But he was scarred. His hips were chafed from the iron belt he insisted on wearing, his back a patchwork of white and pink wounds that snaked across his flesh, jagged rivers of pain.

"Jamie, who dared whip you?" I asked him.

He shook his head, tears lighting his green eyes. "It is a burden

I bear gladly—please let us not think of it or anything unpleasant at this moment. Let me look at you . . . oh, Maggie. . . ." He drew me to him and I reveled in the silkiness of his skin against mine. We pressed against each other with urgency, kissing once more. His lips traveled down my neck, to my breasts, my belly, my legs. My body was aflame with sensation; I was primal, pagan as a priestess at a Beltane fire. Infused with passion, we fell to the ground and with tender urgency claimed what was our right, writhing with love there in the middle of the forest, on a bed of thick, sweet grass surrounded by thistles and wild roses.

At last Jamie was mine.

At Falkland Palace Jamie and I drank in our newfound bliss, having no need of wine or entertainments beyond what could be derived from each other. There we had found a hideaway, a respite from the world. We were not a king and a queen but a man and a maid, simple, eternal, beautiful.

But it was there at Falkland Palace that I learned the truth about Jamie at last. As he was dressing he clasped his iron belt about his fine waist and my heart constricted with pain as I watched him take on this peculiar burden.

"Jamie, why?" I asked him, leaning up on one elbow in my bed, wishing to prolong the ordeal of dressing for a few more minutes.

He arched a questioning brow.

"The belt," I prompted. "The belt, the lashes on your back . . . the nightmares." I cringed as I recalled the countless nights I had awakened to Jamie's agonized cries. "Jamie. Please. I am your wife. Tell me."

Jamie's eyes misted over. He sat on the window seat. "It is a penance, Maggie."

"Why?" I asked again, my breath wavering. Besides keeping mistresses, I could not imagine anything this beautiful man capable of doing that could warrant such cruel observance.

He bowed his head. "My father . . . You recall how I told you that I was used against him. As a child I was kept from him by his enemies. In the Battle of Bannockburn they—they mutilated him, Maggie. They . . . you canna even imagine, you dinna want to imagine . . ." His face was stricken with horror. "And all of it in *my name*. He was made a brutal sacrifice to his enemies' ambitions and *I* was the figurehead to which they attached themselves, hoping that through me they could rule. They learned soon enough that I would be ruled by none but God." His voice wavered with conviction, tears streaming down his cheeks. I crossed to the window and sat beside him, taking his hand in mine while stroking his cheek with the other. "I canna pay enough for my part, the part I played in my father's death. This is the least I can do, for his memory and for God."

"Jamie, surely you dinna believe you were at fault," I cooed. "You were innocent—a child. No one was protecting you; no one had your best interests at heart." I stroked his silky hair, then gathered him in my arms, pulling him to my breast and swaying from side to side. I recalled my father's words, that to be a monarch is to be alone, without true friends. Those who secured Jamie's throne for him did so out of self-interest. I trembled with fear as I wondered what forces could work against us and our future children should we displease our subjects.

"Out of respect for my father, Maggie, I must bear this burden," he told me. "I must continually demonstrate my regret at the treachery and violence that brought the crown upon my head."

"For whom?" I asked him. "For God? If that is so, be assured that He knows, Jamie. You dinna need to torture your poor body for this. You were a child! God knows your regret and forgives you."

He shook his head emphatically, squeezing his eyes shut. His shoulders heaved with sobs. "No!" he gasped. "No! You dinna understand! I must! I must! No matter how many years go by, no matter how fortunate and blessed I become, I must remember what it cost!"

"Oh, Jamie!" I did not know how to comfort him. I never regretted something to such extent that I was inspired to resort to such extreme measures.

I rocked to and fro, humming in soft tones, wondering if there was any way to heal my husband's tortured soul.

It was a way of thinking I did not understand, the need for pain. But Jamie needed it; he thrived off it.

It accompanied him wherever he went, worn like a cloak.

Or an iron belt.

Bitter hot bile rose in my throat, filling my mouth, and there was naught to do but spew it forth into the basin my lady held out for me as she had done every few hours. I could hold nothing down. My stomach grew taut with pain and I ingested nothing but bread and broth.

My throat was raw from retching, my temples pounding. Even my cheekbones throbbed and ached. My breasts were so tender I could not lie on my stomach anymore and no longer got any sleep, for that was my favorite position. I curled up in bed useless, burying my head in the pillows as the physician examined me.

"I'm dying," I told him. "Tell His Grace to find a new queen and she best be fat and hideous. If he chooses Janet Kennedy I'll haunt him for the rest of his life," I said in reference to his favorite mistress and mother of his son James.

The physician laughed. "You are not dying, Your Grace. You are with child."

I sat up, raising my head. My eyes grew wide. "With child?" I breathed in awe.

"You did not recognize the signs?" he asked.

I had never seen the signs before. Besides taking to her bed with exhaustion, my mother was always composed during her pregnancies. If she was ever in such wretched estate she never let on.

"No one told me," I admitted in small tones, flushing in my ignorance. "I have been kept uninformed on a variety of subjects, it seems," I added, thinking of Jamie's children and mistresses.

My lamentation was replaced with a smile as the implication of the physician's news settled upon me. I was with child. I was carrying a prince for Scotland!

"When will he come?" I asked the physician.

"In the winter, perhaps the early spring," he informed me.

I reached down, cupping my flat belly, willing it to curve. How I longed to feel the life stir within me!

A prince! At last I was carrying our prince!

* * *

I commanded those who knew of my condition to hold their peace. I would choose the proper time and place to inform the king.

The moment came in August, when I was three months gone with child. I lay in Jamie's arms in our barge, looking up at the night sky, where a peculiar light was seen streaming against its cobalt backdrop, a cloth of gold thread throbbing and pulsating in a heavenly tapestry.

"It is a comet," Jamie explained. "They are very rare. To see them once in two lifetimes is a miracle. Surely it is a sign from God that something wonderful is about to happen."

The court, floating among us in their barges, pointed and commented on the beautiful long-tailed star.

I nuzzled against his shoulder. "Perhaps it is foretelling the birth of your prince," I said.

I heard his heart quicken beneath his doublet. He looked down at me. "Maggie?"

I nodded. "Late winter, early spring." My lips hurt from smiling.

Jamie proceeded to cover my face in kisses, drawing me across his lap and holding me tight. "Oh, my precious girl, my precious, precious girl . . ."

For ten days the comet lit the sky, convincing us that the baby growing within me would be a prince to rival all others.

The prince sapped me of all of my strength, and though I relished the feeling of him swimming and stretching in my womb, I grew too tired to attend court functions. I lay in my apartments, one hand over my rounded belly, taking in with delight every kick as the entertainment was brought to me. I was surrounded by amusement. English John kept me laughing with his bawdy jokes that he daren't utter before the king, and William Dunbar recited verse. He was as artful as English John. His words settled upon my ears, threaded together with the lyricism of a song and the poignancy of a lover's kiss.

Scotch Dog was there, too, ever solicitous. With his encouragement, I planned the baby's wardrobe and sewed garments with my ladies day and night. They praised my stitches and we fantasized about all the lovely gowns I would have after the baby was born and I reclaimed my figure once more.

Jamie had become caught up in plans as well. He ordered that every man in Edinburgh have a new suit of clothes for the birth of the prince and commanded them to come to the abbey upon the announcement of his birth.

Devout as ever, Jamie threw himself into his prayers, counting his rosary beads even in his sleep. He remained as hopeful as he was antagonized and I could not understand it. He paced the floor late into the night. I begged him to join me in bed, but he refused with a disarming smile. I watched his silhouette in the silvery moonlight filtering through the window and recalled a lion in my father's menagerie, its restless pacing, its wild, frightened eyes. I tried not to compare it to Jamie.

In January I entered confinement, observing the laws set down by my grandmother for ladies of royalty in my condition. I took to my bed. My chambers were darkened and closed off from receiving any outside air, lest it carry harmful contagion, and for the next month no men are allowed within this sacred *gynaeceum*. I was surrounded by women, never my favorite estate, and longed for Scotch Dog and Robert Barton, whom I had fondly come to know as Robin. I missed Jamie and fretted over his whereabouts, allowing tears to slide icy trails down my cheeks as I imagined him passing the month in the arms of Janet Kennedy or romping with his children.

I cradled my belly. The prince was lively, his favorite time to kick being at night, and since night and day had all run together in this strange world of isolation I did not mind. His activity reminded me of life, life beyond the chambers and the life I would soon hold in my arms.

At last in February my waters broke. It was a queer sensation, the warm liquid that poured down my legs followed by the tight, searing pains that seized my belly and caused me to cry out with surprise. The room was filled with at least a hundred people to witness the occasion. There must be no mistakes in birthing a prince; no imposters, no monsters that are switched with a healthy country babe. The onlookers would crowd and cram about my bed and watch me, legs spread and coated in blood, hair matted to my forehead with sweat, as I delivered them a prince. They took my air away; I could not breathe. There were so many of them! I could not stand it. I choked on my screams, trying to retain some kind of dignity during this ordeal. My breath came in spurts, faster and faster till my head began to tingle and hum. Dots of light danced before my eyes till I saw nothing but light, white, carrying me away to a world of colors—blue for the waters carrying my son into this world, red for the blood pounding in my ears and running down my legs, purple for the pain, the pain of royal expectations, the pain gripping my womb. Colors, they swirled and spun around me, faster, faster. I merged with them, floating in and out of their world, reaching, grasping. Peace. What was the color of peace?

And then I was plunged into blackness.

Voices permeated eternal night. My eyes would not open; they were laden down. Had they put the coins on my eyes already, lest they fly open and frighten the mourners?

"A bonny prince!" a male voice cried, but it was a strange cry; slow, drawn out. He was far away, in another realm. I could not get to him. My body would not move.

"The queen . . . near death . . . blood loss," a woman was saying.

I wanted to hold out my arms for the child. They said I had a prince; I knew I would have a prince . . . I could not move. There was no strength. The blackness claimed me. I ran but stumbled, rendered blind. My soul was permitted this exercise, but my body remained still, chained into submission by my hemorrhage.

"Pilgrimage . . ." I heard the familiar low strain of Jamie's voice resonate through my darkness. I wanted to speak, to beg him, *No, do not go.* Not another pilgrimage . . . Must reach him.

I could not.

He left.

They all left.

Blackness . . . blackness . . .

*   *   *

The celebrations ushering in Prince James's entrance into this world were in full tilt when I at last regained consciousness. The baby was christened; the Bishop of Glasgow, Patrick Hepburn, who stood in as my proxy groom at my first wedding ceremony, and the Countess of Huntley were named godparents, and all without me.

I remained abed, weak as a kitten but at last able to hold my son. How bonny he was with his auburn hair and rosy skin! He smelled so sweet, like the milk of a country maid, calling to mind my days in the nursery at Sheen with my brothers and sister, and a knot welled at the base of my throat as I thought of my Arthur and how happy he would have been for me. How different would life have been had he lived. Would he and Princess Catherine have had a houseful of bonny princes by now?

I did not dwell on such unhappy speculations long but instead reveled in my son. Jamie was delighted with me and fussed over the prince as if he were his first child. He was ever solicitous and enjoyed cuddling with the boy as if he were a nurse. I basked in the affection he granted him, reveling in the fact that I had given Jamie what no other woman could: a prince and heir.

Indeed Scotland warmed to me as well; they were thrilled with their fertile queen, deferring to me with new respect. Gifts were sent to me from all over the land and England as well—bolts of fine fabric, plate, jewels. . . . I was in a thrill of delight as I sifted through the material and planned new gowns. I had recovered my figure with a few new curves to spare that served only to compliment me. I was a woman now, a woman, a wife, and a mother.

It was the last title I treasured most.

To celebrate Prince James's birth a great tournament was held at Edinburgh Castle. Jamie was thrilled with Edinburgh's newest installment of brass cannon and could not wait to show them off. In the courtyard the lists were set up and we were treated to a display to rival my father's court. The Lady of Honor was my own attendant Black Ellen, a Moorish girl brought by Robert Barton from the mystical land of Africa and raised by the companion of Jamie's daughter, Marjorie Lindsay. I found great comfort in the fascinating creature since her arrival; she was entertaining and honest, and as we were both foreigners in a foreign land I found I could relate to her in a way I could not with my Scottish ladies.

Ellen entered in a golden chariot, rendering the spectators breathless with her exotic allure. My eyes widened at the sight of the ebony-skinned beauty in her damask gown, which was trimmed with gold and green taffeta. The men were entranced by her. William Dunbar called her Muckle Lips for their fullness and speculated about what it would be like to kiss them.

"The victors will find out," said Dunbar with a sly smile as he ogled her.

A wild encounter ensued, with bandits "threatening" poor Ellen. She was saved by a group of wild men dressed in goatskins with antlers weighing down their heads. They were led by the Wild Knight, who brandished his lance and sword, "defeating" all those who dared oppose him.

"Who can he be?" whispered the ladies, giggling behind their hands.

He removed his helmet, uncovering the tousled auburn hair and sparkling eyes of my Jamie. He beamed as he beheld me.

"My Wild Knight," I murmured, extending my hand. He took it; his was trembling from the exertion. "My Jamie."

"Maggie," he whispered, laying upon my hand the sweetest of kisses. "You have made me a happy man."

I cupped his cheek, wishing to emblazon the moment in my heart forever.

This must be the beginning, I thought, of something grand.

The bells that heralded my son's birth tolled out their heavy mourning song a year later after the baby, my baby, whom I held and rocked and kissed, died at Stirling. Mourners filled the streets, keening and wailing and beating their breasts for the little prince, who was accompanied to his tomb by knights in black livery.

My chest ached, my eyes were puffy, burning from the endless stream of tears that assaulted me day and night. I was with child again and reeling from the myriad of emotions that assaulted me when pregnant, all of them amplified by the horror of my loss. I lay in bed, pounding the mattress, tearing at my pillows, scratching my hands and forearms till little rivers of scarlet appeared bright against the stark alabaster skin. I screamed and raged and cursed; the ladies were in a terror of me.

We were fated to lose. My aunt the Lady Anne Howard had told me this. My mother knew it. All women know it. Babies were born and died every day. Queens were far from exempt.

It did not alter the pain. I was inconsolable. And the one person who could have consoled me had left me, gone on pilgrimage again in the hopes of appeasing God for whatever sin he believed cursed us with such grave misfortune.

"He goes on his pilgrimage and leaves me here to sort through this by myself!" I cried to Ellen, my fast and newfound friend, as she was another slave in exile like me. She sat beside me on my bed, shaking her dark head, unsure of how to comfort one who would receive no comfort.

"The king is a religious man; it is the only way he can see fit to bear it, Your Grace," was all she could say.

" 'Religious man'!" I spat. "Don't you see, Ellen? It is a staged play to him, an act. But an act he has convinced himself of. He is so theatrical! When he wants to be the chivalrous knight he plays it to the hilt! Now he is the grieving father, and though I believe he genuinely grieves, he will play the penitent to the hilt, too!" I scowled. "No doubt he takes comfort in the other children . . . and their mothers, their fertile mothers who are all too eager to spew out more bloody brats to threaten his throne!" I added darkly.

"Oh, Your Grace . . ." Ellen murmured, thoroughly perplexed. Her onyx eyes filled with tears. "Would that your pain could be eased."

I offered a bitter smile. "It will be eased soon enough. As soon as this child is born. I proved myself capable; I will do so again. I will get through this, Ellen. I am a Tudor. What is gone canna be reclaimed; the baby is with God. Until his cradle is filled there will be no rest for me." I began to laugh, an edgy, maniacal laugh. "I must secure the succession. I am the Royal Breeder . . . and breed I shall!"

I laughed with abandon; the sound grated on my ears. My eyes filled with burning tears.

"Oh, Ellen, help me!" I cried. "I'm so afraid!"

"Hold on to me, Your Grace," Ellen ordered, her voice choking on a sob as she gathered me in her arms, breaking propriety in the hopes of saving a queen gone mad. She held me tight, stroking my hair and swaying to and fro. "Hold on to me as long as you need," she added in a husky whisper.

"Jamie . . ." I murmured against her shoulder. "I want Jamie! Bring him home! Oh, bring him home!"

But no one brought him home.

He came in his own time.

Jamie returned, his shirt dried to his skin with blood so that it had to be peeled off. He ordered it done slowly so that he might appreciate the pain. I stood in his chambers watching with dry eyes as his servants flinched, recoiling from the sight of my beloved's back, which bore fresh, angry new wounds. It was a map of rivers and tributaries whose destination was the ocean of his shattered heart; they surged and drove on in pain-ridden streams, coursing, ever coursing, into the fathomless scarlet depths of his despair as Jamie asked himself what more could be done to demonstrate his penitence. He added more links to his iron belt; it weighed heavily about his trim waist and the sweet white skin of his hips bore raw scrapes, bitter hallmarks of his strange self-punishment.

When the servants were dismissed Jamie lay facedown on his bed, staring without seeing at the wall.

"Why did you leave me to do this to yourself?" I asked in calm tones. I had a sincere desire to understand. "While you cried with each snap of the whip I cried here alone in a foreign land with only servants to comfort me. My heart, my one child, was ripped from me while you have five to comfort you with their laughter and their health. But you did not think of this. You thought of yourself, how to demonstrate your regret in this savage way, and God help me, I shall never understand—"

"Oh, my dearest girl, I am sorry I left you, but I *had* to go . . . I had to pay. It was my fault that he died!" he cried, sitting up, his face stricken with genuine despair. "You see? I have cursed the house of Stewart. My participation in my father's death has cursed the line. I sire bastards by the score, but my prince, my heir, perishes and all because of my wickedness."

I sat beside him, taking his hands in mine. "Jamie, have you ever thought to consider that this may not be about you at all? My mother and father lost several children and neither of them did anything to deserve it—goodness, *everyone* loses at least one child! The Howards—Surrey and his son Lord Thomas and Lady Anne, my aunt. They've lost children and all gathered up their strength to have more. It may very well have been God's will to take our prince but not because of something you did." I forced out a joyless laugh. "Why would God punish a baby for your crimes, real or imagined?"

" 'The sins of the father' . . ." Jamie's face was writ with terror.

"Pah!" I waved a dismissive hand.

"Maggie, I appreciate your sentiments, but you are no theologian. You dinna understand the complexities of God," Jamie told me.

"And you do?" I returned, fury flushing my face as crimson as the scars snaking across his back. "You, who prostrate yourself at these shrines and beat yourself bloody, then proceed to bed the nearest wench in sight? Tell me, Jamie, what does God make of that?"

Jamie buried his face in his hands, heaving great broken sobs. "You are right, Maggie," he admitted in soft tones, reaching his hand out. I took it, swallowing a painful lump rising in my throat. "There is something wrong with me . . . I am evil and my ways have favored you with nothing but heartbreak."

"Jamie," I cooed. I wanted to take him in my arms but feared hurting him. Even more I feared he'd derive a perverse pleasure in the pain, so I did nothing but gaze at this twisted creature in helplessness. "Jamie, you can change. You can do anything you want to do. If you are wracked with guilt by your actions, then for your own health and happiness you *must* change."

Jamie rocked back and forth, trembling, his eyes wide with terror. He was afraid, I realized at once. Afraid of change, for change is more painful than the soundest whipping. It may have been easier to remain the way he was, a martyr to his passions. He sinned and sinned again, but all was made up for with the searing heat of the whip, the weight of the belt, and the salve of my pitiable tears.

If there was anyone bound to change in this marriage, I could see with heart-clenching clarity, it would not be Jamie.

๑ 7 ๑

The Stewart Curse

The suffocating heat of summer permeated my confinement chambers and I was slick with sweat, engulfed in darkness once more. All was still; my body would not obey me. I was gripped by pain but could not respond to it; my throat would not emit sound and was as dry as my eyes. I lay, unable to writhe, unable to call out, rendered a helpless slave to a dark force that claimed me once more.

God allowed me the use of my ears and, though I could not respond, I heard the midwife and ladies. I heard the footfalls, running about in a frantic flutter of anxiety. I wanted to ask after Jamie but could not will my mouth to move. I lay. I breathed. Darkness . . . oh, this darkness . . .

"She bleeds," the midwife told the assemblage in urgent tones. "God help me, I canna stop the bleeding!" A cool hand was laid across my forehead. "And the poor child burns with fever."

"God save the queen," someone murmured, their voice far away.

Yes, God save me . . . God save me. . . .

I was enfolded in the darkness; what terrified me moments before became a comfort, a refuge. My womb shuddered and quivered, tensing and relaxing till it pushed something forth, a great wailing thing that was proclaimed to be a princess of Scotland. My legs shook. Something slippery gushed from between them. I was carried on waves of red, my life draining from me. I wanted to see her. I longed to see my little girl. . . .

"Princess Margaret!" Jamie was crying. "We shall name her for her dear mother."

Princess Margaret. I wanted to smile. Was she pretty? I wanted to ask. Was she a lusty Stewart girl?

No one could tell me. No one heard my thoughts and I was alone in the darkness.

I heard her crying for me. I knew it was for me. Her little cries grew weaker and weaker. I could not help her. I could not mother her. She was christened; I heard that from one of the ladies in my room. And when she cried no more she was buried beside her brother, the prince.

Still I could not move; the darkness consumed me. My body was numb, weak. My voice could not be summoned forth, not even to cry for my child, the baby I never laid eyes upon.

Jamie sat at my bedside stroking my face. "Can you forgive me if I go?" he whispered. "I canna lose you, Maggie. God restored you to me last time; if I go, if I do more penance, I know He will have mercy." His lips brushed against my forehead, my cheeks, my mouth. "I love you, Maggie, God, how much! I go to plea for your life."

I needed to summon the strength to beg him not to. He did his penance in sincerity but could never resist the temptation along the way. . . . *Please, Jamie, do not go!* But the words stayed silent, stuck in my impotent throat.

Jamie left. He always left.

"I'm starting to believe that His Grace does have the ear of God," I said in weak tones to Ellen as she sat at my bedside. We were playing chess and she was losing on purpose. "Seems the moment he leaves I recover."

"In body, perhaps," observed my attendant. "But has your heart, Your Grace? There is none to remain strong for. No one would condemn a mother's tears."

I pursed my lips. "I fear for myself, Ellen," I confessed. "I want to cry. Sometimes I lie here trying to will the tears to come. But my eyes remain dry, so dry it is painful. I wonder, have I grown so cold, so heartless, that I am rendered incapable of human grief?" I shook my head in bewildered terror.

Ellen removed the chessboard to scoot closer to me. She took my hand, shaking her head. "No, Your dearest Grace. You are being affected in a different way is all."

"I never saw her, Ellen," I said in soft tones. "I never saw my baby girl. I heard her cry sometimes, even through that strange black mist that claimed me. And I thought . . . I thought she must be crying for me. Yearning for me. And I couldn't be there! I . . . I couldn't be a mother to her. She was all alone. Perhaps that is why she died, because she did not feel my love—"

Ellen's face was writ with pity and I averted my head. "I am certain that is not true. Please, Your Grace, do not punish yourself for this."

"No, His Grace has seized those reins," I said, my voice edgy with bitterness. "No one punishes themselves with greater competence and skill than my husband."

Ellen bowed her head.

"Oh, dismissed, Ellen. I'll not draw you into our hell," I ordered with a wave of my hand.

Ellen rose. "I would stay, Your Grace. I am your devoted servant and friend for life."

I tried to smile, but what twisted my lips could be called nothing more than a contemptuous sneer. "Then you curse yourself," I told her. "For this is hell, and hell is where you'll surely be while serving me."

Ellen shook her head once more, then offered a deep curtsy and retreated, tears glistening upon her cheeks.

I stared with envy at the space she once occupied, longing for those tears to fall upon my cheeks, from my eyes.

Something was wrong with me.

I could not cry. *Please, God*, I prayed, *let me cry!*

* * *

Jamie returned battered and bloody, thinner than before. I was told he added strict fasting onto his exercise in piety, and indeed when he took supper with me in my chambers he ate very little. As he sat in his shift I noted his knees were raw from kneeling at prayer, and he limped into bed. But he held me fast. His tears wetted my forehead and ran down my cheeks, his shoulders quaking with sobs.

I no longer accused him of anything; no questions were asked. I did not want to know in any case. I only stared at this tortured man and upon doing so found at last my ability to cry cleansing, healing tears. I did not cry for the children; that grief had been sorted out in my days of hardness. I bore their loss as my mother bore hers, telling myself over and over as would a chanting monk that God took them for His purposes. Death had always been a reality for me and its constancy was something I well understood. Jamie's life was not.

He could not inflict upon himself enough pain. He no longer reserved his self-flagellation for his pilgrimages but did so at our homes as well. At night I peered inside the candlelit chapel, watching him bring the whip across his back. I flinched upon hearing it snap and whir through the air, starting as it met with his tender flesh. Horror clenched my heart and twisted my gut as I beheld the rivulets of blood streaming down his body, which was wracked with broken sobs.

His wounds had no time to heal before he inflicted more. His face became void of his once contagious enthusiasm, as though he feared to experience any emotion resembling happiness would mean he enjoyed a life he did not deserve.

"This has to stop, my Jamie," I told him in bed one night, grateful one aspect of our lives had not changed but rather became more passionate and loving with each passing year.

"I know," he replied in the intoxicating tone I loved so well. "It is not enough. I have written the Kings of England, France, Spain, and the Holy Roman Emperor Maximilian. I have for years thought that a Crusade would best demonstrate my faith, that if I can succeed in driving the Infidels from the Holy Land God will at last see my sincere wish to be His child. That He will see how sorry I am . . ."

"Jamie . . ."

He offered a heavy sigh. "They respond with well wishes but no real commitments. They are afraid."

"They've every right," I said, angered by this useless goal. "Who has ever met with success in the Holy Land? Jamie, it is a fool's mission. Do not think on it anymore. Think of Scotland, of what can be done to improve *our* land. Surely that will show God the kind of king you wish to be."

Jamie lay silent. "Do you think I am a good king, Maggie?"

"Yes," I said with conviction, for no one was as sincere as Jamie; no one wished to do as much good. Romantic he may have been, misguided at times indeed, but good? Yes, despite everything, Jamie was a good man.

"Yes, Jamie," I repeated, my voice heated with fervor as I seized his chin between my fingers. "You are a good king and a better man. For love of me, please see that!"

Jamie reached up and cupped my cheek but saw nothing. His vision was clouded with tears and self-loathing and there was nothing I could do about it.

In the winter of 1509, just a few months after the birth and death of my daughter, I was with child again; an autumn arrival was expected. I tried not to think of it, even as my belly swelled, even as it kicked and tumbled about in my womb. Panels were added to my gowns. A beautiful cradle of state was placed in the nursery, but I never ventured near it; I did not want to see it. I did not sew baby garments, leaving that task to my ladies.

Jamie went on pilgrimage once more and spent his time at Tain, whipping himself by the shrine of Saint Duthlac. His fervor frightened me; the enthusiasm he once exhibited for hunting and music was channeled into religion, and for his efforts the Pope named him Protector of the Christian Faith, sending a beautiful sword with a gem-encrusted gold sheath and purple diadem. This fueled his passion even more. If the Pope recognized his potential goodness, surely God would, too. Heretics were persecuted, their ashes carried on the winds. I shivered in fear. Jamie would show God, he said, how sorry he was and how devoted he was to the tenets of the Church of Rome. Perhaps those demonstrations would lift the curse on the Stewarts and ensure us a healthy prince. Oh, poor Jamie, my poor, foolish king . . .

When Jamie was not at Tain he dealt with new matters that had arisen on the Border that could threaten the treaty our marriage was meant to represent. Our Warden of the Middle Marches was murdered by a devil named John Heron—called the Bastard by those who knew of his barbaric antics—and two of his companions, who were both delivered up to my husband for their crime. Heron escaped, however, which caused Jamie anxiety. He never trusted my father completely—a Scot—trusted an Englishman no more than an Englishman trusted a Scot and I could not help but wonder if Jamie thought my father was hiding Heron out somewhere, despite my strident reassurance that he would have done no such thing.

And yet if he would order the death of Jamie's mistress Margaret Drummond . . . but there was no proof of that. Why would I think such a thing?

Jamie was vexed further when Father took Jamie's cousin, the Earl of Arran, captive. He had taken Jamie's son the fourteen-year-old Archbishop of St. Andrews (an appointment that still caused my face to flush with rage) to France to study with the celebrated scholar Erasmus, and though the earl had a letter of marque from Jamie permitting him safe-conduct, he did not obtain one to go through England on his return trip a year later.

Father could have ignored it, even I knew that, but instead he had him arrested, fearing that the earl was really in France to restore the Auld Alliance. He sent his almoner Thomas Wolsey as his ambassador, but when he arrived, after many delays and aggravations, Jamie made the portly priest wait.

Wolsey was uncomfortable in my presence and I in his. I did not know what to say, how to deal with affairs of state. I never had to before. Now I sat, with child and wanting nothing more than to lie down, but instead I was obligated to play hostess and diplomat at the same time.

Arran's brother Patrick Hamilton arrived during this ordeal and confused matters by telling me that Father treated him well but then informing Jamie of the opposite. He was obliged to say that, I argued, as he was a Scot. *No, he was saying that to win your favor,* I was told.

I grew weary of it all and awaited a resolution, angry at Father for upsetting the peace between our countries and caught very much in the middle. Though the incidents were eventually ironed out, Arran being returned to Scotland as a means of compensating for England's inability to capture the Bastard, something changed in me. For the first time I became interested in matters beyond myself; I was interested in what it meant to be Queen of Scotland. For the first time I wanted to understand politics and learn how to forge an understanding between the country of my birth and the country of my adoption.

I was told before I came to Scotland that I was to be a daughter of England before I was a wife to my new country, but was there not a way I could reconcile the two? Was there not a way I could be both?

Father never anticipated upon issuing that order how much I would love my Jamie. The balance was a delicate one. I was unsure of my footing and gripped by new fears as at last the realization of my purpose settled upon me.

Determination surged through my veins. I throbbed with it, tingling with motivation. I was an English girl and a Scottish queen and by God I would do my countries proud.

Both of them.

Father was dead. I sat in my chambers numb. All previous resolve was replaced by an acute attack of homesickness. A few months prior Father had sent gifts with his ambassadors, beautiful horses for Jamie and me to ride. I delighted in my new ponies, remembering the palfreys that had been sacrificed to that dreaded fire when first I arrived.

I will never see you again.

We had written. How unhappy I was in the beginning! He reassured me without ever addressing the matters to which I wrote. He reassured me with the knowledge that he was there, in England, my beloved father. He sent part of my dowry, arranged my life and secured peace with Scotland through my marriage. Now he was gone forever, taking his wisdom and caution and stoicism with him. He lay beside my mother in the grand tomb he had obsessively erected upon her death.

Henry, my eager, lively, feisty brother, ascended the throne as the Eighth of That Name. He wed Princess Catherine of Aragon and the world bowed before him, the handsome golden boy. He had great plans, I was told; he would usher in a New Age. At that my throat constricted as I recalled the words of my precious brother Arthur. We had planned to usher in that age together, that sparkling New Age when knowledge and tolerance would flow from the conduits like wine. Did Henry have the same goals? Would he be the grand king Arthur no doubt would have been had God allowed him to sit on the throne? Would Henry do our illustrious father proud?

A few days after my brother and his bride's joint coronation I learned of my grandmother's death. For all her stricture and hardness, there was no doubting her love. I was her special responsibility; no one attended me as she did. No one worried over me as she did. I recalled all the pranks I pulled on her, noting only now the twitch of her lips as she scolded me, the merry twinkle in her eye as she called me "that impetuous girl." Could it be that she saw something of herself in me and admired it? I should like to think so.

I looked out over the Scottish countryside, the rolling hills, the silvery mist hovering over the land like a mourning veil, and dreamed of home, of what was and could never be reclaimed. They were all dying; all leaving me. I shuddered with fear. Was there nothing that lasted?

I will never see you again.

The cycle of death was broken with a burst of new life.

The prince was born at Holyrood on 21 October. I became determined to evade the darkness that danced about the fringes of my soul, waiting to devour me. I would not let it. I would see my son into this world. Weak, bleeding, and quivering, I brought him forth, my beautiful Prince Arthur, named for my brother and the famed king from whom we descended, and clasped him to my chest.

It was a fortuitous name—a good sign. Prince Arthur now stood as heir to the thrones of both Scotland and England if my brother bore none himself, and though it was unlikely lusty Henry would have any problem securing the succession, I admitted to a certain evil hope that perhaps those born of my body would one day unite the two kingdoms.

It was the great sin of those who ruled, the lust for more power, and I was not immune to it. Indeed the acuteness of my longing frightened me.

I watched him grow, strong and lusty and golden like his name-sake. His legs were chubby and fair. I kissed the silky skin; I cra-dled him to my chest. I sang to him. William Dunbar wrote verses celebrating his beauty, and Jamie, his proud, devoted father, al-lowed his back to heal at last.

How much joy the little prince brought us! He cooed and gig-gled. His bright blue eyes sparkled. He rarely cried. The nurses and rockers were enthralled with him; they praised his every move. Never had they cared for such a bonny lad.

There was no indication that we would lose him.

When we did, at Edinburgh on a warm July day just nine months after his birth, we fled the castle. We could not bear to be where our greatest happiness was known, where the memory of his baby laughter still echoed in the nursery.

I accompanied Jamie on his pilgrimage this time. I did not share his enthusiasm for ritual and things holy, but I vowed to make some kind of amends for whatever sin I may have brought down upon our house. I examined my actions, my thoughts, my heart. My pride, I realized, may be what caused God to take him from me. I looked into my baby's eyes and saw a prince, a future king. I dreamed of him sitting on not only the throne of Scotland but that of England as well. It was a cruel thought, a selfish thought, for in thinking it I wished ill upon my brother and sister-in-law. Now they, too, had known the agony of losing children, and as far removed as I was from them, I had played a part in their losses nonetheless. Now God punished me for it. Again. I had to make amends.

And so I prayed. I kissed relics. I inhaled the sickeningly sweet scent of incense. I lit candles. I offered money. Jamie whipped himself bloody. More links were added to his belt. He planned his Crusade with more fervor, ordering the construction of a great ship to add to his fleet in the hopes of setting sail for the Holy Land when the Pope called for him. He wrote other kingdoms, soliciting their participation in his noble cause; no one committed.

There were matters far more pressing than a fruitless Crusade to occupy them. They cared not for the well-intended obsession of a guilt-ridden king nor for the grief of his queen.

Babies died every day, after all.

The Empire, Spain, Venice, and England had formed a Holy League against France by November of 1511 and helped Pope Julius II regain some of his lost holdings. The French had hoped to call for a council in which discussions about church reforms could ensue, but the challenge infuriated the Pope and France was placed under interdict.

While England delivered their declaration of war to the French, I delivered Scotland of a prince, whom we again called James for his father.

I was engulfed in darkness once more, immobilized by the strangling mists. Yet inside the flame the Tudor fire still burned, urging me to live. The baby's cry was lusty; it seemed stronger than the rest somehow. It served as my guide; I followed it. Louder and louder it grew, piercing my ears with its urgency. He needed me. This baby needed me. The blackness faded and I was immersed in the white light of motherhood.

I awakened, drawing into focus the sweet, elated face of my husband.

"The baby?" I whispered, my body tensing in terror.

"Maggie. He lives," Jamie assured me, beaming as he stroked my clammy forehead. "He *lives!*"

"Praise God!" I breathed, relinquishing myself to tears of relief. If we could just get through this first year everything would be all right, I was sure of it. Oh, may it go fast!

Jamie was in a frenzy. England had put us in an awkward position. France had been Scotland's longtime ally and my brother's desire to conquer them had little to do with the Holy League and more to do with regaining England's lost holdings.

"Christian princes fighting Christian princes!" Jamie seethed as he paced my chambers. "No one will emerge the victor. The real battle is in the Holy Land—if only they would see that!"

I shook my head, saddened, wishing in vain that there was another conduit for Jamie's obsession. "They'll not think of the Holy Land if they can gain from the destruction of something much closer to home," I said at last. "But, by the Mass, I wish Scots-English relations did not have to be strained because of it!"

"Ah, Maggie, I am disappointed," Jamie lamented, his face writ with genuine disillusionment. "Your brother has not adhered to our treaty; there are still border raids for which we have no choice but to retaliate. He sacrificed diplomacy in favor of rash action when he had the Howard brothers murder our good Captain Andrew Barton for piracy. Poor Robin . . ." he added with a shake of his head, referring to Robert Barton, who had long been one of our favorites. "And the jewels bequeathed to you by your dear brother Arthur and honored grandmother have not yet been sent. Thus far this Henry is not proving to be half the king your father was in any regard."

"He is so young," I reminded Jamie in a pathetic attempt to keep the peace. "Just a boy. Young men are often lusty for war. He will learn."

"At the cost of men's lives?" Jamie countered. "Not to mention the cost to his own exchequer and his friendship with me, which going to war with Scotland's oldest ally would certainly jeopardize. I would not think he would want to risk war with me. I am far nearer to him than France."

"Of course not," I reaffirmed. "Peace can be negotiated, Jamie. With France and with us. Henry wouldn't dare offend his sister's country."

I cradled our son to my breast, looking down at his rosy countenance. I was with child again and did not wish to contemplate anything unpleasant. Peace was my objective; my children must have a stable alliance secured with England. Oh, heady thoughts . . .

"Wouldn't it have been wonderful if we were born simple people?" I asked Jamie then. "If we did not have to worry about the decisions we make affecting dynasties and starting wars. I'd have been a shepherdess, I think, and would don a gauzy gown to stroll through the fields as I tended my flock." I closed my eyes, riveted by my fantasy. "I'd walk through the heather and run my hand along the top, letting it tickle my palm. And every day would be one of peace, surrounded by God's most beloved creatures." My eyes fluttered open and I offered my husband a smile. "What would you have been, Jamie, had you been a simple man?"

Jamie smiled in turn. His face softened; his brows relaxed. The crinkle in his forehead smoothed as he sat on my bed to ponder. "I suppose I would have liked to have been a sailor," he said. His voice was low with whimsy. "Or an alchemist and spend my days trying to convert base metals into gold. Or a musician, with nothing to do but while away his hours strumming his lute and yielding to fancy." His voice grew softer still. "And you, my Maggie? What else would you have been besides a beautiful shepherdess, had you not been born my queen?"

"Your wife," I answered. "Before anything else, your wife."

Jamie gathered me in his arms. The baby gurgled and cooed while his sibling offered a lively kick within my womb.

I decided then and there that there was nothing else I'd rather have been than Jamie's Queen of Scots.

In November I was delivered of a premature daughter at Holyrood. So tiny, she was no more than the length of my wrist to my fingertips. I was strong enough to reach out to her, to caress the translucent cheek before God claimed her to reside among her brothers and sister in Heaven.

I was almost too ill to mourn. My thoughts were dominated by the possibility of lending aid to France, thus placing ourselves at odds with Henry's England, making my recovery even slower. My limbs were so heavy; I found it difficult to summon the will to breathe. My aching breasts dried and I bled with nothing to show for it. I was nauseated but too ill to retch; the bitter taste of bile was forever in my mouth, stagnant and suffocating. My stomach clenched in pain, but I could not even curl up against it. I was too tired to move. My tears cut slow, sluggish trails down my cheeks, lazy as the rest of me.

"If my brother goes to war with France, you will be against him, won't you?" I asked Jamie one gray afternoon as he sat by my bedside.

"It is very possible, Maggie." His voice was very low.

I closed my eyes, wearied of it all. Yes, I knew. Jamie said as much before. A vision of my father swirled against the opaque background of my eyelids. I was to forge an understanding between England and Scotland, he had instructed. How could I be the least bit successful in that task if they were in opposition? It was more than a matter of countries; it was a matter of family. My husband and my brother, the two people I loved most in the world—how could I be made to choose one over the other? *Oh, there must be a way to avoid this. . . .*

But I could not think of it now.

I was so very sick . . .

❧ 8 ❧

Queens and Warriors

December did not see me any better and the news was even worse. Jamie's intelligence revealed that Henry would tax his people to raise funds for the continued war against France. There was no doubt of whom Jamie would stand with. By 10 December France's Admiral de la Motte anchored at Leith with a ship full of gunpowder, gunstones, eight brass serpentines, by far the most accurate of light field artillery, wine, and, at last, plate and eight bolts of cloth of gold for me.

"Maggie, it is almost certain your brother is planning an attack against us as well," Jamie told me, his eyes lit with the bewildered sadness and anger of betrayal. "He has never taxed his people to this degree. It can mean nothing else. No good will come of it, I can assure you," he added darkly.

My heart sank in my chest; even it had ceased to beat with vigor. "Jamie, no . . . for love of me, dinna speak of it anymore. I am so weak, so very weak. . . ."

My eyes closed and I yielded to the darkness.

I am kneeling before a chest. My legacy from Grandmother and my brother Arthur has arrived at last! I sift through the jewels. They are so pretty! Emeralds, sapphires, diamonds . . . but wait . . . they are melting. What is happening? I recoil in horror. They are no longer glittering and golden; all have transformed into pearls. The adornment of widows . . . I turn. Jamie must be warned. I reach out to him, but he is falling, falling, falling from a tower's great height. . . . I watch him disappear into a bottomless void. No! Jamie, don't go!

I awoke with a start. "Jamie . . ." I murmured. "I want Jamie!"

"He has gone, dearest," cooed my attendant Ellen. "He goes to pray for the restoration of Your Grace's health at Tain."

At once I began to laugh and cry. "Of course," I whimpered. "Of course."

I was slow to get well and no amount of Christmas festivities thrown for my benefit cheered me. The tensions between my adopted country and country of birth ran too high. I hated France and nightly prayed it would sink into the ocean!

As winter progressed my strength returned, surging through my limbs, renewing me and readying me for the battle to come. In February my husband received a letter from Queen Anne of Brittany, Louis VII's conniving wife, promising fourteen thousand French crowns if he stood as her knight, championing her country against Emperor Maximilian, Ferdinand of Aragon, and my brother, Henry VIII, who was the closest. In short, she asked Jamie to go to war against his own brother-in-law and break our marriage treaty. The wench even had the audacity to enclose in her plea a turquoise ring and glove!

I examined the ring in bed, trying it on as I scowled at Jamie, who was pacing by the buffet. "I suppose you canna resist this, can you? A 'knightly errand.' Such utter nonsense, Jamie!" I cried. "She's playing you, you have to know it! She knows you canna resist a romantic overture and now has you right where she wants you!"

"Maggie, there is a lot more to this than you seem to understand—" Jamie began, his tone ever gentle.

"Believe me, I understand!" I threw the ring across our chambers, where it landed with a clatter at his feet. "It's wrapped up in a perfect little box, a mission you cannot refuse, sanctioned by your Pope and a damsel in distress as well. My God, it is tailored for you!"

"Maggie, stop this!" Jamie ordered, sitting on the bed and taking my hands.

I narrowed my eyes at him. My cheeks flushed in fury. "Jamie, do you know these nightmares I have had?" I forced calm into my voice. It wavered in terror as I recalled the dream that stalked my slumber. I stared at our joined hands, at my fingers, all encircled in rings. "I saw my jewels all melt into pearls . . . pearls, Jamie. The ornament of widowhood." I met his eyes, furrowing my brows in agony. I reached up, cupping his cheek and stroking his beard. "And I saw you falling from a great tower *to your death!* You see? These are signs, Jamie, terrible signs of the ill fate that awaits you should you go to war with my brother!"

"Dreams, darling," Jamie said, gathering me in his arms. "They are mere dreams. You are terrified for my well-being and that of the country and rightly so. But you must not let your fear rule you. Now, go to sleep, my sweet." He stroked my hair.

I pulled away, shaking my head. "If you canna abide the signs of my dream, think of your beloved Scotland should you die in this folly! Our infant son will be left to rule with none but me, a poor woman"—surely he couldn't resist the plea of this poor woman!— "to cling to a regency that would be sought after by every noble house in the land! How could you risk leaving us so vulnerable? Is Queen Anne so desirable to you that you prefer her over me?"

I should not have said it. Any chance of winning the argument was lost in that last sentence, for Jamie was on his feet, his eyes flashing in an anger I was unaccustomed to seeing upon his gentle countenance.

"Maggie, jealousy does not suit you," he said in low tones. "You are first and foremost my wife. You serve me, not your brother. Dinna think that I am not aggrieved at the turn of events, but he has given me no choice. He broke our treaty long before I even considered it and now must deal with the repercussions."

"But there has to be a more peaceful alternative!" I insisted. "Can we meet and discuss it? Can we not meet with my sister-in-law Catherine? She and I could forge some kind of understanding, I am sure of it."

He shook his head, his eyes lit with sadness.

"You will regret breaking the peace," I thundered. "By God, you will regret it!"

Jamie shook his head at me and quit the room without another word.

I buried my head in my hands and sobbed. I thought of my jewels, my pretty jewels all turned to pearls. . . .

At Lent we were treated to a visitor, my brother's ambassador the Dean of Windsor, Dr. Nicholas West. As Jamie was on retreat at the monastery of the Friars Observant at Stirling, I was thrilled to receive Dr. West on Good Friday. He brought with him letters from my brother, which I devoured with delight.

"Oh, good Dr. West, you must tell me everything about him!" I insisted as we sat to dinner alone together on Easter Sunday. Jamie had returned but was resting and would be meeting with the ambassador on Monday.

The man offered a polite smile and my heart sank. He did not appear to be a personable fellow and I was disappointed. I had so hoped to work some sort of charm on him that he might see how vital keeping the peace with my country was.

"Tell me of my brother," I prompted with a bright smile. I would still try my best to win through him an understanding with England. I had grown quite buxom and, freed from the mournful constraints of Lent, had donned a lovely gown of pink and gray damask trimmed with ermine to accentuate each curve. My hair was gathered into a chignon beneath my hood and I allowed ringlets to frame my face in organized disarray. I should think I made quite a pleasing presentation.

"What does he look like now?" I asked him. "I haven't seen him since he was twelve."

Dr. West tilted his head as he summoned to his mind a portrait of my brother. "King Henry is as bluff and fine of figure as they come, Your Grace," he told me.

I laughed, certain he was accurate. "Is he very tall? He had the promise of great height when last I saw him. Is he still a marvelous dancer?" Against my will tears burned my eyes as a pang of longing for home and more innocent days pierced through me.

Dr. West nodded. "Ah, yes, Your Grace, he is tall and broad and golden—a veritable Apollo is King Henry. And none are as fleet as he on the dance floor."

"I didn't think so," I said with another giggle as I pictured a golden giant flitting about on the dance floor among a garden of beautiful ladies.

"And how are my sister Mary and Queen Catherine?" I asked then.

"Quite well," he informed me, bowing his head.

For a moment we were silent, each picking at our plates, wondering in what vein the conversation would go next. Beneath the table my legs trembled. I took a sip of wine to calm myself, then offered the ambassador another cheery smile.

"Do tell me of my brother's fleet," I suggested. "Is the *Great Harry* as grand as our *Great Michael?*"

"It is a grand ship," Dr. West answered with a glower.

"I was aboard our *Great Michael* at Leith," I continued. "Oh, it is beautiful, Dr. West, and so fine a ship. Why, most of our forest at Falkland was cut down just to build her. Her walls are ten foot thick—impenetrable!"

"Impressive," he commented, but his eyes were narrowed.

"The ambassadors that saw her that day said that no navy on earth could rival ours," I persisted. "What do you think?"

"Madam, England boasts a fine navy of her own," Dr. West told me in firm tones. He paused, examining me a long moment. "I am certain if your husband requires details, good King Henry would be happy to discuss them. With him."

The smile I returned was frosty.

"Your Grace," Dr. West began. "It is my duty to inform you that King Henry does intend to invade France."

My gut lurched. My face remained impassive. Beneath the table I clawed into the material of my gown, clenching it with a white-knuckled grip.

"It is a dark hour for our countries," I stated. "I regret my brother's decision and what it will mean for our peace."

"Any hope of preserving the peace between England and Scotland is up to you," Dr. West retorted, his voice cold and blunt.

I bit my lip. I wanted to scream at him that I never chose this fate! How could a twenty-three-year-old girl forge peace between two countries? Who would listen to me?

I heaved a sigh of frustration.

"King Henry could certainly help with that," I said at last. "Where is my legacy that he has promised these past four years? The jewels from my brother Arthur and grandmother? Where are they, Dr. West?"

"The king is most ready to surrender them," he said smoothly. "If King James promises to keep the peace and not interfere with the French campaign."

"And if not?" I asked, hoping my voice did not betray my great sadness.

"If not? Then no. He cannot relinquish them."

"But they are mine!" I cried, losing my self-control. "They were willed to me by my brother and grandmother! How dare he keep from me what is mine!"

Dr. West said nothing to this. He continued eating. I stared down at my plate, flushed and disgusted.

The meal continued in frustrated silence; it seemed neither of us would get what we wanted out of it.

Dr. West tried everything from bribery to open threats in the hopes of securing peace between England and Scotland, to no avail. My husband sought to renew the alliance with the French king, who was as wily as his wife and played on Jamie's ultimate desire to lead a Crusade by allowing him to make a levy to fund it. Though Dr. West assured Jamie that King Louis would never keep his promise, Jamie remained undeterred.

Dr. West visited the baby and me at Linlithgow before returning to England.

"He is beautiful," the ambassador conceded as he admired my son. "So golden and rosy, and big for his age."

I nodded as I sat him on my lap, proudly displaying his chubby legs. "As robust as his uncle King Henry," I said. I wanted to say more, about the peace that was now broken, about the inevitable war we had now been thrust into. I wanted to share my fears and lamentations about my broken family. But I could not. It would not be politic.

Dr. West departed, his mission a failure, my attempts at diplomacy all gone awry.

When Jamie joined me at Linlithgow I clung to him, sobbing. I reduced myself to begging, throwing tantrums, anything, anything that would prevent his doomed enterprise.

In my darkest moment I hired an old man to "haunt" Jamie while he prayed at St. Michael's Church. Dressed in a gown of blue and white and carrying a pikestaff, the long-haired old wraith warned Jamie against going to war and seeking the counsel or comfort of women, after which he artfully disappeared, mystifying the attendants by managing his escape without being accosted.

But Jamie knew.

"Oh, Maggie, you are reaching," he told me in bed that night. He offered a slight laugh. "To your credit, you are quite imaginative."

"What can I do, Jamie?" I asked in soft tones, fringed with desperation. "What can I say to keep you from going to war against my brother? I'll do anything. . . ."

"I'm sorry, Maggie," Jamie whispered, kissing me softly. "I'm sorry."

"Not half as sorry as you are going to be," I told him, but my voice was no longer accusatory. It was filled with sadness, all-consuming, terrible sadness.

By May King Louis convinced my husband not only to ally himself with him but to invade England as well when my brother removed to France. It was the perfect strategy, the French louse stated, for Jamie may just gain the English crown for himself in Henry's absence.

Henry embarked for France in the summer and proved victorious, taking the town of Therouanne. In August Jamie sent Lyon King of Arms with our formal declaration of war, listing all of Scotland's grievances against England, which included the withholding of my legacy, the Andrew Barton affair, the John Heron incident, and the border raids.

At Edinburgh my husband prayed, whipping himself with a vengeance in preparation for the battle to come. I watched from the shadows of the chapel and when I could bear it no more I approached him, taking the whip from his hand and holding it at my side, watching my husband's blood drip from it onto the stone floor.

"Sometimes I wonder," I began in quiet tones, "if you are hoping to die so that your pain might end at last. Is that so, Jamie?"

Jamie regarded me, his face tortured.

I shook my head, sinking to the floor beside him and taking him in my arms. "Oh, my love, do not let this be my last memory of you!" I begged, burying my head in his shoulder. "I shall die if all you are to leave me with is the memory of your blood."

Tears streamed down Jamie's face unchecked as he began to sway from side to side.

We removed to our apartments, where our lovemaking was filled with such bittersweet agony that I wondered if I should have left him to his whipping after all. The blood would have prepared me better. The whipping would have allowed me to hate him. But now I was left with this memory, the memory of tenderness, of his caresses, his voice, his breath, his kiss, his warmth . . . his love. . . .

It was unbearable. Oh, it was unbearable. . . .

Jamie named me Queen Regent of Scotland before he left.

"This will not be an easy task, but it is one in which I have the utmost confidence in your abilities to carry out," Jamie told me the morning he would march out.

"I will do my best, until your return, when I will happily relinquish Scotland into your capable hands," I assured him warmly.

Jamie took my hands. "Maggie . . . if I do not come back, the regency will be all the more challenging for you to hold on to. Do you understand what I mean, Maggie?"

I shook my head. I did not want to hear of it; I did not want to understand.

"Maggie, if . . . if you marry again, you will sabotage any chance of keeping the regency. You must think of Little Jamie now," my husband urged, his tone fervent with intensity. "Everything you do from this day on is for him." Jamie's eyes lit with pity. "My poor girl; being the wife and mother of kings, you will never be allowed to live for yourself—not until Jamie is well beyond his majority. Vultures and demons will surround you—they will covet control of the crown like no other and devour each other in the process of trying to obtain it. No one will ever love you, my dearest, not like you deserve." Those words. Where had I heard them before? Ah, yes. My father had warned me of this many years ago. . . . No one would ever love me . . . such was the lonely fate of monarchs.

"To the world, you are a prize to be won, the closest thing to Little Jamie on this earth. Winning you wins him—and he is the ultimate prize. Therefore you must always be on guard against deceivers and those wishing to rule over you and our son," Jamie warned.

I shivered. "I understand, Jamie, truly I do. But please let us not speak on it anymore. You must ride, my love. Ride so that you may return my king and know"—my voice broke—"that I will keep your son and your kingdom safe in your absence."

At this Jamie smiled, offering one last tender kiss.

There was nothing more to be said or done. Our private farewell had been exchanged and there was but to face our kingdom, a united king and queen emanating confidence in the inevitable victory of the battle ahead.

The streets erupted with cheers for him, the bells tolled, the bishops and priests prayed for his victory, and my heart cried out in despair. I clung to him once more before he entered the blinding golden light. He was enthusiastic again, his manner driven and determined, his smile bright, his green eyes twinkling in merriment as he anticipated a glorious battle.

"Come home to me, Jamie," I ordered, taking his hand in mine. "You must come home to me to see your next child into the world." I guided his hand to my belly.

Tears sparkled in his eyes. He leaned in, kissing my cheek. "Oh, my love. I shall return to you. I promise."

He held me fast, planting a firm kiss on my mouth. I frantically tried to impress upon my memory the exact feeling of his body against mine—the way we fit, the way my head nestled in the crook of his shoulder, the way his strong arms enveloped me to his chest, wherein beat his sure, strong, and steady heart.

I did not want to part.

I did not want it to end.

But it did end. Jamie left and I was alone to rule his country.

Jamie raided the Borders as the English raised an army against him headed up by the very men who escorted me on my wedding journey ten years prior—the Earl of Surrey and his son Thomas Howard.

But I was assured their army was smaller than my husband's and Jamie was set to win the day. I waited for him at Linlithgow, sitting by my window in my bower, looking out at St. Michael's Church. I squinted at the horizon. But I knew he would not come. In the few hours sleep found me, my dreams told me so. He stood at the precipice, surrounded by white light. He turned, then walked off. I ran to the ledge to look down but saw naught but the light, the sweet white light.

He was gone.

I will never see you again.

The messenger who greeted me was coated in slick mud. I sat under my canopy of state in my presence chamber, dressed in black, my hair gathered in a chignon under my hood. I sat straight, my head erect. He would want me to receive the news like a queen.

With effort the messenger sank to his knees, bowing his head. "Your Grace, on 9 September the battle was lost." His voice caught. "We were outwitted by the English on the hill at Flodden Field; their weapons and maneuvers were superior, though their numbers were fewer. Everything was against us, it seems—the rain and the mud that had us taking our boots off and fighting bare-footed and the hill that was at first our advantage only to end as our curse." Tears streamed down his cheeks, running off his chin onto the floor, and I was compelled to reach out to him, laying a hand on his dirt-encrusted shoulder. "We lost ten thousand men, Your Grace," he sobbed. "The king among them." He made the sign of the cross, then raised his head, his eyes stricken with horror. "We couldn't find the body. There were so many, lying there in the darkness . . . and by morning most were stripped naked, robbed of their dignity. Lord Dacre found him, or someone he claims to be him, alongside his son Alexander, the Archbishop of St. Andrews, lying together surrounded by their loyal comrades. They—they were going to send the body to King Henry in France on orders of Queen Catherine, but Surrey urged her not to, so they sent his coat instead." He swallowed several times. "You—you want us to send another search party, to make certain the body they uncovered was not an imposter?"

I shook my head, remembering the gentle Lord Dacre, knowing despite our status as enemies that he was an honest man. "No . . . that will not be necessary."

I drew in a breath. I did not cry. I had known this, after all. I was struck numb and found myself thinking less of Jamie than of his bastard son by Janet Kennedy, the young archbishop whose appointment I resented so much. A strange pride welled in my chest as I thought of the young man who fought a losing battle beside his father. I knew that many of the Scots were against going to war, but go to war they did for their king and now all of them suffered for it. There could not exist a noble in the land untouched by this great loss.

But alongside the pride was rage, rage at Jamie for leading his people into this folly, rage at my sister-in-law for daring to suggest that his precious body be sent to France as a trophy of war. My gut churned and I swallowed bitter bile. I never could have anticipated such coldness in a heart I had always found to be so warm and filled with charity.

I swallowed my disillusionment. Now was no time to lament.

Nor could I afford the luxury of hating my sister-in-law at the moment. I could only think of Scotland. I was its regent now.

"We thank you, sir," I told the messenger. I turned to my attendant. "Please send for our son," I ordered in soft tones.

When the baby was brought to me I rose. He toddled toward me, offering a gap-toothed grin and holding out his chubby arms.

"Mama up!" was his first command as King of Scotland. "Mama up!"

I was honored to obey. Stooping down, I gathered my son in my arms, my shoulders convulsing with sobs as I took in his sweet baby scent. I allowed my tears to mingle against his strawberry blond curls as I held him close, then swept him into my arms as I rose.

The attendants and guards, lords, ladies, and servants all removed their caps. Tears coursed down their cheeks as they knelt and curtsied.

"Long live King James V," they chorused.

Long live James V, the seventeen-month-old King of Scots.

❧ 9 ❧

Ten Thousand Widows

I removed to the fortress of Stirling with my baby king, where he was crowned by the Archbishop of Glasgow, James Beaton, on 21 September. I watched as the gem-encrusted crown fit for a man's head was held over that of my son in what all refer to as the Mourning Coronation. Throughout the chapel could be heard nothing but sniffling and sobbing as each witness recalled the loved ones lost at Flodden Field.

I was among them, sobbing for my lost king, shedding tears for the one who replaced him; for myself; for my brother and sister-in-law, who reveled in my husband's death and treated it as a victory; and for the baby I now carried who would never know its father.

As Jamie's will was read the weight of my responsibilities bore down upon me in full. I was twenty-three years old and pregnant. I was widowed. My son was not yet two and he was King of Scotland. As Jamie had indicated before his doomed enterprise, I would rule in our son's stead under the stipulation that I never marry again.

I could not imagine why I would ever want to remarry, why I would ever want to put myself through the agony of loving and losing another person. And yet to never curl against the warmth of another human being in the night, to never savor the comfort only a man can give . . .

Now was no time to think of it. Now there was but to think of my people and of securing peace with England.

I met with my council, comforting myself with the distractions of governing. They were divided; many resented me for reasons obvious. I was a woman, which went against the cherished Scottish tradition of male rulers. What's more, I was an Englishwoman.

" 'Twill not be easy," said the old Earl of Angus, Archibald "Bell-the-Cat" Douglas, as he visited me in my apartments one winter afternoon. He was nicknamed such for offering to attack Jamie's father King James III's favorite Robert Cochrane by pulling his chain from his neck, which led to his and many other of the king's favorites' hangings.

I had always been fond of surly old Bell-the-Cat, though my husband was not. He held him partially responsible for the eventual rebellion against Jamie's father, which led to his death, plaguing Jamie with guilt for the rest of his life. What's more, the earl had married Jamie's lover Janet Kennedy. I never knew if this fact did anything to stop them from carrying on their affair, but in those times when I yearned to recall the few happy days we were afforded in our marriage I liked to think so.

I shifted my thoughts back to the old earl. He was not well. His losses in the battle were extensive and took a toll on him.

"Oh, Bell-the-Cat," I sighed, tears gathering in my throat. "I should like to think I made the right appointments. I have good men about me—your son Gavin and the Bishop of Aberdeen, who will stand as tutor to my son. And with the uncertainty of our relations with England, Stirling seems the best residence, the most resilient. I recall a time when all I had to occupy myself with was what gown to wear. Now I have to think about the price of cannon and the wages of soldiers. And there are so many other crises . . . most of the women in Scotland are widows, most of the children fatherless."

At this Bell-the-Cat flinched. I reached out, taking the withered hand in my own.

"We mourn the losses of your two fine sons," I told him. "And your clansmen."

"Two hundred of them, Your Grace," he said, his voice thick

with sadness. "Two hundred souls gone in one day, along with ninety-eight hundred more. Ten thousand widows."

I shook my head, too awed to speak. No words could do what Scotland lost, what my husband sacrificed, justice.

They poured in, these poor wretches, and I gave them audience, yes, each and every soul. They came to me, their Queen Widow, and I offered my tears and prayers and useless blessings.

"My land is gone!" one woman cried on her knees before me. "I canna inherit, as my son and husband were both killed in the great battle. The looters came and took everything of value," she sobbed without reserve. "And what was most valued, what I begged them not to take, if only for love of the blessed Virgin, was my daughter's virtue!"

"Oh, save us!" I cried, burying my face in my hands.

And on and on they came, all with similar stories of horror, while I sat on my throne of state unable to help, unable to do a thing without aid of council, a group of men who became increasingly frustrating and divided.

There was nothing to give, nothing to restore. All was lost . . . lost.

"What am I going to do, Bell-the-Cat?" I asked my favorite councilor, knowing he had not the answer. "I am awed, dumbstruck as I try and work out how to help our country, a country filled with widows and babies. A country filled with weakness and covered in wounds. I made a useless proclamation in the baby king's name urging the people against these desperate and despicable acts—the looting, the rapes. But no one wants peace. No one wants goodness. No. The women want retribution, rightfully, I believe, but the men? Of course you know what the men want. War. War with England. My brother. Where will that get us but more lives lost? My God . . . what am I going to do?"

Bell-the-Cat squeezed my hand and shook his head. "We are in sorry estate, madam. Sorry estate." He paused. "But ye've got good men."

"Divided men," I said again. "And I can make no decisions of my own without consulting three spiritual and three temporal lords. And the likelihood of them agreeing is . . ." I dissolved into tears, swallowed, then collected myself. "They want to recall the Duke of Albany from France to serve as a military leader. To usurp my regency, I imagine. The King of France wrote to tell me that he will not send him until he knows my wishes. He claims he will not make peace with my brother until I permit him to do so. I know I must make peace with Henry, but France is a powerful ally—"

"Ye best keep the peace with your brother," Bell-the-Cat advised, then erupted into a fit of coughing. "He's already proved what he can do. There may be another way to secure the alliance with France." At this his gaze grew pointed. "Anne of Brittany is not well, you know. The king could be a valuable commodity."

I laughed; the sound was without joy and grated on my ears. "I'd be valuable to him, you mean. Imagine, Louis VII, King of France and King Consort of Scotland. Henry would die."

"It is a possibility not to be overlooked," Bell-the-Cat insisted as he was wracked by another fit of coughing. "In any event, Your Grace, a sound alliance with a good man here at home may serve you well, as another consideration. Someone who will advise you, protect you and our young king."

"Oh, Bell-the-Cat, and lose my regency?" I reached out to him, placing my hands upon his shoulders. I could not bear to tell him I would never lower myself into marrying the poxy and decrepit King of France and I could not think of any good Scotsman to ally myself with either. "You need to return to your home at Tantallon. You need rest, my dear lord, and time to grieve."

"I am loathe to leave you during your trials, Your Grace," he confessed in gruff tones.

"I am loathe to let you go," I admitted. "But you must so that you might return to me strong and able."

He bowed.

"Good-bye, good councilor," I murmured to his retreating back. *I will never see you again.*

Though I received a message from my brother through Lord Dacre assuring me that my sister-in-law sent her love and hopes for peace, my anger resurged, fierce and hot as I imagined her commanding my husband's body to be sent to Henry. She fancied herself a warrior-queen like her mother, Isabella of Castile, who was just as renowned for her cruelty during the Inquisition.

I crumpled the dispatch in my hand in fury, gritting my teeth a long moment before relaxing.

Peace. She wanted peace. Was that not my goal as well? This had to end. Scotland could not take another loss.

I could not take another loss.

If I could just win the support of my council, if I could just convince them that I was not working in the best interests of England but for Scotland. As it was they tried to oust me at every turn and commanded all the greatest fortresses in the country.

"I have never felt so completely alone," I confessed to my Moorish lady, my favorite attendant, Ellen. The bond I secured with her had never been achieved with any of my other women, which made me value her all the more.

We were in my apartments. I rubbed my swollen belly; the baby was kicking now and a lump swelled in my throat as I thought of the father who would never feel it, never see it. . . .

"Poor Ellen, you must be weary of my tears," I said.

Ellen shook her noble head. She was tall and regal in her red taffeta gown. Her tight black curls cascaded down her back in ringlets impossible for a white woman to achieve. To look at her was to be stunned.

"You will endure, Your Grace," she assured me in her melodious accent. "God will grant you the strength. We both came here as slaves, you and I, ripped from our people and our homes. If we can survive what we have thus far, we can survive anything. The worst is behind us."

As I beheld the dark beauty I wondered what else she had survived. For all the years I had known her she had been my confidante but shared very little of herself. I never pried but instead took strength in her wisdom, hoping whatever she derived from me in return was enough to sustain her regard for me.

I reached out, taking her hand. "If only I were not so lonely. I think of him all the time, Ellen . . . I try not to. I try to busy myself with affairs of state—God knows there are enough of them. But at night, when I am alone in my bed, feeling our baby kick and stir within me as some kind of mockery to what was and what will never be, I am tormented by thoughts of him. And I am so angry at him for leaving me with this!"

Ellen bowed her head as she sat beside me on my chaise. "You must think of the new king now and your little baby to come, not as an affront to what was but as your husband's legacy to you and your people. Focus on them. Take comfort in them. You have the power to do so much good."

She echoed the words of my dear brother Arthur, spoken so many years ago, in times so very different from these.

"How can I do good if my council prevents me?" I persisted, knowing she did not have the answer.

"Find an ally," she said, insinuating Bell-the-Cat's blatant suggestion. "A good, strong ally to protect you. Perhaps together you can do right by the people."

"An ally . . ." I sank back into my chaise, thinking.

Who did I know that I could possibly trust?

"Oh, Ellen, would that you had the power I would ally myself to you!" I cried with a sudden rare smile.

"Wouldn't we be the talk of Christendom!" Ellen exclaimed. "Imagine all we could accomplish while the rest of the world was consumed with the scandal of it!"

But our laughter converted to bittersweet tears soon enough.

As Bell-the-Cat so aptly put it, we were in sorry estate.

❧ BOOK 3 ❧

The Douglas

❧ 10 ❧

The Ally

No sooner was I made regent than I was being torn between the interests of my divided countrymen: those in favor of an alliance with England and those who preferred French protection and, in turn, a continued war of revenge on the kingdom of my birth. A peace with my brother, as hurt and betrayed as I felt by him and Catherine, would alleviate the immediate turmoil Lord Dacre was creating on the Borders with the endless raids that served as retaliation for the Scottish invasion. Conversely, it was proposed that John Stewart, Duke of Albany, the son of James III's brother Alexander, who was exiled to France for trying to usurp the throne of Edward IV, be called to Scotland at once. He stood as next in line to the throne after my Little Jamie. It was suggested he would be the most appropriate choice—a strong hand to defend a kingdom he stood to inherit. All the while King Louis VII lurked in the peripheral, trying to decide which purpose would serve him best. He had written his assurances that he would neither send Albany nor make peace with my brother until I wished it.

I could not win. Any choice I made was bound to offend someone and it was all I could do to preserve the smallest decision making for myself, fearing something as minute as wearing the wrong gown would send someone stalking off in a huff. I was a swinging pendulum between one side and the other—the only thing they could agree on was if I swung too far to one side or the other I was showing favoritism. It was exhausting.

And then there was Henry, my brother and current enemy. It was unfathomable. My brother, my enemy . . . How had we come to this? There was no time to reflect. Henry was action and I was reaction. He hounded me endlessly, urging me to stand against the notion of Albany and a French alliance in favor of an alliance with him. After all, he was Little Jamie's uncle and who better to protect the boy-king than his uncle, the King of England? Albany was heir to the throne himself, Henry warned—what would stop him from ousting me and concocting ill fortune against my son, that he might have the power for himself, not unlike Richard III and the poor, accursed Princes in the Tower? The thought of such a horrific tragedy befalling my child sent me into near hysterics as I entertained one frightening scenario after another in an attempt to decide what was best for my son, my kingdom, and, not least of all, me.

No matter what paths the scenarios twisted and turned, all of them ended with making peace with Henry. He was my only living brother, one of the few constants in my life. I could not bear to think of raising Little Jamie to hate and fear his uncle.

And so it would be to that end that I would strive.

In January 1514 old Louis VII's queen, Anne of Brittany, passed. Against my will my chest constricted with a sense of perverse satisfaction. The woman who with a ring and a glove sent my husband to his death now met the same fate and I was glad of it. May she have died with a thousand regrets!

The winter was passing in a blur. With the new responsibilities as queen regent I no longer spent the days in frivolity, planning gowns for Ellen and me or worrying about the next entertainment. We were a kingdom in mourning—there would be no entertainments, not for a long, long time. Even had Jamie survived Flodden, we would not be entertaining. I was eight months gone with child and exhausted most of the time. My back ached, my head hurt, and I had gained more weight than I wanted with this baby. I felt altogether horrid. Moments of serenity, those few times when I did not have to wrack my brain about matters of state, were taken with my devoted Ellen.

"It is being said that King Louis has cast his gaze upon Scotland for his next bride," my Ellen informed me one March afternoon as we sat in my privy chamber sewing baby garments.

"My congratulations!" I quipped. "You did not tell me you were to become Queen of France!"

Ellen's full lips curved into a slow smile. "Your Grace, would it not serve you to wed King Louis? You would be Queen of Scotland and France and be assured protection from your enemies. You would have the help you so need—"

"Not from that poxy old fool," I told her. "He can keep looking." I shrugged. "Besides, now that a truce with England has been secured, precarious as it is, it would not be politic to marry my brother's enemy." I chuckled at the thought. "Henry would have a fit." I sighed. "Now it seems all of my enemies are within our borders. Who can protect me from them?"

Ellen could only offer a sympathetic shake of her head as she continued sewing.

"Ellen, I canna marry anybody," I went on. "My duty is to protect the king and bring him a brother. I must trust that my council is acting in our best interests."

The last phrase was empty. I knew well the council could not be trusted; they protected no one's interests but their own. My one hope was that their interests were intertwined with mine.

"Your Grace, I hate to see you alone, constantly torn in two without a strong shoulder to lean on," Ellen confessed, her voice catching. "You were a woman born for love."

At once tears clutched my throat as an image of my one love swirled before my mind's eye. I blinked it away as his words and the words of my father echoed in my ears. "Ah, but Ellen, who was born to love me?"

Ellen bowed her head. She could not answer.

Nor could I.

* * *

The crowds still shouted blessings to me when I rode through the streets of Edinburgh for the gathering of Parliament. I found myself heaving a great sigh of relief without knowing I was holding my breath. They were still with me. I was still loved. I needed to be loved.

It was my last public appearance before my confinement and I savored the opportunity to meet with my council. It remained vital that I show myself as much as possible before my lying-in; I must be in the foreground of their memories that they might continue to act for and not against me.

It was that council that would forever alter my course.

"My grandson, Your Grace, and the Sixth Earl of Angus, Archibald Douglas." It was Lord Drummond who introduced us. Lord Drummond, the father of Margaret, murdered mistress of my Jamie. Unlike Bell-the-Cat, the new Angus's other grandfather, who was also tied to one of my husband's mistresses, I was not at ease with Lord Drummond. It was never far from my mind that he hoped to elevate his daughter to the throne and was denied the chance. I hoped the tragedy made him more cautious in his aspirations now, even as almost against my will my eyes were taking in the magnificent tribute to all that was good in young men—his grandson.

Archibald Douglas, the newly styled Earl of Angus . . . There he was in a leather doublet with a russet shirt beneath that revealed the muscles of his broad shoulders and upper arms. Ah, he was as strong a lad as one could behold, appearing much older than his twenty-four years. He was big and broad, with his warrior's hands and well-muscled legs, his chestnut hair and beard, and brown eyes that sparkled with alert intensity. He was not as handsome as my Jamie, of course, but there was something about him . . . something dark and wild and helplessly alluring.

Angus dipped into a deep bow before me, placing a warm kiss on my proffered hand.

"He will be taking his late grandfather's place on the council," Lord Drummond explained.

"Our condolences for the loss of your grandfather," I said in soft tones, watching Lord Drummond's all-too-conspicuous retreat. "We were very fond of Bell-the-Cat."

"It was a great loss, Your Grace," Angus confessed in a voice low and strong as Jamie's was melodic. "After losing my father and uncle at Flodden, he and my uncle Gavin were all I had left on the Douglas side. And all this after losing my wife in childbed . . . It is almost unimaginable at times." He offered a quivering smile that caused my heart to constrict. "Pardon me, Your Grace, I still grow emotional." He sighed. "But the turn of events astounds me. Nothing is quite real anymore; I've been going through my days in a dream." He shook his head, chuckling and sniffling as a flush kissed his cheeks a soft rose. "Forgive me, Your Grace."

"You mustn't apologize," I urged, endeared by his raw display of emotion most were too afraid to confront. "We know too well what you are enduring. I know," I added in soft tones.

"Oh, Your Grace, but your position must be far more difficult," Angus told me. "To lose our king and now to be all alone at the head of this rabble." He winked as he gazed about the great hall at the members of council, many of them rough lairds to be sure.

I found myself laughing in agreement but soon found myself choking back tears. How quickly they came! "Flodden cursed our kingdom," I told him. "But We will all endure it together and someday Scotland will be stronger for it. And We are not alone," I assured him with a smile. "We have advisers like you to help Us through."

"Till death, Your Grace," Angus vowed, his fervency matching the intensity of his eyes. "I see it as my sacred duty to hold the interests of your son my king above my own always and"—he seized my hand, bowing before it again—"to serve you in any capacity I can to make your lot easier to bear."

With that he kissed my hand once more, quitting my presence and taking with him forever my better judgment.

"Fair words," Ellen observed late that evening at Stirling as she brushed my hair while I told her of the encounter. "He is a smart man to say them, and at such a sorrowful time when you need to hear them most."

"What do you mean? Are you questioning his sincerity?" I demanded.

"Are you not?" Ellen returned. "Your Grace, you have suffered unspeakable tragedy. Such times make a woman . . . open to charms she may dismiss when her head is clear. It is for love of you I advise caution, please understand."

"I love you for it, Ellen, truly I do," I assured her. "But you didn't hear him speak; you didn't see him. His eyes . . . I canna see a man with eyes like that being a liar. Besides, I thought you would have been happy to note me admiring a man, you who would have seen me married off to old King Louis and wanted an ally for me."

Ellen offered a soft laugh. "He is a king, Your Grace—and in my opinion it is kings that should suit queens and nothing less. The Douglas is a man among many, an ambitious man. And you mustn't forget the Douglases remain one of the most opposed houses in Scotland."

That I knew all too well. After ambition and intrigue led the Douglases to near ruin during the reign of James II, when said king stabbed the conniving and ambitious eighth Earl of Douglas, it was a long climb back into the graces of the Stewarts—and those graces were suspicious at best. But those acts were near seventy years ago—none of it had to do with the young gallant I had seen that day.

I offered a sigh. "Enough of this talk, Ellen," I said in weary tones. "His eyes . . . they seemed true enough, and that is refreshing for one in my position."

Ellen's eyes, those endless black orbs, were another gaze I could count on to be true. But in them all I could see was sadness mingled with fear.

I did not want her to fear for me. I did not want anyone to fear for me. That implied I was not safe. And I had to be safe. I had to be cared for and loved. If I was not safe, it meant I was not loved, that someone could have motives for my fate—and my son's fate—that were less than pure.

I could not bear to think on that.

I wanted to think of Angus's eyes.

* * *

My confinement was as dreadful as the others and I was impatient to be at court, to be where life was happening. I hated the thought of decisions being made over my head, decisions I had no say in. As it was, the March Parliament had limited my power even more, taking control of all the fortresses in Scotland.

But for my part, I still had the person of the king, my son, Little Jamie, and his value surpassed that of any fortress. His rooms were near my confinement chamber and each day he was brought to me, my one ray of light throughout the dread days of solitude and isolation. At two years old, he was a joy, a rambling babe whose chatter was sweeter than the most accomplished minstrel. My eyes followed wherever he went, his slaves, watching him toddling here and there, exploring a world he ruled unbeknownst to himself. How I cherished his innocence—how I longed to preserve it! Somehow I would; somehow I would manage to raise him and his brother or sister as far away from politics as I could, away from those who wished to steer him this way and that, bending him as a willow in the winds of their own devices. No, this would not be for Little Jamie. He would learn to be a king who stood his ground and was firm in his own understanding. He would be his own king, his own man.

But for a boy to be without a father ... He *had* a father, in Heaven. My Jamie would guide him from there. I told myself that. I told myself that would be enough for a growing boy even as I found myself dreaming of a family, a family with a living father and a mother, what every boy—especially a king—needed.

Was it not my duty to provide for the king's needs?

No one will ever love you. ...

No! I refused to believe it. I could be loved, queen or not! Someone would love my son and me. Not everyone could be so misguided as to seek only after power. ... Someone had to have a true heart. And I would find him. I would find him and keep my regency besides, no matter what Jamie's will stipulated. The council would see, they would have to see, that it was for the best interest of the boy that he have a man in his life to guide him, to love him.

And to love me.

*   *   *

Alexander, the precious little Duke of Ross, was born on 30 April. It was a remarkable delivery in that my labor was not the struggle of my previous births. Though it sapped me of my strength, I was alert and able to hold my baby right away. I held the soft, warm bundle in my arms, covering the downy head with kisses.

"I gave you another son, Jamie," I whispered, stroking the silken cheek. "Another prince for Scotland." I held my tears at bay, praying my husband could see our joy from Heaven, praying he thought me a good wife and mother and queen. The longing, sharp as a blade, was almost too acute to bear . . . oh, Jamie. . . .

My kingdom was there when my husband could not be. Little Alexander was their pride, compensation for the miseries and loss of Flodden, a reminder of the innocence and good that could survive even the harshest tragedies. He was a true son of Scotland, and the kingdom stood as his surrogate. It was no small triumph to me that I was mother to the heirs to not only the Scottish throne but, until my brother and the unfortunate Catherine could produce one, the English throne as well. Was it wrong to nurse the hope that it would be through my bloodline that the crowns of both kingdoms would be united, just as my father had once prophesied? Wouldn't Father and Jamie have been proud to see that! Yet to hope for that was to wish ill on Henry and Catherine and I could not make that mistake again . . . yet were they not triumphant at the death of my husband? Did she not want to send his bloodied body to Henry as a trophy? The thought made my blood run hot and justified my ambition. To have my children forge understanding between my homeland and country of adoption was a grand aspiration, a noble cause. There was nothing sinful in taking pleasure in God's will, for it must have been God's will that I be fruitful where my brother was not.

I told myself that, too. But I told myself many things in those days.

"I hope it isn't unseemly, my visit," the Earl of Angus told me when he came laden with gifts for baby Alexander, Little Jamie, and me as I convalesced at Stirling. His brown eyes sparkled with unabashed joy at the sight of the baby in my arms and he rushed forward, reaching out a hand that he might stroke Alexander's head, then drawing back to dip into a bow. "Forgive me, Your Grace, I should not be so impulsive."

"No, you really should not," Ellen said from her seat near my bed. I shot her a quick glance that set her scowling into her embroidery.

"It is all right, my lord," I told him in warm tones. "How thoughtful of you to visit Us; We have been restless for court. And this little one is eager to meet the kingdom—it is appropriate he starts with the best of them."

Angus beamed at this. He drew near, holding a finger out for the baby to clutch. Tears shone bright in Angus's eyes as he gazed at Alexander. "He is a bonny lad, Your Grace," he said, his voice wavering. "After losing my little lamb, it restores me to see life renewed, and such a lusty babe!"

I could not speak. He had lost, I had lost—our babies, our spouses, our fathers—and as he bent over my baby and me something stirred within, something protective and something needing protection. The bond of loss.

"He quite resembles his father," Ellen observed in conversational tones as she regarded us. "Her Grace says so all the time."

"Indeed," Angus said. "It must be a comfort to you, then, I hope."

He understood, I imagined, the mingled comfort and sadness of family resemblance. I wondered if my eyes revealed my gratitude for this—I hoped so.

"It is," was all I could say. "Would . . . would you like to hold him, my lord?"

"It is only my deepest wish!" Angus cried as he scooped the baby in his arms, gathering him to his chest. His deep smile revealed dimples on either side of his mouth as he cooed at the baby, pacing back and forth as we are so prone to do when holding a little one. Through a veil of tears, the scene was softened, the figures obscured, and I pretended just then—for just that moment—that it was Jamie holding our son, Jamie looking upon his sweet face, the proud father, and that we were a family united again. I blinked the vision away. There stood Angus once more.

"And how does His Grace like his little brother?" Angus inquired.

I laughed. "I am not certain," I said, dismissing the royal *We*. "I think he might have been a little put off. He said he wanted a pony."

"As they grow, he will find that little brothers are much better than ponies!" Angus commented as he returned the baby to my arms. "I should not overtax you, Your Grace. You and our little laird must get some rest. I hope . . . I do hope you will permit my visit again soon?"

Again and again and again, I wanted to say. I could only nod and resist the urge to beg him to stay and let me pretend, just a little longer.

But I said nothing and allowed his graceful retreat, while ignoring Ellen's pointed stare as I waited, breath bated, for his return.

He did return, many times, sometimes with Lord Drummond or other members of the court, and always with gifts. But I found myself looking forward to having Angus to myself. He loved to laugh and brought life to my chambers. Sometimes Little Jamie joined us and the two played together, silly child's games, while I held the baby and looked on, cherishing the happy family scene. Angus and I rarely spoke of court matters, only of domestic things— the children, the spring lambs, entertainments to celebrate the birth of Alexander. How I relished those talks and the interest Angus took in the children as children, not as a king and a prince.

May drifted into June and June to July. If I did not regain my figure after the birth of Alexander, I at least regained my strength, and the summer, warm and languid, saw me with my children, Angus, and the court. On 12 July my council signed a document stating they would not divide into factions, that my regency was supported.

"A triumph, Your Grace," Angus told me one evening as we dined in my chambers. "Never has Scotland seen such unity."

"It is true," I agreed. "There has been too much division over the years. I fear my recommending your uncle Gavin to the Pope for the Archbishopric of St. Andrews jeopardized my favor with the council. I must make recommendations based on the quality of those recommended and nothing else, even though I myself consider him quite able and he was much loved by the late king. It's just that I must not be seen to show favoritism to any one family over another."

"The position would have been a blessing for our family," Angus said. "But as it is, His Holiness favors Andrew Forman for when old William Elphinstone passes. That is a battle we can fight later together."

I laughed at this. "Oh, can we, now?" It was both unnerving and exciting, the thought of fighting a battle beside Angus, the thought of having someone to support me.

Angus's smile was soft. "It serves you that the council seems to have overlooked the possible . . . controversy of your recommendation for now and all has been forgiven; the Pope did agree to Elphinstone, which was your ultimate pick, was it not? So you are still in favor. Who could not favor you, when your heart is so pure and well intended?"

I dismissed the compliment with a wave of one bejeweled hand. "I am grateful they have. If we can keep Scotland united for the sake of this little boy then perhaps it will ease his way when he reaches his majority." I cast adoring eyes at Little Jamie, who was making a show of moving chess pieces randomly about the board with Angus, who deferred to His Grace with the utmost respect during their mock foray.

Angus's eyes grew distant. "We can hope. It will not be easy for this little one. So many yearn to control him, and though this document was signed in allegiance to you—in essence him—there are those who will endlessly plot to manipulate him to suit their own ends."

The words frightened me and echoed Jamie's ominous warning to me before he died. "The curse of child-kings," I commented, thinking of Jamie and his grandfather before him. "I will protect him," I vowed, my voice wavering with fervency. "They will not touch him as long as I am regent." I reached out to caress my son's cheek, but my hand never reached its destination, for Angus at once seized it in his. I flinched at his warm touch. I should have scolded him, reminded him of the offense of touching my person without permit. Had Ellen been present, the act may have driven her to slap him outright. But all I could do was hold his hand.

"I will protect him as well," Angus said. "And, Your dearest Grace, I will protect you. If you will let me."

"What do you mean?" I breathed.

Angus lowered his eyes a moment, caressing my thumb with his forefinger. "As your friend, as your adviser . . ." He raised his eyes, gazing into my face through to my heart. "And perhaps more."

I withdrew my hand as an image of Jamie, his eyes so cautious and prudent, presented itself before my mind's eye. I blinked it away. Jamie was gone. It was Angus here with me now, with my children, loving them and entertaining and guiding them. Angus, who was so handsome and fussed over me, making me feel almost lovely again.

I drew in a quavering breath. "Angus, you must be very careful," I warned. "I have not even been a year widowed. Should I marry again, I must consider the wishes of my brother Henry and the council. And, not least of all, the regency—"

"Is all but secure now with the signing of that statement," Angus assured me. "Your Grace . . . Margaret." His tone grew reverent as he addressed the woman and not the queen. My heart began to pound. "You married for duty as a child. A second marriage is usually never under such obligation. Seize your right as a woman grown to choose and be chosen for *love*. We have suffered much, you and I. We have lost more than what is deserved in one lifetime. It may be irregular, but what is regular about the times we live in, when death stalks us all day to day and uncertainty is our only constant?"

"Angus . . ." I began. "You cannot speak of this. You must not. People will not look kindly on our match; they will think you are taking advantage. They will think of the benefits for the house of Douglas and the jealousy will tear the kingdom apart."

"We will make them see!" he cried. "In time they will accept it.

When they see me as your husband, when they see us as a family. Can you not see we are a family, Margaret? Have you not felt what I have been feeling these past months?"

I tilted my head back, resting it against the cushion of my chair, closing my eyes. "I'd be lying if I said I did not feel it," I confessed. "But too much works against us. And you are considered quite young."

"But I am of your own age! And your brother King Henry is young, is he not? And yet is he not a husband? His marriage is unshakeable!" Angus argued. "What is youth, Margaret, really?"

I rose, calling the nurse to take the children. I did not want them present for this discussion and needed a moment to collect myself, to ponder this remarkable circumstance. Had I not been trysting with the idea since meeting Angus? Could it be possible the council would support the action and see it as a boon for the boys to have a living father and a good Scotsman to defend their queen? It was too much to hope and there was far too much to fear.

When I returned, Angus was on his feet. He held out his hands. It would have been rude not to take them in mine.

I bowed my head. "You could have anyone," I told him. "Someone fetching and slim." I swallowed the growing lump in my throat. "Look at me, Angus! I have just had a baby. I am not . . ." Shame gripped me as I thought of my reflection in the glass. I hated to see myself now, my body gone soft and round with the rigors of childbearing. "I am not comely anymore. I am growing stout!"

"You have a woman's curves now, if that is what you mean by that ridiculous tangent," Angus said. There was something new to his tone now, something beyond his fervency. It was akin to authority . . . but not quite. "And I would rather have a solid woman at my side than a willowy girl who would blow away at the slightest breeze. Come now, that was funny. Give me a smile, won't you?"

I obliged. The twinkle in his eye would have made it impossible not to. "You mean, you do not think me . . . fat?" The word sounded vulgar on my tongue.

Angus shook his head with vehemence. "I never want to hear

that word again," he ordered. "You are not just the Queen of Scotland but a queen among women. You are beautiful to me. You . . . you and those two bonny lads . . . are . . ."—his voice softened—"everything to me."

I expelled a breath, not realizing I had been holding it in. He thought me beautiful. How I needed to feel desired again! And he dared see me as a woman, not as a queen. And the boys, he loved them as boys. He thought me beautiful. . . .

"I will," I heard myself whisper.

With this Angus seized my face between his hands, planting a firm kiss upon my mouth. What startled me more than the heat of his lips was the gut-churning certainty that I felt nothing in the kiss, though as a kiss it was quite pleasant.

It would come in time, I reasoned.

Then you are not marrying for love, are you? Was it Jamie's voice or my father's ringing in my head? *And if not for love, your earl's great justification for the match, then why?*

Perhaps to *be* loved. Perhaps because it was the one thing I could choose, or so I thought. And he was so handsome, so passionate. . . .

He thought me beautiful. . . .

Angus insisted we keep our betrothal from the council. It would create a sensation that could curse our union before it had a chance to begin—perhaps even prevent its beginning altogether. It was sound enough reasoning, but something felt strange in it. My first wedding was celebrated with all the pomp and pageantry a Princess of the Blood deserved and had the support of all of my family. Somehow doing something I knew my brother would not support seemed deceptive and wrong. Yet when he found out perhaps he would then be happy for me, perhaps he would understand. . . .

But Henry's understanding was not nearly as important as Scotland's. I could not imagine the reaction. I did not want to. I even kept the news secret from my ladies. I did not want to hear any protests or risk the news being spread about court. It was rather delicious keeping a secret to myself, something I alone could savor. Sooner or later all would be found out and I would deal with it then.

For now I lived in a dream, imagining life with Angus, a quiet life keeping my children safe from the divisive world of Scottish politics till they came of an age and strength of mind to confront such things. And perhaps there would be more children with Angus. . . . As much as I had come to fear and dread childbirth, the idea of starting a new family with Angus was appealing. These would be children who would be mine and not Scotland's, children I could love and protect. . . .

It was, for those few weeks before my wedding, a pretty picture.

❧ 11 ❧

Mistress Douglas

In the oppressive heat of early August, my wedding day stood in such contrast to that of my proxy ceremony to Jamie and my very public reception in Scotland that it was hard to believe any of it was real. We stood in the little church of Kinnoul with none but Lord Drummond's nephew, the Dean of Dunblane, to officiate. Only a handful were present, all of Lord Drummond's picking, as I said my vows in my ordinary russet gown. The brief ceremony seemed over almost before it began; a humble gold band was slid up my finger and it was done. I had said, "I do." I was no longer Mistress Stewart. The thought caused my heart to lurch. I remembered how I had once treasured that name above that of "Your Grace"; it seemed so long ago, when I was with my Jamie and we were happy.

I was Mistress Douglas now. Margaret Douglas. Yet still I was Margaret, the Queen Regent of Scotland. But for how long?

Those were thoughts far too heady as I was whisked away to our secret bridal chambers. It was best not to ponder them overmuch and to give myself over to the moment, subdued as it was. No courtiers laughed and made crude jokes this time; we were alone, save a few servants to attend us and then only when they were sent for.

Angus poured us both healthy draughts of warm spiced wine when we arrived. He was all smiles.

"We did it!" he cried, raising his cup to toast me. "Can you believe it? We will show them all, you and I. Scotland is ours!"

My brows furrowed at the arrogance of his statement. I sat on the bed, cup in hand. "Not ours, Angus," I admonished. "Scotland belongs to Little Jamie. He is ours to protect, for the sake of Scotland. *His* Scotland."

"Of course, my dear," Angus conceded as he sat next to me, clinking his cup to mine regardless of the inappropriateness of his remarks. "I meant nothing by it, only to say how proud of you I am for being your own woman—your own queen. You went against brother and council and followed your heart. That takes true bravery. If your council cannot see that, then they are blind."

I sighed. Though I appreciated his confidence in me, I did not want to think of my brother or the council or their opinions. I knew with a sense of gut-churning dread that they would not think me truly brave at all.

"Tonight isn't about my brother or the council," I told Angus. "It is about us. About our family," I added in soft tones.

"You are right, of course," Angus told me, reaching up to stroke my cheek. His eyes, so sparkling and vibrant, were distracted. "And we are not truly married until our union is consummated. 'Wedded and bedded,' " he quipped with a chuckle. "So enough chatter!"

There was no sensual gentleness in his touch; he clamped his hand on the back of my head, pulling me toward him that he might meet my lips with his own. His kiss was hard, urgent, possessive. I sighed. I should not have expected too much. I had, after all, known the love of a man who was reputed to be one of the foremost lovers of our time. Jamie had known how to kiss a woman. It was for me to teach Angus. I vowed to be more patient with him and, in the hidden part of my soul, that dark recess I did not want to confront, I found it easier to be passionate with him when I pretended he was my Jamie. I would not admit I did it, not even to myself then. But I did.

At once, Angus stood. "We should douse the light," he suggested as he went about blowing out the tapers.

"You dinna have to, Angus," I told him. "I am a woman, not a girl. I know the goings-on and am not shy."

Angus laughed at this. "It is only proper," he said. "And fitting—a secret marriage, a clandestine consummation in the dark!"

And with that the last of the candles were extinguished as I heard him make his way back to me. His arms went around me as he began to kiss my throat and bosom while fumbling with my gown. I closed my eyes, sighing once more.

It was not for the sake of keeping with the theme of our secret marriage that we made love in the dark.

He did not want to see me. Perhaps he was pretending, too. . . .

We had no honeymoon, no entertainments, nothing to commemorate our union other than our frantic, awkward couplings in the dark. Then again perhaps it was just as well. It would not have been a good thing to hide from reality any longer, for reality was a ruthless hunter, ferreting me out at every turn. The sooner I faced it, the sooner would I know what I was up against.

Our marriage was no longer secret. My husband saw to that. With his own men, he stormed upon Lord Chancellor Beaton at Perth and seized the Great Seal. Angus thought it a great show of strength.

"It is the only way to deal with them," Angus assured me in our rooms at Edinburgh when I chastised him for his rash behavior. "We must be decisive. Strong. Determined, and seen never to falter!"

"*We* are not seen as any such thing!" I cried, infuriated with his impetuosity. "*You* are only seen as a fool!"

"This 'fool' is your husband, my dear." Angus's voice contained a hint of warning. "Best that you remember it."

I waved my hand in dismissal. "You have incited the lairds against you! Your 'strength' inspired the Earl of Arran to come to Edinburgh armed with all his men and appeal to the council that *he* might have power over the government. He is a kinsman of Jam— of the late king!"

"Not a close enough kinsman," Angus reminded me. "They'll never give him any power beyond what he has now." He shrugged, shaking his head. "Fine, so we stirred them up, and good that we did! We shall rile them up and take them in hand, showing who should indeed have control of the government!"

"Who should have control then, Angus? You?" I was scandalized. At once I realized it was not Angus who was the fool, but me. Shame heated my cheeks. I began to shake my head. All along this was what he wanted; it was man's oldest ambition: power. . . . No! Surely there was more. His tenderness toward the boys was not feigned, and his sensual nature . . . surely I was being too cautious.

"Us, my dear, us!" Angus cried. "I am the stepfather of the king and you his beloved mother," he went on. "There is no other choice more fitting than us."

I drew in a shaky breath. It had not gone at all like I thought. Of course I did not think of how it would come about. I did not think at all. . . .

"In favor of us they want the Duke of Albany, my husband's cousin, from France," I told Angus. At once I was exhausted. There was to be a battle ahead, the battle of my life, and I was far from ready to fight.

"He is more Frenchman than Scot, raised there all his life in exile," Angus observed. "What could the fate of Scotland really mean for him?"

"He stands to inherit the throne after Little Jamie and Alexander," I reminded Angus. "So it could interest him a great deal," I added with a shudder.

Angus shook his head. "He will not come. Your brother—Henry—he will see to that. Henry will side with us, you will see. He is a powerful ally."

To refer to the King of England as merely Henry, as if they were old mates, incensed me. "Such allegiances are hard won, and harder to maintain," I said in even tones.

"You will of course write and appeal to him while I sort these things out," Angus said. *Sorting things out* referred, no doubt, to warfare. Visions of Flodden and all it cost swirled in my mind; could we go through it all again so soon? "You are his dear sister after all," Angus was reasoning. "You have the commonality of your childhood to warm him and it is in his interests to keep his closest enemy a friend."

"I always write to my brother," I told Angus, irritated that he believed he had to urge me into such action.

"That's my girl," Angus said, his tone affectionate as he stooped to brush his lips against my cheek. "That's my brave, strong queen." With this he made for the door and to the battles ahead. But before leaving, he turned. "And Albany is not your husband's cousin," he told me in firm tones. "*I* am your husband. And I have no cousin called Albany."

Then he was gone.

The council was infuriated by my "betrayal" of daring to marry again; I had, to them, forfeited my rights as queen regent, only valid as long as I remained the widow of James IV as per his will. It was natural now that they should choose another. If I relinquished my regency willingly, they assured me, I could retain custody of my children. As if they had the right to consider taking my children from me, regent or not!

They were determined to oust me from my regency in favor of the Duke of Albany, despite my protests and fears that bringing the duke in too strongly resembled a story that haunted me in my childhood, that of Richard III. Were they willing for my sons, and one of them their own king, to suffer that same cruel fate as my uncles in the Tower should Albany decide to usurp power for himself? Such fears were considered the hysterics of a woman, and mentioning Richard III likely reminded them that the fears belonged to an *English*woman besides. All of my concerns were dismissed.

The Lyon King of Arms William Comyn was sent to tell me the outcome of the council's vote in my presence chamber, which was to end my regency. The man even had the audacity to honor the council's newly appointed title for me—"my lady the king's mother," rather than "Your Grace"—for which my new grandfather-in-law, Lord Drummond, boxed his ears. And rightly; it was a great, unfair offense: I was still the queen and I had care of my children's persons. I would not give up my rightful title or regency so quickly; even my husband, as my appointed co-regent, should have been respected, bold as he was. Why should my personal happiness interfere with affairs of state? What did it matter who I married, so long as he was good to my son? And for all Angus had to learn, he was good to my son. It wasn't Angus's fault that he belonged to the Red Douglases. No one chooses who they are born to, otherwise would I not have chosen a noble family in England other than the royal one, in which I might have lived and loved in happiness rather than for sake of politics?

There was no use rallying against the system at hand. There was but to remain a step ahead of my council and all who opposed me. They became my Party Adversary, for that was what they were—divided, disloyal men, all out for themselves and all of them so willing to take my kingdom and children from me for the simple offense of marrying a man of my own choosing and not theirs. It was a battle of pride, nothing more, nothing less.

In that, they did not realize whom they were up against.

No one was prouder than a Tudor.

October proved an eventful month. My sister, fair little Mary, became Queen of France, a development that rather took me by surprise, as she had once been betrothed to Charles of Castile. It should not have shocked me much, in truth. Mary had everything—famed beauty, the admiration of kingdoms, the unquestioned adoration of my brother and his court, and now she had France. Did it matter if old King Louis was riddled with the pox? She no doubt would take on plenty of lusty young lovers of her own. And should the old man die, she still had the title without any of the adversity I had suffered as a widow. Henry would coddle her, no doubt, and no army would be strong enough or large enough to come to the rescue of his baby sister. . . . Better to be happy for her, I supposed. I could not think of it much, in any event. I had enough worries of my own.

For also in October, the see of St. Andrews became vacant once more, as old Elphinstone passed away; again, no surprise: He was ancient when he was elected. It was my chance to use my author-

ity for good and show my own strength. At once I recommended
Angus's uncle Gavin Douglas to the post. It was my right, the
Crown's right, to do so. Gavin deserved it, after all, as I had
thought before ever marrying Angus. He was not only a gifted poet
with a quick wit but also a most learned man. He had translated
the entire *Aeneid* into English—quite a feat! Despite the fact that I
hadn't read it, it was still admirable nonetheless.

I believed my reasoning for my pick to be sound. Would it not
be prudent for Scotland to see that not all Douglases were of the
"Red Douglases"? That one could perform holy duties and prove
himself an able man and be seen as living beyond the scandals of
his family name? If so, could then my Angus be seen as more? Not
least of all, it stood that whoever the Archbishop of St. Andrews
would be, he would be guardian of the king. It would do to have a
man as close to my son's family as could be.

My nomination, like my every move, went without support,
save for the Douglases and Henry, who whispered in the Pope's
ear on my behalf. His Holiness still favored Andrew Forman, however, and Henry could not influence the fate of the see any more
than I could. The Hepburns, the Bothwells, and a force organized
by Lord Fleming took the castle of St. Andrews by force, placing
John Hepburn, the prior of the castle, in care of the see. Though I
sent my husband and his men in the hopes that they could take
the castle back for Gavin Douglas, the force Lord Home sent was
stronger, defeating my husband's men.

And while I waited for news and pondered every angle of my
situation, my most faithful of attendants, my rare dark jewel,
Ellen, rushed into my privy chamber, stealing me from my reverie.

"Your Grace, forgive my disturbing you!" she cried, breathless.
"But Lord Home has stormed Edinburgh! He has the castle surrounded."

My heart lurched in my chest as my stomach twisted in a
painful knot. I reached out, taking her hand in mine.

"We will escape," I told her. "We will take the children and flee
to Stirling. Angus will find us there."

Ellen's ebony eyes misted over as she offered a quick nod.

I alighted to the nursery, my forced smile bright as I clapped my hands. "Come, my darlings!" I cried to my children. "We shall go on a ride!"

Little Jamie, the king of our land, hopped up and down, his face creasing into a smile. "A ride! A ride! Hurray!"

Swallowing tears, I gathered my babies in my arms, determined that they should not be prisoners in their own domain.

Nor would I.

Far too recognizable to accompany me, Ellen remained behind. I took but two servants and a guard, ordering a coach. It all seemed too easy; no one noticed our departure, and as the coach lurched along the road I held Alexander on my lap and Little Jamie to my side, exclaiming over our night ride and how they would be given sweetmeats at Stirling. Of course the baby knew nothing was amiss and Little Jamie was in favor of a treat. They did not feel my heart pounding against my ribs, or the beads of sweat gathering on my forehead, running down my face as I struggled to maintain even breathing. I must be calm. If not for myself, for the boys. They needed their mother the queen to be decisive and strong, not simpering and afraid.

The hooves pounding behind me alerted me to the fact that we were missed.

"Faster!" I ordered the driver, holding the children closer. "Please," I whispered. "Please dinna let them catch us—"

"Halt there, in the name of His Grace, the King!"

I squeezed my eyes shut, drawing in a breath. As the curtains were drawn, I could not see what was happening, but I felt the coach roll to a stop. I bit my lip.

"Are you or are you not transporting the queen, His Grace, and the Duke of Ross?" a male voice thundered.

"Aye," answered my driver, after the slightest of hesitations. I sighed.

At once the curtains were pulled open by armored hands. Rough faces poked in, examining us with undisguised disgust.

"Right then," the voice continued. "Take them back to Edinburgh Castle; they are not to leave."

"Is that your wish, Your Grace?" the driver shouted. I knew it was for form's sake, to make it seem as if I had a choice.

But I would follow form, if only to make it appear that I still had some power.

"Yes, it is Our wish," I answered in husky tones.

And so we went back, as prisoners in all but name.

We were trapped, and a more sad and solitary place could not be found. I had no one to rely on and few I could trust.

I could think of nothing to do but write to my brother. Angus was right; Henry could be of great help to me. I all but begged him to detain Albany's arrival from France any way he could and to send an army—he could by both sea and land, I suggested—along with supplies. As it were, I could not keep my forces paid and supplied with my own meager income, especially now that the Party Adversary had voted to cease payment for my dower rents. Henry could afford to send an army that would not threaten the Scots. They must keep the peace without molesting the people and their property. I was sure Henry would understand that. He had to. I was his sister, was I not, and now the danger that faced me was very real; I could not risk losing what little respect the people retained for me as their monarch. It was advantageous to everyone if he sent an army; he could not risk his brothers to the north living in a land of lawless bandits. The violence on the Border proved unsettling enough; could he afford all of Scotland to follow suit?

There were only two men I trusted to relay my messages to Lord Dacre, through whom all correspondence with Henry was sent—Adam Williamson and my secretary, Sir James English. With spies everywhere, robbing and assaulting at will, these brave men traversed the wilds of Scotland to make certain that my brother and I could at least communicate.

Angus meantime roamed the countryside with his men, instigating their own reign of terror. Though it was right to intimidate his enemies, I feared for him. He was not loved by the people, nor was his family. Every day I waited to hear of his murder and I cursed myself that I ever allowed my heart to act before my gut. I was fond of Angus, and God knew I found him desirable. But I should not have married him and put him in this position. His life was in jeopardy now and I was to blame.

"My brother says he will help us," I told Ellen as I paced before the fire in my chambers. "He said he would send ships. Oh, where are they?" I wrung my hands, picking at my nails until they bled. "If they take the boys from me, Ellen, I do not know if I will survive."

Ellen could only shake her head. I knew there was nothing she could say to reassure me; my fears were real and Ellen was too wise to try to dismiss them.

At once I heard the doors to my antechamber burst open. I started, gasping. They had come for me! They had come to take my children and perhaps worse.

But as I collected myself, I saw to my delight that it was Angus entering my innermost rooms, Angus and not the enemy. I breathed a sigh, smiling at the rugged soldier making his way to me in long, confident strides.

My heart began to race—how handsome he was! I threw myself in his arms. "Angus, my darling!" I cried. "You've come to save me."

He held me tight a brief moment before disengaging. "I have. Come, there is no time to waste. We are taking the boys and going to Stirling. We will be safe there."

I held my tears of relief at bay as we rushed to collect the children. All the while I could not help but thank God that Angus had come, that I was not all alone.

That must have meant that he loved me, it must have. . . .

Snow was beginning to fall that November night as we made our way to Stirling and Little Jamie delighted in the sparkling white flakes that fell from the heavens. Through his eyes it was a magical adventure, something else I thanked God for. The little boy had no awareness of the idea that he was the center of such conflict and that as many wished to help him, as many wished him harm. I held him close in a moment of wild fear and he squirmed against my embrace.

"I canna see the snow, Mama!" he cried as he wriggled out of my arms to look out the window of the carriage.

I laughed. "We will have plenty enough snow for you to play in at Stirling," I assured him. "You can play all day if you like, when you aren't in your lessons."

Little Jamie's eyes brightened at this as he thrust his arm out of the curtain to catch the soft snowflakes on his fingertips. He giggled.

It was such an innocent moment, and watching him, I somehow knew I would always remember it. How I wished it could last.

Stirling Castle was a safe, strategic spot in the Midland Valley along the Forth, well fortified and well supplied, and my servants there were loyal to me, a hard enough asset to find in anyone. We could hold out there a long while and I could be assured of the safety of my children. Once we arrived, I ordered the portcullis dropped while I wrote my brother once more, briefing him on the situation and begging once more for his help.

There we passed Christmastide and I made the occasion merry for my children, who did not find anything out of the ordinary. I donned a lovely red gown of heavy velvet with gold undersleeves and a matching gold stomacher embroidered with seed pearls, with a matching gown for my faithful Ellen. She was able to accompany me along with some of my ladies who remained out of obligation if nothing else. I trusted none of them beyond Ellen. I was ever grateful for her company and we feasted with music and dancing, a modest entertainment, but it would not do for a queen to pass Christmas by with nothing. I was still a civilized woman despite the fact that I was in Scotland.

Angus seemed to enjoy the festivities; he was boisterous and held a bit of a court of his own.

"He's taken in quite a bit of wine," Ellen observed from where we sat at the high table. Her eyes followed Angus as he leaned in over another lady's plate, laughing as his eyes traveled to her bosom. My jaw clenched.

"He has had a great deal to worry about," I told Ellen. "It is good to see him enjoy himself; we've had little enough to celebrate since our wedding."

I watched the woman tip back her lovely head, offering throaty titters of laughter that I knew were for his benefit, and my cheeks began to burn.

"Who is that woman?" I asked Ellen.

"That is Jane Stewart," she informed me. "Of Traquair. Do you . . . do you know of her, Your Grace?"

"What is there to know?" I asked, offering an open stare toward them that I hoped revealed my displeasure.

Ellen was silent.

I turned toward her. "What do you know of her that I do not?"

Ellen lowered her eyes. "It may be just a rumor."

I drew in a breath, expelling it slowly. "Ellen, by God if you know something of this woman, I should know, too!"

Ellen raised her gaze toward me, sighing. "Only that it is said that my Lord Angus held her in some esteem before he knew Your Grace."

"What kind of esteem?" I asked as my heart began to thud in my chest.

Ellen hesitated once more. "It is said they spoke of marriage."

I closed my eyes, leaning back in my chair. The great hall became warm at once and I longed to shed myself of the burden of my gown, the gown I had thought to be so fetching, which Angus hadn't bothered to compliment once.

Angus, in fact, did not say anything at all to me that night.

"Well, didn't you have a merry evening," I said to Angus when we had retreated to our bedchambers after the festivities. I sat at my vanity brushing my long tawny tresses while Angus lay across the bed, one arm thrown across his forehead, which ached from his enthusiastic intake of wine, I imagined.

"I did," he said, rolling to his side and leaning on his elbow. "It was good to be surrounded with people we care about and who care about us instead of having to look over our shoulders."

"Aye, there were some who cared for you a bit more than others, were there not?" I retorted, attempting to keep my anger in check and remain calm.

Angus offered a wide smile. "Whatever do you mean, my dear?"

"I suddenly become 'your dear' whenever you know you've displeased me," I snapped, slamming down my hairbrush and rising from the vanity. "Who is Lady Jane of Traquair and what is she doing at Stirling Castle?"

Angus averted his eyes. "She is of no import, Margaret," he told me. "Just a lovely young girl who is loyal to you and your cause, I might add."

"Your lover?"

"For God's sake, Margaret, no," Angus said, flopping on his back once more and staring up at the canopy.

"But she was your lover . . . wasn't she?" I hissed.

Angus drew in a breath. "We were fond of one another once. But you've no need to worry. I am committed to you."

"Committed," I echoed, sitting on the bed and dropping my head. "By God, Angus, I have been betrayed and humiliated enough in my life and I will not allow you to do the same. I married you at great risk to my sons and to myself; everything is in jeopardy because of that decision. I demand the respect as a wife and your queen that I deserve."

Angus sat bolt upright, swinging his legs over the bed and rising. He circled the bed and stood before me, arms folded across his broad chest. "You speak to me as if I am one of your subjects and not your husband," he said in low tones. "My God, I believe you fancy yourself still married to the late king, and me . . . I dinna know what you think I am. Have I not defended your decisions before the council? Have I not raised sword and shield to protect your sons, children I love as if they were my own?"

My shoulders slumped. Was I being unreasonable? I sank my forehead into my hand, sighing. It did no good to appear jealous; men hated that. Yet how else was I to express my displeasure and maintain respect?

Angus sat beside me. "I have been good to you and to the children. Remember, you agreed quite willingly to marry me, and you did not have to. We canna go back, so either make the best of it or—"

"Oh, Angus, dinna say that!" I cried as hot tears stung my eyes. I turned toward him, throwing myself against his chest. His arms wrapped about me in a loose embrace. "I am sorry I was cross with you. You have no idea what I have endured. I dinna want to go back there; I dinna want to be disrespected the way I once was; you must realize that."

"And you need to realize that *I* am not James IV," he said. "Understand it and give me the respect that I deserve if you want my respect in turn."

I pulled away, nodding. "I will, Angus, I will," I said, as eager as a child who had been scolded and would do anything to please. I sniffled. "But that Traquair woman. I want her sent away. Please. I may be silly, but . . . please. For me."

Angus sighed once more. I decided he found the argument tedious; it could not be out of regret for sending that little harlot away. We needed no threats to our union; it was threatened enough without her help.

"Very well," he said. "Whatever Your Grace desires."

I wrapped my arms about his neck, ignoring the slight, and held him close, kissing his bearded cheek. He was right; I was married to him now and respect was due him as well.

I would be better, I vowed. I would be the wife he wanted, the woman he wanted, and his head would turn for me alone.

❧ BOOK 4 ❧

Jehan

❧ 12 ❧

The Regent

The winter was as bitter and bleak as my prospects and we relocated from Stirling to Perth. There I awaited and anticipated word from my brother while I watched the children grow. Little Jamie was as agreeable as he had ever been and baby Alexander a blessing. I spent many hours cooing to him and holding him close, but he had begun to develop a mind of his own and wriggled in my lap, longing to crawl about and explore his world whenever he wasn't in swaddling bands. It was a joy to watch him and his brother romp and play. They were my sanity, my strength, and my greatest hope.

In the midst of our routine, word from my brother arrived from Sir James English, my trusted secretary.

"His Majesty your brother has a plan," he told me. "A plan for your escape to the borderlands."

"The Border . . ." I breathed. It would be a perilous journey, and with the children in winter; I could be risking their very lives, and then where would we be? I shuddered. "What shall we do, Sir James? Of course I must go, but how?"

Sir James pursed his lips at this. "I know not, in truth, Your Grace. 'Tis dangerous all over. Why, Williamson was just accosted by ruffians himself. Lord Dacre sent his brother to deal with them, but they are a few of many. Thieves and bandits thrive on the Border. . . ."

That they did; the situation on the Border was volatile and my brother did not help it, encouraging raids. I wondered if we would ever know peace. . . .

Everything seemed to be working against us. The next missive from Williamson dealt a harsher blow. Old King Louis of France was dead, my sister a widow held up in Cluny until it would be revealed if she carried a child, and King Francois now sat on the throne. God only knew what his plans were for peace with England or Scotland. Would he send Albany after all? Would my children be taken from me then?

My head pounded and ached as thoughts turned through it, vultures scavenging on my mind. I could think of nothing but the children and their safety, of my regency all but lost, and of the enemies who would delight in my demise.

I had to get to England with the children. We needed a safe place for them to grow, a place that would guarantee our protection. And yet to raise the King of Scotland away from his homeland seemed wrong somehow. . . . How would he ever know what it was to be a Scot were he not in his kingdom?

I wrestled with these and other grim possibilities even as my brother worked on my behalf, not only by continuing to support my nomination of Gavin Douglas to the see of St. Andrews to Pope Leo X but also by utilizing the Duke of Suffolk, Charles Brandon, in Paris to sweeten the new king to the idea of not sending Albany to Scotland.

Winter melted into spring and with a pounding heart I devoured every word my messengers relayed. When we did receive word, it was the word that would drive the thorns through my skull.

Albany was coming to Scotland. My brother's attempts, Suffolk's attempts, were all in vain.

I should have escaped, I thought over and over in agony. *I should have escaped while I could.* . . .

* * *

Albany landed in Dumbarton and met me outside of Edinburgh. I met him as a queen in state, dressed in my favorite color,
orange, as it so suited my hair.

"To think he was disappointed when he heard I'd married
Angus rather than consider him," I huffed to Ellen as we watched
Albany's approach.

"I must say, he is rather handsome, though, isn't he?" she asked.

I grunted a halfhearted acknowledgment as I surveyed him. In
truth, he was in fact one of the handsomest men I had ever seen, a
tall, lean figure and as sophisticated as I imagined the French to be
(I could not consider him a true Scot), yet he clearly bore Stewart
features. His long face bore a close-cut beard, auburn like his hair,
and his eyes were an arresting shade of gray, both deep and clear as
a loch.

He offered a bow. "Madam." Even his voice was handsome, low
and melodious. Quite different from the Scots brogue I had grown
accustomed to and found I had adopted over the years myself. "I
am Jehan Stuart," he said. John Stewart was what I had known him
as, but his broken English pronounced the name as French as his
signature. "I bid you good health from my wife."

I was taken aback at this. "We were not aware you had married," I said in flat tones, as if it did not bother me at all.

His smile was slow, languid. "Why, indeed I have been married
for ten years, madam," he informed me.

"We imagine she must miss you sorely," I said, wishing to impose the thought in his mind, hoping it would make some difference. Perhaps that would mean he would like to return to her
soon. Perhaps he would not find Scotland in agreement with his
French fancies.

His gentle chuckle rippled like a pebble in a pond. "Indeed, as
I miss her," he said. His eyes were lit with open kindness as he regarded me. "Madam, it is my wish to be a help to you," he told me
then in low tones. "It is my hope we can work together for the
good of His Grace and Scotland."

I nodded. I would not acknowledge the statement more than
need be. I would make no promises, nor trust any of his, should he

make them. He seemed pleasant, but God knew enough pleasant men had brought about the ill fortune of women for generations.

And it was so that I met him, wondering if we were to be friends or enemies or a bit of both. Despite my fears, I found that I liked him.

On 12 July, the birthday of Julius Caesar no less, Albany was given the sword and scepter and my regency. I had lost.

And I was pregnant.

I had been missing my courses since March but thought nothing of it. I had been ill with headaches, and weeping had become a regular occurrence. My burdens were many; my worries seemed boundless. To be with child in addition to all of it sent my mind reeling.

Angus, to my surprise, was thrilled.

"It is just what we need," he told me. "A baby to unite us truly as man and wife, and a brother or sister for His Grace and the young duke."

Angus used the excuse of my condition's delicacy to cease his relations as my husband.

It was just as well; I was too sick and exhausted with worry to be of any pleasure, not that I brought him much to begin with. Our couplings were obligatory on Angus's part. I knew it. He knew I was aware of it. But we both indulged my feigned ignorance.

The baby quickened within my womb as Albany seized power and began his sure, swift justice, or his interpretation of it, on perceived enemies of the Crown. The Pope had rejected Gavin Douglas for the see of St. Andrews and created him Bishop of Dunkeld, sending his nominee, Andrew Forman, home without formally granting him the see.

Gavin Douglas was imprisoned for his ambition. Even my grandfather-in-law, Lord Drummond, was sent to Blackness Castle for boxing the Lyon Herald's ears when he insulted me by the inappropriateness of his address to my station.

For this I had to intervene. Old Lord Drummond was as temperamental as his grandson, though far wilier, I gathered, and yet still I could not see him exiled to some outland castle.

I left Holyrood House to speak to Albany. He received me in his presence chamber, smiling when I entered as though times were peaceful and I were an old friend come to call.

He rose, bowing, ever the gentleman, then offered me a chair and refreshment.

"You are well, madam?" he asked me. To avoid any conflict in how to address me, he called me the uncontroversial *madam*.

I could not contain myself. His nature was as gentle as my husband's was fiery. Tears, never far away as I advanced in pregnancy, burned my eyes. I shook my head. "No, my lord, We are not well," I told him. "Hearing of Lord Drummond's and Gavin Douglas's imprisonment distresses Us greatly."

Albany's eyes were a strange mingling of calm alertness. "I am sorry you are distressed," he said, his tone sincere. "But I am afraid imprisonment is all the mercy I can spare on these men. They have disturbed the law of this land, and you must agree Scotland has fallen into disorder since the death of my dear cousin."

"We do," I told him in honesty. "Yet can my lord afford more enemies?" I asked him, leaving unspoken the well-known fact that Lord Home, once one of the foremost leaders of my Party Adversary, had changed course and backed me for regent after Albany had addressed him in Latin when Lord Home received him in Dumbarton. As Lord Home did not understand Latin, he thought the duke was being pompous and patronizing. The misunderstanding worked in my favor, for Lord Home was now my man.

"I do not wish any more than you to accumulate more enemies, madam," Albany said in easy tones. "But it is for me to restore order here and to remind these feuding houses that they are not the unruly men of the Border, that they are to be civilized upholders of the realm. Many of these men hold titles and exalted positions, yet they behave as any rough clan chieftain. I cannot be seen to show favor to any family above another. I am certain you of all people can appreciate that," he added, his words measured and weighty with their intent.

I rose with an abrupt swirl of my skirts, conceiving of his meaning too well. I stared him down. "You have much to learn about

Scotland, sir," I told him. "It is not France. It is not like any other place in the world."

And with that I excused myself from his presence.

To my surprise, Parliament favored my opinion in regards to the imprisonment of my grandfather-in-law. Yet when discussions opened about who was to obtain custody of my children, my hope wavered. Though I was allowed to participate in the selection of the four guardians of the little king and baby duke, I knew this, like so many moves on the part of men when involving women in a decision, was for form only.

Albany meant to take my children.

The people turned out in droves to witness the guardians meeting us at Edinburgh Castle. There was little time to explain anything to Little Jamie, and we walked hand in hand at the head of our party. Nurse followed, carrying baby Alexander with Angus beside her and our household at a discreet distance.

"Declare the reason for your coming!" I shouted to the approaching party, though I knew their intent. It was a show; everything had become a performance, meant to garner the sympathy and outrage of my people. Who could endure watching children being ripped away from their mother? *Please, Lord,* I prayed, *let them have heart!*

"We come for the king!" was the reply.

At once I nodded. The portcullis dropped, in agreement with my plan. As I was a Tudor, this portcullis was more than a barrier: It was also within my grandmother Margaret Beaufort's coat of arms. If no one else knew it but me, it brought me comfort and strength.

I gazed at the lairds from behind the bars with a cool smile. "By the late king my husband," I cried in a sure, strong voice, "I was made sole governess of him!" The cheers from the people were deafening; the baby stirred within me and I squeezed Little Jamie's hand. "Give Us six days and We shall consider the decision of the council!" I added, then retreated with my household to the blessings of the people.

"Are they going to hurt us, Mother?" Little Jamie's shrill voice asked as we made our way into the castle.

"No," I assured him, my throat catching. "They are not going to hurt us."

My face grew hot; my cheeks began to tingle.

I did not relish lying to my son.

"Margaret, this has become very serious," Angus told me that night in our bedchamber. He was pacing before the window, his face drawn, his steps heavy.

I was immediately irritated. Of course it was serious! It had been serious since my husband the king was slain in the mud of Flodden Field. Was Angus just now noticing this was not one of the games of his training days? I drew in a breath, trying to contain my patience.

Angus ceased his pacing, standing still, shaking his head. He parted his lips to speak, stopped, then began once more. "You may want to consider giving the children over," he said, his tone soft.

My mouth fell agape. I stared at him, trying to conceive of why again I had married him in such haste. Looks alone could never sustain any kind of feeling, I decided then, steeling myself against his sensual mouth and pleading liquid brown eyes. I shook my head, rising from my settle.

"Are you mad?" I hissed. "You married me insisting that you could help protect me and the children from this very thing! And yet now we meet opposition and obstacles and you are ready to surrender? What kind of man are you?"

"Margaret!" His voice was sharp and I started. "You are with child. Think about *our* baby. Think about your health. What good would it do to have all of your children go without a mother? So we give them over. It will not be forever. Just until we can gather enough support to take them back."

I brought my hand to my mouth, stifling the urge to scream at him. I shook my head against the logic, sound though it may be. "How can we hand them over? What would they think? They would see it as a betrayal," I told him. "They would feel abandoned and alone. Their father has already passed; for us, the only true family they know and love, to leave them over to Albany and the council . . . they would never understand." I began to cry. How

I hated my unpredictable onsets of emotion during times when I needed calm the most. "If we give them over, they could grow to hate us."

Angus shook his head at this argument, approaching me. "A child never hates their mother, no matter who she is or what she has done," he assured me. "And even if they were angry, they would come to understand the decision in time, when the king is met with the challenges of his own rule and his own children." He opened his arms, expecting me to fold into them as I had so eagerly in the past.

Instead I backed away, shaking my head with more vehemence. "No," I breathed. "My children are all I have. You canna ask this of me."

Angus's arms fell to his sides, limp. "You have our baby," he told me. "You have me."

"Dinna do this, Angus," I urged him. "Dinna make me choose."

"Dinna put this all on me!" he cried. "As if it is *me* asking you to choose and not Albany and the council! As if I am solely responsible for what has come to pass! I offer you a solution that may not be easy or pleasant, but it may be our only choice until we have the men, the arms, and the support! And yet you say *I* am making you choose when ultimately I *do* have the best interests of you and the children always in mind?" His eyes sparkled with unshed tears.

I pursed my lips and turned away. By God, I could not stand a man's tears.

At once I decided what I must do.

I squared my shoulders. "I am going to Stirling," I said, my tone hard. "I am taking the children and going. You may do what you like."

"Margaret!" His tone was urgent, desperate.

I closed my eyes, drawing in a breath, letting it out slowly. "We will not speak of this anymore, Angus," I told him, raising my hand to silence him as I would any subject.

And then I left him, going once more to collect my children and flee to the only safety I had known in Scotland, my beloved Stirling.

*   *   *

Though we made it to Stirling with Little Jamie thrilled to be a part of another midnight riding adventure, Albany and his men were in pursuit. From inside the castle I watched as we were surrounded by the forces led by the Earls of Cassilis and Lennox. Angus; my newest supporter, Lord Home; and my brother-in-law George Douglas defended us with their own riders, skilled and able horsemen from the Border.

Angus offered a sound option for my strategy. If they were to battle in earnest, he told me to place Little Jamie with his crown, robes, and scepter on the castle's very walls. Surely this would move them; they could not make war against the person of the king. I shook my head at the thought, remembering too well stories of other child-kings jeopardized in times of violence, children who included my uncles, my late husband, and his grandfather before him.

Albany made his intent more than clear when he arrived with a force seven thousand men strong with "Mons Meg" at the head of it. I shuddered. "Mons Meg" was the utmost cannon in the land—none could withstand her might.

My forces fled at the sight of her.

I crumpled to the floor of the bower, Ellen at my side. "Your Grace!" she cried, seizing my arm. "Your dearest Grace," she whispered, pulling me to my feet.

My legs quivered as I clung to her. "It is over, Ellen," I breathed. "I canna have my children witness bloodshed and curse them for life. I have to give them over."

My boys, my boys, will you ever forgive me?

Ellen began to sob. "I know," she choked.

I drew in a shaky breath, disengaging from my faithful maid. "We will do so with honor, Ellen. I will do so like a queen."

"You are nothing less," Ellen assured me, reaching out to tuck a stray wisp of hair behind my ear.

Nothing less, and nothing more.

Before we went out to meet Albany, I knelt before my son the king, dressing him in his robes of state myself. I reached out, stroking his baby skin.

"I may not see you for a while," I told him. "You and baby Alexander will be staying with the Duke of Albany for a time," I explained, swallowing an onset of tears. "But only for a time, till Lord Angus and I can fetch you. You must be very good for the duke and his men and show them that you are king. You must look after the baby and show him how to be a strong little prince. We must be brave, hmm?"

"I am brave, Mother!" he assured me with an earnest nod of his head.

I drew him to my breast, squeezing him as tight as I could without hurting him. "Know that I love you, Jamie!" I cried, allowing my tears to fall. "I love you with all my heart, all my soul, and I will do anything to keep you safe."

"I love you, Mother," he said, his voice small. His lips quivered as I pulled away.

I shook my head, blinking my tears away. "No tears, lamb," I urged. I took Little Jamie's hand, placing in it the keys to Stirling Castle. "When you see my Lord Albany, you will give him the keys to the castle," I explained. "Because this is our decision, to let him in with peace and dignity. We must go to the duke as a queen and a king. Always remember, *you* are king and no one else."

Little Jamie swallowed, clutching the keys to his breast and offering another grim nod. How great was the burden set upon the tiny shoulders of this three-year-old king! I could not think of it. I could not afford to meet the duke and his men in tears. I rose, taking my son by the hand and nodding to Nurse, who held the baby for me.

It was time.

Albany, given word of my intent, waited with his men outside of Stirling Castle as I made my way to him with my children. I drew on every bit of strength inside of me, holding my head high as I let go of Little Jamie's hand, urging him toward the duke.

Albany knelt before my son, bowing his head as Little Jamie extended his hand with the keys to the castle in it. Albany took them with solemnity.

"Please," I said to the duke, my tone low and steady. "We beg you to show mercy to these innocent children. And to my Lord Angus and his forces. Please."

Albany raised his head. To my shock, his gray eyes were lit with tears. "I know what this is costing you, Your Grace," he told me. "The king and the Duke of Ross will be treated in accordance with their stations, I promise you."

I closed my eyes a moment, willing my tears to hide a moment more. Composed, I opened them. The duke was still kneeling before us. All I could see was the artillery behind him. At once his promises faded in the dust the horses kicked up, swirling and blowing away in the bitter wind.

I nodded to him, then turned away.

I could not watch him take them from me. I could not bear to see them go.

ᐳ 13 ᐸ

The Flight

I returned with great reluctance to Edinburgh to offer my half-hearted signature on the agreement supported by Parliament, confirming that the Duke of Albany now had charge of my babies. Though I was reassured I could still see them, Albany made it plain that it may not be wise given my husband's defection, one Albany never spared mercy for. He feared Angus and I would escape with the children, and despite whatever motherly feeling I retained, I could not be trusted. As outraged as I was, I understood as one who bore the burden of rule the practicality of his decision even while I cursed him for it.

I was twenty-five years old and had been married a year to Angus. It should have been a happy time of raising the boys while preparing for the little one I now carried. I should have been planning my confinement and great entertainments for after its birth. As the child would be a sibling to the king, it would have been a grand affair.

But there was none of that. There was running, always running, nights filled with panic as horrific imaginings gripped my mind, causing me to wonder who my enemies were, if I would even live out each week, if my children were safe and cared for, if I would ever see them again. I wondered if the letters to Henry and Lord Dacre were intercepted. Henry was only to trust letters signed "your loving sister, Margaret R," but a few of the letters sent in which I sounded agreeable to the fate of my children I was forced to sign as such. Not knowing this, Henry and Lord Dacre chastised me for my decision, telling me the gravity of my mistake, as if I hadn't a grasp on it. And yet they were men, what did they know of how my choices came to be? Henry had command of armies and still had no children; he had no concept of what it meant to fight for them, to make unbearable decisions one could never imagine being faced with. And Lord Dacre commanded border reivers who could wreak havoc like no other kind of soldier should anyone interfere with his loved ones.

They could not possibly understand. No man could.

I had lost my children, my regency, and the respect of my kingdom. I lost respect for myself.

I was now eight months gone with child and exhausted. But there was no rest for me, no respite in a darkened cloister of a lying-in chamber.

Henry and Lord Dacre had developed a plan. I was to come to the Border, to Lord Dacre, who would then escort me into England, to Henry and his court, to the prospect of support. Dreams of a glittering triumphant return to Scotland at the head of a well-paid, well-fed army swelled my heart. Why else would Henry assist my escape if not to send me back to Scotland stronger and able to oust Albany, thus taking back my children? No matter the beginnings of understanding that were being forged between Albany and me, the thought of having my children back was irresistible.

I would do anything.

Sending coded messages in response, I agreed to the escape.

Albany granted me permission to retire to Linlithgow for my confinement. The jostling of the coach that transported me jarred and jerked my belly and I gripped it as if it were a foreign thing, some awful mass attached to me that caused nothing but pain and sickness and utter inconvenience. How I wished to have this baby so I could move about with more freedom! I could not regret my estate, but how much easier would it have been if I were not with child!

Once we reached the castle, I sought the refuge of the lying-in chamber, developing a "sudden illness" that made for good enough theater on my part to inspire Albany to allow Angus a visit, just as I had intended.

When Angus appeared in my chambers, I found myself smiling. Gone was my anger from our last encounter. He was working toward the goal of regaining custody of the children; he was doing what he promised he would do. I could see that now and could not bear to harbor resentment against the father of the little one stirring in my womb.

"Are you well, Margaret?" he asked. He looked older. He had always looked older than his years to me, but there was something different about him now. He was becoming seasoned, learning to accommodate himself to disappointment and opposition and the rigors of warfare. He was becoming a man.

I offered a weary nod. "Well enough to make for the Border," I told him.

He leaned over my bed, offering a light kiss on my forehead before drawing back. He stroked my forehead, offering a faint smile. "You are a brave one, Margaret. Keep being brave."

I nodded, reaching up to take his hand in mine, too overcome to speak. It was so rare to share a moment of tenderness with my husband I found myself treasuring the words.

"Are you ready?" he asked, tilting a thick black brow.

"Aye," I said in firm tones.

There was no time for tenderness now. Now was the time for action.

Night had fallen. I was not allowed a coach; it could not negotiate the wilds of the Scottish countryside with its many steep hills and winding paths as well as the sturdy reiver's Galloway horses. There was but a handful of armed servants to accompany us until we were just beyond the town of Linlithgow, where Lord Home, my unlikely new champion, met us with his own small force.

We were to ride for our very lives.

I had been an able equestrienne when not with child, but it was another matter altogether riding in my heavy gown with the burden of my belly. As we rode, I could not help but be in a terror of losing my balance and falling, then losing the baby as a bitter consequence. I held on as if the ground were covered in writhing demons waiting to take the baby and me to the depths of Hell with them, willing myself to remain atop my horse and keep up with my lord husband.

We arrived at the Douglas stronghold of Tantallon, where I collapsed into bed, clutching my aching belly. My ankles were swollen, my hands calloused from their death grip on the reins of my horse, and nausea clutched my throat. Despite being allowed to lie down, I could not rest. I thought of the children, as always, hoping they were safe, wondering if Little Jamie had said anything amusing or if the baby had done anything new. Would I miss it all? His first steps, his first words . . . I could not bear such reflection.

I thought of my ladies, Ellen in particular. She could not come with me; she could not even be made aware of my escape. Though I trusted her like no other, I could not trust her with this. I could not put her in the position of having to lie to the duke or his men. Nor could I put her in the position of having to tell them the truth.

Angus joined me in my bedchamber, rousing me from my reverie with more news.

"Albany is in pursuit," he announced, his tone thick with frustration. "We must flee to Lord Home's castle of Blackadder immediately."

Even as I sat up and allowed Angus to assist me with my boots, I trembled and moaned with pain. "Oh, Angus, I feel so sick and tired. The baby is going to come soon, I know it," I told him, voicing for the first time my fears, that this child would come and hamper all plans of escape.

Angus shook his head with vehemence as he helped me to my feet. "You must not say it, Margaret. You must not even think it. The child can wait till we get to England. Hold on for me, eh? Hold on just a bit more."

I sighed and nodded, as if I could somehow control the advent of my labor, and we set to ride again. In our haste, my jewels and gowns were left behind. Yet they made a far easier sacrifice than the children.

* * *

As we made for Blackadder we were met by a messenger.

"The duke amassed a force of forty thousand," he informed us, breathless. "He intends to take Blackadder."

"Damn, damn, damn!" Angus cried, flicking his reins with a wild shake of his head. He inclined his head toward me. "We have to get to Berwick Castle, Margaret, d'you hear? Can you make it?"

Through tears the night kept concealed from my husband, I offered a strong "Aye!"

And so we rode. My legs ached, my back was stiff, and the baby kicked up a fury. Despite the rough terrain, the bumps, and the rollicking gallop of my horse, I managed to maintain my seat and my grip, keeping my eyes forward, ever forward, till at last I saw Berwick. We had made it! We were all but in England!

I tipped my head back, smiling with a sigh of relief. Soon I would be in a nice, warm bed. Soon I would have food in my belly along with the baby. Soon I could retreat into the only sanctuary I knew—sleep. Oh, how heavenly it all sounded now, far more grand than gowns and entertainments!

But even as I dared to relinquish myself to such sweet fancy, our messenger met us again with more unwelcome news.

"The Governor of Berwick will not admit you without safe-conduct from King Henry," he told us. His blue eyes were wide, as if fearing a reproach.

"Even to his own sister, man?" Angus cried, incredulous. He bit his lip, his eyes scanning the horizon. The first ruddy strains of dawn lit the hills, coloring them a deep amber. Morning was in pursuit, as unwelcome as Albany and his army.

"Even so," the messenger replied.

Angus bowed his head. Lord Home, always a rough old man, cursed.

"We best get to the priory at Coldstream," Lord Home decided after he had exhausted his string of expletives he felt described the situation best. There was nothing to do but agree; I needed to rest. We could not very well camp about in the wild like reivers.

We turned our horses about and rode to the priory, where at last I could take my longed-for rest before the ordeal began again.

* * *

At the priory I fell into a fitful slumber. I had hoped that after the difficult ride and my constant fretting sleep would overcome me in that dark, quiet completeness I cherished, but it eluded me. Lord Home's mother arrived to comfort me and I was grateful for the presence of an older woman. And yet it served to remind me of the loss of my own mother. I ached for her with a longing as acute as that for my children yet was grateful that at least I stood the chance of seeing them again. As for my mother and so many loved ones who went before me, I would have to wait.

Meantime the best way to serve the memory of the dead was to live.

Lord Dacre had arrived, and in him I saw the hope to do just that.

I had not seen him since I was a child entering my kingdom, when he had thrown the entertainments with the god-awful bear-baiting. It seemed like another lifetime, as if it were someone else's memories I was stealing a glimpse of. Casting my gaze upon his kind countenance reduced me to stilling my quivering lip and blinking back tears. It was happening; safety and support were within my reach at last. But to achieve that safety, Lord Home, my husband, and our party had to remain behind just now.

It was an agonizing good-bye. I had come to like the colorful Lord Home, who would have razed his own castle rather than give it over to Albany. I found Lord Home to be a noble, loyal man, a hero. And my husband, for him to leave now . . .

"We will get to you soon, Margaret," Angus promised, squeezing my hands. "Be well," he whispered, leaning in to kiss my cheek. I longed for something deeper, but I supposed he was clinging to propriety.

"Be safe," I said in turn.

No other words of love were exchanged.

We rode to Lord Dacre's castle of Harbottle, in England now. I was beyond exhausted. My belly was taut, stretched to its limit, and felt lower than before. My legs quivered and at times my right leg plagued me such that I cried out at the pains, sharp as hot daggers shooting from hip to ankle. My head ached; my swollen hands and feet throbbed. I was grateful that the first destination upon my arrival was a warm, soft bed, where I remained for days, with Lord Dacre making frequent visits in the hopes I would regain my strength for the rest of the journey.

"You will be delighted to know," Lord Dacre told me, "that the king and queen have sent you many beautiful presents to my home at Morpeth with Sir Christopher Garnyshe."

I brightened at this. I could in all honesty never resist the thought of gifts. Gifts meant love and I needed to be loved.

"Oh, Lord Dacre, do tell me of them!" I begged, delighted as a child.

Lord Dacre smiled. "You will soon see for yourself, Your Grace, once we reach Morpeth," he assured me.

The words no sooner fled his lips when I crumpled over as a sharp, searing pain seized my abdomen. My hand shot out, reaching for something, anything, and finding Lord Dacre's strong hand in response, his hazel eyes wide with fright. I clung to his arm as if it were the only thing that would keep me in this world. The next one was calling; I was sure of it.

"Your Grace!"

Warm liquid rushed down my legs, seeping into my covers and gown. My cheeks burned as I raised my head, looking into the Warden of the Marches' stricken face. This would set everything back. . . . I shook my head.

"No," I breathed as another pain gripped my womb. "Oh, Lord Dacre, no. . . ."

Somewhere I heard the frantic voice of Lord Dacre calling for assistance, but sweet blackness, that longed-for blackness that would sweep me away on a tide of dreams, enveloped me. The voices faded away into nothingness, and then so did I. . . .

"This is far from a suitable place to bring in a bairn," Lord Dacre was saying when again my eyes fluttered open. The chambers were humble, drafty, and without décor, something that would not have perplexed me in the least before. We would have been removing to the luxury of Morpeth and I could have stood a few days in this rough and wild place had my pains not started. But everything was halted. I lay overtaken by guilt and pain and despair. I was an obvious inconvenience to my host and I prayed the pains would stop, that my labor would hold off just a bit longer.

"Her waters have already broken," an older woman I gathered to be a midwife was informing him. "The bairn will arrive regardless of this castle's suitability."

At once my belly quaked with another pain and I cried out. Lord Dacre, thrilled to be out of my reach, I was certain, fled the chambers and I was left to the strange old midwife and less than a handful of servants.

One lady brought a cool cloth to my burning forehead, dabbing gently. "There, there, Your Grace, do not fear," she said in soothing tones. "All will be well. We will take care of you."

My head lolled from side to side as I clenched and unclenched my fists. It could not be an easy birth, of course. That would have been right. No, I was fated to bear this child in a rough border castle and suffer as I had with my earlier births. If only it could have been as it was with baby Alexander. How swift his birth was! The thought of him soothed me somewhat and all I could think of was bringing him a healthy brother or sister.

Despite the chill of the castle, I was burning up. Even the sweat that glistened off my body did nothing to cool me. I longed to tear at my gown and blankets and let the air hit my naked skin. But that would not be proper.

My only relief came in the blackness, and when it beckoned I ran to it with the eagerness of a lover.

She was born 8 October, a sturdy lass with a tuft of hair as red as my own, another Tudor rose whom I would call Margaret at the urgings of Lord Dacre, for "she so resembles Your Grace," he said. It mattered not what she was called. She had the great misfortune of being born a girl, and my heart sank. She was soon in the care of her nurses. I was too weak and ill to hold her and pay her as much heed as I had my boys. I wondered what Angus would make of her. It wasn't that I would have minded a daughter, but in these rough times I feared for her. Would she survive? And if she did, what path lay before her as a Princess of Scotland and daughter of one of the most unloved men in the land? Oh, my poor, sweet lamb . . . I could not bear to think of her fate. I could not bear to think of my own.

Though I was ten days after her birth able to sit and read letters from Henry and Catherine, I was still too weak to be moved. My leg aggrieved me and my exhaustion never seemed to abate. But in November, when Little Margaret was but a month old, it was decided we must risk the journey southward. I knew there was no choice but to press on, but my pain and weariness were so great that I could not abide even a litter for the progress. I was carried aloft on the shoulders of servants on my day bed. As we traveled we were met by more lords of the land who joined our party. We stopped twice for me to rest, once for five days, when I all but slept straight through, waking only to eat and offer my daughter a feeble smile.

When at last we made it to Morpeth I was relieved. We were in civilization now and I was received as a queen should be. Lady Dacre was gracious and kind and informed me she was readying the castle for Christmas. I was eager to be a part of it, though it would be from my bed that I would be so, at least till I gathered more strength.

Lord Home arrived with Angus and a party of loyal Scots lairds come to see the baby as promised, and my husband at last was able to hold his daughter.

"She's beautiful, Margaret!" he exclaimed, clasping the little girl to his breast. His eyes regarded her with a new gentleness, one I had never seen before. True, his dark gaze lit with fondness when admiring my children, but this was different. I imagined he thought of the child he had lost before and in her saw his hopes for the future of a new dynasty realized.

"You're not disappointed, then," I said, but watching the pair I knew he was not, and for that my affection toward him was renewed.

"Of course not!" he assured me, never taking his eyes from Margaret's face. "Though you could have waited a bit longer to arrive," he told our daughter in the exaggerated tones of a smitten father. "But I think you are as stubborn and impatient as your mother!" he teased.

I laughed, relieved for the lightness of the moment. "Indeed," I agreed. "And as ambitious as her father!"

Angus shot me a glance at this, his brow furrowing. I had offended him. "Angus, I didn't mean it," I told him, reaching my hand out.

He sighed, shifting his eyes to the baby once more. He did not take my hand. It fell to my lap. He was soon cooing at the baby once more and I sighed in relief.

Perhaps he had let it go.

The day Lord Home and Angus had arrived was also the day Christopher Garnyshe, the sweet courtier charged with bringing me the tidings from my brother and sister-in-law, bestowed upon me my gifts. I was carried in a plush chair to the great hall, resplendent with festive Christmas décor; pine boughs wrapped about the great beams with beautiful new tapestries that must have been new, so clean and vibrant were their colors. There were gold plate and cups and scrumptious-looking dishes of silver on the table where we would soon celebrate our Christmas feast. But the most wonderful thing of all was that, to my astonishment and delight, my new wardrobe from my brother was on display for me.

"Oh!" I cried, wishing I had the strength to leap from my chair and run to fondle the pretty things. There were bed hangings, meant I imagine for the confinement chamber I never knew, little clothes for the baby, and my favorite gifts of all—gowns! There was one extraordinary piece of cloth of gold and another in a light silver shimmering material called cloth of tinsel. It was astounding!

"See!" I cried to Lord Home. "My brother hasn't forgotten me. I certainly shan't die from lack of clothes!"

The men laughed, but there was something in their eyes, something sad and guarded, and at times they whispered and nodded to one another as if agreeing upon something. *They pity me,* I thought. My cheeks flushed with the heat of anger. I should not be pitied! I should be admired! And soon, in these gowns and more I planned to have made, I would be. I would regain my strength and become the queen I knew was inside, a beautiful, strong queen who would return to Scotland one day with her new bairn and reunite her family and kingdom!

Twelfth Night came and went. The winter days passed in a windy gray blur. Convalescence was slow. My right leg had become a curse, and I could not bear to stand upon it. I was weak but could not eat to gain strength; I had no appetite. Though I was glad to be losing weight so my husband could at last see how becoming I could be, I knew that I needed to eat enough for clarity of mind and the physical strength to endure the rest of the journey to London.

Lady Dacre fussed over me, seeking to coax my appetite with comforting foods—almond milk, boiled mutton, and different pottages brimming with vegetables. I could eat none of them to anyone's satisfaction. I picked at things here and there, but my stomach ached and I grew nauseous when the pain was at its height. Little appealed to me.

What's more, I wanted to go home. I wanted my children. They needed to meet their baby sister and I needed them. I needed to see that Little Jamie was as bluff and bonny as ever and that baby Alexander was thriving.

To pass the time while I struggled to heal, I regaled Lady Dacre with stories of my children and my Ellen. Lady Dacre had never seen a Moor before and was fascinated by the dark beauty. I told her of the matching gowns we used to wear for entertainments and this amused her. I missed having gowns made for my favorite lady, and to remedy this Lady Dacre encouraged me to pay mind to my attire once more. Nothing made a woman feel as well as having new dresses! I was compelled to agree.

I ordered new gowns in addition to the beautiful wardrobe from my brother. It would do to suit my slimmer figure, I reasoned. And after all I had endured, I certainly deserved some finery to take what joy I could from. I would have more satin kirtles, a beautiful purple velvet confection lined with cloth of gold, and another of a stunning velvet as red as rubies, accentuated with the softest ermine. I would enter London every inch a queen, and in those gowns I would feel beautiful again.

As the dressmakers worked on my gowns, I had my ladies show me the dresses from Henry. They would bring the dresses to my bed sometimes twice a day, and I would reach out, fingering the beautiful materials and sighing, fantasizing about the day I could wear them and dance at the court of my brother. I couldn't wait for Angus to see me in them. I knew he would find me truly beautiful then. It would erase any doubts he would have about my fitness as his wife.

I hoped.

One day in early February I was admiring my gowns while Lady Dacre was trying to convince me to eat a creamy bread and apple pudding she had Cook make when Lord Home entered my chambers with Angus.

I brightened at the sight of my handsome husband. He had been so good with the baby and so solicitous of my health that I put our previous grievances aside. Lady Dacre made a gracious retreat in deference to the men.

Angus offered a slow smile. "It is good to see you up, my dear," he told me in gentle tones as he leaned in to offer his customary kiss upon my forehead. "Are you feeling well? Stronger?"

I nodded. "It restores me to look upon my lovely gowns and think of happier times," I said. "I canna wait to don them for you."

Angus sat on the bed beside me, taking my hand in his. "You will steal my breath away, I am sure," he said. His eyes were so soft they seemed almost lit with tears, and I thought it sweet that he would be so moved by the imagery.

At this Lord Home cleared his throat.

"Lord Home," I said by way of greeting. I imagined he was not too comfortable with our loving banter, so attempted to adopt a more regal bearing. "Any word from Scotland?"

"My mother has been taken prisoner to Dunbar Castle," he began. "Didna even let her ride a gentle horse! She had to gallop through the country like a commoner and God only knows what they feed her at the castle." At this he swore an oath. "It's me he's after, by God! It's a hard sort of man to take revenge against some-one's mother, innocent old woman that she is."

Anger heated my cheeks at the thought of poor old Lady Home being dragged through the wilderness like a dog. How I detested Lord Albany! What could he have been thinking!

"We are much aggrieved at the thought," I told Lord Home with sincerity.

At this he and Angus exchanged a glance.

"What else?" I prodded, knowing this could not have been all.

"The duke has taken my estates of Tantallon and Borthwick," Angus said. "Without those rents it will be hard to finance our cause," he went on. "And what's more, he refuses to release my uncle Gavin, even though the Pope has ordered it so he might serve as the bishop he was ordained as."

"To not even listen to the Pope!" I cried. "For shame!"

Again, Angus and Lord Home found each other's eyes; it seemed as though they were each trying to urge the other to speak.

Perplexed, I sighed. "Sirs," I began. "Something else has happened."

At this Lord Home sat in my bedside chair next to Angus, who tightened his hold on my hand, his thumb stroking my forefinger with a new sense of urgency. He was sweating. A deep flush colored his cheeks and forehead crimson.

"My dear," he began. He pursed his lips, swallowing hard. "Oh, my dear—"

I squeezed his hand in turn. "Angus, what is it?" I cried. "The children? Are my babies well?"

Lord Home bowed his head at this, shielding his eyes with his hand.

"By God, someone tell me!" I demanded, as frustrated as I was frightened.

Angus's liquid brown gaze found mine. Tears spilled onto his cheeks. "My dear . . . it is the Duke of Ross. Alexander . . . he's . . . he's . . ."

"He's dead," Lord Home finished for Angus.

My breath caught. I withdrew my hand, bringing it to my chest, where my heart throbbed and ached at once. "No . . . no . . ." I breathed, closing my eyes and shaking my head. "Oh, God, no! No!" Angus gathered me in his arms as I sobbed.

"He is lying!" I insisted. "It is a ploy, a trap of some kind! My child canna be dead! It is an evil trick to lure me back, that he might capture us!" I pulled away, blinking back tears, almost convinced that this could be true, hoping it was. "That is it, isn't it, Angus? Surely that is what you will tell me next. Tell me. Say, 'The duke is alive, however, and is quite well.' Tell me, Angus!"

Angus furrowed his brow in helplessness, shaking his head, reaching out to cup my cheek in his large, warm hand. "I am so sorry, Margaret."

"Lord Home!" I cried, jerking my head away from Angus's hand, turning my gaze to the older man. "You must know something Angus does not. That is why you are here. Tell me my son is alive and well. Tell me this is an evil ploy on the part of that devil Albany!"

"I'm afraid it's true, Your Grace," Lord Home said with a shake of his head, his gravelly voice as gentle as I had ever heard.

I shook my head with vehemence, squeezing my eyes against hot, stinging tears. "When?" I whispered.

Angus drew in a breath. "18 December."

"18 December!" I cried. "But that was two months ago!" My mouth stood agape as a horrible awareness settled upon me, realizing that the party from Scotland had known when they arrived to see baby Margaret that my son was dead. They had known and allowed me to play with my new wardrobe like a child while they talked of my pitiable case. Those glances at Christmas had told the tale too well. Why did I not sense it then?

"You knew," I seethed. "You all knew and let me go on like a fool, a great, pathetic fool!"

"Your Grace," Lord Home began. "We couldna borne telling you in the estate you were in. We had to wait till you were strong enough to bear it. And you are strong enough now. Strong enough to get to London to gather the support you need and return to avenge his death." He rose. "And we did pity you," he added in soft tones. "We pity anyone who loses a child. Lord knows we have all lost enough in our lives. But we dinna think you are pathetic, Your Grace. We think you are . . ." He swallowed, lowering his eyes. "We think you are quite strong."

"A great good strength does me," I spat, my tone hard. "Thank God I am so strong, strong enough to outlive my children. God can keep that kind of strength."

Lord Home offered a sigh. There was nothing he could say and he knew it. He bowed. "I will give ye some time alone with your husband," he said then, grateful for any kind of escape, I imagined. "God keep you strong, Your Grace. Strength is all we have and we need it now, all of us."

I watched him retreat through a veil of tears. I cursed my strength and I cursed God. How could a loving God do this? How could he take that which I loved most?

"I suppose he was here to make certain you did tell me the truth," I said, angry that such a precaution must be taken and wondering what it said about Lord Home's faith in my husband.

"He wanted to be here," he said. "So you knew that he supported you."

"All the support in the world won't bring my baby back," I returned. I leaned my head back against the pillows, closing my eyes, willing to mind images of my baby when last I saw him so bonny and pretty. "He was fine when I left him. He was strong and bluff as his uncle Henry." I choked on the words as I thought of Little Jamie. "Does anyone know how fares the king?" I opened my eyes, frantic that the same fate should befall Little Jamie. "Is he well? Is he very afraid? Has anyone comforted him or made him understand what has happened? Oh, God!" It was too much. All of it was too much. Little Jamie in Scotland alone trying to make sense of his baby brother's death with none but the Duke of Albany and his appointed staff to comfort him? As poor as my estate was, his was so much worse. My heart ached to be with him. Baby Alexander's battles were over before they began; he was with the angels, with his father, my parents, my grandmother, and God. The suffering was for us now, for Little Jamie and me, and I could not get to him. I could not help him.

It was then I hated the Duke of Albany like no other.

It was his fault my baby was dead. He was no better than Richard III! I would make the world see that; I would expose him for the evil snake of a man he was.

He would pay for his sins against the houses of Stewart and Tudor.

By God, he would pay.

Angus could not comfort me; no one could. I lay alone, the covers drawn to my neck, refusing food and drink. What I longed for no human hand could give. Oh, Alexander . . .

The men drifted in and out of my chambers; none could speak to me, none wished my tears upon them. None knew how to offer true comfort, not even my Angus. True, most of them had lost their own children time and again, but their children were not princes. Their children did not hold the fates of kingdoms on their tiny shoulders. Their feeble words and consolations could do little to restore me.

Lent was spent not only in deprivation of the finer things in life; I had grown used to that. Mine was a sterner penance. My sons were gone, and the distance between my baby girl and me was of another, subtler kind. I could not bear to hold her or even to look upon her overmuch; when I saw her, I saw her brothers, the one forbidden to me by Albany, the other forbidden to me by God. Whenever I beheld her, I could only but think of her future. Would she one day meet my eyes with the pain of her own agonizing choices as a reflection? Would she lose her children and her loves like me? I could not bear the thought of it; we were all but repetitions of the vicious cycle born unto women, living one another's lives, crying one another's tears, over and over again.

At Morpeth, I learned of another highborn daughter's entrance into the world. My brother and Catherine of Aragon became the new parents of a living princess at last, a little lass they called Mary, for my sister, of course. I imagined since my Margaret's birth they found I had enough of a namesake and extended the courtesy to the family favorite, as out of favor as she was with her forbidden marriage to Charles Brandon on the heels of the King of France's death. My sister Mary's star rose further in my brother's eyes when she bore Brandon a bonny son in March.

If anything, the Tudors were proving their fertility at last.

As if to echo that thought, spring, silent as the snowflakes of its predecessor, was upon us. The days grew longer, the snow began to melt as the earth renewed itself and, with it, hope for my journey southward.

Lady Dacre, my most faithful and tolerable visitor, came to my side as she had so often these past months. She stroked my hair and held my hand, but even her gentle touch, always hoping to solicit a response, could evoke nothing from me. I could not cry anymore. I could only think of getting back to Scotland, to Albany, and exacting my vengeance.

"The only way to get back to Scotland," Lady Dacre told me, "is to get first to London. You must get your strength up, Your Grace. Get to London and see what His Majesty can do for you to help you. Then you can return to your child the king and set things right."

I turned my head on my pillow to gaze at the gentle woman who had offered nothing but hospitality and comfort. For the first time I squeezed the hand that had been holding mine. Tears hovered, a painful swelling in my throat, but I could not let them fall. I could spare no time for tears now. She was right; I needed to get to London. I needed my brother, my family.

I drew in a breath. "Is there any word on the arrangements?"

"My lord husband corresponds with His Majesty to see how soon a party and the proper horses and litter will arrive," she informed me in her gentle tones.

"Thank you, Lady Dacre," I told her. "I want you to know how much I appreciate all you and Lord Dacre have done for me and my baby princess. Were I someplace else," I added with a sigh, "I do not think I would have been able to endure."

Lady Dacre's hazel eyes softened with tears at this, and she reached out to stroke my cheek once more. "We love you, Your Grace," she said.

It was then my tears, so masterfully hidden of late, began to flow unchecked. How I longed to hear those words! They loved me. Not because I was a queen, not because of my power, or lack thereof. They loved me because I was a woman in need, a mother, a wife, and in me perhaps they saw their own helpless women. For that, or despite it, they loved me.

I reached up, covering the hand on my cheek. I could not speak. No words would ever convey the gratitude that swelled in my heart just then.

It was a good and rare thing to be loved.

In an attempt to gather strength for the journey, I began to eat a bit more. I took in supper with my husband, Angus, while awaiting word of the arrangements.

"It will be good for us to get to court," I told Angus. "I think you will like my brother and he you. I am certain he will have grand plans in store for our pleasure. It will be so nice to pretend for a while that things are . . . well," I added in soft tones. "And we will all be together for the first time in thirteen years! Mary and that new husband of hers Charles Brandon—what a scandal that was, him marrying her without my brother's permission, and even after Henry asked him not to propose! She was fresher in her widow-hood than I! It's a wonder they're even welcome. Of course my brother will forgive our little sister anything," I prattled in cheerful tones. Light conversation was so rare these days I was eager to make the most of it. "Though Brandon is said to be quite hand-some," I went on, as if handsomeness could expiate any sin. "And Henry, of course. They call him the 'handsomest prince in Chris-tendom.' " I chuckled at this. I did not think I would ever be able to think of him as anyone but Henry, the boy I had once hit with a stick for his teasing. "But of course, they have not seen you yet," I added, hoping to inspire my husband's affection.

Angus sighed at this. I noticed he ate little of his fish stew.

"Eat, darling," I urged. "We canna have two of us weak and ill."

He pushed his trencher aside, then took my tray from me, sit-ting on the bed beside me. I stiffened. The last time he had done so he had told me the news of my baby.

"What is it, Angus?" I asked. I could not bear more secrets. "If it is bad, tell me quickly!"

Angus drew in a breath. "I . . . I am not able to go with you to London."

I furrowed my brow, folding my arms across my breasts. "What do you mean, you're not coming with me? Why?"

"Margaret, Albany has offered terms by which I can keep my estates. If I leave now, I could forfeit everything and be exiled forever," he said. "I have lost much. I canna lose my homeland, too."

"*You* have lost much?" I cried. "Was it not my baby that just died? Is not my living son motherless in Scotland still? And *you* have lost much!"

"I've lost a child before, too!" Angus cried, rising. "You think your situation is so remarkable? And was not the Duke of Ross my stepson? Do you not think his death affected me at all? A cold-hearted man you must take me for!"

"I was not saying the loss of Alexander is greater than the loss of your first bairn," I said, angry he should read my words such, angrier that he should take my tragedy and make it about him. "But you canna say you are more deprived than I am at present! How can you go back to Scotland now and send me, your wife, alone to London with our baby, as if you didn't care what happens to us at all!"

"You are hardly alone," Angus reminded me. "And you are hardly a common wife. You are the Queen of Scotland, for love of God, going to meet your brother the King of England! It isn't as if you are being sent alone with no guards to protect you. Besides, at the court of Henry you will be treated well and entertained; you will hardly miss my presence."

"It isn't about that," I returned, shaking my head at him. "This is not a progress for pleasure. We are going to discuss the fate of my son, of Scotland. How can you not be by my side for that?"

"If I accompany you, I may never get to see Scotland again." Angus's tone was low. "Then where would we be? How can I help shape the fate of Scotland if I am exiled from her!"

I shook my head. "You are afraid. You would rather bargain with the devil than stand beside your own wife. I am ashamed of you, Angus. You are a coward."

Angus bowed his head. "Maybe I am," he said, his voice husky. "But I will better serve you, my king, and our interests if I am a coward within the kingdom. Perhaps if you could trust me, you could see that."

"I see no such thing," I hissed. "You are afraid of losing your precious estates and the esteem of Albany and his cronies. You would rather stand with a horde of wrongdoers for the strength of their numbers than stand with any one person, no matter how isolated they are in their rightness, for to do so could risk losing a future political opportunity!"

Angus's eyes flashed almost onyx at that and I knew I had him.

"Someday," Angus told me, "you will regret what you have said."

"Until then," I hissed, "God keep you, my dear husband."

The anger faded from Angus's eyes, replaced with a sadness I did not want to acknowledge.

"God keep you, my dear Margaret," he said.

And then he was gone.

ᕷ 14 ᕷ

The Reunion

Though Lord Dacre's kind eyes reflected sympathy over my husband's desertion, he was far too polite to voice his opinion. There was too much to do, and even I could not ponder it overmuch. We were to set out to London at last. Soon I would be with my brother and he would set things right, perhaps even have some words for my derelict husband.

Our progress, reminiscent of my long-ago journey to Scotland, gathered a large party of well-wishers to accompany me home. I was feeling rejuvenated with purpose and impatient to arrive at my brother's court. Each long-suffering plod of the exhausted horse's hooves, each stop we made along the way, was a torturous hindrance to my goal. Lord Dacre rode with me to Newcastle, where the mayor and my sister-in-law's equerry Thomas Parr met us. Though I was grateful to be greeted with the proper ceremony and courtesy, I saw all stops as unnecessary. I was feeling as well as could be and wanted to keep moving!

We made it to Stony Stratford in Buckinghamshire, where I drafted a quick note to my brother conveying my eagerness for our reunion, resting before we pressed on. I was so close! I could barely eat or take rest for excitement, though we did at our last stop of Enfield, where we stayed in the comforts of the Lord Treasurer's home. This, too, lengthened the journey beyond what I found reasonable, though I exuded nothing but gratitude to all of my hosts.

Inside I was mad with anticipation. My heart raced, my face tingled in giddy, girlish delight; every facet of my being longed for London, for my family, for home.

I rode in on a gentle palfrey, a sturdy white echo of others, the ones my father had sent with me to Scotland that were destined to perish in a fire. I willed the vision out of my heart, that and my late husband's remedy of new white palfreys. Jamie had always been good at making up. . . . I wondered if Angus would ever be compelled to the same chivalry his predecessor had practiced with such ease.

But my arrival was not about either husband and I forced myself to think of the present. At Tottenham Cross my brother met us at last.

He was a sight to behold, and far different from the little brother I had battled wills with as children. His hair and beard shone golden red, a beacon of light for this weary traveler, and his smile exuded confident radiance. Henry stood strong and tall, rippling with the muscles of a young warrior and decked in the regalia of his station; he shared my love of fashion and would never appear in public as anything less than a king. Looking at him, I knew he was everything my father hoped he would be. My face ached from smiling as I took him in.

We were not permitted a personal greeting yet; I was received as his sister the queen in his booming voice, thunderous and thrilling to hear as I realized with a laugh that anytime I thought of my brother speaking it was still in his child's voice. I longed to throw my arms around him and talk of times gone by and times yet to come. But, as the last, sweetest, most tantalizing leg of my journey, that had to wait . . . for now I had to be content with a meeting of monarchs.

We rode to Baynard's Castle at the head of a grand welcoming party Henry assembled for my reception. As we rode I could not help but offer my brother the happiest of smiles; the crowds were too boisterous for us to converse, but the joy on our faces rendered words inadequate as it were. I could not take my eyes off Henry; I longed to impress this memory in my mind for as long as I lived; who knew when we would see each other in a time of such bliss again?

When at last I was shown to my apartments, we were afforded our longed-for moment of privacy. I threw myself into Henry's arms, taking comfort in his strong, hearty embrace. Being held by a member of my own family once more served only to remind me of who was not present, and the thought of Father and Mother, Grandmother, and old Archbishop Morton coaxed forth an onset of tears. My shoulders quaked with sobs as Henry stroked my back, clucking endearments in my ear as he would to a distraught child.

Collecting myself somewhat, I pulled away, my arms still entwined through Henry's as I gazed into his ruddy face. His blue eyes were lit with tears in turn, but his smile was irrepressible; the imp he was as a child was quite alive in the man.

"Forgive my tears," I said, my first words to my brother in the privacy of my chambers. "It's just there is so much to take in—and so much that is no longer here."

Henry shook his head. "I know," he returned. "But too many wondrous events have transpired these past few months to think on that, my dear sister. We've three bonny Tudor babes in our nursery! Think of that! Your precious little Margaret, our little princess, and another Henry in the Brandon boy! Now how is that for good fortune?"

Listing the babies present drove the thought home again of those who were not, those who never would be, and I fought the urge to cry again. Henry must have perceived this and took me in his arms again.

"Ah, Margaret, I'm so sorry. We've lost much," he cooed as he rocked from side to side. "It does no good that your husband couldn't even accompany you," he added to my chagrin. I could only imagine how disappointed Henry was in Angus. "Done like a Scot," he uttered again, his now famous phrase for my husband's betrayal.

"I am just so happy to be with you," I said, hoping to avoid the topic for now.

"And I you," Henry said as he pulled away once more. Now he

took the time to assess me, and heat flushed my cheeks as his gaze traveled from my hood to my slippers. "Well, at least they fed you well in Scotland," he offered, which I chose to take as a compliment. I was not nearly so stout as I was months ago and was too proud of my newfound figure, curvaceous as it was, to take it as anything less.

"That they did," I said. "But it was your Lord Dacre who restored my health best after the birth of baby Margaret," I told him, to appeal to his pride.

"I am glad of it," Henry assured me, squeezing my hand. "And now we are to be all together again for a time!" he exclaimed with a joy so contagious I could not help but smile in turn. "We shall keep you merry here in England, Sister. We have ordered feasts and entertainments to celebrate your arrival; we shall dance together as we did when we were children!"

"I will cherish every moment," I told him in truth. Unlike when I was a child, I knew now that such moments were to be treasured beyond the most coveted jewels.

They were stolen all too often as we grew.

My sister, Mary, came to see me in the company of my sister-in-law Queen Catherine. I was not prepared for my reaction to either. Mary was slim and fair as ever, even for just having borne a child, and it was easy to see why she had maintained her position of favorite despite any scandal. She had a special talent for being the mildest, most agreeable person to one's face no matter how she followed her own convictions behind one's back. With her ethereal features, fair hair, and light eyes, she was every bit the opposite of her sturdy older sister, and seeing her caused my bones to ache with my own inadequacies. Her carriage and manner were fluid as a dancer's, her speech soft and sweet as honey. I moved about in a brash, heavy way no matter how big or small I was at the time and my speech had become foreign in my own ears next to those of the English around me; I rolled my *r*'s and had assumed many of the phrases of my adopted homeland, sounding grating, guttural, and northern.

I had become a Scot.

Catherine, conversely, was not the beauty my sister was, and this lifted my spirits somewhat. She had also grown a bit stouter and her expression revealed the all-pervasive exhaustion afforded by continual loss. I offered her a cool smile and stiff embrace. Never far from my mind was her triumph over my late husband's slaying. Seeing her confirmed I would never be able to think of her with the fondness of our childhood connection again.

But together we sat and spoke of lighthearted things. No one spoke of Mary's outrageous debt to Henry or of the rumors of Henry's philandering on Catherine. Nor did they mention Angus and his scandalous desertion or the loss of my little Alexander.

The visit was steeped in formality and falsehood.

It was as if we had never met, had never shared any common bond, and were now forced together out of necessity; we danced the dance of diplomats and courtiers—ever superficial, ever polite.

Ever strangers.

– 15 –

His Sister's Keeper

I was distracted from the disillusionment of my reunion with Mary and Catherine by the extraordinary sport my brother had arranged for my pleasure. He alighted to the tiltyard with my new brother-in-law, Charles Brandon, and Nicholas Carew to challenge the best jousters at court, who included the Earl of Surrey, our former uncle Thomas Howard, who had since lost my dear aunty Anne and all of their children and wed the daughter of the Duke of Buckingham. My heart lurched at the sight of him; his extensive losses once more reminded me of my own, of Henry's, and even to a lesser degree Mary's.

It was no wonder we had become a cold lot.

I refused to dwell on such dark matters that day, however, and watched my brother and his knights in their revels. They had donned rich black velvet covered in golden honeysuckle branches that caught the sunlight, shining so bright that I found myself flinching against it now and again. Their opponents wore gold-fringed blue velvet, looking worthy of their noble company indeed. They were a spectacle of strength and handsomeness and my heart swelled at the sight.

Of course my brother won the day. It would be no other way.

The next afternoon was another feast for the eyes. Henry and his men were outfitted in purple velvet trimmed with ornate golden roses, while his other knights and lords were dressed in stunning yellow with cloth of gold borders. The challengers shone brilliant in white and gold. It was as if I were watching the sun tilt with the stars. My heart leapt as each blow was delivered, and the crashing of lance against armor, hoof against earth, along with the cries of the men and the spectators set me to shivering with delight. As I watched I was reminded of my first tourney, when as a little girl I had passed out the tokens to the winners. How distant did those days seem now!

My brother's display jostled me into the present as once again he took the day, and ended the festivities with him and Brandon besting each other, performing tricks and an improvised form of jousting that displayed their remarkable skill at the sport. I was as impressed as Henry intended me to be and praised him that evening in Catherine's apartments, where we feasted.

"Ha!" Henry laughed after receiving my compliments. "See if that coward Angus will come and meet me on the field—would he do so well?"

My cheeks burned. "Not so well as my brother, I am sure," I said, knowing it was the expected response.

"No, and no other bloody Scot with him!" Henry cried in triumph.

Henry delighted in insulting my husband and my kingdom, doing so ever since my arrival at any opportunity. Though I was grateful for his support and expected most brothers would regard anyone who mistreated their sister as I had been as cowards and traitors, it smarted just the same. But I vowed to keep my peace for now; I was a guest in his land, after all, and I needed his help. It would not do to indulge in petty quarrels and I took to enjoying the remainder of the evening as best I could, taking in the delicacies, the wine, and the company, reminding myself as always that such time with my family would not last forever.

As with all good things, the festivities of that beautiful May drew to a close. The party was over. It was time to attend to my queenly business once again.

*   *   *

One of the lighter pastimes of those days was to attend the nursery with Mary and Catherine, where we would fuss over our bairns as if we were ordinary mothers in an ordinary family. The women prided themselves on their children's development, but as my daughter entered each new stage my heart throbbed and ached for Alexander and Little Jamie.

One afternoon when Catherine deigned not to join us, Mary noted my quivering lip as I beheld her son.

"Sister . . ." Her tone was gentle, her gray-blue eyes brimming with unshed tears. "I am so sorry for what has come to pass, for your poor Alexander and the king . . . I cannot imagine being separated from little Henry as you are from the king now."

"You dinna—do not," I stammered, attempting ever since my arrival to lose my Scottish accent. "You do not want to imagine it. I hope you never have to endure it." I turned from the sight of the children and sat in one of the plush velvet-trimmed chairs, taking my sewing in my lap, pretending to examine its stitching, blinking away tears of acute homesickness.

Mary approached, resting one of her slim-fingered hands on my shoulder, again reminding me of the refinement and delicacy I lacked. I swallowed hard, covering her hand with mine and telling myself she couldn't help being so dainty.

"Oh, Mary . . ." My voice was husky. "I want to be happy here with baby Margaret, but all I can think of is Alexander and how he will never reach another milestone. And thinking of that makes me wonder what ones Little Jamie is reaching without me. I feel so guilty fussing over these children not knowing if my son is being cared for and loved properly. I dinna—do not know if he has the same nurse, if she is warm and kind, or if he is embraced and snuggled with and treated not so much as a king but as a little lad."

Mary shook her head. "I wish I had the answers for you," she confessed. "It must be unbearable."

"It is," I said, knowing that voicing my thoughts only heightened my longing, knowing that my sister, like most, could do nothing.

Mary sat beside me. "What are you going to do about Angus?" she asked, and despite the unpleasantness of the topic, it was preferable to discussing the children.

I shook my head. "I don't know."

"Do you love him, Margaret?"

I closed my eyes. Did I? "I am no longer sure if I ever did. It's just that he made me feel so pretty for a time; it is always nice to feel wanted by someone so handsome." This was something I knew Mary could not relate to. Everyone had wanted Mary; everyone had found her beautiful. "And I believe he loved the boys," I went on. "Do you love Charles?"

Mary's face softened. Part of me hoped that she did not, that it was a move as impulsive and desperate as my own. But her eyes revealed otherwise and I hoped my own gaze did not yield my disappointment. Not that I wanted her unhappy . . . I just wanted someone to commiserate with, someone who did not see me as pathetic.

"I do," she told me. "But I do not know if what we did was right," she said then as if intuiting my thoughts. "We caused a great scandal, and though Henry has been merciful, our debts keep mounting. We owe Henry so much as it is . . ." she sighed. "It is staggering."

"I am sure I will be indebted as well," I offered as a bit of consolation. "I receive next to nothing from Scotland and Henry will have to support me as my station requires. I just hope he can do so without a grudge."

Mary smiled at this. "I am sure he will; we are his sisters."

But I am not his favorite, I hesitated to add.

"We are to be leaving," she said then. "Charles and I are going to the country. We can no longer afford to be here; the tourney has set us back even more and being here will only remind Henry of his burden."

I understood that pressure all too well. I wondered how long it would be before my own welcome wore itself out.

Despite the awkwardness and inherent rivalry in our relationship, I was reluctant to see Mary go.

"I feel as if I am just getting to know you again," I told her. "Or perhaps for the first time. I should be used to good-byes," I added in husky tones.

Mary pursed her lip and bowed her head. "As we all have been," she said as she rose. "But take heart. We are luckier than most. Many royal families never live to see reunions such as ours."

I rose in turn, offering my sister a fast, tight embrace. For all I knew, it could be our last.

"Indeed." I forced myself to agree. "We are . . . lucky."

Without my sister, Mary, to be the buffer in our conversations, Catherine and I were left to ourselves. Prior visits had been easier to endure; Mary, as if sensing the tension I experienced in our sister-in-law's presence, steered the topics to the children and court gossip (nothing too scandalous; Catherine's sensibilities tended toward the pious). Now that Mary had retired to the country, more to my regret than I had anticipated—I had begun to like her; in her I recognized a vulnerability and sweetness that both Henry and I lacked, which I knew endeared us both to her, fostering a sense of protectiveness in me I did not demonstrate for many—visits with Catherine were forced and awkward.

"Your Grace," Catherine began one balmy afternoon, having never called me by name. She was alone, which was rare; she almost always had her closest ladies at her side.

I was too tired and hot to sew and preferred to cool myself on the chaise of my apartments with an ivory-handled little fan my mother had told me long ago was from a Crusader. I was disappointed to see Catherine in my rooms, but as she was my hostess, I knew I could not refuse her. I offered a languid smile, hoping to reveal my sleepy state and inspire her to cut her visit short.

Catherine sat, stiff as she always was. I wondered if she ever allowed herself a moment's relaxation.

"Your Grace," she said again. "I feel as if you have been avoiding me."

I ceased my fanning, drawing in a breath, expelling it slowly. "We have seen each other often, Sister," I told her. "With Mary in the nursery, at the entertainments, and of course at Mass."

Catherine lowered her eyes. "I understand we have seen each other. But we have not spoken much, not of anything . . . true."

I clenched my jaw at this, swinging my legs over the side of the chaise to right myself. "I do not know what you expect me to say," I confessed, my tone guarded.

"About Flodden, about King Ja—"

"Do not say it," I cautioned. "There is no use going back. What's done is done."

Catherine never lost her composure. "I want you to know I am sorry about James."

I shook my head. It was not as easy to remain calm. "How sorry are you, Catherine?" I challenged. I did not want to address her by title. We were two women now, and one had been quite wronged. "Were you sorry when you wished to send his body to Henry, as if he were a stag, as if it were all a great sport?"

Catherine had the grace to bow her head at this. "I was regent in Henry's absence. I was trying to show our strength, to keep the confidence of our people boosted. I acted as a queen, not as your family, just as King James acted when he invaded our kingdom. He did not regard us as family then, did he?"

I rose, turning my back to her and heading to the window, watching the swans glide through the sun-kissed sparkles of the Thames, envying their beautiful simplicity.

"My husband had his reasons," was all I could think of to say, though in truth none were good. The reasons for war never were.

"I had mine," Catherine returned. "But I do recognize how it could have been perceived by you; I did then and do now. And I am sorry for it."

"For what good it does, I accept your apology," I said. "But it changes nothing. My husband is still dead, by the hands of your countrymen."

"Because he invaded and we were defending our homeland," Catherine reminded me, and though I knew she was right in her line of logic, I hated her for it nonetheless.

"Still, he was your brother-in-law," I told her, turning to face her once more. "For whatever wrong he did, and however the conse-quences played out, he was your family. To triumph over his death, to gloat, and to even entertain the idea of sending Henry his body was barbaric. That was unforgivable."

"So you cannot forgive me, then." Catherine's voice was soft. She lowered her eyes to her folded hands. "Even though in the end, I did not do it. And still you cannot forgive me for the error of my thoughts, which I now confess to you? Was not James a Christian king?"

"Don't let's make this a matter of faith," I snapped, irritated she would enter that vein. "What does faith have to do with it? Did it stop my husband from committing adultery? Did it stop the armies from slaying each other, forgetting 'thou shalt not kill' so easily? Or are you insinuating that I lack faith? I know exactly where I stand with God. I am more faithful than all of you who declare yourselves His devout children as loudly as you sin."

Catherine flinched. "So you insinuate in turn that I am a hypocrite?" The furrow of her brow and light in her dull blue eyes revealed genuine hurt. I could not bring myself to regret my words.

"We all are," I admitted. "But I do not like being told that someone is more faithful than I. My husband used to visit his shrines with all the enthusiasm of a monk and none of the discipline. He had a lover waiting for him at almost every one.

"I may not demonstrate faith the way he did, but I do believe in God. I believe He will always be there to take everything I love most from me; in that I have the utmost faith." My voice caught on the last word.

Catherine shook her head. "Then I pity you. That is the wrong thing to have faith in. You must hold faith that God hears your prayers and cries two tears for every one you shed, and that tragedies arise from us being born in a sinful world, not from God's desire to inflict them upon us. God is faithful; it is He who gets us through those tragedies. He rewards long-suffering. He rewards steadfastness."

"Then I look forward to it, for surely I shall be duly rewarded," I said in flat tones. I hated these types of discussions; they bored me and were often used to obscure or manipulate a more relevant point. "But I do not need your pity, Catherine," I went on. "I do not need anything from you."

"Yet you seek refuge in my kingdom." Her tone became as cool as mine.

"Not your kingdom," I reminded her. "Your husband's. My brother's."

Catherine averted her head, as if the thought of her power being more limited than she imagined struck her, perhaps even frightened her.

"And you can be assured that I would never revel in the glory of a victory over England, especially one that resulted in the death of my family," I promised her. "In that I am capable of deporting myself as a queen and a sister, not one or the other."

Catherine pursed her lips. "Yet clearly you cannot as easily reconcile being a queen and a mother," she said, her tone low.

My jaw fell agape. The audacity! "How can you say that?" I breathed.

"I only mean to say, were I in your position, nothing would tear me away from my child." Her tone was matter-of-fact, as though it were that easy.

"Do not speak so soon, my dear sister," I warned. "You never know when you will be in my position. For your sake and the princess's, I hope you never are. But," I added in hard tones, "if so, you will remember what you said to me."

Catherine sighed, shaking her head. "There is no use explaining or defending myself. You will see it your way; I, mine." Her voice softened. "I did not mean to insult you; I do not know your heart, so should not question it." She clicked her tongue. "Nothing has gone as planned. I came hoping to make peace with you, not renew bitterness. I hoped you would forgive me." Her voice caught. "Margaret," she said my name for the first time since I arrived, "can you appreciate that I seek your forgiveness as I know I must, and that I do with a sincere and contrite heart? . . . Can you forgive me?"

I sighed, sitting once more. I did not know if I could forgive her, because I still hadn't forgiven Jamie for dying. I hadn't forgiven myself for marrying again. I could not yet forgive Angus for betraying me. Nor could I forgive Catherine now for judging me. With all that weighing on my conscience, how could I with a sincere heart forgive her for her past transgression?

"I want to," I said in truth. A painful knot of tears swelled my throat. "But I do not know if I can. I am sorry."

Catherine rose. "I appreciate your honesty," she remarked. "I suppose it does no good for me to remain then." She offered a smile; I could not say it was unkind. "I had hoped to be at peace."

Peace. I had searched for that since Jamie's passing. I resented her need for it, as if her declaring it somehow eclipsed my own.

I nodded. "It is my wish as well," I said softly as she quit the room.

Soon after our conversation, I was relocated from the castle of my childhood to Scotland Yard, as fitting a Scottish monarch.

I was no longer a sister in need. I was yet another dignitary in Henry's court and would be treated as such.

Henry did petition the council in Scotland to reject Albany's regency and exile him once more. Of course this was as offensive to them as any plot could be, and they deemed Henry's proposition treasonous. Thus incited and insulted, he ordered Lord Dacre to renew warfare on the Border, which meant more raids, more bloody skirmishes, more property stolen, and more lives lost. I hated to see it done but could not fathom a better way to pressure the lairds to just action on behalf of Little Jamie and me.

Henry's attention to my cause was wearing on him, however, and my presence was another grating manifestation of those tedious efforts. I irritated him and, to be frank, he did me. His arrogance, his showiness, all of it was as if to flaunt his good fortune in my face and remind me that I was at his mercy. He was no longer toasting my presence. Long since ended were the receptions and entertainments welcoming me to his court. I wasn't the favorite, as I was well aware, but now it showed.

As I was not receiving income from Scotland, I had hoped Henry would supplement me to support my household. I wrote to Henry's most influential adviser, Cardinal Wolsey, in the hopes that I could appeal for the means I needed to survive with the dignity of my station, to no avail.

One ray of light shone in that the jewels and wardrobe left behind during my flight from Tantallon were itemized and returned to me. Not one pearl, gem, or garment was tampered with or stolen. Which meant that the Scots still retained some kind of respect for me. My fine jewel-encrusted hoods and cloth of gold sleeves, my gem-studded collars and hats, my rosaries and pendant pearls, were preserved with the utmost care. If these articles had been treated with such delicacy and honor, then so must my Little Jamie. I could only pray.

The Scottish council had promised to send my dower rents as well, and this lifted my spirits. The less I had to depend on Henry the better. But autumn wasted into winter, with no money ever sent. I was in as desperate a state as I ever was. It would all have been much easier to manage had I never fled Scotland. Time had dulled the urgency of why I had left, clouding the danger I had been in with homesickness. I found myself regretting the decision to come to England. If I had only stayed, perhaps I could have been reunited with my son by now. . . .

I found more and more that I was beginning to think of Scotland as home. I had spent as much time there as I had in England, but being that I was grown for much of that time, I remembered it all the more. I missed the clear lochs, the rolling hills, the craggy paths and trails, the morning mists. I missed Stirling and even Edinburgh.

I missed Little Jamie.

I had left my home an English princess, returning a Scottish queen. More and more I realized I was a foreigner in my own homeland. I started to resent my accent and manner less, seeing it now as a connection to my son, the King of Scots. I longed for him, oh, how much!

Where he was, there also was my home.

Another Christmas had come, my second without Little Jamie, and my finances were dire. I had no money to even reward my most faithful servants for the holiday season, and I was ashamed of my estate. Though I had all the accoutrements, I was far from a true queen; it was as if I had been consigned to playing make-believe, with my baby, Margaret, little more than a glorified doll. And Henry was tired of hosting such a charade if it were not his to play. Since he was proving to be of little help, I appealed once more to his trusted Cardinal Wolsey, hoping he would at least see the gravity of my case and make the necessary loans, for I would pay him back when my promised rents from Lord Dacre arrived. I was a woman of honor, after all.

Despite my situation, I was invited to Greenwich Palace to celebrate Twelfth Night with Henry, Catherine, and the court. There it was made clear to me that my brother had more than enough money he could have spared for my expenses. Even clearer was the fact that he did not want to waste it upon me when he could instead hold yet another lavish entertainment, for which he had become so renowned.

This display was called The Garden of Esperance. Towered with ornate gilt rails, the garden sported silk flowers and satin greenery, sparkling with golden accents. On a large central pillar were a bush of white and red roses for the house of Tudor and a pomegranate tree for the house of Aragon. Six knights accompanied by six of the fairest ladies in magnificent gowns and apparel that would have fed a family for a month each took to a splendid sequence of dances that I had to admit were choreographed to perfection. No one fell out of step; it was as if I were glimpsing a garden of the fey, where there was nothing to worry about, nothing to ponder but the next step in a never-ending dance of richness and beauty. Oh, if reality could have been so simple . . .

After the pageant, the garden was wheeled out and we were treated to a banquet as abundant as the garden was exquisite, in which two hundred dishes were served (yes, I counted). It was almost debauched in extravagance, and though I did enjoy it, I could not help but make this point with as much subtlety as I could.

"It is a spectacle beyond belief as always, Henry," I complimented him, knowing the surest way to appeal to him was through his vanity. "To be among such grandeur, I admit, makes me long to treat my own household this season. They have served me so well; it is a pity they canna be rewarded more suitably."

Henry shook his head as he dipped an artichoke leaf into a silver dish of melted butter. "I don't know what you expect from me, Margaret," he said in light tones. "It isn't as though you are still wed to James IV." He sucked the meaty bit of the leaf noisily before discarding it on the floor. "You are the Queen Dowager, not even a regent, yet I cannot help but notice you still wish to live as if you were a queen in full state."

I glowered at this. "Henry, I'm not asking for much," I said, matching his light tone, fixing a smile on my face in the hopes no one would observe the strain between us. "You are the King of England, after all. No one is more powerful, more formidable! Henry . . . you can do anything," I added sweetly.

Henry smiled at this, reaching over to pat my hand. "I can do a lot," he admitted. "But some things are even beyond my power, Sister." He chuckled. "My naïve sister," he added with a more robust laugh.

My shoulders slumped. Perhaps I was naïve. I was reminded of my own lack of power at every turn. To know the same applied to Henry, my larger-than-life brother who could make a garden in winter, was disheartening.

No matter his lush displays of wealth and power, Henry was not magical; he could not work miracles. It occurred to me his words with the Scots on my behalf had little effect. And the control he did have he guarded jealously. He would spare me no more than what he deemed necessary, and our versions of necessity were wildly disproportionate to each other.

The epiphany made the celebration far less merry.

Henry paid my financial estate little heed after the holiday season, though a treaty he and Cardinal Wolsey made with Albany would allow me my beloved Stirling and unlimited access to Little Jamie. Beyond that, however, Henry busied himself with hawking well into spring, until matters came to a head in London. It seemed English workers were resenting foreigners in the city, feeling as though they were stealing their livings. On May Day riots erupted, most of them against the Spanish and Portuguese. Henry sent his most able warriors, the Howards, against them, hanging, drawing, and quartering the instigators. It was a gory display; scaffolds by the city gates illustrated the fates of those who disturbed my brother's peace. At the trial, in her own display of pious theatrics, Catherine begged Henry to show clemency on the rioters. The remainder were pardoned and tossed their halters in the air to my brother's benevolence. *Good show, Harry!*

It was clear to see that Henry had his own matters to deal with in his realm. The new treaty that promised me a reunion with my son was his greatest achievement in my case and I was grateful. And more than eager to leave.

At last the arrangements had been made; I was to go home. We set out on 16 May, Henry riding with me for four days of the journey. I'll never be certain if guilt over his lack of financial support during my stay in England compelled him to it or if it was another of his shows, but Henry doled out to me rich gifts in farewell. I received more tapestries, gowns, plate, jewels, cloth of arras, sturdy horses, and even money for the journey. Whatever his reasons, I wasn't going to refuse.

When he left my progress, we embraced. Henry's arms enveloped me in one of his great bear hugs and all was well between us again. I looked up into his face, at his sparkling blue eyes and impish smile, and reached up to stroke his cheek.

"Thank you for all you have done, Brother," I told him in sincerity. "I hope I wasn't too much trouble," I added with a laugh.

"You're a Tudor," Henry said, his thin lips stretching into a wide grin. "And Tudor just may be indistinguishable from 'trouble.' " He squeezed my hands. "But be that as it may, it was good to have you and good to see you."

"Henry?" I asked. "Do you remember the last time we said good-bye, when I first left for Scotland and you told me about the seventh day to take in my mind, where you would always be there to protect me?"

Henry squinted a moment, as if trying to see into the past. He smiled, shaking his head. "I'm sorry, Sister. I do not recall."

I sighed. Maybe it wasn't as memorable for him; with all he had been through since, I couldn't expect it to be. Still, it saddened me that so tender a moment was not remembered by him as it was treasured by me.

Henry reached out, squeezing my shoulder. "I wish you well, Margaret. I truly do," he said, his tone wistful.

"The same, Henry," I returned, tears caught in my voice. Somewhere deep within I knew, just as when I parted with my father before my marriage, and Jamie before Flodden.

I will never see you again. . . .

❧ 16 ❧

The Return

At York, to my delight, I learned that Albany had departed for France, taking the brothers and oldest sons of the foremost houses in the land to secure that none would attempt to overthrow him in his absence, an intelligent strategy, I must say. He left Scotland in the care of the Earls of Arran, Huntley, and my Angus. My heart lurched at the thought. Was Angus working for me, hoping to use his new power for my cause, for Little Jamie?

I was plagued by this and other worries as we rode northward. The treasury of Scotland was dwindling; my expenses after Flodden were exhaustive and confronting my financial woes once again was daunting. No one, least of all the Scots, would understand why I had spent as I did, and I drafted a letter to Henry explaining the situation, in the hopes that after our warm farewell he would be sympathetic. I did not want to push him, however; I knew his help was fickle and self-serving when offered.

When we reached the Border, it looked as if Flodden were upon us once more. The land was desolate, burned, and ruined from raiding. Barns and homes stood broken, dilapidated. What new hell was I entering? Was it wise to return to this barren despair?

Only the thought of my son spurred me onward to Berwick Castle, where Angus himself came to meet me.

Despite everything between us, my heart still thrilled at the sight of him; he was as dark and handsome as he had ever been. I was determined to put his abandonment behind me. Perhaps he had been right to return to Scotland, to be a presence there and garner whatever power and sympathy he could in my absence. Perhaps it had all been part of a more intricate strategy.

I offered my brightest smile. "Have you seen the baby, Angus?" I asked him as we made our way into the castle. "She's beautiful, just like her papa," I added, hoping to renew whatever affection we had known, though in truth baby Margaret was all Tudor.

"I canna wait to see her," he said, though he did not meet my eyes. We reached the apartments designated for me during my stay. He reached out, taking my hand, our first touch since meeting.

"How is Little Jamie?" I asked. "Surely you have seen him."

Angus smiled at this. "I have and he is bonny, truly."

"Oh, time canna go fast enough!" I exclaimed. "I long to be with him, to hold him, and make known how loved he is."

Angus nodded, but he seemed half-engaged in the present.

I swallowed. "Angus, I forgive you," I blurted. And I did. "I want to start over. We can be a family again with baby Margaret and Little Jamie. We can put things right now."

Angus glanced at my face a brief moment before returning his dark eyes to his boots. "There have been some changes in the year and a half you've been gone," he informed me. "You know that Lord Home has been executed, his clan outlawed."

My throat tightened at this. I had learned of this; it was a distressing display of Albany's rule and a loss of a man who had become a great ally, as unlikely as that was.

"A lot has come to pass," I agreed. "But I am here now. I am recovered from the baby's birth and my illness; I am ready to fight."

"There isn't so much a need for fighting as there is . . . collaboration," Angus said. "In that, I think you will agree."

I drew in a breath, expelling it in a heavy sigh. "I dinna want to think on it now, Angus," I confessed. "I will address each issue as it arises. For now, I want to think of you and the baby, and of seeing Little Jamie soon."

"And so you shall," Angus said as he made to quit the room. "I will let you get some rest."

"You're leaving?" I asked, furrowing my brow in confusion. "I thought you might want to stay. It has been a long time. . . ."

Angus shook his head with a small smile. "Now, there's plenty of time for that, my dear. Rest now."

"You dinna want to stay and rest with me?" I prodded, feeling a desperate fool.

Angus sighed. "My dear . . . Come, I'll tuck you in." With this he led me to my bedchamber, drawing the covers down before helping me out of my gown. I slid between the warm blankets, snuggling in as he drew them to my neck, tucking them around me and pressing a kiss against my forehead. "There. Settled?"

I nodded with a smile. "Won't you join me, keep me warm?"

Angus pursed his lips. "I have matters to attend. You have been through much. Just rest. For me?"

I nodded again, the obedient wife once more. "Of course, darling," I conceded, watching his strong back retreat.

Changes, indeed. Everything, to my dismay, seemed unremarkably the same.

Little Jamie was in the care of the Archbishops of St. Andrews and Glasgow at Edinburgh and I went there straightaway. I could not get there fast enough. In a matter of moments, I would be holding my son.

I was refused entry. There was plague, I was told, and Little Jamie was moved to Craigmillar. Once again I set out for another ride, hoping this wasn't some kind of scheme to keep me from him, which would stand at odds with the new treaty.

But, to my relief, I was allowed to see him. The lairds and his attendants were present; no one would leave me alone with him, driving the point deep within my breast that I was held suspect of kidnapping my own child. I had to content myself that at least I was allowed to see him.

He was now five years old, slim like his father but robust with health. While retaining as much dignity as I could, I ran to him, taking him in my arms. He stood stiff in my embrace.

"Jamie, darling," I cooed. "It is me, Mother." I knelt down beside him, stroking his hair, his face, taking in the feel of his baby skin, his child's scent. Tears caught my throat. "I know it has been a long time. I have missed you so! But now we are together and I can see you again often. Did you miss me, Jamie?"

He first looked to the lairds, then shifted his gaze to me, offering a slow nod and shy smile. My heart clenched. Damn those men's influence to manipulate a child's heart for their own interests!

I took him in my arms again, rocking to and fro. "I'm sorry I had to leave you," I whispered against his cheek. "And I am so sorry I wasn't here when baby Alexander died."

He trembled in my arms at this. I held him tighter.

"It is hard for you to understand," I went on, swallowing the tears rising in my throat, "but all I have done I have done for you, for us. I love you more than anyone or anything and I always will. Everything I do is for you, to keep you safe and to keep you king."

"Yes, Mother," was all he said as I drew back.

My visit was brought to an end and as I left I cursed myself for ever leaving him, for leaving Scotland, and for the forces that were driving my son and me apart.

One of the few joys of returning was seeing my Ellen once more. She was as beautiful as when I first saw her, fuller of figure, but it suited her; she appeared healthy and, as always, I cherished her calm, clear perspective on life. Our reunion at Stirling was warm. I was grateful to have my favorite confidante at my side at long last.

"Oh, Ellen, why is it that everything looks better when we're away from it?" I asked her as we sewed in my apartments. I was sewing garments for Little Jamie. It would please me to see him wear clothes sewn by my hand and grate on the lairds, meeting two objectives at once.

"Distance and time always alter our view of things," she told me. "It's why people live in the past; they see it as better. In truth, even then they lived further back in their own minds, where everything is forever good and innocent. Our truest happiness is known when we are but babes. Still, we must try to make some kind of life in our present. Otherwise we miss all the good that is around us now, longing for things we can never have."

I pondered her words, knowing them to be true. In Scotland I wanted to be in England; in England I wanted to be in Scotland. With my husband Jamie, I wanted the love and devotion of a man who would never betray me; with Angus, I wanted Jamie. It was a torturous existence and I knew it was not exclusive to me.

"The present is as confusing to me as it ever was," I said, my tone taut with frustration. "Scotland is as barbarous and bloody as ever in its divisiveness. The Homes murdered Deputy-Governor De la Bastie, even having the gall to tie his head by its hair to the saddle of his horse, as if killing him wasn't enough. Now Lord Hamilton, the Earl of Arran, is his replacement and he suspects my Angus as playing a part in his predecessor's murder. He's arrested Angus's brother George."

"What do you think, Your Grace?" she asked me. She had abandoned her sewing, engaging me with her ebony eyes, fully attending the conversation while I fumbled with my needle, dropping it and recovering it over and over, fidgety with anxiety.

"I dinna know what to think," I confessed. "Angus and the rest of the Douglases have always had their share of enemies. And Lord Hamilton was a bit of a pirate in his day, but he has become loyal to me."

"I think you like pirates," Ellen teased. "As it is, Robert Barton is your comptroller." Her eyes grew soft when she said the name of one of my favorite storytellers from my early days in Scotland. I remembered that it was he who captured the Portuguese ship Ellen was on as a slave. He had rescued her and brought her to Scotland with another Moorish beauty, named Margaret after me.

"Yes, but Robin was a *privateer*," I returned with a smile, utilizing my dear friend's pet name.

"Oh, yes, a marked difference." Ellen laughed. "A pirate with papers!"

We giggled at that and it lifted my spirits to laugh and tease as if we were young girls at court again.

"I hate to see Lord Arran at odds with my husband and his family," I said, returning to the topic at hand. "I dinna know what to make of Angus, Ellen. He is so cold to me."

To this, Ellen bowed her head, saying nothing.

Her silences had always revealed more than she intended, or perhaps exactly what she intended. She knew why Angus was cold; perhaps everyone did.

For me, I was content to live in ignorance a bit longer.

I did not want to know.

To my utter surprise, I received a letter from Albany stating that I should appeal to the council for the return of my regency. His correspondences had been warmer to me of late. Perhaps he was plagued by the guilt of baby Alexander's death, though in truth I no longer blamed him for it. Perhaps Scottish politics had been too much for him, with the constant feuding and clan rivalries. Or perhaps he was accepting that he was a Frenchman at heart and wanted to remain in the home of his former exile. Whatever the reason, this turn of heart rejuvenated me.

I took this news to the lairds of my council, suggesting that Angus be my co-regent; nothing like this boost of power would prove my desire for a happy marriage more. After our triumphant ride into Edinburgh together with a train four hundred horses strong, our ears ringing with the cries of the loving crowds, the hope of being received well as regents seemed reachable.

My appeals were denied to a man.

"Angus," said Lord Arran, "is not an honorable man."

I shook my head at this, taking to my apartments again to wonder why. Angus was rash, his moves bold. But was he without honor?

It was in my apartments that I was paid a visit by Robin Barton. He was a handsome man, I had always thought, with his cut figure, dark curling hair and thin mustache, skin tanned from years at sea, and bold green eyes. His stories of his adventures had delighted me as a young girl, and his loyalty touched me as a woman.

Ellen remained with me for his visit and I noted the softness in their eyes as they regarded each other. Robin sat across from me in a stiff-backed chair, folding his ankle over his other knee and lean-ing forward.

"Your Grace," he began in his gruff voice. "What do ye know?"

"About what, Robin?" I asked, knowing somehow that he was to be the bearer of bad tidings and steeling myself against it.

"About Angus," he finished. "About the goings-on while ye've been in England."

My heart began to pound. I lowered my eyes, clenching my hands on the arms of my chair. "I know nothing," I breathed.

Robin drew in a breath, expelling it in a *whoosh*. I could see he was uncomfortable in his task.

"It is my unfortunate duty to make plain to you what he has done," he said. "And I dinna like it any more than you," he added with a wag of his finger. His eyes softened. "Your Grace, Angus took up with his old love, Lady Jane Stewart of Traquair. He lived with her for the whole of your departure. On your lands and on your money."

The words were a lance in my side. I clutched my churning belly, squeezing my eyes shut, praying it was a dream, praying I would open them and Robin would begin telling a story of the sea, something far removed from these days that only grew darker and more complex.

I shook my head and felt Ellen behind me. She wrapped her arm about my shoulders, drawing me to her. I grew stiff. I could not begin to fathom what I had been told, even if I had suspected he dallied with the girl well before I left Scotland. But to live with her on *my* lands, on *my* finances! The depth of his brazen disre-spect boggled the mind.

"He's taken the rents from both Methven and Ettrick Forest," he revealed.

I offered a shaky sigh. "Oh, Robin . . . I am a great fool. No wonder I am mocked and laughed at. No wonder the lairds re-jected my proposal. God curse me for even thinking to name him co-regent!" I dipped my head in my hand, humiliation heating my cheeks. "I am fated to be the last to know, always. Such a fool, such a fool . . ."

"Not a fool," Robin amended. "A woman. Ye canna condemn yourself for falling in love. It happens to the best of us and always throws reason over the ledge."

"I did not love him, Robin," I confessed. "I loved love."

Robin lowered his eyes. "Ye canna be faulted for that, either."

I straightened myself in my seat, wiping my eyes and squaring my shoulders. "Well. I commend your courage for telling me," I told my friend. "Now I must decide what to do. . . ."

"Appeal to the lairds of the council for assistance; perhaps they can help restore the stolen funds," Robin suggested.

I nodded, taking this in. "Then what?" I asked in flat tones. I wished for him, for Ellen, for anybody to take the helm of my life and steer me away from danger. The thought of going it alone was exhausting and at once all I wanted to do was sleep.

"You're asking me?" Robin retorted. "Ye dinna want to know what I think, Your Grace."

"I do," I urged him. "I want you to be honest. Even if I disagree, I will respect your honesty. It is a trait found in few enough men."

Robin met my eyes with his own stormy green gaze. "Divorce him." His tone was hard.

Divorce, that most dishonorable of estates. I could only imagine how such a notion would be received. And yet already I was courting that most appealing of solutions. But was I bold enough, brave enough, to take such action, to name our marriage false before Christendom and the world?

Anger clenched my heart and twisted my gut.

Yes, a voice inside me declared. I was every bit bold and brave enough. I was a Tudor!

Before action against Angus could be taken, I summoned him to Stirling for a meeting alone in my presence chamber. I could not go forth if I knew there was any chance of reconciliation, if there was any possibility that the rumors were not true. His set jaw and hard eyes confirmed without a word that they were.

I remained calm; I would make it known who was queen and who was the overreaching subject.

"Why did you marry me, Angus?" I asked in quiet tones, dispensing with the irrelevant and getting to the heart of the matter.

"I could ask the same of you," he retorted, his tone high with tension.

"Answer the question," I urged with exaggerated patience. "Please. We've nothing to lose now; I know of your transgressions against me. Tell me the truth."

Angus sighed. "You want the truth? I married you because my grandfather wished it. He thought it would serve our family well. He was wrong. It only tore Scotland in two and took me from the woman I truly loved, causing me nothing but aggravation and turmoil."

The words struck me to the core. Even though I knew they rang with indisputable truth, my ears ached with each one. But I had asked him to be honest. I could commend him at the very least for that.

"So now you are reunited with your true love," I observed. "On my lands and with my money."

"Money and lands that are as much mine as yours," he spat. "I went through the dread ordeal of being your husband and gave you a daughter; it is the least you can allow me."

I would not permit myself to flinch at his brazen hatred.

"I answered your bloody question," Angus went on, irreverent as ever. "So answer mine. Why did you marry me? You did not love me any more than I loved you; of that I was reminded every time you referred to your husband and didn't mean me but King James. Every time you referred to me by title and never my own name." He laughed. "Did it ever occur to you to call me Archibald and not Angus?"

I considered this. He was right; I never could bring myself to call him by his given name. Why was it? Did the barrier of a cold title help insulate me against hurt I must have intuited as inevitable?

"I was lonely," I confessed. "I was afraid of ruling Scotland by myself and feared for the safety of my children. I wanted to feel admired; I wanted to feel loved." I had nothing to lose in my honesty, but how it shamed me to admit the paltriness of my own desires. "So," I went on with a sigh of resolve. "We have admitted we have no love of each other. Why not end this travesty? Why not appeal for a divorce?"

"I have always known you thought little of our daughter as compared to your golden sons," Angus seethed. "But for you to so easily bastardize her shames you beyond what words can express."

I knew there were ways around that but would not argue with him. I shook my head. "I see," was all I said to that. I swallowed an onset of tears; I'd be damned if I would allow them to fall in front of him. "I am sorry for everything; I need you to know that. It would have been easier, for baby Margaret's sake if no other, for us to behave with civility and peace. But if you refuse to, then all I can do is pray for you and wish you and . . . the lady of Traquair . . . well."

Angus's eyes softened a moment at this, before returning to murky depths of disdain. "Good-bye, Your Grace," he said in quiet tones, offering a swift bow.

"Good-bye . . . Archibald," I whispered, watching him retreat and, with him, any hopes of saving the marriage. We stood in direct opposition of what our Lord commanded. We entered into the sacred estate of marriage not with loving hearts desiring to work through any obstacle life threw our way as friends and lovers.

As far as I could see the sin was not in a divorce but in that very union. We had entered into marriage lightly.

✎ 17 ✎

A Woman of Scandal

My estate grew bleaker by the day. I had begun to pawn my jewels and was even dismissing my servants, hardworking gentlemen and ladies I could no longer afford to pay. It was humiliating and no way for a queen to live. Even my dear friend Robin condescended to loan me five hundred pounds of his own money.

" 'Tis a gift," he assured me, and with bowed head and flushing cheeks I was forced to accept.

"I am at my wits' end," I confided. "I have appealed my cause to my brother, to Wolsey and Albany, to the Pope, to everyone who could have influence. Henry and Catherine have written me, actually scolding me, saying I'd bring scandal to the Tudor name if I divorced Angus." I held up a letter from Henry, waving it in front of Robin before reading an excerpt. "This is what he says: 'Remember the divine ordinance of inseparable matrimony, first instituted in Paradise.' The thought of divorce to him is 'wicked delusions, inspired by the father of evil, whose malice alone could prompt you to leave your husband or unnaturally to stigmatize the fair daughter you had by him.' " With a disgusted click of the tongue, I tossed the letter aside on my writing table. "All this after Henry has a son with one of his mistresses! Hypocrites, all of them! And Angus refuses to make any terms; he sees it as his right to my land and income as my husband, despite the fact that he continues to live with that woman and the child she bore him openly on *my* lands of Newark!"

"It is a shameful ordeal," Robin conceded.

"Even my old friend Lord Dacre sides with Henry," I went on miserably. "If my daughter Margaret is bastardized by it, as Henry implies, it makes her less of an asset to him and Angus," I added, my tone thick with irritation. "She's fated to be a pawn, just like me. . . ." My tone grew soft with regret.

Robin shook his head. "One thing I will say, Your Grace, is ye've conducted yourself admirably. Every bit a queen."

My chest swelled at the compliment. "I have at least tried to be charitable to Angus," I agreed. "I will not speak ill of him or his mistress to anyone, at least in public," I added with a joyless chuckle. "His actions speak for themselves and I won't lower myself to acknowledge his overt sins. All I want is what's due me— my lands, my rents, and my dignity."

"All of which is more than deserved," Robin noted as he rose from his chair. "Keep being strong and keep your course," he advised me. "It may be a long struggle, but God will set things right. He knows all."

I took comfort in the words. Robin's piety never extended beyond the simple, as with my own, and that was what I appreciated. True piety, I believed, was meant to be modest. God knew our hearts, and no showy displays for the benefit of others would convince Him more than a simple, sincere appeal to Him.

So, along with my brother and Dacre, Albany and the Pope, I commended my cause to God and hoped He would, as Robin assured, see justice done.

I knew now that I had one thing to live for, beyond seeking love for myself, beyond seeking the restoration of my finances and rightful lands, and that was Little Jamie. He was my light, my hope, and my ultimate cause. I saw him as often as I could and was relieved to find he was growing more comfortable around me as we reacquainted ourselves. Though we were never allowed to be alone, I delighted in his quiet, scholarly nature. Though I told

Henry many a time that he resembled him, in truth it was my brother Arthur that Little Jamie brought to mind. For this I was grateful; the less he resembled Henry and perhaps even me, with our rashness and bold impetuosity, the better.

Angus, too, had access to my son and I resented this; I could not imagine the hate he filled his head with and prayed Little Jamie would remain strong in his own ideals, his own thoughts. The curse of child-kings was the influence of the men around them, and weak spirits often caved to their ambitions.

It was Little Jamie I kept in the forefront of my mind and heart as I continued to pursue my divorce. I wanted him to see his mother as strong and true, as someone who wouldn't allow herself to be used and abused. Thus by seeing me so I hoped it would inspire him to be the same.

Letters flew between me and the various lairds entrusted with my suit. Henry and Lord Dacre continued to chastise, even sending a friar to illustrate the errors of my ways, whom I indulged with politeness and privately scoffed at. Henry was reaching if he thought I could be moved by one of his men, especially if they didn't come with money.

And money, as Henry continually illustrated, was no issue for him. His glistening triumph, the meeting with King Francois of France called the Field of Cloth of Gold, was an extravagance beyond the imagination, dubbed such because of the extraordinary use of cloth of gold shimmering from every corner of the venue. The one advantage in my brother's friendship with France was my elevation in their eyes. King Francois, at my brother's urging, was now leaving Scotland to the Scots, which in turn I hoped would grant me more much-needed influence. So I congratulated my brother on his garish display and commended his tenacity. I had little use for Francois as it were.

There was only one jewel that I needed plucked from the crown of France . . . and that was the Duke of Albany.

Angus was doing nothing to further his cause. At a skirmish that had been called Cleanse the Causeway, he instigated an attack against the Hamiltons, the clan of whom the Earl of Arran was head. Their support, along with Robin Barton's, of the Leith merchants over the burgesses of Edinburgh incensed Angus and the ensuing violence killed the Earl of Arran's brother along with seventy men. This, and the fact that Angus was seizing offices for himself and his family, was enough to incur resentment among the other lairds.

Though I was loathe to see anyone hurt, I could not help but delight over Angus's sabotaging of himself. It was the perfect time for Albany, whom I would welcome as an ally and no longer an enemy, to return to Scotland.

Albany came in November of that year 1521, and again I was struck by his elegance, his cool demeanor, and his tactful yet decisive statesmanship. The Constable of Edinburgh handed him the keys to the castle upon his arrival, reminiscent of the days I urged my Little Jamie to do the same, but Albany, ever the gentleman, handed them right back.

After giving him time to settle in his office once more, I began to meet with Albany to discuss my cause. I was always in my finest. On the wintry afternoon that everything changed, I met him in a deep blue velvet gown trimmed with soft gray fox fur and kirtle of gray damask, complemented with a simple strand of pearls I wore in memory of my Jamie. The gaze of appreciation I noted in Albany's deep slate eyes was not lost on me.

We sought the refuge of his privy chamber, closeted from the spying eyes and ears that surrounded us. I now knew he served as my only hope, not only for my cause but also for Little Jamie's, that Albany's power could serve as his best protection, and better to work with great power than against it.

"Madam," he began. He seemed uncomfortable today, shifting in his chair, crossing and uncrossing his legs. Something was on his mind. We sat before a crackling fire drinking hot spiced wine and I smiled at the sound of his melodic voice. "About the baby . . ." he went on; his voice was low. "About the Duke of Ross . . . you have to know that I would never have wished him ill nor had any foul plot inflicted upon him."

A lump rose in my throat; it still pained me to think of baby

Alexander's death, all these years later. It was clear it still pained Albany as well.

"I know that, Jehan," I said, making a point of addressing him by the name he preferred. "In truth, though I may have said it in anger before you even came to Scotland in the first place, I have never likened you to a usurper. Yours is not a merry duty; it will be its most challenging now."

Albany nodded. "And the Earl of Angus," he went on. "You are determined to appeal to Rome?"

I nodded. "I am. God forgive me, but it is the only way. We canna live like this. And it is the height of injustice that he should be allowed my rents and my lands. I could afford to give him one residence; I won't begrudge him that. But everything? No," I added with an emphatic shake of the head.

"I am here for you," Albany assured me, and no words were sweeter. "I regard it as a debt," he explained, assuaging my anxiety over a possible betrayal. "You need to understand that Scotland has always been my first priority since taking on the regency. It is to maintain the peace that I have been compelled to the decisions I have, not as any personal offense to you or your right as mother to your children."

"I do understand," I admitted. "I have not always agreed and I have not always liked it. But we are statesmen. And I do understand the sacrifices and agonizing decisions that such a role entails."

"More than most, I imagine," Albany ventured, his eyes soft. "As to our current situation, you should be informed that I have removed Gavin Douglas from Dunkeld."

"He has done nothing but abuse the generosity and endorsements I gave him in such good faith," I muttered, irritated that the man I had admired and called friend also served to be as much a traitor as his nephew Angus.

Albany nodded in agreement. "He has sought refuge at the court of your brother."

I sighed in exasperation. "Of course he would."

"The Douglases have been removed from their posts. And for the moment you may not have to worry about your lands and rents," Albany went on with a note of languid cheer. "Angus is in exile. He has fled to France."

"Ironic," I observed with a smile, marveling at all Albany had accomplished in such a short time. "You have switched places, it seems."

Albany lowered his eyes at this, and I flushed. I had not meant it to be interpreted in a flirtatious manner . . . yet I wouldn't *not* let his mind wander in such vein either. What was I thinking? Albany was my friend; I could see that now. I was not about to lose a friend for sake of attraction, not ever again. And yet, for whatever my womanly wiles were worth, dull and dowdy though they may be now, I was not averse to utilizing them for whatever favor I could gain.

"Thank you for all you have done," I said in sincerity, hoping to offset the awkward moment.

"Do not thank me yet," Albany cautioned with a smile. "Your brother is far from pleased. I have received a letter from him; he accuses me of pretending to the throne, of abusing and manipulating you, and, of course, of unlawfully gaining custody of His Grace. He has all but declared war, madam."

I shielded my mouth with my hand a moment, repressing a gasp. "I should have known. He sent Clarencieux King of Arms to scold me. There are the most wicked rumors. . . ." I was ashamed to name them. It was being said that Albany and I were lovers. Part of me found I was disappointed that, for once, the rumors were not true. But being thus, I was indignant. I never liked rumors even when based on truth. That my dignity and honor should be so besmirched without any right was infuriating.

"I have heard the rumors," Albany said. "Let them think what they will; they will find enough fuel for their hatred regardless of what we do. Keep pressing forth, doing what you feel God is steering you to do. I truly believe that right always wins out in the end. It may take a while. Sometimes the end isn't even in our lifetime. But I do believe that." His eyes revealed the conviction of his words and I admired him more for it.

"I wish I had your optimism," I confessed. "It always amazes me how people regard matters of faith and life. We all endure the same tragedies, yet some of us turn to coldness, to doubt, while others, like you, retain a kindness and purity of heart that I envy."

"I would not say you are cold," Albany assured me.

"I dinna know what I am now," I admitted, bowing my head, amazed to be revealing my soul to this man. "I find myself swinging on the pendulum of extremes. Some days I hate the world and the people in it; other days I am filled with hope and charity."

"Be assured, madam, whatever you are," Albany said, "I would not have you any other way."

My eyes stung with tears at the simple sweetness of the sentiment. I met his soft gaze and in it found no sense of regret or unease in his confession.

And I loved him for it.

Whatever I may have felt for Albany, there would be no addressing it. I would be chaste and honorable; I would never fall to the side of the rumors and give my brother and those who spread such wickedness the satisfaction of seeing them made true. The fondness I bore Albany was pure; he would be one of the only men in my life who could in truth be described as noble. And I wanted to keep it that way.

We had enough to worry about without complicating our friendship with the joys of the flesh. And yet there were days when we would stroll the grounds together, arm in arm, and I found myself stumbling just so he would help me right myself. It was these small things that sustained me—his touch, his voice, his low, subtle laughter, his company. And when we weren't caught up in the tensions of the realm, which was rare, we took time to take in a few of the things we both enjoyed: music, hawking, riding. Albany was competent at all three and especially gifted in music.

If I close my eyes now, I can still see Albany standing straight and rigid before the window, hands linked behind his back as he sang a French ballad, his low baritone resonating through my body like the hum of a bell. I would watch him, how he closed his eyes, feeling the music, letting it carry him away from this wretched place. No part of him would move, save his lips and his eyes when he sang, and yet never had I witnessed a performance more filled with conviction and emotion than his. Not even my talented Jamie or brother, Henry, was as gifted as this duke. Even I, with my appreciation for music and performing, would not dare to sing when Albany did. It would seem, somehow, disrespectful and intrusive on a moment too beautiful to last. It was almost holy.

Albany did not sing often; in truth, in those days we did not have much to sing about, but I would sit, enthralled, during those times when he did treat me to his songs.

Albany may have been the only person I had ever known to make me appreciate anything around me. I had been rushing through life, just trying to get to the next day, hoping things would be better, and had never slowed to dwell in the moments I did have.

One afternoon when we took rare bits of leisure, I was impatient with my hawk. We were hoping to hunt for some small game and it seemed to me my hawk was taking its sweet time. I stamped my foot and clicked my tongue in exasperation.

"Madam. Stop," Albany said, coming behind me and resting his hands gently on my shoulders. "Look up. Enjoy this moment. Watch how graceful the bird flies; look at his command over the wind. Look at the trees, at their majestic stillness. Listen to the sounds of the forest. Take it in."

"My seventh day," I murmured, thinking of Henry and that day long ago when we bid each other farewell when first I came to Scotland, the good-bye he no longer recalled but that was forever etched in my memory. "When I was little, my brother told me whenever being queen was too much, that I should close my eyes and be still, and take a seventh day, where we would be waiting for each other to lend comfort and strength."

"A lovely sentiment," Albany observed. "There are seventh days all around, those moments of calm and tranquility we must seize because there are very few times when life is not too much."

I leaned back against his chest. The world seemed to pause. The trees indeed were silent giants standing guard over their woodland subjects. The hawk soaring above glided across the sky with no effort at all. Then all at once I could not take any of those things in anymore. All I could appreciate was the beating of his heart, his hands on my shoulders, his warm breath against my neck.

Oh, Albany, Albany, had things only been different . . .

My brother meant for war. Gavin Douglas wasted no time in fueling his anger, telling Henry that among Albany's infamous offenses, he manipulated me into my desire to divorce Angus, stole from the treasury, sold off religious offices, and dressed Little Jamie shabbily, to boot! It would have been laughable had Scotland not been in such danger.

As winter progressed, Clarencieux King of Arms spent his time between the courts of my brother and me, relaying our mutual displeasure to each other. Henry also accused Albany of coercing me to respond to his letters in the sure, strong tone I had adopted in my correspondence with him. I assured him, through the poor messenger, that this was not the case, but I knew Henry would believe whatever suited his purposes at the time, and the affair became tedious and exhausting.

Even the Estates of Scotland had assured Clarencieux in a formal declaration that Albany was the lawful governor and tutor to Little Jamie. It was good to have them on my side once again. My side was the king's side and it was he who was most important, he who must not lose himself in these delicate dances of power.

The steps of the dance grew more complex by the hour.

"Ellen, I am confused," I confessed to my most faithful maid, who kept me company in my apartments. I was too anxious to sew, but Ellen, with her calm elegance, worked on a tapestry that would feature a scene of birds—doves, hawks, and eagles, all flying together, as if to achieve one aim. It captured all of my hopes for England and Scotland, to fly their banners together in peace.

"Why are you confused, Your Grace?" Ellen asked, her musical voice calming as a ballad.

"I am torn between my brother and Albany," I told her. "For the sake of the king, England and Scotland *must* be at peace, and it is to that aim I am loyal, more so than to any one man. They may interpret things differently," I added with a sigh. "But my goal is peace, however I can attain it, for a stable realm for my son."

"It is a worthy goal," Ellen assured me.

"But how to achieve it without seeming to betray everyone I lo—I am bound to?" I shook my head. "I rode to Carlisle with Albany; I appealed to Lord Dacre myself. Our army was too afraid of another Flodden to attack and Dacre called for a truce. I believe he thought our forces larger than they were. I urged my brother Henry to offer a five-year peace and he did—can you imagine, five years of peace? In that five years so much good could be accomplished! It could have led to another five years, and another after that!" I smiled at the thought, now lost to me as all my other dreams had been. "But the lairds of Scotland renewed the Auld Alliance with France and will have no peace with England. And I am the sister of Henry, so I am the enemy. The Borders are ravaged and I am to blame. I report to Henry and to Albany; I betray both in the hopes that peace might be gained for all. There are times when I am unfair to both; I make Albany sound worse than he is to Henry, and the same of Henry to Albany. I feel if I please everyone, if I tell them what they want to hear, then both will strive for peace more ardently."

"Who, then, are you loyal to?" Ellen asked. The question startled me.

"The king, to Little Jamie," I answered, as if it were obvious. "And I will do whatever it takes to secure his realm. Let them call me fickle and changeable. They do not know what it's like to be mother of a king. They do not know what it is like to be me."

"Are you not afraid that if you continue to play both sides all will turn against you in the end?" Ellen asked. She was by far the only person who could afford such audacity; she knew I would forgive her anything. She, more than any adviser or counselor, gave my conscience a voice and, with her quiet prompting, forced me to examine my innermost heart.

"Yes," I told her in truth. "I am afraid of that."

"But if all you say is true, and I do not doubt your word, Your

Grace, then you are sure of your course and are not in truth confused at all," Ellen pointed out.

I laughed at her reasoning. It was true. "I suppose I'm not," I agreed. I offered another long-suffering sigh. "Perhaps then it is approval I seek." My tone was wistful.

"Whose?" Ellen prodded. "Surely not mine. With what little influence I have, you canna expect to gain anything by my endorsement."

"Maybe that is exactly why I seek it," I said. "Because you have nothing to lose and nothing to gain. You simply know what is right and what is not. And I need to know from you, from someone who isn't in the thick of it, if what I am doing is right." My heart pounded. I realized I put more store in her opinion than anyone else's in my life. "Do you . . . do you think that I am right in what I do, Ellen?"

"You want the truth." It was not a question. I nodded, urging her to speak. To my anguish, Ellen shook her head. "I do not think it is right, Your Grace, if you will forgive me. I think someday you will have to choose a side, or you will lose the respect of both."

I nodded again, taking in her words, knowing she was right and knowing with as much certainty that what she was asking me to do was impossible.

Ultimately, her opinion, as I knew it would, changed nothing.

Maybe that, too, is why I sought it.

❧ 18 ❧

The Crown of Flames

"I am leaving for France," Albany told me. This time he called upon me and my heart stirred as it always did at the sight of him, though he appeared weary and careworn. "They demand to know what happened, why we lost control at the Border. It is my hope to return with more men and more arms."

I nodded. "I expected so."

"Did you?" he asked me. "Because I do not know what to expect from you, madam." Albany's tone revealed a genuine sense of hurt. "I know you keep the English abreast of our military situation, just as you keep us abreast of theirs." His slate gray eyes made an appeal his words would not.

"When I married King James," I began, reaching out across my writing table to take Albany's slim hand in mine. I found in it a ready, strong grasp. "When I married the king, my father told me to remain a daughter to England before I was a wife to Scotland. Ever since I have endeavored to be both. But my father never prepared me for what being a mother to Scotland would be like, nor the sister to England. Everything has changed, except one thing: I was meant to bring peace between both kingdoms." I bowed my head, still holding the duke's hand. "To that end I will work, by whatever means necessary."

Albany nodded. "Then I suppose this is no more than I should expect. Thank you, at least, for your honesty." There was a sense of mourning in his tone. He sighed; it was a warrior's sigh, one of pure exhaustion mingling with the dread of more battles to come.

"Be safe, Jehan," I urged, squeezing his hand.

He disengaged, reaching up to cup my cheek. His eyes, those anguished stormy orbs, were the saddest I had ever seen. I leaned into his hand, reveling in the closeness. His lips parted as if to speak, but no words ever came. He dropped his hand. I longed to seize it, to press it to my cheek once more, to take him in my arms, anything that would assuage his grief and my own for the impossible position I now found myself in.

But he turned. And walked away.

It was a sight I was growing used to from the men in my life.

No sooner did Albany leave than I was struck with smallpox. My skin was on fire, my throat raw, and welts made itching, festering roses upon my flesh. My strength was sapped, reminiscent of my many births, yet there was no joyful end to reward me for this hell. Ellen braved tending me, but most of the court stayed away for fear of contagion. Imprisoned in fitful slumber, I gave way once again to the dread blackness that overcame me so many times before. . . .

All is smoke. I am running through it; it is so thick, filling my lungs, burning my eyes. . . . Jamie appears, my Jamie! I am here, Jamie! Oh, Jamie, how I have longed for your direction. . . . But as he reaches me it is not Jamie I see, but Albany. I reach out to him only for him to fade into the smoke, curling around him like the fingers of a dragon's whisper. Angus appears then, his lips twisted into his confident smirk. I stretch my arms out only for him to become enveloped in the dusky haze and at once Angus transforms into old Bell-the-Cat. I smile at my beloved councilor in greeting as he is enveloped in smoke, taken from me again.

At once my father is there. The smoke that swirls around us dissipates at once and we are bathed in blinding white light. He is stretching his arms out, holding in his hands a crown of fire. Emblazoned upon it is a thistle entwined with a Tudor rose.

"This is who you are," Father says.

"I dinna want it!" I cry. "I want a home, a husband, and a family. Please give it to someone else!"

Father shakes his head, smiling as he is absorbed into the light, part of its brilliance, and I am alone.

All that remains is the flaming crown. . . .

As my strength ebbed back into me, a slow tide of resilience I came to rely upon throughout my life, messages about the state of the realm were relayed to me. I found them far more preferable than the messages from the beyond, no matter how discouraging they were.

Henry had sent his most able soldier, the Earl of Surrey, Thomas Howard, to the Borders. It was clear Surrey did not regard me as his former niece anymore. I was something to be taken care of, and not in the nurturing sense. I was a matter to be dealt with. Surrey was as changeable as anyone, being a Howard. I knew that family switched allegiances to whoever wore the crown at the time, from Edward IV to Richard III and then to my noble father. They set their sights, always high, accordingly. In this, I suppose, we were alike but were both reluctant to admit it.

Surrey laid waste to the Borders with more ferocity than ever and raided the town of Kelso, burning homes and ravaging the land. Though I was saddened at the devastation, I reminded Surrey that if he was planning to make any impression on the Scots lairds, it was them he must attack at Edinburgh. The loss of life of the peasants on the Borders mattered little to them. But what would motivate a Scots noble more than an attack on his homeland was the common persuader of most men: money.

In turn, Surrey urged me to view my son, now eleven, as a king near his majority. It was time that Little Jamie sued for peace with his uncle in England himself. Backed by Henry's strength and my son's new independence, I would be viewed with more favor from the people.

Despite a passionate speech Little Jamie wrote himself being read before Parliament at the Tolbooth, which I drew enough strength to attend and listened to with a chest near bursting with pride, his pleas for peace with England fell upon deaf ears. All that was granted him was new guardians and more freedom to hunt and hawk around Stirling.

Surrey's response to the lairds' decision was to blow up the abbey at Jedburgh with gunpowder and burn the town. It was 20 September, and Albany had returned from France with the promised men and munitions. There was hope for a victory yet, and my allegiance would be with the victor. Despite Ellen's caution and Albany's regret, I remained a good sister and told the English of Albany's forces, of his magazines, his cannon, and his weaponry. If my lot must be cast with the English, I would not let them go into battle in ignorance.

Albany marched on Wark Castle on a day as stormy as his eyes, with Frenchmen as his front line, dragging their cannon through the mud and the muck. As the weather escalated into a violent blizzard, Albany and his army were forced to an understated retreat.

My poor gallant duke had lost. And thus I knew before long I would lose him, too.

Despite the instability of the realm, I was afforded a few delights, chief among them being able to keep company with my Little Jamie at Stirling. I was at last able to stay with my son and I relished it. Little Jamie, the reason I lived, was a lad to do a mother proud. He was born to be king; it emanated from him, it *was* him. He was as talented in music as his father and me, as athletic as his uncle Henry (with far more grace and cool, self-assured elegance), and as studious as his uncle Arthur. He was regal, growing handsome, and I knew deserved to reign in his majority sooner than expected. It was as if he knew his would be a more challenging lot than that of most kings more fortunate to reign at a more suitable age and somehow his mind and body adapted, maturing beyond his years; perhaps it was in his breeding.

We often spent time in his apartments with his tutor David Lindsay, a faithful friend who had known Little Jamie since he was a bairn. There we would sing and play games; Little Jamie would recite his lessons, impressing me with his memorization and insightful perspective on the realm.

There, with his little court, we indulged in one of my favorite pastimes: singing. I strummed my lute and sang to him the ballads his father taught me and some from home. Little Jamie had a clear, strong voice and was as fast a learner in verse as anything, and I loved harmonizing with him.

One afternoon after I finished one such ballad called "Edward," I was treated to a hearty round of clapping by the King's Carver, young Henry Stewart.

"That was amazing, Your Grace!" he blurted, his lips spreading into a full smile, revealing bright, straight white teeth. He ran a hand through his tousled blond locks, flushing at the breaking of protocol.

"You seem surprised, Master Stewart," I quipped, unbothered by the breach in etiquette. "Did you not know we could sing?"

His tanned cheeks flushed a deeper shade of rose. It was rather endearing. "I did not, Your Grace, if you'll pardon me. I have never been here when you and His Grace were singing; this is the first time I have heard you. Your voice is . . . well, I already said, it is amazing!"

I laughed at his awkwardness. "Do you sing?"

"I do," he admitted.

"He does sing, Mother," Little Jamie informed me. "Quite well; We have heard him when We go riding."

"You ride with Master Stewart?" I asked; I had thought I knew all of my son's companions and this surprised me.

"Why, yes," Little Jamie said. "His company delights Us."

I smiled at this. "Well, join us in a song, won't you?" I invited. "I adore music; it is a Tudor weakness."

"Music is never a weakness," Henry Stewart ventured. There was something in his boldness that charmed me. It wasn't cocky, like Angus. It was unbridled, innocent. Young. "Music pulls us through life!"

I laughed again. His wide blue eyes sparkled with merriment.

He did not look at me as if I was stout and scarred from the ravages of smallpox. I cannot place how he looked at me. But I welcomed it. I thought his company was going to delight me, too.

My joys were predicated by pain, always. In this, I was kept in check, I suppose, by God, by my son's government. By myself. I was enjoying my time with my son and my newfound friend, Henry Stewart. But in these gains was a loss, a loss I foresaw but never prepared for.

Albany was getting his longed-for wish.

He was returning to France.

Again I welcomed him into my chambers while he said his farewells. Though he was still invested as regent, his powers would be challenged when he was not in the kingdom, as they always were. He knew it and so did I. But the advantages of this would not be dwelled upon as yet.

Now was not a time for scheming and strategy. Now was a time for good-bye.

I greeted him wearing a soft mauve velvet gown with a cream satin kirtle. I would never tire of velvet; it was my favorite material and suited my complexion, softening it, and I could almost believe my scars escaped notice. I felt beautiful in velvet and I needed to feel beautiful; there were few enough other pleasures afforded me.

"You look exhausted," I observed of my old friend, gesturing for him to take a seat in one of my fine velvet plush chairs before my warm fire. We had spent many a long afternoon in front of crackling fires, talking and sipping wine. It should not change now, even if it was his last visit.

"I am," he confessed, in his handsome low voice. He leaned his chin in his hand, regarding me with soft eyes. "I once said that I'd rather have my legs broken than return here," he added with a slight chuckle that revealed no humor.

"I have felt the same," I said. "But Scotland was our destiny, it seems. We canna fight her, so we fight for her."

"Strange, isn't it?" he returned. "And now I am leaving at last. My wish will be realized. I will serve France in the capacity I am needed as I hoped to do. And yet I am sad."

"Why sad, my lord?"

"For having to leave you," he admitted, his voice soft as an angel feather. My heart lurched. Tears stung my eyes. I blinked them away.

"Oh, my dear lord, why now? Why tell me now?" I breathed.

"Whom would it have served to tell you before?" he challenged. He sighed. "You not yet rid of Angus, my popularity here waning by the hour. You had bigger things to worry after and so did I. We would have complicated it and neither of us needed more complications."

"I would have been too much for you," I assured him, attempting to lighten the moment with humor. "As I always am. You would have been unfaithful and I could not have borne it. Not from you, whom I esteem as the finest and noblest of gentlemen."

"It isn't that you would have been too much," Albany told me. "It is just that you never found a man who was enough for you."

I smiled at this. "How cruel is life," I said, feeling it a pointless observation. We knew well how cruel life was, better than many. "So that is why everyone leaves," I added, my tone thoughtful. "Because they are not enough and I am too much."

"A man needs to feel he is like the king of something," Albany told me. "A peasant, the king of his hearth, of his fields . . . A queen needs a king and nothing less. A lesser man cannot bear the competition with the kings who surround you—Henry and James. He will become undone by his inferiority, even if he does not mean to be."

Ellen had once told me the same, in a manner of speaking. As had my father. And my Jamie . . .

"I suppose I expected more from those I loved," I said. "I wanted to be viewed as a wife, not a queen."

"You, madam, are always a queen," Albany said with a slight chuckle. "You cannot even pretend to be otherwise. And," he added, tilting one of his well-sculpted brows, "beware of expectations. They ruin us. When we expect anything of anyone, we are asking them to fail."

"Do I expect too much, then, in hoping a man can be faithful to me?" I asked, feeling wretched, cursing my vulnerability revealed so naked and raw before this man.

Albany shook his head. "I daresay, madam, you should not expect faithfulness, friendship, or anything at all. But if you get it, treat it as a fleeting gift, the rarest of jewels, as you have been to me. A rare, fiery jewel." He rose, approaching me and reaching out to tuck a coppery lock that had strayed from my hood behind my ear.

"I am rare enough to admire from afar, but too fiery to keep," I said brokenly, clinging to his hand, pressing it to my cheek.

"Maybe that is what makes you shine above the rest," he told me.

I looked up, meeting his dove gray gaze, unable to hide the tears welling in my eyes. "I would rather be ordinary. A pearl or a diamond," I said, fingering the strand of pearls I wore forever about my neck.

"Pearls are for mourning, and diamonds are hard and unfeeling," Albany told me.

"But people love them," I countered. "And people keep them."

"I will keep you." Albany's voice was soft as he laid a hand across his breast. "I will keep you here."

It would have been any courtier's perfect line, but from Albany it rang with the utmost sincerity.

I wanted to beg him to stay, to marry me, and promise him we could rule together. He was closer to a king as a duke than an earl; he would not compete with Henry or Little Jamie, he would rule by my side. But I knew better than that. I would never take his dream of returning home to France away from him. I would not disgrace myself or our friendship with such pleas.

I would let him go.

Albany stooped down, tilting my chin up with his fingertips. With the greatest gentleness, he leaned in, pressing his lips to mine in a warm, soft kiss. There was no lust in it; it embodied our respect, our friendship, our honor.

Long after Albany departed I sat before my fire, my hand pressed to my lips, clinging to the moment.

It was the sweetest kiss I had ever received.

*   *   *

If Henry and I agreed on anything, and we seldom did, it was that Little Jamie's minority should be ended. It was time he ruled as king in full; it would save him from the ambitions of the men who surrounded him and perhaps compel Scotland to further solidarity. Henry's letters were full of grand schemes. He wished to break his daughter the Princess Mary's betrothal to the Emperor Charles V and instead forge an alliance between her and my son. Though I considered this, I was also aware any betrothal between the cousins would offend France greatly, and I never knew when I would need France as an ally.

I mulled this and other things over in the company of Little Jamie and Henry Stewart, whom I called Harry. I could not bear to address him as I did my brother; while many called him Harry, I never had. Henry was my brother. Harry was my friend.

I began to spend more time with this young Harry, maybe to distract myself from pondering what might have been with Albany and remembering what had been with Angus. Or maybe I was set on proving I could still capture the heart of someone handsome and virile. Harry was six years my junior, but the age difference mattered little; we enjoyed each other, and the rapport he had with Little Jamie was genuine. I could not have asked for more. We began to ride together, hawk together, sing and read together, sharing our time and meals, most often with the king, but sometimes not. When I needed to discuss the matters of Little Jamie's future, I preferred Harry alone.

"I canna imagine wedding him to Mary," I told Harry one evening as we took a quiet supper in my apartments of game hens in a cream sauce, with sweet wine, rich cheeses, and bread to accompany them. "If I agreed to such a union, Henry would control them both to suit his own ends and I could not bear that. Little Jamie needs to stand on his own, which is why it is vital that his minority be ended."

Harry laughed at this.

"What's so funny?" I asked, irritated that such a serious matter should be scoffed at.

"Nothing funny, Your Grace," Harry said, his full mouth still spread into a wide grin. "It's just that if you want His Grace's minority to end, should you not desist in calling him 'Little Jamie'? I do not think it makes him feel very . . . manly."

I began to laugh as well at the thought. "I suppose I've never thought of him any other way," I admitted. "I never will," I added softly. "He will always be my little one. But you are right. I should call him Jamie now . . . Jamie. . . ." I lowered my eyes as an image of my late husband, the other Jamie, the only Jamie, flashed in my heart.

"I think he'll appreciate it," Harry said. If he had read my wistfulness, he did not show it, and I was grateful to him.

"He confides in you, doesn't he?" I asked, with a knowing smirk. "He put you up to this suggestion, did he not?"

"He . . . may have," Harry responded, a mischievous smile on his own lips.

"I am glad he found someone he can trust," I said in earnest. "He has had few enough in his life, men he could count on and admire."

"I am a lowly man," Harry said. "I am unworthy of his admiration. But I am very content for his friendship, however he esteems me."

"He holds you in high esteem," I said. "Which, of course, inspires me to do the same."

"Again, I am unworthy," he said. "You must know I hold you in high esteem as well."

I laughed. "Oh, I can almost hear it. As 'more than a queen, as a woman as well,' isn't that right?" I challenged.

Harry furrowed his brow at this. "I do not think I could ever see you as anything but a queen, Your Grace. A woman, of course. But you are a queen and I would be a fool to consider you as other women."

I considered this. It was honest and, being that it was a rare enough trait in men, I relished it.

"Could you see yourself loving a queen, then?" I asked him, cursing myself for revealing my feelings before he did, yet not caring. I had nothing to lose anymore; I had already lost the respect of great nations, what did it matter if I lost his?

"I already do," Harry said, his tone matter-of-fact.

"Do you?" I asked. "In what respect, then? As the mother of your sovereign or something more? All the time we spend in each other's company and with Jamie . . . why do you do it? You could spend time with Jamie without my company. Why seek me out? Ambition?"

"I am ambitious," Harry admitted. "I admit that I want to raise my station in life. Who doesn't? Yet do I love you as more than the king's mother? Of course." His tone was so offhanded, as though he were revealing things I should see as obvious, that I laughed. He was without condescension; it was as if he seemed surprised I had not already come to the same conclusions.

"So if I raised you high above the rest," I went on, "you would enjoy that, wouldn't you?"

"Who wouldn't?" Harry returned again. "I told you I have aspirations for my future; I won't lie. But I think, if I may be bold, that you are afraid that I wish to intertwine my aspirations with notions of romantic love with you, when in fact that is not so." He tossed his head a moment, his unruly blond hair flipping up over his eyes and to the side, revealing his earnest, engaging blue gaze. "There are many ways a man can elevate himself. I keep company with the king; I could of course wait for him to promote me. I do not need to romance his mother. I spend time with you because I like you."

"Why?" I asked, uncaring as to whether I sounded vain or not. "I am far from a fair young maiden. I am thirty-five years old. You are twenty-nine. You could have anyone."

"So could you," he returned. "You are a queen and a Tudor princess. Could you not suit a king, a wealthy duke?" I did not know if he implied Albany but chose not to acknowledge it if he did. "Why would you want a man of low station such as me?"

"Because I like you," I said. "I enjoy being together. I like that you are honest and full of life; I like that you are kind to my son, that you always treat us with respect. I like that you are fun."

"I feel the same," Harry said. "You never care what anyone thinks; you say what you want and do what you want. You ride well; you are good with the bow; you have a beautiful voice; you are clearly strong and intelligent. I like those things about you."

His manner lacked a courtier's charm; he was not like Angus, full of fair words and dramatic declarations. He was simple; he was honest. And it was rare to be genuinely liked by someone, rather than tolerated for my station under a thin veil of respect.

"I find that I am often too much for a common man," I warned. "I have been told only a king should love me. And even so, it is rare to find faithfulness in a king let alone a man of lower station. I have been much humiliated in my life, as well you know after Angus's betrayal. I do not know if it is because being married to a queen was too much for him, or if it is simply man's nature. But given that I have been with a king and with a great laird and was betrayed just the same, I will venture it is the latter. So. I won't expect you to be faithful, Harry. All I expect is that you do not humiliate me publicly."

"What are you asking of me, Your Grace?" Harry's tone was soft.

"I am asking you," I began as I rose from my seat at the dining table, rounding the corner to take his hands in mine, "to call me Margaret."

Harry squeezed my hands. "Margaret . . . what do you want of me?"

"Just you," I said, pulling him up. With Harry I wasn't a queen teetering on old age, a queen without power, without prospect. I was desirable and daring; I was taking control and I liked it.

Harry rose and wrapped his arms about my waist as I wrapped mine about his neck.

"Just you," I whispered as I drew him toward me in a kiss that, if not passionate, was enjoyable.

And that was all I wanted. To enjoy the company and affections of a man; to feel . . . *alive*.

With Harry, for a time, I did.

"It seems Angus has fled to my brother's court," I told Harry one evening after receiving the disturbing series of dispatches from my brother that revealed his plans.

Harry was naked from the waist up and I admired his torso, rippling with lean muscle as he leaned on his elbow in my bed. I lay next to him, my long coppery locks spilling over my creamy shoulders, reading my brother's letters.

"He has the audacity to like Angus," I spat, disgusted with Henry's fickle ways. "He wants to send him back here for a reconciliation, that we might back Jamie in his rule together when his minority is ended."

"You aren't considering it, are you?" Harry raised his brows.

"Why? Do you fear losing me?" I asked, not without a trace of delight. The thought that he would worry about our affair ending pleased me somewhat.

"Of course I do," Harry said. "I do not know where we are going, but I am enjoying it."

"Well, you do not have to fear," I assured him in sugared tones. "I will not reconcile with Angus, no matter what Henry dangles before me. He has no idea the machinations of Scotsmen's hearts. To elevate the Douglases again would turn clan against clan again and upset the balance of power."

"Power that should belong solely to His Grace," Harry said.

"Exactly," I agreed, touched that he should recognize it as well and not include himself in that balance as Angus would have done. Angus would have said the power should belong to "us." Meaning him and Jamie, not him and me. Me he would have flattered till his ends were met, then discarded me as he had countless times before. Oh, how wonderful it was that Harry was not such a man!

"I have written to Henry," I went on. "I have told him my fears and urged him to detain Angus. I will not have great jealousies stirred up once again and destroy the allegiances I have worked so hard for." I sighed. "We need to get Jamie away from Stirling, away from his French guards. We will take him to Edinburgh and there the minority will be officially ended. Even Lord Hamilton, the Earl of Arran, agrees."

"Then we shall do it," Harry said. "And I will help you however I can."

"I know you will," I said, and I did. "But dinna do it for me,

Harry. Do it for Jamie. Whatever happens to us, I never want you to lose your affection and allegiance to him."

"He is my king, Margaret," Harry assured me. "No matter what happens, I will never lose sight of that."

Somehow I knew he spoke true. Whatever confidence I had, or lack thereof, in a happy, lasting future with Harry, I knew he meant my son well.

I was learning, as Albany had instructed, to let go of expectations. There was only to think of Jamie's happiness and safety. What little pleasures I could steal for myself meantime, I would. But none would eclipse what mattered most and that was Jamie. And for whatever Harry would prove himself to be, he was at my side knowing that.

That was all I needed.

19

The Mothers of Kings

We rode with Jamie into Edinburgh, where he was invested with the sword, scepter, and crown. He was king as he was meant to be. Acknowledged before his peers as a man, despite being a lad of twelve. Henry lent to me the support of Thomas Howard, the newly styled Duke of Norfolk, elevated from Earl of Surrey upon his father's death. With him and his men just beyond the Border, the statement of the might that backed the decision to invest Jamie with his full powers of state was made clear. Norfolk was the son of the victor of Flodden. What destruction a Howard could wreak upon Scotland was now legendary. No one would cross me now.

When Jamie presided over his first council, it was decided that Albany's regency would officially draw to an end. Only Lord Chancellor Beaton, the Archbishop of St. Andrews, objected, for which he was imprisoned. I would not have anyone threaten my son's power. He was king now; no one would rule over him, not even my dear Albany. Jamie's power must be felt and respected; if the only way was out of fear, then so be it.

Henry showered Jamie with gifts for his elevation to power, creating him a member of the elite Order of the Garter. He sent Archdeacon Thomas Magnus with five cartloads of treasure. In my apartments we ogled the fine gifts—beautiful lengths of cloth of gold and Jamie's favorite, a sword inlaid with the finest jewels and gems.

"Look, Mother! En garde!" Jamie cried as he pretended to wield the sword, slicing it through the air with a great *whooshing* sound. I laughed at the sparkle lighting Jamie's often earnest eyes. He had seen so much in his short life; to watch him play with a sword as a young lad should clenched my throat with tears.

"Your uncle Henry thinks very highly of you," I told Jamie. "Do you like your presents, darling?"

"Very much," Jamie said, still gawking at his sword, turning it over and over in his hands to watch the light catch the shimmering rubies and emeralds flashing from its hilt.

"Why not take your sword and show Davie?" I suggested, referring to his tutor David Lindsay.

"I will accompany him," Harry offered, and I nodded my gratitude, watching my two favorite people retreat companionably, leaving me alone with Magnus.

"Our brother is very generous," I said to the archdeacon. "What news have you brought with these fine gifts?"

"His Majesty wishes to remind Your Grace of the proposal of marriage he has offered between the Princess Mary and His Young Grace," Magnus informed me.

"His Majesty!" I laughed. I had forgotten that Henry fancied such glorified styling. I rather liked it and noted to call Jamie the same.

As to the marriage proposal, I began to reconsider. It would not be unfavorable, though it threatened to present obstacles in the future. Yet the peace it could create with England, which was my purpose in life other than being Jamie's mother, was a tantalizing prospect. Jamie and Mary's children would be heirs to both thrones. . . . A united England and Scotland. Was it possible? Would my father's prophecy come true through them?

"Thank Our brother for his generous offer," I told Magnus. "It will be considered. Though it also must be considered the great barrier it could cause with France."

"A worthy deliberation, Your Grace," the archdeacon said in even tones. "His Majesty also wishes you to consider reconciling with your lord husband. He has a sincere desire to serve Your Grace and the king."

My cheeks flushed at the thought. How long would my brother push this most vile plot? "That will not happen," I said, hoping to put an end to it. "We have more immediate concerns, sir. First, that Lord Albany will not be sent back; Lord Arran and I have exposed ourselves to great danger by ending King James's regency. We should like Our son to have a guard of two hundred men who will protect him at all times, not only from that but from Angus's designs. If you do not think that he will threaten Our son's power, you are wrong. We urge you to convey to His Majesty that the return of Lord Angus will be a great impediment to peace. He should be kept in prison."

Magnus's eyes widened at this. I detected a trace of mockery in them, as if he did not believe my fears rational but he was intelligent enough to keep such a conclusion to himself.

Magnus was dismissed and I sat pondering how to keep Angus at bay and how to convince my brother that the threat he presented was very real.

Once again, when there was no one I trusted to consult, I turned to my Ellen, who remained faithful and steadfast at my side. Alone in my apartments, the other ladies who drifted in and out of my life dismissed, we sipped mulled wine on my plush velvet settee before the fire, not even indulging in the charade of sewing. I almost felt naughty, giggling and talking with her as if we were girls again and plotting our matching gowns for the next entertainment.

"Not only Henry is badgering me," I huffed. "He has Lord Dacre, Cardinal Wolsey, and Norfolk haranguing me with their interpretations of morality as well. It is quite taxing listening to their opinions when three of the four of them consort with mistresses regularly."

Ellen laughed at this, but the laughter was interrupted by a cough that quaked her shoulders and brought tears to her eyes. Alarmed, I leaned forward.

"Ellen, that does not sound good; shall I have my physician sent for?" I asked. I could bear much but not the thought of my dearest friend in any discomfort.

Ellen waved a hand. "Do not worry; Robin has sent me his. He takes good care of me."

Robin . . . why, yes, Robin Barton. I did not acknowledge what this could imply; Ellen deserved whatever happiness her unusual position could grant. That it should lie with Robin, the man who saved her from a life of slavery in Portugal, seemed fitting to me, perhaps even ordained.

"I am grateful to him," I said, reaching out to take her hand.

"Enough about me," Ellen urged, her voice husky. "You were speaking of your brother and the lairds harassing you."

"Oh, yes, that," I returned, eager to distract myself from the thought of a sick Ellen and get back to the topic at hand. I sighed. "Angus is coming. Norfolk detained him at Newcastle, but of course he is for our reconciliation as well and could only keep him for so long. He is on his way. And if he thinks he will get the best of me this time, he is wrong."

"What will you do, Your Grace?" Ellen asked. As always, she questioned me more so I could puzzle things out aloud. I suspected it didn't much matter to her what I did, so long as she had my friendship. I was grateful to her for that.

"Whatever I can," I said. "Albany, bless him, is still pushing my suit in Rome, that the Pope might grant our divorce. Angus must learn his place. It is not in my heart, or, for that matter, this realm."

"What of your daughter?" Ellen's eyes were soft.

I lowered my gaze. Even to Ellen I could not reveal my guilt over young Margaret, who grew up with her nurses and tutors and had very little interaction with me, save for a random petting and fussing here and there, while I worked to secure her brother's realm. I hoped she wouldn't hate me for it someday, but were there a different way to pursue matters, I was hard pressed to find it. I loved my daughter, of course; she was a beautiful little girl with her Tudor red hair and willowy build, so reminiscent of my sister, Mary. But I did not want to be reminded of her, how she could suffer for the malice borne between her father and me as surely as if it were another sibling, filled with a life of its own.

"Margaret loves her father," I told Ellen. "I of course will not discourage it. But I will try as best I can to protect her from his influence, as I must protect Jamie. It will be Jamie whom Angus goes after; a girl is of little consequence in the grand scheme."

Ellen flinched at this. Again I found I could not meet her eyes.

Yet I had proved, had I not, even as a queen, that I was of little consequence in the face of the ambitions of men? Station was not discriminated against in this; it was fact.

The world did not belong to women, except for what they could do to further their men. In this, my lot had to be cast with Jamie, as it always had. Such is the only fate for the mothers of kings.

When Parliament opened, my wrath was unleashed upon my brother's envoys, Roger Radcliffe and Thomas Magnus, while I prepared to send three ambassadors of my choosing to England. I was mad with rage over the fact that Angus had made his way into Scotland, that my brother's realm had encouraged it. Could no one see that reconciliation was beyond possible? Letters from Angus, hopes to manipulate me, were sent back to him unread. I would not indulge my brother or Angus's fantasy that we could rule alongside Jamie as man and wife. Those days were over; Angus's chance to make things right had long since passed.

Jamie and I were at Holyrood House when we learned of Angus's arrival.

"He has scaled the walls of Edinburgh," Magnus informed us. "His only wish is to sit in Parliament as his ancestors before him had, and, of course, to reconcile with Your Grace, if you would open your heart to him. He has," he added, raising his brow, "four hundred followers with him."

"You think to intimidate Us with this, Magnus?" I cried, enraged that such tactics be used. "We may have been foolish in Our younger days, but no more. We will not be bullied into subjugating Ourselves to Angus's ambition!"

"I am certain he longs to be reunited with his daughter as well; he has not seen her in a great while," Magnus returned.

I shook my head, beyond irritated that he should dare play that card. Margaret was my business; I would not have her used against me as another manipulation ploy.

I was distracted from Magnus's impotent pleas by the ruckus of horses' hooves and men clanking in their armor beyond the castle walls; it was Angus, no doubt, hoping to impose his force upon us and take what he considered his.

"We want as much guard assembled as is at Our disposal," I ordered.

"We've less than five hundred," Harry told me. "I am afraid this castle is not as well armed as others," he added, his handsome face drawn with concern.

"It matters not; We will do what We can," I assured him. "Turn what cannon We do have on him and his men."

If Angus wanted to know my true feelings on matters, I could think of no surer way to communicate them than with cannon.

"Your Grace!" Magnus cried, scandalized. "To turn the cannon on your own lawful husband? Surely this is not advised!"

"By God, man, will you go home and quit meddling in Scottish matters?" I cried, whirling on Magnus in a flurry of orange velvet skirts. "Fire one of them, at least," I ordered my men, who rushed to do my bidding.

One great booming round was shot, resonating through my body and causing the floor to tremble beneath my feet. My heart thudded at the sound. I truly did not want to cause carnage, but what had Angus driven me to? He could hardly be said to listen to reason. At times the force of warfare was the only language men of such passions understood.

To my regret, the cannon served to end the lives of a woman, a priest, and two merchants. All innocents, and all dead for a message that was lost upon proud Angus, who retreated with his party on the king's orders later that afternoon.

I readied Jamie, who was by now used to fleeing in the night, and we rode in a procession illuminated by torchlight to the safety of Edinburgh Castle. As we rode I composed a defiant letter in my mind to my brother.

He would no longer assist any Scottish subject, unless by the express orders of my son, the king. I was through asking for Henry's help, only to be betrayed and manipulated for his own ends.

I was the Queen of Scots, was I not?

I laughed as a new thought occurred to me. Ellen was right.

I had at last chosen a side.

Whether it was due to my display against Angus, which scandalized the rest of Europe and I am certain sent Henry and Catherine into a fit of shock, or if it was because I was simply too stubborn to fade into the background as other lesser women had done, Parliament backed me in my suit for the regency. I was the Queen of Scots, acknowledged and respected at long last.

Perhaps I had been wrong. Perhaps if they fought long enough and hard enough, there was a place for women in this world.

I took to wielding my new power with certain exactness. Harry was promoted to Captain of the Guard and I courted Rome about my divorce with renewed vigor. I perpetuated an old rumor that would invalidate my marriage to Angus, that my Jamie had lived through Flodden for a time and I hadn't learned about it till it was too late. I regretted espousing such a lie; I knew in my heart the moment Jamie had died, with a sickening, all-consuming knowledge that eclipsed all doubt. But His Holiness did not have to know that. It was a divorce I wanted and I would get it, whatever had to be said or done. To my good fortune, I could still call Albany my friend and he did all he could to promote my suit as well.

Meantime it was learned that King Francois of France was now being held prisoner in Italy after the Battle of Pavia. His mother, Louise, wrote to me, offering me the pick of her granddaughters for Jamie and a restoration of the Auld Alliance. She pointed out my brother's fickle nature, his numerous betrayals to both France and Scotland, and the breaking of his daughter Princess Mary's betrothals to both the Dauphin and the Emperor. I admired Louise's shrewdness. It was true my brother had a pattern of breaking promises, and she assured he would break them to the Scots as well. Though I was mildly offended that it was my family she was insulting, her reasoning was not beyond my imaginings, especially after the scathing letter I had received from Henry chastising me for my treatment of Angus. The letter sent me into a fit of tears for an hour; that Henry could talk to a fellow monarch, sister or not, with such judgment and disrespect was appalling. My embassy in England had come to nothing, but here France was prostrating itself at my doorstep. It was a worthy consideration.

Albany, by the provisions in the Treaty of the More between France and England, was forbidden to enter Scotland during Jamie's minority, though I could not imagine that Albany would ever wish to return. I was glad that we were no longer beholden to the French; if we were to consort with them, it was of our choosing, not our obligation.

However, despite strides being made in my cause, and allies both in Scotland and abroad, the threat Angus posed to my son was still imminent. In order to preserve the peace of his realm, I was forced to thoughts of reconciliation once again.

"It would be in name only," I assured Harry, who was wild-eyed at the suggestion. "Harry, it is for the sake of Jamie, for the sake of peace. You must understand that he comes before anything, before my happiness, before us, before everything. The divorce, believe me, is just a matter of time. But in the meantime, is it not better to keep one's enemies closest?"

Harry shook his head. We were at Edinburgh Castle. Parliament was about to open and we were about to perform the masque of our lives, that of the peaceable family. I was not about to make this harder on Jamie than it had to be.

"Someday," Harry said, his tone wistful, "when King James is old enough and has full command of himself and this land, I hope you will do things just for yourself and learn to have your own life."

"Ha!" I laughed, immediately wishing I could take it back. He was serious and the hurt in his eyes that I should mock him constricted my heart. "I can never have my own life, Harry. Queens never belong to themselves," I added softly.

Harry's shoulders slumped and he bowed his head.

"Please dinna look at me like that, Harry," I urged. "I defy all convention to live with you, and display you on my arm to the world with pride; everyone knows who truly has my heart. There will be time for us someday, I promise."

I turned away, finding myself shaken that I had sounded too much like the men in my life who made such false promises to me. I had always hated lying to those I loved.

The opening of Parliament was an affair as tense as a bowstring, the very air alive with animosity as Jamie and I led the procession that included the Earl of Arran holding the scepter, the Earl of Argyll holding the sword of state, and none other than Angus holding Jamie's crown. Edinburgh was made ready in case Angus and his throng of Red Douglas supporters and clansmen grew hostile, but they seemed to desire peace as much as we did, not that I trusted their reasons. Still, I preferred it to putting my son in any jeopardy.

It was decided that varied lairds would have custody of the king's person in rotation. The Earls of Argyll, Lennox, and Angus would each host the king. I was loathe to making such an agreement, but the peace of the realm was too precarious, and I needed to capitulate where I could. But I knew I had made a grave mistake.

When it was Angus's turn, he refused to relinquish the person of the king. Jamie was his prisoner at Edinburgh. I received from my son two missives—one, at the command of Angus, I knew without doubt, that stated he was happy in the care of his beloved stepfather.

The other was a simple, short plea. Jamie needed my help. He wanted to be free of Angus, as free as I longed to be.

It did not take me long to decide what to do. I rode from Stirling at the head of an army with Arran, Argyll, the Earl of Moray, and even old Archbishop Beaton, who now saw it prudent to ally himself to me, reminiscent of old Lord Home's defection to my cause years ago.

To my horror, Angus met us with an army of his own, Jamie riding at his side. It was a brilliant ploy, one he had also adopted years ago when he urged me to place Jamie dressed in his robes of state and crown on the wall of the castle to dissuade attack against his person. My army could not bear to attack if Jamie's life could be threatened.

My eyes met those of my son, those tortured brown orbs, and I prayed to convey my love to him, my desire to protect him against the monster I had been fool enough to ever take up with, and my regret at ever submitting to the council's decision that his custody should be shared with anyone but me, his mother.

Jamie shook his head, the side of his mouth lifting in the most subtle of smiles, as if he hoped to reassure me. I pressed my hand to my breast, squeezing my eyes shut. *Oh, Jamie, Jamie, I am so sorry!*

We were forced to retreat.

Angus deprived Jamie of everyone he had known and loved. He dismissed David Lindsay, Jamie's beloved tutor and one of the few constant fixtures in his life since he was a bairn, replacing him with his own brother George. Angus made his uncle, another Archibald Douglas, his treasurer, and he created himself Chancellor, taking the Great Seal from Lord Beaton. It was Angus's Scotland now and I cursed my brother as I never had before, that he should have ever allowed him to cross the Border again.

Yet I did not lose hope. More attempts were made to save Jamie from Angus. The Earl of Lennox, a man much loved by my son and prized for his loyal friendship, went to battle in my son's name at Linlithgow. The dear man was slain on the field. I could only imagine my son's distress; a man he had known and loved well had lost his life for his cause. It seemed after the death of Lennox the Earl of Arran gave up altogether and retreated from public life along with old Beaton.

Oh, how weighty was the crown on young kings!

Meantime Angus made a show of educating Jamie in the manner he saw fit, taking him to preside over cases at the Justice Ayres. *May Jamie learn enough about law to best his keeper,* I prayed when I heard.

This was one of the best lessons he could have taught in comparison to what else Jamie was learning from him.

"He makes sure the king is able to hunt and hawk," David Lindsay reported to me, his eyes wide with sadness. "But he also encourages him to gamble and seek the company of . . ."

"Of whom?" I asked, horrified that my son should take to such reckless pursuits at such a young age. Though he had been declared of age at fourteen years old, he had not been released from Angus's clutches any more than before and was as captive to him as ever. As time was passing, months into one year, and then another, I feared for what his influence wrought upon my studious, gentle son. He was just sixteen years old, still young, still malleable to the ambitions of evil men.

"Of lowborn women," David informed me delicately.

Whores. Just like his father. Ah, how clever Angus was, that he should steer my son so, exploiting the weakness in both the Tudor and Stewart bloodlines that ran deeper than the Tweed.

"Something must be done," I pleaded as I paced my apartments at Stirling. "He canna be brought down to a debauching degenerate, steered from his duties by pleasure so Angus can rule in his stead. God rot that man's wicked soul for leading my son's into such peril!"

Though it could be argued living with a man who was not my husband put my own soul in equal jeopardy, I was not about to indulge that thought. I was not encouraging every woman who came my way to do the same; it was by necessity that I lived, eking out what little happiness I could. As soon as I was granted my divorce by Rome, all would be remedied as it were. There was no comparison to Angus, I reassured myself. I was still a good woman, a good mother, a good queen.

Harry was sitting before the fire, his long legs stretched out, his arms folded across his chest. "Sit and be calm, Margaret," he urged. "Nothing will be solved if you make yourself ill."

I did as I was bid, sitting across from him, but wringing my gown in my hands, twisting the material and pinching it in my fidgety state of nerves. As I attempted to collect myself and rid images of lewd women guiding my son into the depths of sin, a messenger was announced.

The man appeared exhausted as he made his way into my presence, offering a deep bow. "News from the Vatican, Your Grace," he said in a thick Italian accent.

My heart thudded. News from Rome, from the Pope. I closed my eyes, readying myself for the worst.

"His Holiness, Pope Clement, has granted your divorce," he began. I had to restrain myself from whooping out loud, bidding him to continue. "It is on the grounds that Lord Angus was precontracted in marriage to the lady of Traquair. Because you did not know of this at the time, Lady Margaret Douglas is still considered legitimate."

"God bless him!" I cried, rising, previous anxieties held at bay for a time. "Clement, he couldna chosen a more suitable name!" I praised. "Good sir, your journey has been long and arduous, We are sure. You are Our esteemed guest and shall be treated to the finest meals and most comfortable apartments. Bless you, sir!"

The man bowed again and was dismissed while servants were ordered to carry out my good wishes for him.

I turned to Harry, clasping my hands to my breast in delight. "The sun can still shine in the darkest of hours, Harry!" I cried. "I am free!"

Harry rose, gathering me in his arms and holding me close. "Not for long!" He laughed as he picked me up off my feet and whirled me about. When he set me down again, he leaned in, kissing the tip of my nose. "Not for long," he whispered again.

I leaned up, looking into his handsome face, bright and hopeful as the sun, and counted my blessings. Soon I would be his wife, I would belong to someone once again in the eyes of God and the realm and no longer be looked down upon for living with him in sin. I would provide a stable home and good, loving stepfather for Jamie and even little Margaret. We would be together soon, a real family in a real home. We would be happy soon.

Soon . . .

*   *   *

I set the wedding for March. It would do my heart good to have a happy occasion in the bleakness of winter. I cared not if it were during Lent. Lent never cared much for me anyway and I could see little use in all the deprivations; if such exemplified Catholic values, Jamie and I should have been canonized long ago.

As I planned my wedding, I kept Henry in England abreast of the atrocities done to my son—his deprivations, his restrictions, and Angus's tyrannical hold on him and the realm. My brother loathed upstarts; I could not imagine him sanctioning these antics. But, I had learned, Henry had troubles of his own.

"Can you believe it, Ellen?" I asked as Ellen and I were shown swatches of fabrics for my wedding gown. Ellen was lying on one of my chaises. She had been ill of late, and I did not want her to stand on ceremony for my account and made her comfortable in my rooms so I could still enjoy my favorite's company.

"Henry wants to appeal to Rome for a divorce from Queen Catherine," I said, barely able to refrain from giggling. "He says that their marriage is invalid, on the grounds that she was married previously to our brother Arthur. He cannot bear living sons with Catherine because God is cursing him for living with his brother's widow, he says."

Ellen smiled. "Irony is quite the jester," she quipped. "Considering all you told me he said about your marriage to Angus and you living with Harry."

"Well, Henry has a code of conduct for the rest of the world to follow, then a separate code for himself," I returned, my cheeks hurting from smiling. "I want to be sympathetic to my dear brother, truly I do—" At once titters of laughter escaped my lips. "But I just canna!" I blurted with a burst of laughter.

"So whom is His Majesty putting the queen aside for then?" Ellen inquired.

"A lady called Anne Boleyn," I answered. "She is in some way related to the Howards." I laughed again. "And knowing the ambitious and hardheaded Duke of Norfolk as I do, I can only imagine he is thrilled to promote their match. Ah, well." I dismissed the subject with a wave of my hand. "If anything, I feel a bit vindicated. Henry is as much a slave to the passions of his heart as I am.

I canna really condemn him. I know I will never get an apology from him as to my own choices. But"—I shrugged—"I suppose being the Christian sister that I am, I can forgive him a mite easier. I only hope he will remember me for that."

"What will happen to the Princess Mary if they are granted a divorce, and the marriage plans?" Ellen asked then.

"I had not really thought on it," I replied as I fingered some cloth of gold, deciding then I should have it made into the kirtle for my gown. "The bastards of my husband James IV all did quite well; a child of a king is always the child of a king," I remarked, finding technicalities tedious when they did not serve my purposes. "To have a solid peace between England and Scotland is my greatest desire and I will espouse whatever agreement to further that end. Och!" I held my hands to my temples in mock pain. "But I am not to think of Jamie's wedding today! Today is about my own!"

Ellen laughed at this and we dissolved into the chatter of two friends planning a happy occasion. I settled on deep crimson velvet for my gown, with cloth of gold accents and rubies sewn into the stomacher, with pearls, my tribute to my late husband Jamie, embroidered on the neckline. For Ellen, who would attend me, we decided upon beautiful yellow velvet, with red satin accents and amber sewn into her stomacher. Her gown would be cut much the same way as mine, so we would complement each other. "If we were a painting, I would title us 'Mirrored Opposites,' " I told her with a laugh. It was as if we were in the days of old again and I savored the moment.

"Will young Lady Douglas be here for the wedding? What will she wear?" Ellen asked me once we had settled on the designs with the dressmaker.

I flushed at this, bowing my head. "No . . . she will stay at Edinburgh. She has stability there that I do not like to interrupt, with her tutors and her nurses."

I did not want to admit, even to Ellen, that I had not thought of my daughter.

❧ BOOK 5 ❧

Harry

❧ 20 ❧

The Captive King

We were married in the chapel at Stirling. It was an understated affair, but not quite as clandestine as my wedding to Angus. This time I felt as a noble bride should. I was elated in my luxurious gown; I was restored and lovely again and happy in my choice for a groom. Harry was decked in a crimson doublet trimmed with brown fox fur, his black boots shining such that I could almost see my own reflection. He stood at the altar, blue eyes shining, full pink lips spread into his carefree grin.

I did not know what lay ahead for us and would not think on it then. There was only to be suspended in that moment, of being made whole again, of being what I was meant to be: a wife.

We exchanged vows. Rings slid up our fingers. Harry gave an awkward laugh when I could not quite get his past the knuckle. When at last I forced it with a little push, I said, "See? It will bend to my will as any subject should!" Harry's smile faded at that, but I dismissed it.

It was done.

The feast commemorating our union was also quiet, and David Lindsay recited some poetry as our entertainment. I did not much feel like dancing; I wanted to be alone with my husband. We took to our chambers and held each other into the night, making love without guilt. Harry was kind and tender, as he always was; he did not make me feel ashamed of my body or my age. He made me feel like I belonged to something.

Perhaps now I could be at home.

No sooner had we settled into nuptial bliss, which may not have been altogether blissful, distracted as we were by Jamie's cause, did Angus lay siege to Stirling, an act made more cruel by making Jamie attend it. He rode beside Angus, his face, so like his father's, somber, his lips set in a grim slash. There was nothing we could do; I would not send an army against my son. Angus knew that.

The air was chilly, the wind whipping against my cheeks as I met the party beyond the castle walls on foot with Harry and our own meager guard. My heart thrilled at the sight of Jamie even as it knotted in fear. And Angus, he was as handsome as ever; it set me in awe, it still does, that I could regard him as such even at his darkest hour. And, at that same hour, I could even still admire him for his tenacity. Perhaps it was the statesman in me, that I could separate things as I did. I had always admired Albany, even when he was against me . . . and now Angus; perhaps, despite everything, we still had more in common than he liked to admit. . . .

"We call for Henry Stewart," Jamie said in a strong tone thick with regret. As the words fled his lips, I shook my head. I knew he was being coerced; what Angus was threatening him with, I had no idea.

"You can break free, Your Majesty," I urged him in hard tones. "You can do it now!" I reached out my hand. Jamie, still on horseback, tightened his hands on the reins. They trembled. He averted his eyes.

My hand fell to my side.

"I love you, Your Majesty," I whispered. I did not know if he heard me, but his deep brown eyes flickered a moment, as if fleetingly he was released from some evil spell.

"Dinna make it harder than it has to be; have you not made his life hard enough, shaming yourself before God and country and everything in between?" Angus spat. "Give up Stewart and we'll be on our way."

Harry stepped forward. Angus's guard seized him roughly by

the arms, dragging him into their midst. I reached out, my throat seized by sobs I choked back. I would not let Angus see me cry ever again.

"Please, please dinna hurt him!" I begged, which earned me a hard look from Harry and an abrupt shake of his head. I imagined he did not want me to humiliate myself by begging anything of Angus. But Harry was all I had; I would humiliate myself for him. I was growing used to it, as it were. Angus had put it aptly; I had shamed myself before the world, what more could begging for mercy on my husband's behalf do to my already-sullied reputation?

Jamie swallowed; his Adam's apple bobbed in his long throat. His face was stricken, his brow furrowed. His eyes as they regarded me were lit with pity and tenderness and I clasped my hands to my heart as if I could will into him my love and shameless strength.

Jamie turned his horse and the party rode off, Harry with them. I stood, watching them become little specks on the horizon.

I was sick with fear. As far as I knew, they had thrown Harry into a dungeon; I could only imagine their designs for me. We were not safe at Stirling, not without Harry. Margaret, my daughter, was fortunately with her own household at Edinburgh Castle or surely her father would have taken her as well. For once I was grateful she was kept in the background of my life. Perhaps there was a kind of reprieve in anonymity.

"Ellen, what does he mean to do to him? Will he kill him?" I asked as we readied ourselves to flee the castle. I knew she didn't have the answer, but she was my Ellen and she would listen to any rhetoric I uttered.

By now it was made known that Harry and I were married. I wondered if Angus's motives were more about his wounded pride and the feeble grasp he held on my son than about protecting Jamie's interests.

Dressed in homespun, I rode with Ellen and a handful of servants away from Stirling, into the forest, where we hid in a crude hunting lodge. I did not know what Angus meant to do, if he would come for me next. It was not inconceivable to believe that he would have both Harry and me killed, thus securing his power base and hold over Jamie for good. No . . . I could not imagine that; slaying the mother of the king would not win him favor. The Scots could not even be so barbarous. And Angus, he could not hate me that much. . . .

One evening a ruckus was heard outside of the lodge. They had come for us; we could not hold out against any battle. They might as well have claimed their victory. When the door burst open I steeled myself against what was to come, offering a quick prayer to the Lord that He might forgive me my many trespasses, recalling, strangely, when I had been made to confess to old Archbishop Morton all those years ago, trying to shock him with my great list of "sins." Oh, if those had been the greatest of it, I would have been guaranteed a mansion in Heaven surely. . . . As it was now . . .

But it was not Angus or his men; it was my own Harry.

I abandoned ceremony, throwing myself in his arms, knocking him off balance.

"You escaped!" I cried against his shoulder, pulling back to admire his travel-weary face, which was caked in dust and blood and grime. "Did they hurt you?" I asked, reaching up to trace a jagged cut on his cheek.

His eyes were distant. "No . . . no, they did not," he assured me, with a half smile that I did not believe. He took my hands. "We are going back to Stirling, Margaret. We will fortify it and stand strong against Angus."

"But he already imprisoned you; might he mean us more harm?" I wondered, tears clutching my throat. Though grateful for my husband's miraculous escape, I could not foresee the same fate for my son.

"You are the mother of his child, Margaret; no matter his personal grievances or ambitions, he will remember that," Harry assured me. "Have faith, Margaret, and return with me."

"Of course, Harry," I agreed as we made ready. "I will go anywhere with you."

Harry closed his eyes, squeezing my hand, expelling a great sigh.

I wondered if it was all becoming too much for him, as I had always been too much.

I wondered how much more it would have overwhelmed him to know I had missed my courses.

I was pregnant.

At Stirling we readied the castle as much as we could, fortifying it as Harry recommended. Whether Harry had a premonition or had some signal from Jamie he did not confide; it was not long after that Jamie sent word. He was escaping! We must await his arrival and lower the drawbridge, preparing to raise it as soon as he crossed over.

"Can it be true?" I asked Harry, holding the precious message to my breast. "Will he soon be here with us? Is it almost over?"

"It will only be the beginning," Harry told me. "The beginning of the glorious rule of James V. This part is almost over, Margaret." He turned to me, offering a smile that had become fringed with sadness since his imprisonment. "Soon our lives can truly begin."

I cupped my belly, knowing those words to be truer than ever. I would not tell him till the quickening. By then, everything would be better and we could celebrate our joy without any encumbrances.

I waited through the night, my body rigid with tension, my ears pricking at every horse's hooves that could be heard pounding in the distance, at every innocent clank of armor. At last, a lanky young man arrived, windswept and dusty, dressed in the rugged apparel of a yeoman.

Jamie!

We raised the drawbridge immediately as I embraced my son, now a tall young man with a beard no less! It was the closest I had been able to see him since his imprisonment. Even those few futile times we met on a field of potential battle, I was never able to take him in as I wanted to. I could not stop looking at him, touching his face, and running my hand through his silky auburn hair. How like his father he looked, so lean, with a poetic handsomeness that no doubt would be made immortal in ballads and break women's hearts. I wondered how many had been broken already.

"Oh, Jamie, at last!" I managed through tears of joy. I took him in my arms again, my body quaking with sobs. I felt Jamie's shoulders shake and began to cry harder. "Almost three years, it's been," I whispered. "I will never let you go again, Jamie, never!"

Jamie pulled away then, wiping the tears that were trailing through the dust on his cheeks. He cupped my face in his hand a moment. "Believe that you have always been with me, Mother," he assured me, and my heart warmed at the sentiment, something else his father would have uttered with ease. "And when Angus laid siege to Stirling, I wanted nothing more than to be with you, than to break from him. But I could not, not with his army; it was not practical. I had to play it out as I did."

"I understand, darling, truly I do," I told him, and I did. I knew more than anyone how difficult decisions were to make when literally under the sword.

Though Jamie was king, I ordered him to sit and take wine while he regaled us with his daring escape.

"After all the attempts and battles fought in my name, it is not what I would call worthy of a ballad," Jamie admitted with an arresting smile that was his father's alone. "But after Lennox died, I knew I could not let his murder be in vain. I would honor him and all those who tried to rescue me and save myself. I would at last be king. I prayed to my father and my grandfathers before me, that they might lend their strength, their guidance, their"—he winked—"savvy. And they did. We were at Falkland Palace—"

"Oh! Your father's favorite!" I blurted before I could help it, thinking of the beautiful castle where I had known such passion, and noting, with a painful lurch in my chest, that Harry's expression darkened.

Jamie nodded. "Yes, Mother, indeed," he said indulgently. "I was with James Douglas of Parkhead and asked for the forester of Falkland, the Laird of Fernie, as I thought perhaps a bit of sport in light of all we had been through would lift our spirits. I decided we should go deer hunting the next day," he went on in a strong voice laden with authority and confidence from his adventure. "I said we should go to bed early, since the hunt would start at seven in the morning, and before bed toasted the men and our luck for the next day; I made quite a few toasts, letting the wine do what it does best. After they went to bed, I waited for just a bit, then disguised myself and rode off into the night with my two most valued servants. And you know the rest!"

"Oh, Jamie, how brave you were!" I praised him, once again unable to resist stroking his hair and patting his face. "Your father would have been so proud of you!"

"I am proud of you, Your Grace," Harry interjected, bold enough to break protocol at this triumphant moment. "After my own narrow escape, I can only imagine how difficult it was, hoping to God every noise you heard behind you wasn't them on the pursuit."

"Too right, Harry," Jamie concurred. "And I am certain they are in pursuit as we speak. Which is why we should set to action."

"Jamie, you must rest, darling, you've been through so much," I cooed, ever the solicitous mother, for which I earned a sharp glance from both Harry and Jamie.

"I know I will always be your little lamb, Mother, and I love you for it," Jamie told me. "But I want to issue a proclamation. Angus and the Douglases are not to be within six miles of Stirling. Within six miles of my person, for that matter. Ever. We will see that it is done."

I nodded, my heart swelling with admiration for my son. He was decisive, single-minded, and every bit the king he was born to be.

"The Douglases will be punished," Jamie said then. "And you who have supported my cause with such devotion and at your own peril will be rewarded. You, Harry, will be created Lord Methven."

Harry's eyes widened at this. "Your Grace, I am touched and honored. And unworthy of such esteem. I canna thank you enough for your kindness."

"Those who advise me will be men of my choosing," Jamie went on, dismissing Harry's thanks with a wave of his slim-fingered hand. "I want my Davie to be Snowden Herald. And I shall create my schoolmaster of old, dear Gavin Dunbar, Chancellor of Scotland."

"Jamie, you have been thinking much about this," I said, a bit awed still that my son was not the long-limbed youth Angus had first taken prisoner nigh on three years ago.

"It is what I must think on, Mother," Jamie said, his tone hard. "I am king."

It was, perhaps, though I did not know it then, as much a warning to me as a reminder to himself.

When the Douglases rode back to Stirling we were ready. The premier earls of Scotland, including dear Arran, who I believed had been beaten down by this struggle, rode with Harry and me to meet them. Angus, his brother, and his cousin were little more than a glorified group of thugs to me, and I made sure to meet him in a beautiful dove gray velvet gown trimmed with ermine. Despite being married, I allowed my most stunning feature, my coppery hair, to flow free down my back, and it whipped about me in the wind. I was as a Celtic goddess of old and I laughed at the comparison. Angus was nothing now.

"His Majesty, King James V, expressly orders that neither you, Lord Angus, nor the clan Douglas and their supporters shall be within six." The herald even had the good sense to hold up six fingers at this, and the condescension in the gesture caused Angus to grimace as I knew it would. "Six miles of His Majesty's person."

Angus, eyes narrowed, mouth bowed like a petulant child, drove me a hard stare, to which I only offered my prettiest smile. *Look what you lost,* I thought as I steered my horse closer to Harry, holding my belly in a gesture that, if not obvious to Harry, sent the message to Angus that another man's seed was sprouting within me.

Angus shook his head.

They made their inglorious retreat and my heart swelled—the reign of the Douglases, over at last!

"I am not certain you should ride against Angus, Jamie," I advised my son in the privacy of his chambers. Jamie had set to the task of his kingship with admirable competence, already corresponding with my brother in England in the hopes that the ever-precarious border situation could be stabilized.

Jamie sighed. I was beginning to get the feeling he was impatient with me and indulged my opinions for form's sake.

"Darling, you've been through such an ordeal. Perhaps if you just sent him and his supporters into exile, that would be right. Nothing hurts Angus like being separated from his beloved Scotland," I informed Jamie.

"Mother, I was his prisoner for nearly three years," he said. "He was a usurper, not unlike the stories of Richard III you and Davie scared me with when I was a child. I was fortunate to escape him alive. What he did, and for those who supported him, was treasonous and they will all be held accountable."

"What do you mean to do, Jamie?" I asked. An icy hand clutched my heart. I knew well the toll revenge took and did not want to see it embitter my son.

"I mean to sentence him, Sir George, and the Douglas of Kilsprindie to death," Jamie told me in even tones. "I have the backing of Parliament, Mother. Angus is running to Tantallon, wetting his breeches in fear, I imagine. I mean to go after him with my own men. If he won't meet his death with dignity, he will meet it at the end of my sword, or be torn apart with my cannon." Jamie shrugged. "I won't make a fuss either way," he added lightly.

"Jamie!" I cried. "You canna mean to do that! He is the father of your sister. Jamie, show mercy. It is a true king of greatness that can show mercy on his worst enemies. Please . . ."

"So that he can gather an army and rise up against me again? Are you willing to take that chance, with *my* kingdom?" Jamie returned, his dark eyes flashing. I flinched. Of course, I had known it was his kingdom. It had always been his kingdom; was that not what I had always been fighting for?

"Mother, the decision has been made." Jamie rose from his writing table. "No antics, please. No theatrics, and no schemes." He smiled; it was his father's smile and his father's tactic whenever we disagreed. Jamie meant to offer me some kind of pleasant consolation. I steeled myself against it. "Now. Why don't you have yourself some new gowns made? I shall have two new gowns, fashioned as richly as you please, ordered for you. Set to picking out the materials with Mistress Ellen. You would like that, wouldn't you? Of course you would."

I bowed my head. After all my years of fighting for my son, he was dismissing me as if I were some frivolous maid irritating him.

"Yes, Your Majesty," I said, not without a bit of sarcasm. "Thank you, Your Majesty." Before I made my retreat, I paused, my back turned in a deliberate rebellion to protocol. I inclined my head slightly in my son's direction. "Remember. You are sixteen years old. You need to rely on men with experience, men you can trust, to guide you in the ways of battle, that you might keep a clear head and a strong plan."

"If I have learned anything from Angus, I have learned one thing," Jamie returned in cool tones. "I trust no one."

I understood; after all he had been through, why should he? Yet I was stricken just the same.

A messenger kept us abreast of the situation as my son rode against the Douglases. I was sewing in my apartments with my ladies while he informed us of the latest.

"He borrowed cannon from the castle of Dunbar, Your Grace," the young man told me. "But of course Tantallon was strong against the attack," he added, nodding to me as if we were in on this summation of events together. "The king was forced to re-treat, but the Earl of Argyll won the day for him in the end."

"His Majesty is safe?" I asked, reaching out, squeezing my Ellen's hand in mine. It felt bony, where once it had been plump and warm. Now a strange coldness had settled into her that caused me to tremble more for her sake than my son's. I dismissed my momentary worry, squeezing her hand harder.

"Yes," he answered. "His Majesty is safe."

The tension stretching my shoulders taut relaxed. The throb-bing pain of anxiety in my brow eased a bit. "You are dismissed, thank you," I said with a smile. "Ladies, you are all dismissed, save for Ellen."

After the flurry of skirts and sewing was packed away and the ladies left, I turned to Ellen.

"My poor son was humiliated, I am sure," I told her. "I hope he isn't taking it too hard."

"Still," Ellen reasoned, "it is a good lesson for him to learn. He must not react rashly among these clansmen and he needs to take some counsel."

"I had told him as much," I said. "But," I added with a sigh, "he is sixteen."

"Sixteen . . ." Ellen's sigh was not as light as mine; it was fraught with a deep sadness that seeped straight into my bones. "Were we ever so young?"

"It feels a lifetime ago," I said.

"So . . ." Ellen offered a sly glance at my belly. "The king has triumphed, at least for the moment. There is nothing preventing you from telling Lord Methven of the little bairn now, is there?"

"Ellen, how long have you known?" I countered with a laugh. I could never resent her intuition.

Ellen shook her head. "Your Grace, I know you better than anyone."

"It's true," I said, my voice heavy with the wistfulness of nostalgia.

At once it struck me to the core that as well as Ellen knew me, I did not know her at all. I swallowed an onset of tears. Was it too late? Or was it not meant to be that kind of friendship for us, with shared secrets, hopes, and dreams?

Perhaps it did not matter.

"Your Grace, may I be dismissed? I am a bit tired," Ellen told me, then, her hand fleeing to her breast a moment, before resting again in her lap.

"Of course, darling," I told her. "Get some rest, my friend. . . ." I bit my lip as she rose, watching her wobble a bit on her feet as she packed her sewing away. "Ellen . . . is there anything you need?"

Ellen offered her sweet smile that seemed to hold so much more knowledge than mine, as if she were in on some divine secret I could only guess at.

"No," she assured me. "There is nothing you can do." She approached, leaning in to offer a soft kiss upon my forehead. "Except, Your Grace . . . remember Lord Methven. He needs you."

I nodded. "Yes, of course, I could never forget my dear husband," I said.

I didn't know what she meant. I should have. But I didn't.

Perhaps I chose not to.

Alone that night, Harry and I dined in my apartments on roast peacock, one of my favorites, and I made a fuss over Jamie's battle against Angus, attributing all the glory to him, of course, a fantasy in which Harry was kind enough to indulge.

"I am hoping he will drive them out of Scotland and not carry through the death sentences," I told Harry.

"You still are fond of Angus, aren't you?" Harry asked me then.

"How can you even think that?" I challenged, my voice light. "He is young Margaret's father, however. It seems unchristian to see him dead. He was wrong for what he did to Jamie. But I was wrong for what I did to him. I wonder if he knows that."

"What did you do, Margaret?" Harry tilted a brow. He was not quite accusatory, but his voice was tense with caution. "Was it that you were a widow with child, vulnerable and alone, and fell to his charms? Was that so great a sin?"

I shook my head. "I know what he did; I know what his grandfather did to push him. It was wrong of me to ever take him in. He could not handle it. He could not handle me."

Harry lowered his eyes, staring at his plate, which was for the most part untouched, something quite unlike him. His appetite was almost always ravenous.

"Anyway, Harry," I said, reaching over to take his hand in mine. "Dinna let's worry about Angus tonight when there is so much to celebrate. Jamie's victory . . . and our child."

Harry's full mouth fell agape. He raised his blue eyes to me; they were softened with tears. "Really?" he breathed. "Margaret, are you sure you can bear it? Are you well enough, strong enough?"

I waved a hand in dismissal of his outrageous implication of my age. "Many women bear children in their thirties and survive."

"But you are almost forty," Harry interjected.

"Dinna remind me," I muttered. "I have borne many and I have always come through, no matter how sick I have been." I patted my belly. "It has quickened," I said with a smile. "I feel it is God's reparation to us, Harry."

"And a sign that you need to slow down now," Harry told me, his voice firm. "It is time to step back a bit from public life, from the king. He has good men around him now, and of course I will always guide him in what modest ways I can. But now it's time for us to concentrate on our family, on us. We should retire to Methven Castle; you can set up a confinement chamber there and we will be away from all this. I want you and our baby to be well, to thrive. We can get young Margaret from Edinburgh, if you like; I am sure she would love to be a part of her new brother or sister's life, and wouldn't you like to have her beside you again?"

My heart lurched at this. "Harry . . . it is so wonderful, what you are saying. But to leave Jamie when his grip on his throne is so precarious and new . . . I dinna know if I can do it. And I feel strong and lusty. I can bear public life as I always have. And young Margaret is happy where she is; there is no need to disturb her just yet, not till I go into confinement; then perhaps she can come and spend time with me and the baby when he is born."

Harry's shoulders slumped as he sighed. He bowed his head. "Margaret, His Majesty is so strong willed, just like you. He will never let his throne go, even at his tender age. And the men he has chosen to surround himself with are wise. He seeks counsel from France, from your gracious brother the king, and from so many more. I am certain if he needs us he will make it known and we will be there; if you canna, I surely will in your stead. But you are of an age now where you need to rest more, in your condition. I want you to be safe, Margaret; I want the baby to be lusty as you are."

I patted his hand. "Eat your peacock, darling, and stop fretting like an old woman," I teased, flinching as he furrowed his brow, knowing I had insulted him. "Harry, I appreciate what you are saying and it is noted, of course. But please trust me. When it is time for confinement we can go to Methven Castle. But for now, we need to be close at hand for Jamie. We need to be a solid presence in his life; Scotland needs to know we are behind him and that the roles we play in his life are not small ones."

"But Margaret," Harry said in tones soft with hurt. "*He* is the king, isn't he?"

"Of course he is!" I declared with another laugh, made edgy with nervousness. "But he is just a boy, Harry. He needs us."

Harry rose from the table.

"Harry, you haven't finished your supper. Sit down, won't you?" I gestured to his plate. "Come now, this is our celebratory meal!"

"I prithee pardon, my lady," Harry said in cool tones. "But I am not much for celebrating tonight. . . . I wonder how His Majesty will take the news of being a brother again. As it is he has . . . three or four? At least four bastards of his own, all with different ladies."

My stomach turned to rock. Nausea gripped my throat. It was my life all over again, a mockery of my life, and Jamie was not James V but James IV. I shook my head.

"You are jesting," I said, attempting a chuckle that strangled itself in my throat. "You are jesting! Harry, I just informed you that you are to be a father and this is how you act? My God, you ungrateful little man!"

Harry approached me, leaning forward to kiss the top of my head. "A mother and grandmother in one year. Isn't that something?"

"Oh, get out!" I cried, rising from my chair, causing it to jostle on its legs. "Get out, anyway! I shall celebrate alone, as I always do!"

Harry's bow was stiff. "Then I bid you good night, my lady. Enjoy your supper and your . . . celebrations. . . ."

Harry quit the room and I sank into my chair, laying my head on my folded arms and sobbing.

❧ 21 ❧

The Princesses
of Scotland

In November I was preparing for Christmas early from my confinement chamber at Stirling. I wanted to have a good Christmas with Harry and Jamie and the new baby, despite the unpleasantness revealed the night I informed Harry of our blessing. Jamie's matters would resolve themselves when he married, and I was considering more and more my brother's proposition of his daughter, Princess Mary, for his bride. His children by his mistresses would be heaped in honors, just as his half brothers and half sisters were by his father before him, and his ladies well compensated as royal mistresses always seem to be, the lucky little wenches. Marriage would tame him, and if he was able to sire so many children there was no doubt it would be fruitful. The sooner to get him wed, the better. I resolved to make it a priority.

But as to Christmas, I hoped to make at least part of Harry's wish come true and bring Margaret from her household to celebrate with us at Stirling. I would throw a feast and perhaps even a masque. We would all be happy and at peace and Harry would let go his silly desire to retire to Methven. All would be restored. I would spoil Harry and the children with the best of everything in my power to procure. It would be a happy Christmas.

I regaled Ellen with my plans, hoping to rouse her from her

malaise. She always had a good head for planning things, and perhaps a new gown would cheer her as well, if I could afford it. I hated asking for money, but I wasn't above it, especially at this crucial time of preserving my family and marital peace.

One day as we chattered under the pretext of sewing garments for the new baby, we were interrupted by Harry bursting into the room without ceremony. He was breathing hard, his forehead and cheeks ruddy and glistening with sweat.

"Harry, how rude of you to come so unkempt," I said, mildly annoyed that my time with my truest friend was interrupted. "What is it?"

"Your Grace." He bowed as he approached me. "Mistress Ellen." He offered another nod in her direction, which she returned. "I wanted you to hear it from me first," he told me. My heart began to thud. Sweat mirroring his own began to gather at my hairline.

"Harry, this is serious, isn't it?" I breathed. "Something has happened." My stomach began to twist as I swallowed back burning bile. "Jamie. Is Jamie all right?"

Harry squeezed his eyes shut and nodded with a sigh I detected exasperation in. "Yes, the king is fine, my lady. It is Margaret."

"Margaret?" I screwed up my face in confusion. "What on earth could be wrong with Margaret? She has not taken ill, has she?"

Harry shook his head. "No, she is not ill. She has been taken by Angus, Your Grace. He has fled Scotland with her."

My hand flew to my breast as the baby offered a hard jab to my bladder. I doubled over. "No . . . oh, no . . ."

My daughter, the little fair stranger I had borne Angus . . . he had taken her, as he had taken Jamie, as he had taken everything, and I did not protect her, I was not there.

I had failed her as I had failed so many times before.

"What are we to do?" I breathed. Ellen took my hand, rubbing it. Mine was limp in hers. "Oh, God, Harry, what are we to do?"

"She is at Berwick," Harry said. "You may wish to consult His Majesty King Henry on this; perhaps he can be of help."

I nodded, numb. "Yes . . . yes, of course." I turned to Ellen, reaching out to pat her cheek. "Leave us, darling," I said, and she rose to do my bidding. Once we were alone, I reached out my hands. Harry took them.

"Harry . . . if we had gone to Methven, like you said . . ." I could not speak. Tears choked me. "Oh, Harry—"

Harry shook his head, drawing me from my bed to hold me near. His steady heartbeat beneath his doublet was strong, reassuring. I nuzzled against his shoulder.

"It is not your fault, Margaret," he told me, stroking the back of my hair. "It is not your fault."

But I knew better. Harry was being charitable, that we might keep the peace, which had been so delicate of late.

It was completely and entirely my fault.

My labor pains began on my birthday; it was a bit early but not dangerously so. I bore down, anticipating another dreadful birthing experience, wondering how I could ever pursue young Margaret and Angus if my recovery was as slow as when I had Margaret. With Ellen and my ladies and a competent midwife, I endured. It was a blessing that it proved not to be as hard as I dreaded, and my fair-haired little girl was brought into the world with relative ease on 29 November.

I took her in my arms, grateful I was able to hold her so soon after the birth, unlike many times before when I had been too ill to hold my other children. She was tiny and pale, thinner than her siblings.

"What will you call her?" Ellen asked me.

"I rather like the name Dorothea," I said. "Harry fancies it, too."

"It is a lovely name," Ellen assured me, reaching out to take the baby. "Now get some rest while Lord Methven is fetched. He will want to see his new little angel."

Weariness overcame me as soon as the word "rest" fled Ellen's lips, and I sank back into the pillows. "I hope he is happy. Perhaps next time it will be a boy . . . but of course perhaps God is sending me this little girl to replace young Margaret. . . ."

Ellen cocked her head, scrunching her nose up and regarding me as if I had said something strange.

I closed my eyes and allowed sleep to carry me away, to lands where I could see the other babies I had borne, babies who were no longer here. . . .

My family was as broken as it had ever been. The months passed, Christmas falling short of my expectations once again, as no one was in a celebratory mood and I was still weak from Dorothea's birth. Though I wrote to Wolsey, my brother's adviser, and my brother himself, no one would venture to rescue my Margaret. Instead, Henry arranged that she be brought to his court and be raised beside the Princess Mary. She was gone. I had lost her as surely as if she had died, and I knew I would never see her again, as I would never see the court of England again. She was the daughter of an English princess and would be raised to be a good English maid.

Was it a kinder fate than what Scotland could offer?

I wanted to think so.

"I never talked to her," I confessed to Ellen one night while I rocked Dorothea in her ornate cradle Harry himself helped fashion for her. He did not seem the least bit offended that I had given him a girl; in fact, he seemed mad for the little golden-haired cherub. As for me, I spent as much time with her as I could; I would not repeat with Dorothea my mistakes with Margaret, mistakes that haunted me almost every waking moment.

"Did you know? I never talked to her," I repeated, referring again to Margaret. "I canna even remember one meaningful word we have ever, ever spoken to one another, beyond letters and such. Oh, I fussed over her as a babe and whenever we saw each other as she grew I petted her, of course. But . . . I never really *talked* to her. She is thirteen years old and I have never even talked to her!"

"I know, Your Grace," Ellen said. Of course she knew. She knew everything, every dark recess of my soul, which I was certain was now damned, if it hadn't been before. "I know," she said again, in her cooing voice.

"At least I have Dorothea," I sighed, looking down into the cradle where lay the sleeping babe. Tears clouded my vision. "At least I have her. . . ."

"Lessons abound, Your Grace," Ellen said.

I was tired of learning them.

By the next summer I had recovered well. I was still stouter than I hoped to be, but I was now forty and could not expect much. I was lucky to have lived to forty, as it were. My brother, in a comic twist of irony, was making any attempt he could to further his cause of divorcing Queen Catherine in favor of Anne Boleyn.

"What do you make of that?" Ellen had asked me one evening as we were preparing to receive an ambassador from the Vatican to assess our perspective on the situation.

"I find it hilarious," I said. "In light of the vulgar things he said about me, and to me, when I dared go against convention and divorce Angus. He didn't even wait two years before seriously pursuing his own divorce. Ah, hypocrisy . . ." I chuckled. "Only my brother. He can justify any move he makes and never see the parallels between himself and those he criticizes for the same choices."

Ellen echoed my laughter. "Poor Queen Catherine, I wonder how she fares."

I shrugged. "I couldn't care less. After her triumph over my husband's death, and her joining in my scolding for the Angus affair, I see it as divine retribution. I wonder how above me she sees herself now that her own daughter is kept from her and she canna do anything about it, especially after her criticism of me when I was separated from my boys." I remembered the conversation at Baynard's Castle too well, when she dared imply my unfitness as a mother. *Divine retribution has a bitter taste, doesn't it, Catherine?* I thought with a sneer.

Ellen sighed at this. "I will remember her in my prayers; I canna help but feel sorry for her."

"You were always better than I," I told her with mock petulance. "And you are the only person I dinna begrudge for being so. But! Enough about my brother; I shall be embroiled in discussions about him all weekend. You are coming, are you not? We are going to the Highlands, Ellen; they are so beautiful! You would love it. It is so different there, not bleak and rocky like it is here. Everything is green and beautiful and steeped in traditions of old."

Ellen drew in a shaky breath. "I will remain behind and look after Dorothea, along with her nurses," she told me. "Let you enjoy your time with Lord Methven and His Majesty."

"Very well," I consented, though I was sad to leave my dearest friend behind. "You don't know what you will be missing!"

"All the better, then," Ellen said. "This way I shall have no regrets."

For some reason those words struck me and I wondered if Ellen had any regrets thus far.

Surely no one could have as impressive a catalogue of regrets as I.

Oh, the Highlands! They always surpassed my expectations with the lushness of the foliage, so green it seemed almost painted on by some faery hand, and the kindness of the Highlanders as they received us into their strange world. We were met with cheers and blessings as we made our progress to where we would meet the Earl of Atholl. It was the old days for me again, my days with my husband Jamie, when life was merry and the kingdom was at rest.

My son, Jamie, was as beloved as his father and as handsome. The young maids fawned over him as they struggled to be the first among the throngs that lined the roads, waving and shouting, hoping he would cast his gaze upon them and favor them as he had been rumored to favor many a lass. Though it grated on me, I could not begrudge them; it elevated a woman's status in life to be loved by a king, and if she was fortunate enough to bear him a child, she would be rewarded. And my son was rewarding many women. He now had five children by five different mistresses.

At least he had established the fertility of the house of Stewart.

The Earl of Atholl had built a marvelous reception hall of woven birches and green timber that smelled so fresh, I inhaled as if it were the sweetest pomander. Tapestries hung from the roughly hewn walls, the windows were glazed, and we stood on a floor strewn with a carpet of sweet-smelling herbs and flowers. It was a marvelous marriage of courtly elegance and the simplicity of the forest.

"Oh, but it is just wonderful! It is like the court of Robin Hood!" I exclaimed as I was seated to table, which was laden with the finest foods and wines. I was eager to sample everything, from the breads, to the mutton, moorfowl, capercaillie, swans, and rabbits, to the blackcock, partridges, ducks, and, my favorite, peacocks.

We sat to devour the magnificent bounty before us and the papal nuncio was quite impressed. Harry was impressed with the scene as well; however, what seemed most captivating to him was not our surroundings but the Earl of Atholl's young daughter Janet. With her curling black hair, skin pale as cream, and elfin green eyes, even I could not deny that she was a great beauty.

I never had any luck with women whose names began with the letter *J*. My Jamie had loved a Janet Kennedy, and Angus had his Jane Stewart. No, *J* names were never good to me. My heart clenched in my chest. It was Jamie and Angus all over again. Perhaps it was all men.

I did my best to ignore Harry's flirtatious statements about his hunting prowess, and Janet's overindulgent laughter. I sighed, trying to excuse it. Here I was, stout after the birth of a child, and none too appealing to my own self let alone a man. And hadn't we had a bit of a rough start, with our marriage steeped in the intrigues of Jamie and the court? Didn't Harry deserve a bit of a diversion? I had told him I did not expect faithfulness from him; I had told him long ago. I only asked that he not humiliate me. Thus far, the flirtation was subtle enough.

In any event, what were the odds that he would see her again?

I told myself this as I ate helping after helping of the generous earl's fare.

But as we stood at the night's end watching the lodgings go aflame in a blazing bonfire, as was Highland tradition, it was nothing to the fire lighting my husband's eyes.

* * *

We returned to Stirling to find Dorothea ill with fever. All thoughts of Highland seductresses were put aside as we tended our daughter.

"Why didn't they send a messenger to us?" I demanded as I held my daughter, who was so hot her flesh was scalding to the touch.

"By the time a messenger would reach you, you would have been on your way back," Ellen told me.

" 'Tis a childhood fever, Margaret," Harry assured me. "We've all had them. She will be fine, you'll see."

But I knew too well. I bathed my daughter in icy water myself, hoping to abate the fire in her humors to no avail. Her blue eyes began to roll in her head and her body jarred and jerked with fits.

Harry paced the rooms as we waited for the physician.

"She is bound to recover," he insisted. "She is bound to!"

I knelt on the floor beside my daughter, whom I placed in the center of one of the carpets that she might move freely without harming herself. She flopped about like a fish and I covered my eyes with my hands. I did not want to see this. Oh, I did not want to see this. . . .

At once the flopping stopped. Dorothea was still.

I met Harry's stricken gaze as he knelt down beside her, reaching out to feel the pulse of life. He searched her neck, laying his big hand on her tiny chest. I shook my head. Harry rose, as if burned by the fever now ebbing with the life force from the little body. He looked upon me, blue eyes wide in horror.

"Oh, Harry . . ." I looked up at him, appealing with my eyes that he might take me in his arms, that we might comfort each other. "Harry, darling—"

"Sometimes," he said, his voice low, "I do believe you are a curse."

He turned on his heel and quit the room, leaving me to keep vigil alone over our dead child.

"It is because of Margaret that God took her," I told Ellen in my apartments the night after the interment. Harry would not attend Dorothea's burial. She was laid to rest beside her half siblings after services subtle and unfit for a Princess of Scotland. The coffin was so small. . . .

"Why do you say that?" Ellen asked me.

"Because I failed her," I explained. "I failed her as a mother and I failed Dorothea, too. I should never have gone to the Highlands. We never should have gone," I added, thinking of Harry and the earl's fair daughter.

Ellen rose from her chair and gathered me in her arms as I at last began to sob for the first time since Dorothea's passing.

"You did not fail," Ellen told me. "You have always done what you thought was best at the time. You have always done the best with who you are and what you had. You must hold on to that."

I shook my head. "I wish I could believe that," I confessed brokenly. "To Harry I am a curse. Maybe I have always been a curse."

"No, darling, no . . ." Ellen soothed. "You have been a blessing to me," she told me.

"Jamie," I breathed. "I must not fail Jamie. I must do right by him at least; I must protect him. He is all that is left to me."

"But, Your Grace, you still do have a living daughter," Ellen told me.

"It is too late for us," I sobbed. "It was too late the moment she crossed the Border."

Ellen stroked my hair and back, rocking to and fro. "It is never too late," she told me. "You have been as good a mother as possible, considering the circumstances." How gracefully she lied! "And you have ever been a faithful and good mother to His Majesty. Now you must just take care of yourself."

"Yes, I best," I spat, my tone hard with bitterness. "I am all I have."

❧ BOOK 6 ❧

Margaret R

❧ 22 ❧

Distractions

I did not see Harry much after Dorothea passed. He called upon me now and again out of formal obligation, but his heart was no longer there; his blue eyes were distant, longing to be elsewhere. The Highlands . . .

One evening when he came to me I presented myself in a warm brown satin gown trimmed with otter fur, making certain my hair, which still shone coppery despite my age, was worn long as he had once preferred it. I ordered a dinner of his favorite roasted fowl and greeted Harry with a smile.

"We should not carry on as we are, Harry," I told him, reaching out to take his limp hand in mine. "We have so much to live for. Jamie is such a triumph! He's restored my lands that Angus stole and named you governor of Newark Castle. He even had that border terror Johnny Armstrong hanged. He is putting Scotland right, Harry. We should put our marriage right as well."

Harry bowed his head. "Of course I want peace with you, Margaret," he said in soft tones.

"Then stay with me tonight, Harry," I urged, hoping he would respond to my aggressive passions as he had in the past. "We lost our precious Dorothea, but we can still have more children. It is not too late. I am still lusty with health."

Harry withdrew his hand as though I were as fevered as Dorothea had been the night we lost her and he was at risk for contracting it. He shook his head. "Margaret, no. Whatever you may think, I do worry after your health and how taxing it would be to bear another child. And perhaps it is your age that cursed Dorothea with such ill health. I do not want to risk that upon future children."

"But that is ridiculous!" I cried, rising, balling my hands into fists. "It is just that you dinna want me anymore, do you, Harry? You've found another, younger maid to warm your bed and now you want to put me aside, isn't that it? It's Janet Stewart, isn't it?"

Harry rose. "I do not want to hurt you, Margaret, please believe that."

I laughed, tossing my hair over my shoulder. "Of course not, they never do." I shook my head, dismissing him with an impatient gesture. "Go to her, then. I am sure I have only been an impediment to your plans. Go!"

Harry offered a blow and I sank to my seat once again.

Somehow I had known the night would play out that way.

Perhaps in some perverse sense, I had planned it thus all along.

I threw myself into the reign of my son with more enthusiasm. I had nothing else. And whether he liked it or not, I would be there to advise him against the foolish impulsivity of his youth and give him the clearheaded guidance he yearned for, even if he did not know it.

One of the foremost priorities, in my mind at least, was Jamie's impending marriage. My brother had sent Lord William Howard to court to discuss a possible alliance with the Princess Mary.

I received Lord William in my apartments at Edinburgh Castle, thrilled to discuss such a delightful enterprise.

"Lord William!" I cried to the smiling young lord, so different from his darker, more brooding older brother, the Duke of Norfolk. "How happy We are to see you! Tell Us of England and Our brother. Tell Us of his court. Is he well? What news of the divorce from Queen Catherine?"

"Still a confounding, difficult endeavor, Your Grace," Lord William said with a grimace. "Let us hope we can make these arrangements with more ease. Is His Majesty in favor of a wedding to the Princess Mary, then?"

I offered a half smile. "Our son seems to have his own ideas. We are still working toward making the sense of that end clear to him."

"Ah, I see," Lord William replied with a laugh. "Well, then, I suppose it would be best to discuss the matter with him directly."

I was reluctant to agree to this, but then Jamie was king. It would be good to allow him to think he had say in a matter as important as his marriage.

Lord William rose. As he bowed, he said in a light voice, "And the Lady Margaret Douglas, Your Grace . . . I am happy to report that she is thriving and doing well at the court of His Majesty, King Henry."

Her name jarred me. I was ashamed I hadn't asked of her. There was too much else on my mind, as there had always been where Margaret was concerned.

"Ah," I answered, matching his light tone. "That is good . . . that is good."

I did not cry till after he quit my rooms.

"I will go to war with Henry if I have to!" Jamie told me, his cheeks ruddy with rage as we discussed the matter of my brother's insistent support of Angus in his apartments. Despite my trying to steer the conversation toward the lighter fare of marriage, Jamie would not be dissuaded. Talk of Angus inflamed him. "Do not think I am above going to war against my uncle if he keeps undermining the peace of Scotland!"

I shook my head with a heavy sigh. "Nothing will surprise me. Brothers war against brother, son against father . . . nephew against uncle is nothing new," I said, my tone weary. "But please, Jamie, think of Scotland and the peace I have worked for these past thirty years. Please think of that, of how hard won it has been."

"Of course I want to maintain the peace, Mother," Jamie told me. "But I will not tolerate betrayal. By anyone."

"I have offered myself as mediator," I said. "I want to honor the treaty of Berwick; perhaps we can renew it. England is too mighty an enemy to have at one's border, Jamie. We canna afford it."

"I know, Mother, I know, by God," Jamie answered, his voice thin with impatience. "Meantime, what of the English court? You know more than I, I am sure." This was not true; Jamie was indulging me, but for the sake of indulging his need for distraction I told him. Anything to be relieved of the topic of Angus.

"Henry wrested his wish for a divorce at least from the English people," I informed him. "Though His Holiness was none too eager to grant him a thing, and excommunicated him."

"His soul is in peril, then," Jamie observed, wide-eyed. For as much of a profligate my son was proving to be, it amused me how prudish he could be when the occasion called for it. He was not as different from his uncle Henry as he thought.

I laughed. "Well, he separated from Rome and made himself head of the new Church of England, with one of his own as Archbishop of Canterbury. So I imagine he sees his soul as quite reconciled with the Lord, Jamie." I could not help but admire my brother's tenacity and great strength of will. He managed to carve out a way where no way seemed possible and was ruled by no one but himself. Had I only been as strong . . .

"So he married his Anne, then," Jamie said.

"Yes," I said. "And she is even expecting a prince already," I noted.

"Well, I suppose all is as he wants it now and he can address English matters of policy with more focus."

"Indeed," I agreed. "Perhaps one of those matters should be your own marriage, Jamie. To the Princess Mary?" I could not keep the hopefulness from my voice.

"Mother, you canna be serious," Jamie said with a laugh. "With the king remarried, the princess is now illegitimate. I have advised the Duke of Albany and Lord William Howard of the same. The marriage is not to be considered."

"How can that be? My daughter Margaret is recognized even though Angus and I are divorced," I pointed out.

"King Henry wants no one standing in the way of future male heirs, Mother," Jamie told me. "You must know that."

I suppose I did. "Well, then," I said, not without a bit of sadness in seeing my long-held dream of the cousins wed dying. "What did Albany say?" I asked then, my heart still thrilling after all these years at the thought of him.

"He has proposed his niece by marriage, Catherine de' Medici," Jamie informed me.

"Oh, an Italian," I said with a dismissive wave of my hand.

"A very wealthy Italian," Jamie told me.

"She'd never survive Scotland," I told him.

"Albany was told the same thing," Jamie returned with a laugh. "But what think you, Mother, of Margaret Erskine?"

"What, a Scotswoman?" I was scandalized at the thought. "What on earth could she offer you?"

"She is a noblewoman, Mother, and the mother of my son," Jamie told me. "I think she could offer me a great deal. I am very fond of her."

"Perish the thought," I said. "What has love ever gotten us? You are better off with a foreign princess who can give you an alliance and a good dowry."

Jamie sighed at this. "Sometimes I think you have been through too much, Mother," he observed, his tone thick with sadness. "It is making you cold."

I pursed my lips at this, too afraid to speak past the painful lump growing in my throat. "Well. Be that as it may. If you won't take my good advice about marriage, then perhaps we can at least set to organizing a personal meeting between you and Henry." I blinked away the onset of tears, allowing myself to be captivated by the new dream. "Oh, but I would love that! It would be a great spectacle, like Henry's Field of Cloth and Gold with King Francois long ago. Wouldn't it be wonderful? An historic meeting between two great monarchs."

"Now, now, Mother, dinna get ahead of yourself," Jamie cautioned, but he was smiling. "It would be a great thing, were we able to achieve it. But first, we must achieve some sort of lasting peace, else a personal meeting could go drastically awry."

I would not lose hope for it, though. Ah, but wouldn't Father be proud! If I could achieve such a meeting between the two men I loved most in the world, it would be my greatest glory. . . . Peace, lasting peace, between our realms, orchestrated by me. My dreams would have all come true, marriage or no marriage between Jamie and my brother's daughter. My purpose would still have been fulfilled.

I could die happy then.

As I prayed for peace between my son and my brother, a messenger delivered more heartbreak from England. My sister, Mary, was dead. I prayed for her soul when I learned of it, saddened as I recalled her wistful beauty, wondering if she had found happiness with her Brandon after all, wondering many things. I recalled the years when I was jealous of her beauty and her fortune; she had gone after the man she loved and won him, with little consequence from my brother. Had it been worth it then? I knew little of Brandon. I knew little of her.

Now I was Henry's only sister left; for a Tudor nursery once so full, it was now down to the two of us. It made the necessity of peace between our realms all the more urgent for me. I could not bear the thought of being at odds with my only sibling.

Anne was delivered of a baby girl in September of that year, and though my heart ached for my brother's disappointment, I rejoiced just the same. They called her Elizabeth after our mother and I was told she had the Tudor red hair, perhaps a Heavenly tribute to her aunt Mary in Heaven. Elizabeth was said to be a lusty bairn and I was assured her birth meant more babes would soon fill England's nursery again.

I wondered if my Margaret saw the baby and what she thought of her.

I did not hear from my daughter enough to know one way or another.

In 1534 the treaty of Berwick was renewed between Jamie and my brother. It would not be long before, I hoped, a meeting could be arranged between uncle and nephew. As the treaty stood, both Henry and Jamie swore to peace as long as they lived. May their reigns be long!

"I canna help but feel complete," I told Ellen. We had just arrived at Stirling from Edinburgh and I was glad as always to be at my favorite residence. "Everything I have worked for has come to fruition; I have at last realized my purpose."

"Well, good," Ellen said, her voice laden with weariness as she sat, a bit heavily, in her plush velvet chair, pulled before the merry fire I insisted remained stoked in my rooms regardless of the season. It reminded me of the many days I spent before fires, with Albany, with Jamie, with my brother Arthur . . . fire cheered me; it restored me. As I was born under the sign of fire, this did not surprise me. I was one with it.

"Now perhaps this means Your Grace can take a bit of much-needed, well-deserved rest," she said.

"Rest?" I waved a hand. "Really, Ellen, you speak to me as if I am an old woman! Rest!" I mocked with a laugh. "Not while Jamie is unmarried and has that ridiculous notion of wedding Lady Erskine. No, I must find him a proper bride. And I still must arrange the meeting between him and my brother."

Ellen regarded me a long moment, then shook her head. Or perhaps I imagined she did. Her smile was as indulgent as always.

She offered a long sigh. "Perhaps you will allow me, then, to take some rest, Your Grace."

"But of course!" I told her. "Do you need to nap? You may go to your apartments and rest as long as you like, only come back later so we might sew together and take in a bit of music."

"No," Ellen said, her voice unusually firm. I started at the sound. "Your Grace, I mean, I would like to retire from court life. I would like to go home."

"Home?" I screwed up my face in confusion. "What do you mean, home? Your home is with me."

Ellen bowed her head. "I would like to go to the Lindsays. It was Marjorie Lindsay who took me in as a child, and I have . . . family there. I would like to retire with them."

"But, Ellen, that is just foolish," I said, incredulous that she should suggest such a preposterous thing when we had so much to do. "Whom will I consult on gowns? You know I hate my other ladies; I have no use for any of them, they are all flighty, false-hearted fools. I need you. And the Lindsays, you dinna really know them, not like you know me. You wouldn't be happy there."

"Perhaps Your Grace would allow me to be the judge of that," Ellen told me. "Your Grace, you dinna really need me. What am I? Your Moorish lass. I am nothing to the great minds who advise you. And wouldn't you like to repair things with your lord husband?"

"Ellen!" I snapped. "Dinna throw Harry at me at a time like this, just to distract me from you weaseling your way out of my service, and after all I have done for you! Really!" I huffed, folding my arms across my chest. "I'll hear no more talk of it; it is sheer foolishness. I will permit you to take rest whenever you like, though," I added in softer tones. "I know we are none of us as young as we once were, though I'm hard pressed to let it stop me," I said with an air of superiority. "You can go rest now, if you like, and we shall go on as if this unpleasant topic has never been discussed."

Ellen rose. I averted my eyes from the tears glistening in her ebony eyes.

"Thank you, Your Grace," she said in low tones.

I waved her off, still miffed at the audacity of her suggestion.

Too many had already left me. I was not about to lose the best friend I ever had.

"News of England, Your Grace," Lord William Howard informed me. I smiled in greeting as always when meeting with the handsome young ambassador. We were in my apartments today. I was thinking of returning to Edinburgh of late to attend to the matter of Jamie's meeting with my brother; for two years now he had teased me with the prospect and I was tired of him putting it off. My brother was willing to meet him at York, but stubborn Jamie would not venture farther than Newcastle. It was obvious now that Jamie did not intend to meet with my brother, on the advice of his council, a party that was standing more and more at odds with me by the day.

"Good, perhaps my brother has agreed to pay me back the money I spent on a suitable wardrobe for the meeting that never happened," I said, irritated that Henry was silent on the matter of my funds. I was to appear the mother of one king and the sister of another; I would not be seen in rags!

"I am afraid His Majesty has been occupied with rather serious matters," Lord William said. "Queen Anne Boleyn has been executed for adultery and high treason."

I glowered at the thought of a woman executed. The image never sat well with me. "Our poor brother," was all I could think of to say. "Is he well?"

"He took a hard fall in January at a joust," Lord William told me. "It has caused him much grief. And Princess Dowager Catherine passed in January, you know," he added then, as if this perhaps figured into Henry's current state.

I could not help but feel for the woman I had regarded almost the whole of our lives as my sister-in-law. As I had never met the Boleyn creature, I was not as inclined to regard her as family. And though my bond with Catherine was precarious at best, she was still yet another fixture of my youth to perish, proving herself as mortal as the rest. I wondered what this bespoke of my own life's impermanence.

"We had heard," I said, my tone heavy with mourning. "First Our dear sister Mary, now Catherine. I feel as though I am the last of something." I blinked several times. "There is something more, isn't there?"

Lord William nodded. "I am afraid it regards your daughter, the Lady Douglas."

My heart lurched at the name. "What of Margaret, Lord William?"

"She is being held in the Tower of London," he said. "She . . . she fell in love with the wrong man, it seems. She was betrothed without the permission of the king. He—the young man—is imprisoned as well." He closed his eyes at this, swallowing hard. "He is sentenced to death," he added, his tremulous voice soft with the horror of it.

"Who is this man?" I asked, anger hot as wine coursing through my veins at the impulsive act of my daughter, who should have conducted herself as a good English maid in my brother's court and instead went on to shame us both.

"My brother Thomas," Lord William revealed, lowering his eyes.

"Norfolk?" I asked, grimacing.

"No, my other brother Thomas, the Younger," Lord William hastened to correct me, for which I was eternally grateful. I could not imagine my daughter succumbing to the considerably lacking charms of old, hawk-nosed Norfolk.

"Well, we are much aggrieved for both the Howards and for Our daughter," I said. "We canna abide Margaret disobeying Our brother after he has hosted her with such kindness, raising her as his own. It is most unseemly and ungrateful and We are ashamed of her; We shall disown her if she canna deport herself with the dignity of her station," I added, my tone hard with severity. "It is obvious she has had little guidance from her own father."

Lord William's expression was pitiable at this and I dismissed him. Only after he left did I succumb to trembling and pacing before my fire as I wondered after my daughter's fate. Would she be put to death as well? Surely Henry would not risk it, for putting to death the sister of the King of Scots could bode war, and Henry did not want war, not after renewing the treaty of Berwick. No, he would not put her to death, I assured myself.

I sat before my fire, rocking back and forth, staring into the flames, praying with all my soul that my daughter be wise, that she be kept safe from my brother's wrath.

Oh, Margaret, Margaret, you foolish girl. We know each other not, yet how like your mother you are. . . .

❧ 23 ❧

The Distant Drums

I returned to Edinburgh to be with Jamie. I would take comfort in the only child I had and hoped I would find in him reassurance.

"More than ever I believe it imperative that you meet with my brother," I told him. "Your sister's life could be in jeopardy," I urged Jamie. "He must be made to see how vital peace with Scotland is, and how risking the life of your sister could thwart the treaty of Berwick."

"Margaret is safe, Mother," Jamie informed me, his tone thin with impatience. He met me in my apartments. He would not even suffer to see me alone, but allowed Harry in the room with him—Harry, whom I went without seeing for months at a time,, and only by chance when we did meet.

"She is?" My heart was pounding heavily in my chest. I put my hand to my breast as if I could still it. "You are sure?"

"Yes," Jamie told me. "I have been assured this is more of a chastisement for her behavior and no real harm will come to her," he added.

"Thank God!" I exclaimed, closing my eyes a moment. "What of Lord Howard?" I asked then, pitying the young man who had the misfortune of loving my equally unfortunate daughter.

"Still imprisoned, but the death sentence has not been enforced," Jamie said. "He is none of our concern. There is other news, Mother."

By the wistful light in his eyes I discerned it was nothing good and stiffened in my chair, drawing in a deep breath. "What now?" I asked.

"The Duke of Albany, Mother," Jamie told me. "He's . . . he has passed on."

The room seemed to be moving. My heart thudded against my ribs in a violent rhythm. Albany . . . Albany . . .

"No!" I cried. "Oh, Jamie, no!"

"I am afraid it's true," Harry interjected.

Jamie bowed. "Perhaps I will leave you to discuss this alone," he said, pressing my hand with a brief kiss before making an all-too-hasty retreat.

I began to sob. "Not Albany!" I cried. "Oh, not my Albany . . ."

" 'Your' Albany," Harry stated with a sigh. "You really loved him, didn't you?" His tone was soft.

I could not help but nod. I did love him. And now he was gone, denied me forever.

"Always the men you canna have," Harry noted then, and I flinched. "I suppose there is something about the forbidden that keeps such love forever sweetened. It is never tainted by the hardships of reality."

"You would know," I snapped, my cheeks hot as I thought of his Janet.

"I suppose it is better for John Stewart to never have known your love," Harry said then. "Perhaps you remained as tender in his memory as he does in yours."

"Jehan . . ." I whispered though tears. "He . . . he called himself Jehan. . . ."

Harry bowed to this. "I crave your pardon, Your Grace," he said in smooth tones.

"Oh, Harry, I want to be alone, won't you just let me alone?" I hissed, impatient with his mocking banter. "No . . . fetch Ellen for me. Yes. I would like Ellen beside me now."

Harry sighed, his shoulders slumping.

But he had no sarcastic retort and I was grateful. He left to do my bidding.

Ellen entered the room, wrapping her arms about me and holding me as I sobbed for Albany, for my dear Jehan.

"Oh, Ellen, do you remember how he used to sing?" I asked her. "Did you ever hear him? His voice was so strong and low. Oh, Ellen!"

"There, there, Your Grace," Ellen soothed in her soft voice. "He is with God now, and his wife and daughter. He is in a better place," she assured me as she pulled away.

I looked into her face. "His daughter? Oh, yes. I had forgotten." I wiped my eyes. "I supposed I always hoped there would be a chance for us," I admitted in soft tones. "I always seemed to miss my mark, didn't I, Ellen?"

But Ellen was not listening. She was gazing at a point just beyond my head and sinking to the floor, her mouth forming a perfect O.

I rose from my chair, stooping beside her. Her eyes were fixed, staring beyond me still as I shook her shoulders.

"Ellen! Ellen!" I cried, holding her to my chest. She was heavy, limp in my arms. "Oh, Ellen! Oh, God, help me!" I screamed. "Please help me!"

Servants rushed into the room, sweeping my Ellen up and removing her. I followed, ordering a physician's immediate assistance. I was eager for a report as soon as possible.

Harry, having heard the ruckus in the hall, joined me as we progressed to her rooms.

I linked my arm through his. "Oh, Harry, Ellen canna be ill, not when I need her so much!"

"Yes, God forbid she take ill when you need her," Harry spat, pulling away from me.

"I canna expect you to understand," I cursed as I made my way into her rooms. The physician who met me there only shook his gray head.

"I am afraid her heart is failing," he informed me. "Should be no surprise; she lived much longer than expected. She has been unwell for many years now."

"She has?" I asked, mystified as I rushed to her side, taking her hand in mine.

"She hasn't long, Your Grace," the physician told me.

"All right, then, leave us," I said in harsher tones than I meant as the physician and servants quit the room.

"My people," Ellen murmured. "I hear the drums . . . home at last . . ."

"Your people?" I returned. Though it had always been obvious that Ellen was from a distant land, I never thought of her as having people. I never thought of a lot of things.

"Your Grace . . ." Her voice was barely audible as a trace of a smile curved her full, dark lips.

"Yes, my darling?" I squeezed her thin hand in mine. Had I not noted how thin her hands were becoming? Why did I do nothing? Why did I push it aside, as if it would go away?

"Listen, Your Grace," she said then.

"To what?" I cried, my voice growing shrill with panic. "I dinna hear anything, Ellen!" I was desperate at once to hear what she heard, to be part of her world, a world I chose to ignore in lieu of keeping her tethered in mine.

"Just learn . . . to be still," she told me. "And listen."

"Of course, I will, Ellen, only stay to teach me!" I begged, reaching out to stroke her forehead. Already it was cooling; already the life was leaving her. I wondered if she would meet Albany and my children and my sister, and all those I longed to see but was deprived of.

"Oh, Ellen, Ellen," I cooed, leaning in to kiss her dusky forehead. "Dinna leave me, Ellen, please dinna leave me. . . ."

But her eyes were empty. She had left me for her people and the land of the distant drums.

And I was all alone, listening.

I quit her room, moving as if prompted by unseen strings. I was numb, my body going through the motions of walking, of breathing, of what seemed now to be the useless act of living.

Harry had been waiting. He caught my elbow. "Come now," he urged in soft tones. "We must leave her to be attended to."

"I want a grand funeral arranged for her," I announced, stifling my tears. Ellen would want me to be strong. "She shall have the best gown, the best of everything, as my dearest friend."

"Her funeral shall be as her family sees fit," Harry told me in harsher tones as we made our way back to my apartments.

"What do you mean? I am her family!" I cried when we were alone. "I am all the family Ellen ever had!"

Harry leaned against my writing table, shaking his head. "Are you really so blind, Margaret, or are you just that selfish?"

"What do you mean?" I demanded, mortified Harry should choose such an inopportune time to scold me.

"She had a daughter in care of the Lindsays," Harry told me.

My heart seemed to slow. My breath caught in my throat. "What do you mean, a daughter? I never heard that; she never said. How do you know this?"

"Because, unlike you, I stopped talking long enough to listen, to inquire after *her* life and what was important to *her*," Harry told me. *Listen, Your Grace . . .* "As you could not, as her 'dearest' friend. Did you know there was another Moorish lady, a Margaret?"

"Yes, she was named for me," I said dumbly.

"That is irrelevant, but I suppose that is the first thing you would think of," Harry said. "Did you know why she was not close to Ellen? They were from different tribes. Is that not ironic? The one person she could have claimed as a friend, who knew of her people and her lands, was from another tribe, thus forbidden to her. They honored that even here, even in Scotland, the land of warring clans. We are not so unlike the Moors, are we? But why would you care? You know nothing of your friends, let alone strangers."

I sank into my chair. "Harry, why are you telling me this now?"

"Because, as Ellen's 'friend,' it would serve you to know a few things about her," he returned, his tone icy.

"Oh, but Harry . . ." I breathed, unable to take it all in. "A daughter . . ."

"A daughter you would not let her go to—you 'needed' her too much," Harry said, his tone laden with disgust. "As you need everyone too much. You needed her to death. So at the very least, if you held her in any esteem at all, let her daughter lay her to rest as she sees fit. I will take it upon myself to inform Barton of her death."

"Barton . . . you mean, Robin?"

"Who else would I mean?" Harry shot back. "He first brought her to Scotland; they were especial friends. He has a right to know."

I could not speak, I could not think. All this time, Harry knew more of my Ellen and her world than me.

"If I had only known, Harry, I swear to you I would have let her go to her daughter," I said. "You can imagine, me being separated from my own daughter, I would have care of such things."

"Ha!" Harry scoffed. "Poor Margaret means no more to you than this child of Ellen's does now. They are both just as much strangers to you and better for them that they are."

"Harry, why are you being so cruel to me?" I demanded. "First about Albany and now my dearest friend—and she *was* my dearest friend regardless of how you mock me—she is gone and you . . . all you can do is antagonize me!"

"I am not antagonizing you," Harry told me, his tone softer. "I am being honest."

"I did not know she was sick, Harry," I said then.

"Do not insult Ellen's memory more by lying," Harry said. "You have known she was ill for years but were too selfish to part with her. My God, I could see how ill she was every time I looked at her! But you, Margaret, you see what you want to see."

I sank my head into my hands, my sobbing renewed with a vengeance. I hated him for his cruel words. I hated him more because he was right.

"Maybe now you will see, Margaret, that it is time to slow down, to retire from public life yourself before it is too late for you as well," Harry said then. His tone grew soft. "You can come with me to Methven Castle. I am willing . . . I am willing to try to repair things with you."

"After everything you have just told me this very night?" I returned, seething that he dare propose such a thing now. "After you made it clear you have no respect for me as your wife, let alone your queen?"

Harry shook his head. "I feel sorry for you, Margaret." I searched for a hint of mockery in his voice but, to my mounting frustration, found none. "You will never learn from your past, will you? You will insist, with that Tudor stubbornness, on sabotaging any possible chance at happiness."

I bowed my head, sobbing brokenly.

"Cry, Your Grace," Harry urged, the mockery I could not find before now abundant in his tone. "Cry for your Albany and cry for your Ellen. But before them all, cry for yourself, for you are more pathetic than the lot of them."

With that he retreated, leaving me to my tears, my pathetic, useless tears.

24

King Jamie

There was nothing to be done but think of the present and who was left in it. I pushed my mourning for Albany and Ellen aside. They were never far from my thoughts, as it were. When I lay in my bed alone at night, with no letters to write, no missions to set upon, they came to me whether I wanted them or not, taunting me with my memories, where they were young and bonny while I was cursed to grow old alone on this earth.

But for now there was Jamie and I would concentrate my waking energies on him. I would renew my pleas for a meeting with my brother, and Jamie's marriage prospects needed tending. He needed me.

I would show Harry that I was not needy but needed as well.

Jamie was less than enthusiastic when he received me.

"Mother, it isn't prudent to meet with Henry at this time," he told me. "You need to come off these plans. We have come to an agreeable truce; be satisfied with that. You've endured so much lately," he added in gentler tones. "You need to stop and rest. You need to think less about me and more about yourself. Think of your own marriage."

"Do not advise me about marriage, Son, when you yourself are not yet wed," I urged him.

Jamie indulged me with a smile. "I hope to be wed soon,

Mother, to Lady Erskine, whether you approve or not," he told me, in a tone that did not match his sweet smile.

"Your council will not approve, let alone me," I said in hard tones. "We have been through too much to see you married to some common woman. She has nothing to offer you, Jamie! You are *king!*"

"Yes, I am king!" Jamie cried, pounding his fist on his writing table with a resounding thud that caused me to start. "*I* am king," he said again, his tone softer. "And I will decide whom I will meet and when, and whom I will marry and when."

I rose. "Then you do not need me after all." I dipped into a low curtsy. "If I may be dismissed?"

Jamie nodded. "Go rest, Mother. Please," he urged as I made my retreat.

It was as if I were an old cow everyone wanted to put out to pasture.

What did I have to live for now?

I met with Lord William Howard to discuss Jamie's stubbornness.

"He will not bend to compromise!" I cried in frustration. "He has his own ideas and canna be persuaded for the good of the Anglo-Scots alliance! Do you know I told him I would even go to York in his stead, but that would not do, either."

"It is unfortunate, Your Grace," Lord William agreed. "But he is young and the young do tend to have their own ideas, I am afraid."

I sighed. "Oh, Lord William . . . sometimes I feel it best for me to leave him to them. Perhaps Henry would have me back in England and I could be with my daughter again. She could do with a mother's guidance. King James is a man now. He will make his own fate. I am so weary." I swallowed tears. I was quicker to them than ever now. "I am weary of my lot in life. I am weary of Scotland."

Lord William said nothing. I was grateful to him for that.

We both knew there was nothing to be done.

* * *

Robin Barton interrupted my woe by calling on me at Edinburgh. Upon seeing him, I dismissed my staff, abandoning ceremony to throw myself into my old friend's arms.

Dignified as always, Robin suffered my embrace with his own arms awkwardly about me as he patted my back. He pulled away to guide me to my chair as if I were the guest and he the host.

"Ellen . . . ?" I began, recovering myself enough to speak. It was the first time since the day she died that I said her name aloud.

"Aye," he said, intuiting my thought. "She has been interred."

"Was she buried well?" I asked. I did not inquire as to the arrangements after Harry humbled me. I was afraid to intrude now. It was clear Ellen was as much a stranger to me as my own daughter. I denied myself, therefore, any rights those more intimate with her were allowed to enjoy.

"Aye," Robin told me. "She has been laid to rest at Over Barnton. And there is no more to be said of it."

I nodded in understanding. "I am glad you came, Robin," I told him then.

"I am worried about you, Your Grace," he confessed to my surprise.

"Why are you worried about me, Robin?" I asked in an indulgent tone.

"Albany is gone; Ellen is gone," he added in a softer tone. "And your husband . . ."

I offered a wry chuckle. "What of my husband?"

"Do you know where your husband is, Your Grace?" he asked, with a deliberate tilt of his dark brow.

"Do I care?" I spat before I could help myself. I offered a bitter smirk, shaking my head. "Well . . . Where is he, then?"

"Living on your lands, off your rents, with Janet Stewart and the child he got on her," he said.

I drew in a breath, closing my eyes a long moment. "It is no more than I would expect," I told him then. I almost laughed, so reminiscent it was of the time he imparted similar news of Angus. "Well. You always seem to know the whereabouts of my husbands, poor man, and are always in the undesirable position of having to tell me," I observed with a chuckle devoid of amusement. "I have too much to worry about now to think on that overmuch, Robin. I expect after divorcing Angus, a second one shouldn't be as difficult. I will set to suing for it directly, with the king's help."

"The king, Your Grace, left for France," he said then, his gruff voice low. I suppose, in his sailor's way, he was trying to be gentle.

"What?" I breathed. "What do you mean, France?" My voice rose in panic.

"He learned Lady Erskine was married to Lord Lochleven and his hopes for a Scottish marriage were dashed," he informed me. "He goes to France seeking a bride. He didna want you to know; he was afraid you would upset yourself. He wants to leave you regent while he is gone," he added, as if that was supposed to soothe me.

"So you came here to tell me all this," I said, my tone hard. "I thought we would discuss Ellen and the old days, but no, you came on my son's bidding. You are my son's man."

"Of course I am, as you are his subject as well. And there's no use revisiting the old days; they are gone. Those who trap themselves in nostalgia may as well bury themselves with the dead." Robin's tone was matter-of-fact but still kind. "I came, Your Grace, to help you however I can. Because I am your friend."

At once no words were ever sweeter. "Well," I said with a rueful smile. "I suppose I am in need of that. Thank you, Robin."

He smiled then, a pirate's smile, and it warmed my heart.

He had always been my most loyal friend, never swerving from my cause.

No wonder Ellen loved him so.

With the setback of a storm that sent me in a panic over the possibility of losing my son at sea, Jamie's travels did not go as planned, but he was able to venture forth again in September, determined to procure a French bride. While he was gone, I set to pursuing my divorce. I hoped the fortune that smiled upon my brother would also favor me and proceeded to gather the opinions of forty learned gentlemen regarding the validity of my marriage.

If my brother could have a marriage of twenty years declared invalid by university men, then there was no reason I could not do the same with a shaky marriage of less than ten.

Jamie married a Frenchwoman on New Year's Day, the daughter of King Francois, Princess Madeleine. While I attempted to keep my son's realm secure, Jamie and his fair bride were toasted at the French court, enjoying every luxury life had to offer. They did not return till the spring. It was none too soon; I missed Jamie and was eager to put our differences aside now that he had found a wife. Besides, I needed his support in my divorce.

I met them at Leith with the rest of the court and watched with my breath caught in my throat as the slim, tall young maid stooped over to grab two fistfuls of earth in a gesture I found haughty and pretentious but the crowd loved. It was a blatant statement signifying who was now Queen of Scotland. I suppose it was her right. More and more, I heard it whispered in the galleries and the gardens, "Here comes the Old Queen," whenever I passed by. After all I had done for Scotland, this was what I was reduced to: the Old Queen. Scotland, it seemed, was ready for the beauty and vibrancy of a young queen.

She might have been fair, but I could not say young Madeleine was especially vibrant. She had a fragile look about her that frightened me.

"Jamie, she's consumptive," I told my son when at last we were afforded some privacy amidst the happy chaos of their arrival. "Did Francois not tell you? Surely he must have known. Her lips are bluish and she has a dreadful cough. She's terribly thin, Jamie. I would fear getting a child on her; she may not live through it."

"He did worry after her health here," Jamie confessed, referring to the King of France. "But, Mother, you must tell me you remember what it is to be in love. I loved her from the moment I set eyes upon her. It is our love that I pray will keep her strong, despite the harshness of Scotland. If we keep her warm and well fed, she will be all right. She must be," he added, his voice taut with desperation.

Whenever love was mentioned in any conversation, there was no use imposing reason, so I let Jamie believe as he would.

"I wish you both well, of course," I told him in sincerity. "Davie is preparing a lovely coronation for her," I said, referring to David Lindsay, now Lyon King of Arms, who was relishing his new role and had been planning a magnificent coronation since learning of the wedding. "I hope she will be well enough to enjoy it."

Jamie nodded, but it was clear to see he was distracted. "And you, will you be well enough for the coronation?" he asked me then. "Can I trust you will conduct yourself accordingly and stand beside your lord husband, my beloved stepfather, and desist from making a fool of yourself with these divorce proceedings?"

"Jamie!" I cried, scandalized. "Surely you have heard what Methven has done to me! Stealing my lands and my rents, living with that Janet Stewart and their son! He gave her a son," I added in wistful tones as an image of Dorothea presented itself in the mists of my mind. "How could you allow me to suffer it? I have the opinions of forty learned men, Jamie, forty of them! They seem to favor the idea of a divorce."

"Well, I, Mother, do not," Jamie told me, his tone hard. "Is there someone else again, Mother? Is it Angus?"

"Angus!" I cried. "What on earth could you mean by that?"

"I have heard you speak fondly of him; the years have corrupted your memory against all the wrongs he committed against us. In that, nostalgia proves to be a fiercer enemy than any border warrior," he said, echoing the words of Robin Barton. "I thought it relevant to ask."

"Of course it isn't Angus," I assured him. "I will always be fond of him, I canna help myself. He is the father of my daughter and I loved him once. I will always be sorry for what passed between us; we were both the victims of bigger ambitions. I would be a fool to harbor a grudge against him. It is high time you forgive him as well."

"Dinna even suggest it," Jamie snapped. "After everything he put me through, I am appalled at the thought. I will hear no more of Angus, except to say that I am glad you are not planning to reunite with him. So. We have established there is no one else. Then what purpose could a divorce serve, other than put your own soul at peril?"

I furrowed my brow, disgusted with talk of my soul, disgusted that I had revealed my vulnerability regarding Angus, a man I should hate but could not.

"Jamie, I have my pride," I argued then. "Harry humiliated me; he's stolen from me. He is no better than Angus, no matter how kind he is to you."

"Pride is not enough, Mother," Jamie said. "Otherwise I'd have been to war a thousand times on matters of pride. I am stopping the proceedings, Mother, and it is in your best interests that I do."

"Jamie!" I cried, shaking my head. My cheeks flushed hot with anger. "How can you do this to me? I deserve to be treated with respect; I deserve some happiness in my old age, especially after all I have done for you, after all the fighting and scheming and planning so you could keep your crown!"

"It is because of that that I am stopping these proceedings," Jamie told me, his tone gentle. He reached across his writing table to take my hands in his. "It is because of your fighting, your scheming, and how you tirelessly have sacrificed through the years to preserve my crown. Dinna think I am not appreciative of your toils on my account. But, Mother . . . I will not have you regarded as some kind of farce. You are better than that. Live quietly, take enjoyment from what you have, but *please* stop making a spectacle of yourself! I want you to be respected and remembered for all you have done for me and for Scotland. I will speak to Harry and make sure he does right by you; I of course dinna sanction his behavior. But, I pray you, by carrying on as you are, you are humiliating yourself far more than Harry Stewart ever could. For me, for Madeleine, and your future grandchildren, please stop humiliating yourself. I will not have my children's grandmother thought of as a fool."

Tears seized my throat. "Harry has encouraged this, has he not? He has bribed you! He made you think I was leaving him for Angus and bribed you to stop the proceedings so he could continue to use me!"

Jamie shook his head, his eyes wide and lit with something that could have been tears. I chose to ignore them and looked down at my hands, which kneaded and wrung my gown in frustration.

"Mother . . . I love you. I am worried about you," Jamie told me then.

"I am a grown woman!" I cried, rising. "I do not need anyone worrying after me! I am so weary of everyone's worry!"

And with a whirl of skirts, I quit my son the king's apartments without waiting to be dismissed.

If Jamie would not grant my divorce, my brother would. I would go through him. I was through with Scotland, through with this "farce" of a life my son insisted I maintain. I had written my brother informing him of my plight. My only desire was to live as a princess, in the manner our father ordained, and not be made to follow my son around as some common gentlewoman, living a quiet, subtle life so as not to embarrass him. Surely my brother would understand, and I his only living sister. Surely he would want to protect me.

Letters to Henry were not enough; they often went unanswered as it were, as distracted as he was by his new bride, Jane Seymour, and his fervent desire for an heir. I would take my appeal to him in person. I was still strong; I was still robust with Tudor health. I would make for England. It was the old days again, the days of night flights to the Border. I readied myself and had my most trusted servants procure a Galloway for me, one of the sturdy border ponies. I would only need one armed man, and silenced with a few jewels, he was easy enough to come by.

So began my ride. I rode as if I were a girl again, as if not plagued by pain in my joints, migraines, and shortness of breath. It was exhilarating feeling the wind against my face again, feeling the muscles of the horse work beneath me as he brought me closer and closer toward my refuge. I was happier than I had been in a long time, on that night ride.

Without stopping we navigated the craggy trails of the Border, making it into Berwick. But when I heard the pounding of hooves behind me, I knew I had been caught, that my dream of finding refuge in England was just that, a dream, and that I had further humiliated myself before the eyes of Scotland, living up to my son's assessment, that my life had become a farce, that I was a fool.

"Your Grace?" a strong male voice shouted. "Your Grace, Margaret, Dowager Queen of Scots, and party?"

I slowed my horse to a stop. "Yes, it is us," I admitted in small tones.

"I fear you may be lost, Your Grace," the man who I realized was Lord Maxwell said as he caught up to me on his own chestnut stallion with a party of guards and servants. He offered a kind smile. "Come, I will escort you back. 'Tis dangerous on the Border, you know. . . ."

"Yes . . ." I said, my tone thick with a new exhaustion not born of the ride. "Thank you, Lord Maxwell."

Thus ended my flight. Lord Maxwell, with the utmost politeness, escorted us back to Edinburgh, graciously maintaining the façade that I had been lost.

It was to Jamie's credit that I was not treated as a runaway queen mother gone mad.

The matter of my flight was never addressed and for that I was grateful. It seemed Jamie at least did not wish to see me further humiliated. There were other matters to attend to now that I knew I was reduced to living out my days in Scotland, so I put the fantasy of rescue from my brother out of my head. Jamie needed me now, as it were.

His young bride had perished from the consumption, as predicted. Jamie's love was not enough, after all.

My heart ached for him. It was clear there had been genuine feeling between the two of them, and though I did not have the opportunity to know my short-lived daughter-in-law well, she had been a regal creature and I was certain would have made a good queen, had she been robust enough.

David Lindsay's grand plans were all put asunder, and he wrote a beautiful lament for the queen. Scotland was plunged into mourning. Edinburgh, which was to have come alive in cloth of gold for her coronation, now held vigil over her casket in colors of darker, more somber hues.

My heart also went out to poor King Francois, who lost a daughter in our fair young queen. What a terrible plight, sending a princess away a queen, only to lose her.

Another parent and child, each destined to never lay eyes upon the other again. Such is the fate of princes.

Whether it was his grief that had driven him or it was his sincere resounding vengeance against the Douglases that motivated Jamie's next move I would never know. It had been in the making before the death of Madeleine, to be sure, but came to fruition after. That was the execution of Lady Glamis, Angus's sister Janet Douglas.

She had been charged with treason and witchcraft. Her treason was in communicating with her exiled brothers. Her witchcraft was in the supposed plan to poison Jamie, a plan with no evidence other than what my son had concocted. So like my brother, Henry, who was rumored to have done similar to his poor Anne Boleyn and Catherine . . .

"You know it is not true," I told Jamie in his apartments the night before Lady Glamis was to die. "Whatever it is, Jamie, whatever is causing this hatred in you and this fear, if it is the death of Madeleine, I understand. If it is your resentment of Angus, I understand that, too. But it isn't enough, my dear heart. It isn't enough to kill a woman for. Please . . . Jamie, if you are anything like your father, you will regret this. It will haunt you. Please. Put a stop to this."

"By God, Mother, let me do what I must do!" Jamie cried, meeting my eyes with a gaze as fiery as the stake. "The people must know who sits on the throne of Scotland—the Douglases must know most of all. My rule is absolute and above question."

I shivered. "Jamie . . . everyone knows you are king in right. There isn't enough evidence to carry this wicked thing through. Imprison her, exile her if you must, but please, not—not this. Lady Glamis is your sister's aunt; she is a good woman. She has a young son of her own."

"Who will watch," Jamie seethed. "He will watch what becomes of those who are traitors to the king."

I shook my head, reaching out to take his hand in mine. He withdrew it, rising.

"Jamie, we have both suffered so much," I pleaded, tears clutching my throat. "Dinna let's make another innocent suffer for what we have endured."

"Once and for all, Mother, you are going to see who is king!" Jamie shouted. "Now you are dismissed!"

I dipped into a curtsy on legs wobbling with fear.

"I will pray for you all, Jamie," I said, thinking of the poor woman I had once known as a sister-in-law and the child who would be motherless, and all for my son's fear and anger—the two very worst enemies of mankind.

Janet Douglas, Lady Glamis, burned on the stake the very next day.

I refused to witness the execution.

All I could imagine was the fire reflected in the eyes of an innocent young boy, now motherless, and I thought of Jamie. I knew the image was forever burned in his heart. I wondered if he was satisfied, if this mere woman's death made his reign feel more secure now.

I would never know either way. Jamie never spoke of it to me again.

❧ 25 ❧

The Stewart Legacy

Jamie waited almost a year before marrying again. In keeping with his wish to restore the Auld Alliance, a bit to my chagrin, it was to another French bride. But she came to us this time and I was grateful Jamie did not have to go fetch her, as he did with the last unfortunate. This Marie de Guise was rumored to be a strong, healthy woman and I prayed this was so. My son did not need any more heartache. Since the deaths of Madeleine and Lady Glamis, he had grown serious and brooding.

I wrote to my brother, hoping he would furnish me with money for clothes suitable to meet my new daughter-in-law, but, as had become typical, received no response.

It was Harry, of all people, who was sent to fetch me from Stirling, that we might share in the entertainments welcoming the new queen to court as if we were a united front. I was sure this was designed to spare my son any embarrassment over his mother's exploits.

"Where is your Janet?" I asked Harry when we had settled into the coach that made for Edinburgh.

"She is behind," Harry told me. "Margaret . . . I want you to know I am sorry."

"I only asked one thing of you when we married, Harry," I told him. It would be a long ride, I decided; best to say what I had to say now. "One little thing, and it was too much for you. Oh, I expected you to be unfaithful; I have not yet come across a man who was not. Do you remember what I asked of you?"

"You asked me not to humiliate you," Harry answered in soft tones.

I said nothing.

"And I did anyway," Harry went on. "And for that I am sorry. You were right when you said you were too much for any common man. I should not have married you. But I did and should have been honorable to you; you deserved that, at least. It is my hope I can be honorable now."

"Jamie is behind this," I accused in hard tones.

"His Majesty deserves to have parents that care for one another and can conduct themselves with honor," Harry said. "And since his father is not here, I am the closest thing to a father on earth that he has. I owe it to him to respect his mother."

"So are you leaving Janet and your little family you have with her?" I asked with a sneer.

"They will remain away from court," Harry told me. "And I will keep company with you more. Margaret—" Did his voice break? I gazed at him, startled by the abject sincerity of his tone, wondering if it was wise to believe him, if it was wise to believe in any man. "I do care for you. I feared for you when I heard you tried to ride to England. It was beneath your dignity and could have put you in so much danger. I realized then how low I had brought you. I am sorry for it, Margaret, and I want to offer you a truce. Can we be at peace with one another? Can we be friends again?"

I pursed my lips, closing my eyes a moment, drawing in a breath that I released slowly. I reached out, taking Harry's hand and squeezing it. "I suppose it is all a woman in my position can ask for," I said. "A truce it is then, Harry."

Harry squeezed my hand in turn. We said no more on it.

But our hands remained entwined the rest of the journey.

I was presented to Marie de Guise alone. She was an astounding beauty, a tall, graceful woman with curling dark hair and large, attentive blue eyes. She emanated strength and confidence. I had no doubt she would be a healthy and able mate for my son. Relieved at this thought, I offered a low curtsy.

"Maman," she greeted in her thick French accent, rising from her chair to seize my hands in hers and right me. "How glad I am to meet you at last!" She kissed me on my right cheek and then my left.

"I am ashamed to meet Your Grace in this condition," I babbled, her calming, sure presence unnerving me, making me feel big and awkward and foolish. "You see, I had written my brother for proper attire, but of course was provided with nothing, as is the usual. And your husband, I am afraid, has not done his mother justice."

"*Mon Dieu,* but men know nothing of the expense involved in keeping their women beautiful, no?" she returned in a voice sweet as warm honey. "We will make certain to keep you here at court and I will personally see to it you are kept in attire befitting your station, Maman."

Well, I thought with a grateful smile, *she is off to a good start.*

"I need you here, you know?" she went on in a light tone. "You can help acclimate me to Scottish ways and make certain I do not cause offense. And you can tell me secrets about His Majesty that I can use against him in arguments!" she added with a laugh that rippled like a pebble skipping across a pond.

"I will be most happy to comply to that," I assured her, touched to be included in a jest, as if I were an intimate. "I am happy you have come to Scotland, Marie. You will make a good wife, I am certain of it."

"With a good *maman* as my guide!" she cried, taking me in her arms in a robust embrace. "Now, in your chambers you will find some gifts I have ordered for you. Perhaps you would like to retire there and take some rest before the entertainments begin?"

"Yes," I agreed, suddenly extraordinarily weary. "Yes, I should like that."

With that I was dismissed and removed to my chambers, glad that I came to Edinburgh, glad that my son chose this kind woman who would be not only his wife but also my ally.

* * *

"Are you happy, Mother?" Jamie asked me as we feasted him and the new queen at the entertainments celebrating their marriage.

I smiled, taking his hand in mine and squeezing. "Very, Jamie. She is a good woman, a strong woman. And she makes you smile again," I added in soft tones. "You?"

"I am," he told me, patting my hand in turn. "It is the beginning of a new era in Scotland, an era of prosperity. And an era for peace—for you and me especially, I hope."

"Of course for us," I assured him. "More than ever I want to be at peace with you, Jamie. And for you to know I always support you as my son and as king."

Jamie leaned forward, pressing a kiss against my cheek. "I know," he whispered. "I am grateful to you, Mother," he said, his light tone bearing the softest trace of wistfulness. Before I could respond, he pulled away to join his bride and companions on the floor for a dance.

My eyes were diverted from my son and his court by Harry, who sat beside me, allowing his cup of wine to be refilled. I caught him admiring me and pretended to demur under his gaze. I was in a beautiful new gown, one of the gifts that had awaited me in my chambers from my daughter-in-law, of vibrant deep orange velvet that set off the copper still shining through the gray streaks in my hair, my head dressed with a crown befitting my station as the Dowager Queen on the insistence of Her Grace.

"Well, now what are you going to do?" Harry asked in cheerful tones.

"What do you mean, what am I going to do?" I returned, casting a fond gaze on Marie and Jamie as they alighted to the floor in the fleet dances of France with a group of young courtiers whose names I no longer knew.

"Now that you have nothing to fight against," Harry supplied.

I seized my cup of wine and raised it to Harry. "I am going to appease all of you worriers," I told him. "I am going to rest."

We clanked our cups and laughed.

All at last was right. Jamie was married to a sturdy, lusty woman who would be my friend and give me legitimate grandchildren and heirs to the realm. England and Scotland were enjoying as much peace as they could. Harry and I achieved some sort of friendship, and I had, as Harry pointed out, nothing to fight against or for.

At last.

I turned my eyes to Jamie. For a moment it was not my son anymore but his father dancing in his place. The woman beside him was not Marie de Guise but I, tossing my long red locks about as I showed off before the court. I shook my head, squinting, and in our place stood the children once more. It was beginning again, another dynasty, another life of heartaches and triumphs that they would share and I would only observe. I was content to observe.

"You know, Harry, I have been thinking," I said then, more to myself than to him. "All my life I have been searching for my place, as either Tudor or Douglas or Stewart. But I was never any of those women. This is who I am."

"What do you mean, Margaret?" Harry asked with an indulgent smile.

I reached up, fingering the crown on my head. At once it was weighty with meaning. I thought of my father in my fevered dream where he presented me with a fiery crown stating, *This is who you are.* How then I did not want it but could never seem to escape it.

"It suits you more than any wedding ring ever could," Harry told me, noting the gesture. "You are every inch a queen."

How often had I been told that? How often did I not believe it? Yet it was my place. It was indeed who I was born to be, who I now accepted myself as being. A woman too much for any common man, a woman who at times was too much and not enough for a king. A woman whose search for a constant in life always led her back to herself.

"I am, Harry," I admitted, my tone rich with contentment. "I am every inch a queen."

I was, and ever had been, Margaret R.

And it was, for once, enough.

Author's Note

Though I utilized all of the research as was at my disposal at the time, this, as with all of my works to date, is a dramatic interpretation meant to entertain. It is not intended to be consulted for scholarship. For a deeper study of the historical, military, and political events surrounding Margaret Tudor's life, please look to the "Further Reading" section I have provided as a starting point.

Robert Barton did bring two "Moorish lasses" to the court of James IV in the early part of the first decade of the sixteenth century. It is true that Margaret Tudor enjoyed choosing gowns to accentuate the beauty of "Black Ellen." The fates of the dark ladies, whose origins were likely in Guinea, remain unknown. They faded off the records of the Scottish treasurer in the 1520s.

Robert Barton remained an integral member of the government of James V till his death in 1540.

Margaret Tudor did claim to have had dreams prophesying the death of James IV. She spent her last years in relative peace with Harry Stewart and was active at the court of James V at the indulgence of her very patient daughter-in-law. She proved a great comfort to James V and Marie de Guise during the mourning of their two infant princes. Margaret died at Methven Castle in 1541 of a stroke, missing the birth of the princess who would become the ill-fated Mary, Queen of Scots, a woman whose life would parallel her grandmother's in many ways.

Margaret left her possessions to her daughter, the neglected Margaret Douglas, but her wishes were never carried through and her humble estate reverted to the Crown. Her last words were an appeal to be remembered to the Earl of Angus, whom she believed she had wronged. Harry Stewart went on to marry his Janet, and the Earl of Angus wed Margaret Maxwell. Margaret Douglas married the Earl of Lennox and remained involved in court intrigue for the whole of her life. Her imprisonment in the Tower of London in 1536, where her first love, Lord Thomas Howard, ultimately perished, would not be her last.

James V died in 1542, a year after his mother. He remained haunted by the execution of Janet Douglas, Lady Glamis, for the rest of his days.

Despite a turbulent life that some have regarded as an embarrassing sequence of bad judgments, Margaret Tudor had the last laugh, albeit posthumously, when the union between her grandchildren fulfilled her father's long-ago prophecy. Her grandson by Mary, Queen of Scots, and Henry, Lord Darnley, son of her daughter, Margaret Douglas, became not only James VI of Scotland but also James I of England when he inherited the throne from his cousin Elizabeth I.

England and Scotland became one kingdom at last.

Further Reading

Chapman, Hester W. *The Thistle and the Rose: The Sisters of Henry VIII.* New York: Coward, McCann & Geoghegan, 1971.

Dawson, Jane E. *Scotland Re-formed, 1488–1587.* Edinburgh: Edinburgh University Press, 2007.

Harvey, Nancy Lenz. *The Rose and the Thorn: The Lives of Mary & Margaret Tudor.* New York: Macmillan, 1975.

Mackie, R. L. *King James IV of Scotland: A Brief Survey of His Life and Times.* Westport, CT: Greenwood Press, 1976.

Moffat, Alistair. *The Reivers: The Story of the Border Reivers.* Edinburgh: Birlin, 2008.

Perry, Maria. *The Sisters of Henry VIII.* Cambridge: Da Capo Press, 2000.

Thomas, Andrea. *Princelie Majestie: The Court of James V of Scotland, 1528–1542.* Edinburgh: John Donald, 2005.

THE FORGOTTEN QUEEN

D. L. Bogdan

About This Guide

The suggested questions are included to enhance your group's reading of D. L. Bogdan's *The Forgotten Queen*.

DISCUSSION QUESTIONS

1. Margaret Tudor learned early that she was destined to be Queen of Scots. How did the knowledge of the daunting responsibility before her affect her?

2. Describe Margaret's relationship with her family and siblings as children. Whom was she closest to? Why or why not?

3. Did Margaret love James IV? Did he love her? Was he a good husband, in the context of the times?

4. How did the deaths of her children affect Margaret?

5. Margaret loses James IV as a young woman while with child. How did this tragic circumstance affect her? How did it factor into her marriage to the Earl of Angus?

6. Describe the relationship between Margaret and Angus. Was there any love there?

7. At one point, Margaret is forced to flee Scotland and leave her children behind. Was this the best option? Did she have any other alternatives?

8. Was Margaret a capable regent? Why or why not?

9. Did the Duke of Albany do right by the royal children?

10. Describe Margaret's feelings toward her sister-in-law Catherine of Aragon. Why did Margaret resent her? Is it understandable? Why or why not? Were these feelings ever resolved?

11. Throughout the novel, we see Margaret go through a series of changes regarding her emotions toward Angus. How did she ultimately feel toward him? Why?

12. Margaret often finds herself playing both sides while trying to secure James V's throne, between that of Scotland and that of her brother, Henry VIII. Why did she do this? Whose side was she on ultimately?

13. Describe Margaret's relationship with Harry Stewart. Compare and contrast it to her previous relationships with James IV, Angus, and the Duke of Albany. Who was the love of her life?

14. What was the turning point or points that contributed to the deterioration of Margaret's marriage to Harry? Was this inevitable?

15. Compare and contrast Margaret's relationships with her daughter, Margaret, and son, Jamie (James V). Was she a good mother? Why was it difficult for her to resist meddling in the rule of James V when he came to power, yet (seemingly) easy to let go of her daughter, Margaret Douglas?

16. Describe Margaret's relationship with Henry VIII as adults. Did Henry do right by his sister?

17. Margaret was told by several that to be a queen and to have true love was next to impossible. In the context of her time, was this true? Is it true of people in power now?

18. Margaret acted often out of impulse, necessity, and at times seemed impervious to the needs of others. In regards to her regency, marriages, and children, did she make the right choices? What could she have done differently? Did she fulfill what she viewed as her purpose in life?